The Fading Glow

Sovereigns of the Dead: Book Two

Vista McDowall

Library of Congress Control Number: 2021900975

ISBN: 0-9795113-6-4
ISBN-13: 978-0-9795113-6-3

For Mom, for your unwavering support and eternal love.

The
Kingdoms
of
D'Ehsen

PROLOGUE

Jagger's eyelids glowed red, but he didn't dare open them. Not when the darkness of purgatory still plagued his mind.

"Look at the sunrise," came the blind man's voice. A firm hand took hold of Jagger's. "You have survived the night."

Opening his eyes at last, Jagger stared out at the world. The overgrown trees of the swamp sagged with vines and trailing branches, their roots concealed beneath the mud and moss. In the shadows, he thought he saw a shimmering image of a woman before it faded, fog evaporating in sunlight.

As if reading his thoughts, the blind man said, "The mist-folk won't bother you again. Not while you're with me."

A thousand questions flooded Jagger's head, and he opened his mouth to speak them. Nothing came out. His tongue worked – he coughed, and laughed – but it refused to form words when he tried.

The blind man smiled. "I told you, there is a cost to returning to life after death. Yours is your voice."

A small price to pay. Jagger stared in wonder at his scarred hands. In purgatory, they had been whole and pink like the hands of his youth. Now, the stumps of his pinkies were long healed, his pockmarked skin telling of many years of violence. His skin felt moist, as if there were a layer of extra water between it and his muscles, and had a slight bluish tinge in the light. Timidly, Jagger stood and tested his legs and arms, feeling the pull of his flesh.

Already, the memory of purgatory had been clouded by the

sunlight drifting down through the trees. A wisp of it remained in the back of his mind, a constant reminder of the sacrifices he would make to rejoin his wife, Raven, in the final death of Lyael.

Who is this blind man? Jagger wondered. The blind man appeared young, no older than thirty, with a mop of dark hair and Gallic olive skin. He had a cane resting on the log beside him, and his milky eyes stared eerily in Jagger's direction.

"My name is Darian, and I am a servant of Death," the blind man said, responding to Jagger's unasked question.

How did he find me?

Darian's small smile unnerved Jagger – a difficult feat, after Jagger's long, terrible murdering career. "Something on the wind told me that you needed my help."

Jagger pulled away, eyes narrowing. *How...?*

"We are connected, you and I. I found you in Autorus's domain and pulled you back to Earda. I can see from your eyes, hear from your ears, and yes, I can detect those thoughts that flow most prominently to the fore of your mind."

Could anyone else do this? Read my mind?

"No. Only me."

Oh. Jagger chewed his lip, mulling over many considerations. After a moment, he directed a strong thought toward Darian. *How can I reach Raven? What do I have to do?*

"Autorus has kept count of each soul you sent too early to the afterlife. You must repay that debt."

Why me? Does every murderer get this chance?

"No. Your soul is filled with remorse. I heard it, and I found you. Death is as unjust as life; there are a hundred thousand other souls trapped there who I could have rescued. But I chose you."

Why?

Darian cocked his head. "Because I have a purpose, and you will help me with it."

Running his fingers through his lank hair, Jagger stared into nothing. *This is madness. I'm still dead, I'm just dreaming, this is all a mad dream, any moment I'll wake up and–*

"It's no dream, Jagger. This is life, as real and raw as it can be." Indicating the log, Darian gestured for Jagger to sit. Once he did, the blind man continued, "For each soul you sent to Autorus, you must selflessly help another. This will take many years, and Autorus may not count some as you believe they should be. You will not age, you will not succumb to hunger, thirst, or disease; no weapon can permanently harm you, for you will always rise until your task is done. When I die – and trust me, I shall die before you do – you will find another to guide, and live on until Autorus calls you home."

Jagger stared at the blind man, disbelieving. *I'm undead,* he thought. *I can't die again, not until...*

Gods, how many years, how many souls would it take? But it all would be worth it if he saw Raven again in Lyael. Clenching his fists, he brought up an image of her in his mind, fixing on it. *Whatever it takes, I'll find her again. I'll do what must be done, I'll atone for whatever sins Autorus deems fit, just as long as I get to hold her once more.*

Nodding sagely, though to which thought Jagger couldn't tell, Darian climbed to his feet. "We have a long way to travel, Jagger Cross. There isn't time to delay."

Where are we going?

"To find the woman who travelled with your old friend."

Oh. And then, *That bitch stabbed me.*

PART ONE

CHAPTER ONE
Cara

One by one, the lanterns in the city extinguished, snuffed by hand or magic. The festival of colors beneath the plateau diminished as the sun rose, its pale light illuminating a changed populace. Shutters remained closed. Once-thriving markets were deserted. The people, awake and afraid, did not dare come outside.

Prowlers had invaded the Cascade Palace, the center of nobility and wealth; what hope had the rustic folk if their own earl barely escaped the slaughter?

Messengers moved down the plateau and into the city, each carrying news of the dead to their families. The quiet streets would soon fill with wails and moans, for many widows had been made that night.

The dawn's light did nothing to dissipate the horror in the ballroom. Cara surveyed that once-glittering hall, not quite sure what she was looking for. Hope, perhaps, that the previous night had been but a dream.

Yet the carnage left behind dissuaded any such wish. Though servants worked to clear the marble floors, bodies still lay haphazardly where they had fallen. Bloodstains dried into dark puddles. Prowlers, Realm's Protectors, and nobles lay side-by-side, monster and man united in death. Their bodies painted the room in a macabre display, each a demonstration of a final breath, final thought, final terror.

A young girl scrubbed at the stairs, her face pale and

drawn. More than one servant had tears on their faces as they worked. Some part of Cara wished to help them, but she didn't stir from her place at the top of the stairs. Many of the frightened glances were directed at her.

I'm one of the monsters they fear.

Cara turned away and rubbed her tired eyes. She hadn't slept that night, even after burning her battle-soiled clothes and scrubbing her skin raw. The lavender soap had done nothing to erase the memory of death, a phantom that lingered on her skin.

She ran her hand over her head, her fingers tracing over the short strands of her hair. After Mavian's dark lightning had hit her, much of her long, curly locks had burned away. In the heat of battle, she hadn't noticed. A servant had kindly evened out the various lengths, but little had been spared. Cara's head felt strangely light, and she knew that this, too, separated her from the other women of the palace.

Once, she had wanted to be like her lady: beautiful and delicate. No longer. Cara resolved to embrace this new self, just as she had embraced the beast that lurked in her belly. If she must be a weapon against the undead, then she would become that, and only that. Such frivolities that she had once dreamt of would be cast aside.

In the peripherals of her vision, Cara saw a steward lurking. She beckoned him over, and he bowed. "My Lady–"

"I'm no lady."

He corrected himself swiftly. "Maid, the king has summoned an emergency council. You are wanted there."

She couldn't refuse the king's summons.

Though still dressed in breeches and a loose tunic – the first things that had come to hand before she left her rooms – Cara followed the steward. If the king wanted to see her, he would see her as she was.

As they walked, Cara asked, "Has any news come of my friend? The one in the infirmary?"

"I'm afraid not, Maid. His condition has not improved."

Cara reached for her braid before she remembered its absence. She settled for playing with her tunic laces instead.

Sandu had still not awoken, and with each passing candle, she feared the worst.

She had to put Sandu from her mind as they arrived at the council chamber.

The grand double doors were carved with impressive friezes. Guards stationed to either side opened them for her, and she walked into the room. A series of tables were arranged in a half-circle on the dais in front of her, some empty, others occupied by lords. The king himself sat in the highest chair in the center, his brow wrinkled beneath his crown. As soon as she came to the center of the room, Cara gave a wobbly bow.

"Maid Gellder." At King Henrik's words, the others fell into silence. Cara noticed that none of the four earls were present. The king spoke, "Have you come to swear fealty?"

"I have come because I was summoned, Your Grace."

"Then you will not swear?"

Cara didn't move. "I am your loyal vassal. I gave fealty when I emerged from my mother's womb, and I will swear again if you so wish it."

"Good. What do you know of the events of last night?"

"I know as much as you do, Sire. I did not confirm that Earl Seastone was *fampir* until last night, though I knew of Lord Strilu's. With the imminent threat of Mavian and his prowlers, I thought it best to wait until after the Masque to bring my knowledge to light." This was only partially the truth; Cara had tried to warn the king, but he hadn't listened to her. This, she supposed, was not the time to bring that up.

"Do you support these *fampir*?"

"No."

"Despite being kin to them?"

"I am kin by birth, not by choice. I do not approve of Autorus's creation walking among us." Cara glanced at the suspicious faces that surrounded her. Not one seemed convinced of her loyalty.

After a moment's appraisal, the king gestured to an empty seat near the dais. As Cara moved to sit, the other lords watched her, as if waiting for her to spring. Cara wondered what in the world she was supposed to do in the face of their political power should they decide to turn against her. Once she sat quietly, though, they returned their attention to the doors.

Druam Strilu entered alongside Edsel Hawk, the Earl of Stonetree. The lords stilled, hushed, ready for the storm to break. Cara could feel the weight of the king's glare even though it wasn't directed at her.

The doors closed behind the earls. Druam stepped into the center of the room, his head high, no emotion clouding his expression. He spared a short look at Cara but didn't greet her.

"Good morrow, Your Grace," Druam said. "A little early for council, don't you think, after last night's events?"

"Last night's massacre," the king said heavily. "You are not here as my friend, Strilu, but as a traitor. There are many witnesses of your monstrous heritage."

"I am *fampir*, yet I am no traitor."

"How long have you lived? Hm? How many kings have died while you still lived, aloof in your palace?" King Henrik spat the words.

Druam paused, apparently thinking. "Too many to count over the centuries, Henrik." The lords gasped at his informality, and even Cara leaned forward, drawn by his charisma. "You are merely the latest in a long line of proud men, none of whom I deemed worthy of immortality. I have seen firsthand the Eadron invasion of D'Ehsen, I witnessed the first Lofalins brought as slaves to our shores, I spoke to the men who formed Demarren from Skallish ashes. When you are dead, your face, too, shall blend with the others of the past until it is no more than a passing recollection. Yet would all be forgiven if I gave you immortality? Is *that* the reason for this mock trial?"

Despite the greedy gleam in his eye, the king said, "You are a foul creature of Autorus. I want nothing to do with such evil."

"Death is no more evil than life. Were you to request my blessing, I would not grant it to you."

"And why not? You have kept knowledge from the crown for a thousand years–"

"Seven hundred and eighty-nine."

"Don't correct me, treasonous snake!" King Henrik's eyes bulged.

Cara admired the king's persistence, but Druam was an ocean of calm, washing over every obstacle in his path. *How many kings have had this very argument with him?* she wondered.

Druam's expression finally darkened, his mouth turning down, his eyes burning with a hint of his *fampir* blood. "You are only a child to me, Henrik. You are my king because I have no desire to rule in your stead, but you are mistaken if you believe I will grovel. You call me traitor. Where is Earl Hjalder? He fled in the night with all his people. Why, I wonder? Perhaps because *he* is the one who plans to take Dotschar for himself. He is allied with Mavian, yet you waste your time lecturing *me*?"

"Rask is not my concern this moment–"

"He should be! It is thanks to him that your kingdom will collapse. If he hasn't already, he will secede and invade your lands. It is because of Rask that our good friend is dead."

And it's because of you that Renna is gone. Cara narrowed her eyes at Druam.

Cara turned to the king. She had heard the news as it passed through the palace. The queen's father, Earl Stillmeadow, was the greatest casualty of the Masque. Though Cara cared little for the loss of a man she'd never met, the nobles' mood was somber.

The king shouted, "Ulmer perished defending *your* palace from *your* cousin. And what of you, Earl Stonetree? You stand beside this monster; do you claim to support him?"

"Stonetree has always been allied with Seastone," the other earl said mildly. "I see no reason for that to change now."

Nausea rose in Cara's throat. Stonetree was her earl; he had passed through Kell once and greeted its residents. She'd always believed him to be a paragon of justice, but now she knew him to be with the undead menace. Every passing moment, she regretted not killing Alex and Druam when she'd had the chance.

The king appeared equally distressed. "You knew, Stonetree? You knew what he was, yet you said *nothing* to the crown?"

"Yes. I admit that to be true," Earl Stonetree said.

"Then you are a traitor, too. We will hold trial–"

"Enough!" Druam's voice carried commandingly over the king's. King Henrik paused, and in the silence, Druam said, "There will be no trial, no mockery of justice to steal our lands and degrade our titles. We are not dogs to be held on your leash."

Druam paused, and all held their breath. The heaviness swept Cara up, and she realized that the first waves of the storm had come. Druam spoke, "We are not your enemy. Unless you drop this sham, we the Earls Seastone and Stonetree will secede from your kingdom."

Exclamations arose, the lords shouting, "How could you, Strilu? You have no right!"

King Henrik made his way around the high table. The hubbub quieted as he came to face Druam, close enough to touch. In a low voice that nevertheless carried, he said, "You mean to carry out this threat?"

"We do." Druam met the king's eyes without flinching. *Why would he?* Cara thought somberly. *This is but one of a hundred fleeting sovereigns to him.*

"You believe Rask plans to turn on us?"

"He already has," Druam said. "He showed his false loyalties last night."

The king was silent, and all held their breaths. A glower darkened his eyes, his lips pushing together. At last, he said, "We would gladly accept your help in ousting the traitor Rask from our kingdoms. We will revisit the matter of your immortality once peace has been regained."

Druam and Edsel gave small bows. The lords whispered as the king returned to his seat. Before more could be said, the doors opened again, and a white-faced steward stepped into the room.

"Your Grace, Your Distinctions, my lords," the steward started. He gulped, "We've received word of forces landing on our eastern shores. Skallish and Demar, we believe."

The air thrummed as his words sank in. Cara straightened in her seat, her glance darting between the king and Druam. The king's fury settled first on Druam. "If your wife hadn't hidden her magic–"

"She'd be dead in Demarren," Druam said coolly. "Henrik, *think*. This force must have been well on its way long before the Skallish Ambassador confirmed Gwen's power. Perhaps they are allied with Rask."

The king cursed. "I must return to Con Salur with all due haste. Druam, Edsel, rally your forces. You will march on Rask while I take care of these foreigners."

Druam bowed, then turned to Cara. She quailed as every eye followed his gaze. "I ask that the *sulpari* stay with my army. She belongs with her kin."

Cara swallowed, her throat dry. She stood, determined not to quiver under his subtle threat. "I stand with the living, Earl Seastone. You are not among them."

He inclined his head, his expression unreadable. "Your defiance is admirable, but momentary." Cara's lips tightened and she didn't respond. *Let him believe he holds the upper hand.*

With that, Druam and Earl Stonetree swept from the room. Cara sat slowly back in her chair, her hands shaking. The king called for quiet, and all eyes drew to him. He took a deep breath. "Maid Gellder, will you stand with Druam against our enemies?"

Choosing her words carefully, Cara said, "My duty is to obey my king, but I cannot forget Mavian Strilu. He is just as dangerous as Rask. When he is dead, I will be yours to do with as you please. My loyalty is to you, not to Earl Seastone."

The king regarded her with a judging eye. Cara lifted her chin, determined not to waver. At last, King Henrik spoke, "Do what you will, and do not betray us."

"My fealty is true, Sire."

At last, after much discussion, Cara was released from the council. She retreated to an empty alcove above the gardens, her head swimming. All the lords now knew her loyalties, even if they didn't trust her. *I'll prove myself to them and the king.*

First she would kill Mavian. It was his fault that Renna had been taken from her. *Except Druam was the one who murdered her.* The king may have forgiven the earl, but she would not. *Once Mavian is dead, I'll rid the kingdom of Druam and his ilk.* Her heart faltered a bit at the thought of destroying Alex, and she hardened it. *He lied to me. He's* fampir. *No matter their smooth words, they have killed many to satiate their bloodlust.*

Once she regained herself, Cara meandered down to the infirmary. Or, she intended to, before one of Druam's stewards waylaid her. He was a small, stout man called Master Eigbrett. He stopped her at a staircase, his hand firm on her arm.

"My Lady, the earl requests your presence in his study."

"I'm not a dog to be called to heel," Cara said, moving to push past him. Even with her strength, she found the steward an immovable pillar. She looked at him, really looked at him, and saw a hint of red gleaming in his eyes. "You're *fampir.*"

Master Eigbrett smiled. "Yes. His Distinction's most trusted adviser for centuries. Now, will you come peacefully, or must I use force?"

With a sigh, Cara followed him back up to the main palace, up and up majestic staircases until they reached the earl's quarters. Eigbrett led her through an antechamber to Druam's study, which she'd only stepped foot in once on her arrival to Riverfen. But she was no longer the frightened girl in a strange new place. She wouldn't be cowed.

Druam stood next to the window, gazing out over his city. His shoulders slumped, his hands squeezed tightly together behind his back. His dark hair, normally slicked back, hung lank around his ears. When Cara entered, he turned to face her.

For a moment, they regarded each other silently. Cara refused to speak first, and met his eyes with no fear. *He has no power over you,* she told herself, though it was hard to believe while she stood in his study, in his palace, overlooking his city. He controlled everything from Riverfen to the mountains.

Finally, he said, "You're as stubborn as your mother."

Cara gaped at him for a second, thrown off balance. Of all the things she expected him to say, that wasn't one of them. "Beg your pardon?"

"Your mother. Always, her stubbornness and independence shone through. You're just like her."

"And what did you want with her?"

"I wanted you."

Of course. "Then why didn't you claim me all those years she was away?"

"We have an arrangement. Though I expect our terms must be revisited in light of recent events." Druam sat behind his great desk, rubbing his temple.

For a moment, Cara hesitated. Despite her attempts at strength, the young girl deep down, the girl who had always wondered, came to the fore. "You know my mother. What of my father?"

"He is – or was – *fampir.*"

"I know. But who is he? What was his name?" In that moment, had Druam given her the answers she wanted, Cara may have been swayed to forgive him. Her mystery of twenty years resolved if he just–

"I don't know." Druam shook his head, and Cara deflated. The anger in her belly, fueled by the beast, rumbled again. Druam continued, "There are many *fampir,* and not all from my line. Alex once tried to catalogue them, though I don't know how far he reached in that endeavor. I never knew him, and your mother never spoke of your father. I'm sorry."

It doesn't matter, Cara thought, persuading herself. *Whoever he was, he was* fampir. *It's his fault that evil lives in you.* She looked away from Druam for the first time, quelling a melancholy that threatened to wash away her anger. She needed that anger now more than she needed pity. Druam regarded her with those cool blue eyes that threatened to read her heart.

"You believe me to be wicked," Druam said.

"Yes." Cara saw no reason to lie about it. "And I will not follow you, no matter your honeyed words."

"What makes me so terrible?"

"You are born of Autorus. You should be dead. It's unnatural."

"So are you."

Cara glanced down, ashamed that he was right. The beast inside her *was* unnatural, and as much as she reveled in its power, guilt devoured her. She said at last, "I don't kill to survive."

When she finally met Druam's gaze, she found it far too understanding. She started to speak, but he held up a hand. Reluctantly, she listened.

"Look out the window, Cara. When lit, the lanterns illuminate my city by the thousands. Did you know that my home, Belleslye, had a festival every year? The Valadi tribes would gather there with lanterns and torches and candles. It was a festival of light." Druam's eyes took on a faraway gleam. His voice was soothing, low and warm, hypnotic. "Until the Eadrons came. They burned our city, raped our wives, murdered our children. I left home to join the fight and protect my family. But when my brother and I returned to our village, we found that the *fampir* got there first. They slaughtered everyone we knew and loved. We pursued them far beyond the borders of Valadi lands."

Despite herself, the story drew Cara in. She leaned forward ever so slightly, her palms gripping the sides of her chair.

"Verdon and I found the *fampir* who killed our parents and siblings. But we were young and inexperienced. We were turned into our very enemy before we could stop it. When we woke, with fresh eyes and blood on our lips, we got our vengeance. We trapped our sire's mate in an eternity of suffering."

Druam sighed. "Her death did not bring back our mother or father. My sisters were still cold in the ground. My kin were exiled from their lands. Still I have carried hope. I have lived now for nearly eight hundred years and built a city in remembrance of my people. Each lantern down there carries a name: a mother, a father, a daughter, a son, a brother, a cousin, a friend. I have spent my eternity mourning my people, remembering the names forgotten by time. Is that so ignoble?"

Cara's breath caught in her throat. She shook herself, urging the beast to give her strength. It flared in her belly, hot with fury, and she took respite in it. *He killed Renna. Mass graves would overflow if all his victims were numbered together. He may speak of beautiful things, but there is nothing worth saving in him.* The beast agreed with her.

Druam's expression was open, hoping. She'd never seen him so vulnerable before. *No matter his story, he is still my enemy.*

Cara said, "All your years were stolen from others, your successes riding on the backs of many more unnamed souls than ever you remembered. Your tragic history will not sway me."

"Have you ever broken a horse?" Druam's expression turned stony and cold. "It takes time, but even a strong-willed creature will ultimately give in."

Her hands clenched at her sides. "So you'll keep me until I do what you want?"

"As long as it takes."

Her angry eyes met his icy blue ones. Neither looked away. Cara gritted out, "Alex will not stand for this."

"Alex has already left."

That surprised her. "Where to?"

"On a fool's quest for a fool's love. He will not help you, Cara."

She would not convince him. He was a centuries-old being, accustomed to taking what he wanted. Cara stood, leaned her knuckles on the desk, and bent down so her face was inches from his. "You will not break me, Strilu. You will not keep me here for long. I'm going to kill Mavian, and after that, I'm coming back to kill you."

Druam's lips quirked. "Many have tried before you. All have failed. I look forward to your attempt."

Cara glared at him. The beast uncoiled in her belly, and she held it down. *Not yet, my friend.* "May I leave now?"

Druam waved a hand, and she strode from the room. *Perhaps it would be easier to just do as he says.* He had eight hundred years of experience and knowledge, and she a child's perspective by comparison. Yet she couldn't forget him sliding his sword through Renna as easily as a butcher slaughters a pig. Even if she perished in the effort, she could not forgive herself if she let him live.

CHAPTER TWO
Sandu

Sandu dreamt of his mother and grandmother. They sat beside the campfire, the glow flickering on their colorful scarves. Behind them, the wagon stood dark against the stars. Paint brightened its old wood. A savory scent drifted in the air of chicken and spices cooking in the pot.

"Come now, my boy," his grandmother called. "Come, drink and sing with us. It's been far too long."

Sandu obeyed, accepting the flask. He sipped at it, the honeyed mead sweet on his tongue. "This is Da's brew, isn't it?"

"Oh yes, my dear," Mumma said. Her smile lit her whole face, her eyes crinkling at the corners. "His best one."

"Where is Da?"

"He hasn't joined us yet," Nan sighed. "Though I don't think we'll have to wait too long."

"We've waited many years for you," said Mumma. "Oh, but you're still so young! Barely a gray hair in your beard, not balding yet." She cupped his face in her warm hands. "What happened, my son? Why are you here?"

"I don't know." Fear shot through Sandu. "Isn't this just a dream?"

Nan clucked. "Dreams are the path to death, dear boy. Don't you know that?"

"I'm not dead!" Sandu cried. He flung himself away from the two women. "I'm...surely I'm still alive?"

"What do you remember?" Mumma asked gently.

"Nothing." Memories fled his desperate grasp. He couldn't recall a thing. "Am I really dead, Mumma?"

"Perhaps not," she sighed. Just as when he was a child, she ruffled his hair and drew him close to her breast. "We have waited for you and your da. We haven't passed on, not truly. But you are near to us, near enough to touch."

"If you want to live, you must wake up, boy!" Nan shouted, the willow switch she'd always carried whipping through the air and smacking Sandu's wrist. "Wake up! And don't you come back until you're old and gray like me!"

✳

Sandu jolted awake with a start, his heart pounding. He could still feel the switch's sting on the back of his hand. Yet as he looked around, something felt wrong. A strange smell made him wrinkle his nose, then it dissipated, leaving only the scent of the fresh hay on the floor. The corners of his vision wavered for a moment before righting themselves. He touched the blankets over him, scratchy and warm. They certainly *seemed* real. But again, so had his family's fire.

He staggered out of the small bed, through the low doorway, and into the kitchen. Fresh bread cooled on the sill, and outside he could hear giggles as the children played.

He sighed. He was home.

Tambrey bustled through the door, a stained apron tied over her dress. She saw him and screeched with joy. Her arms folded around him. "Oh, my love! You've woken at last! I thought I'd lost you to the fever."

"What fever?" Sandu's head hurt. He couldn't remember any fever. Though he also couldn't remember the day before, or the day before that, or how many days had passed, for that matter. His gut told him he was forgetting a huge chunk of his life, but he didn't know what was missing. With Tambrey hugging and kissing him, he decided not to worry. Not at that moment, at least.

"You were so sick for so long! Your father's barely slept."

She sat him down by the table, chattering all the while. "We had to use the last of our silver to pay for a healer, but the gods proved true, and you're awake! How do you feel?"

Scratching his head, Sandu watched her. When she gave him an expectant look, he said, "Odd. I feel odd. I feel as healthy as ever, and I don't remember being sick."

"Well, it lasted so long, and you were unconscious for most of it. I'm not surprised." She kissed him again, and he savored the sweetness of her lips.

How long had it been since he'd last kissed her? *Years and years*, came his thoughts. Yet he couldn't have been sick for years...could he?

"Where's Da?" asked Sandu.

"He'll be here soon; he just went out to market."

She spoke true, for not a minute later a healthy baritone voice burst into hearing, and the children outside shouted with glee. Tambrey and Sandu went out into the bright sunshine. Their twins, a boy and girl, laughed and skipped about the yard as Cadel Barrow, Sandu's father, opened the gate. Cadel's mouth dropped into a small 'o' before he grinned and rushed at his son.

"My boy! How glad I am to see you awake and well. We've been nothing but worried."

"So I've heard." Sandu sank into his da's embrace, yet couldn't shake the feeling that something was off. Wasn't there gambling, and prison, and bounties? He still couldn't piece together the memories.

"Come, Sandu, let us break bread and celebrate together!" Da boomed. He threw an arm around Tambrey, and they went into the house. The children followed after giving Sandu a quick hug.

Sandu paused. His nerves pricked. He slowly went in, his eyes hard on his father. "What did you call me, Da?"

"What do you mean?" Da poked Tambrey. "He must still be addled."

"Come and join us, Sandu," Tambrey said, taking his hands. Her blonde hair glowed around her pale face.

Sandu pulled back though it broke his heart. "You called me

Sandu."

"Of course, love, that's your *name*."

"No, it's not," Sandu said, backing away from her. "It's the name I gave myself after you left me and told the twins I was dead, after Da went to prison. My real name was Bartholomew Barrow. This isn't right, I shouldn't be here."

Before she could stop him, he ran out the door. He found himself not in a small town, but a grand ballroom. Above, crystal chandeliers twinkled and shimmered while dancers in grotesque masks twirled around, their hands grabbing at him. Dressed now in elegant robes, Sandu was swept up into the dance, his confusion growing.

A dancer flashed past, her lips curled over long fangs. Her partner had blood on his chin. Another dancer ripped off his mask, revealing a prowler's horrid countenance. All the dancers now had the prowlers' unmistakable features. They closed in around Sandu, their red eyes boring into him. He screamed and reached for his axe, and found nothing but cloth at his hip.

The prowlers sprang at him, biting and clawing. His flesh ripped and tore as he thrashed. Sandu's throat grew hoarse from screaming. His hands fell to his sides, his limbs stilling. When he shut his eyes, he found no solace within.

A cold blue light beckoned to him. It pulsed as a voice spoke from within: "Be at peace. Let your soul wander while your body suffers."

Sandu was entranced by the voice, though he moved slow as molasses. He tried to reach out, but couldn't find the strength. The voice called softly, "Be not afraid. You will find rest with us."

His mind was melted butter, his thoughts fleeing before they could form. The voice didn't feel quite right, yet it was so calm, so peaceful, so irresistible.

From behind him, another voice, this one painfully human, said, "Come on, Sandu. Pull through. I need you."

The voice in the blue light sounded angry for a moment before resuming its tranquil tone. "Listen not to the other. You will find only pain there. With us, you shall be free."

"Am I dead?" Sandu managed to say.

The perfect voice caressed him. "You cannot truly die with me, you–"

"Hang on, Sandu," the human voice interrupted. "You're strong, fight it off."

A small part of Sandu recognized the human voice, however he couldn't recall who it belonged to. It sounded nothing like Tambrey or his father, yet he intimately knew it. He craned his neck to see the voice's owner, but saw only blackness.

"No!" The blue voice hissed. "Listen not to her, she–"

"I know her," Sandu said, turning away from the blue light.

"She lies!" The cool voice rang with fury, its facade crumbling. "You belong to me."

The human voice came again. "I need you. Don't you die on me, Sandu."

Sandu's mind collected itself, sorting through his memories to find the name.

"Cara?" Sandu asked, reaching toward her voice. "Cara, is that you?"

The blue light vanished, and Sandu fell into darkness, his cries lost amid the burdening black.

✳

Sandu woke to the smell of soap. Everything was sore and bruised, but when he experimentally lifted an arm, it moved easily. Long cuts and scrapes covered his hands, all thoroughly cleaned and scabbed over. He lay in a bed with fresh linens and a down pillow. A well-dressed man sat in a chair beside the bed, his dark hair slicked back. When Sandu shifted, the man's head snapped up, blue eyes fixing on him.

"Ow," Sandu said. His head hurt when he tried to move it.

"Look into my eyes," the man ordered. Sandu obeyed, his thoughts fuzzy. The man nodded in satisfaction. "No red."

"That's...good?"

"Very good. The curates thought you may turn prowler after your shouting and fever last night."

"I saw my mother and grandmother, and then I thought I was home. There was this light." Sandu struggled to find the right words.

The man nodded. "Autorus beckoning your soul to join him. It is a difficult temptation to resist."

"How do you know that?" he asked. "Who are you?"

"Your head must be more addled than we believed. I am Druam Strilu, Earl of Seastone."

Oh gods, he came himself. Sandu tried to bow, but the earl waved him to rest. Sandu settled back into the pillows as Seastone said, "I wondered if those who turned prowler saw Autorus, as I did when I became what I am. Yet he only took a piece of me, enough to tie me to his domain. Perhaps he would have taken all of you, leaving your body to wreak havoc on the living." The earl's eyes were thoughtful. The blueness of them reminded Sandu of the cold light, and he shivered. Seastone's eyes were sharp. "How much do you remember?"

Sandu tried to think, his memories taking a long time to coalesce. At last, he said, "I remember seeing Alex, and Cara, and there was a ballroom." The images of grotesque dancers made him groan, and he couldn't quite parse out the real memories from the false. "Mavian showed up, and we were fighting the prowlers. Some of them cornered me, I think. That's all I can remember."

"Cara saved you. Mavian and Chadron escaped."

"He's still out there?" Sandu swallowed. His stomach, though empty, roiled with nausea.

"Not for long. Cara will pursue him."

"Oh." Sandu couldn't fathom why the earl had come to his sickbed. Why would he converse with someone so low? "I should go with her."

"Indeed you should." Without warning, the earl grasped Sandu's chin, forcing their eyes to meet. In a singsong tone, he said, "*As you travel with Cara, you will encounter creatures of the wild which speak to you. You will answer their questions truthfully and completely. You will have no memory of them, and you will not remember seeing me today. As far as you know, I have done everything in my power to block your and Cara's escape from my palace. Now sleep, and when you wake, you will think it the first time you are conscious since the Masque."*

Sandu instantly fell asleep, all his concerns melting away in the smooth deepness of the earl's voice.

When next he woke, Sandu felt sore but refreshed. He stretched, all knowledge of the earl's visit forgotten. To his pleasure, Cara and Captain Dirgard hovered at his bedside, watching him with concern.

"How do you feel?" Cara asked.

"Fairly good. Like I've slept for days."

"That's because you have."

Dirgard came forward. "The earl sends his regards and regrets that he can't visit himself. He's offered you a permanent position in the Realm's Protectors."

Sandu opened his mouth to accept, but Cara caught his eye and shook her head. Confused, he said instead, "I'll have to think about it. I thank him for the honor."

Dirgard nodded. "There's something else, too. It's about your father."

Sandu sat up straighter, his palms tingling. The captain's expression was pitying.

"When I thought you would die, I looked into your next-of-kin."

Tambrey wouldn't care, Sandu thought. *But Da always wanted to see me again.* He said, "Da's in prison."

"I know." Dirgard gestured at Cara. "She told me that he was held by Sir Vlasimir. Thankfully, the lord hadn't left yet, and I spoke with him."

The prickling in Sandu's palms traveled up his arms, leaving goosepimples. He hardly dared breathe. "Da...is he..." *Is he dead? Is he free?*

The pity in Dirgard's eyes near confirmed the worst, and Sandu waited for the dreadful truth. After a moment's hesitation, Dirgard said, "I don't know if he's alive. Vlasimir sold the debts of all his prisoners to Sir Chadron Elliot in D'Clet. They were moved there some months ago."

The dungeons at Sir Vlasimir's fort, though crowded, were at least clean and sunny. But rumors had it that D'Clet's dungeons went deep into the mountain, cold and mildewy, filled night and day with screams and moans. *If Da's alive, he won't last long.*

Dirgard patted Sandu's hand sympathetically. "I wish the Earl Seastone could use his power to free him, but since Sir Chadron and Earl Hjalder's betrayal, I doubt they'll listen to him. I'm sorry, friend."

"Thank you for telling me." Sandu took a deep breath and met Cara's eyes. "Don't let me keep you, Captain."

With a final handshake, Dirgard departed. Once his footsteps had faded away, Sandu turned to Cara. "Are you alright?"

She nodded. "I was beside you last night. You spoke a lot in your fever." Hurt filled her eyes. "Did you have a wife and children?"

"Yes." Sandu's voice broke. "Tambrey, and our twins, Eaton and Elvy. But I gambled too much. Da took my place in prison, and she threw me out."

"Why didn't you tell me sooner?" Her hand closed around his.

"I'm a coward, Cara. I told you that a long time ago. And admitting to you that I lost my family was a hard thought to bear." Sandu gripped her hand tightly. "I have to go to Da. I have to free him; he can't die in that prison on my account."

Cara looked down. "There are bigger problems in the world, Sandu. Mavian and the *fampir* must be destroyed. Nothing can get in the way of that. And we don't know if your father is still alive."

"I did everything I could to get back to you and help save Renna. Surely you understand? This is my Da, it's my fault he was imprisoned in the first place, and I'll not see him die because of my own cowardice. If you knew your father, you'd agree with me!" As soon as he said it, Sandu regretted the words. Cara drew back, her mouth tightening. Immediately, Sandu said, "I'm sorry. I shouldn't have said that. But Mavian will still be out there, and so will the *fampir*. They're immortal, you have time to kill them. Da's time might be running out. Please, help me save him. You know I'll follow you to the ends of Earda, but first him. Please, Cara. Please help me free Da."

She sighed and frowned. "Alright. I'll go with you to D'Clet, and I'll help you rescue him. But if I see Mavian, I'm killing him."

What happened to mercy? When did she become so bloodthirsty? Rather than risking her anger by questioning her, Sandu merely said, "Thank you. So, what's the plan?"

"Druam won't let me leave without a fight. Once you're recovered, we'll pack and head out the servants' passageways in the hours before dawn. First we'll raid Alex's room for coin and anything else that might help us."

"Can't we just ask Alex for it?"

"He left. It's just us two again."

"Oh." Despite Alex's many lies, Sandu still harbored a soft spot for his friend. He wished he could have spoken to him one last time, but the world didn't always work in one's favor. "What do we do after we escape?"

"Stay low and travel fast. Get horses if we can. Pray that Druam doesn't send troops."

Sandu nodded, his throat tight. *Gods, I just seem to get myself into mess after mess.* "Let me rest tonight. We'll start preparing tomorrow."

"Good." Cara clapped his shoulder. "I'm glad you pulled through."

"Me, too." Distantly, Sandu thought about the dream with his mother, the contentment at being by Tambrey's side again. *Fictions and fables. That's all they were. That's all they can be.* He wondered what would have happened had he given in, and shuddered at the thought. Cara wouldn't be there comforting him; she'd be busy killing the prowler he'd become.

CHAPTER THREE
Cara

Cara left Sandu to rest, a large weight lifted from her. In the days between the Masque and his awakening, she had done little except pace her rooms and stare longingly at the hills beyond the city. Druam had not yet sent for her, which was a small reprieve. Though she could have escaped, guilt assailed her at the very thought of leaving Sandu behind.

Now he was awake, if not perfectly hale, and their preparations could begin. Cara itched to leave the dreadful city behind them.

Cara returned to her rooms, too focused on her plans to notice the man waiting on her couch until he made a little noise of irritation. Startled, she looked up, almost sure that it was Alex.

Her heart dropped a little when she realized that this was the wizard from the Masque. Laris Stanthorpe, Master of the Peddler's Guild, the one who had sent a bounty after her so many months before. Cara's hand instinctively dropped to her sword hilt. She gripped it tightly as the beast agitated within her.

Unlike the night of the Masque, Laris didn't wear a long robe with sleeves that graced the floor. He was dressed like any other merchant. If not for his stark-white hair and beard, he would have appeared a typical dandy. A dandy with power at his fingertips.

"What do you want?" Cara asked.

"I sent for you," Laris said, low and dangerous. "Thrice I sent for you, yet you ignored me. Did you not forget the Masque? You knew we would have words."

Indeed Cara had received his summons. She had torn each one up with great pleasure. She said, "Seems a lot of people want words with me. Doesn't mean I want to give them the satisfaction."

"Do you know who I am, Maid Gellder?" His hard grey eyes burned into her.

"Some wizard with delusions of grandeur?" Though every muscle was taut, ready for action, Cara drifted to a side table and perused the dishes heaped with food. She presented a careless attitude as the beast strained at the bindings she had put on it.

"I'm the only reason you're alive, whelp. Your mother and father so very much wanted a child, but his *fampir* blood prevented it. I made it possible. You owe me your life."

"Shall I pay in coin?" Cara popped a grape into her mouth.

"Ignorant fool! You defy the last living sorcerer. I could tear your tongue out with a word, freeze your heart with a thought. You cannot stop me, so I suggest you cooperate."

Shivers crept down her spine. Cara tried to act confident. "What do you want with me?"

"Power." Laris stepped forward and took her chin in his long fingers. "Others see you as a brute, a weapon only. Yet I know there is more in you than meets the eye. You see, Maid Gellder, I've lost something quite precious to me. I mean to get it back."

"Why do you need me? Why not one of your bounty hunters?" Cara tried to pull away, but his grip was surprisingly strong. He held her still.

Laris's grin sent goose pimples across her flesh. "Because *you* are the only one who can help me regain it."

Cara swallowed hard. She remembered how easily Laris had struck down the prowlers at the Masque. He could do the same to her. She gathered her thoughts before asking, "Let's say I agree. What do I get out of it?"

"Your freedom." Laris amended, "Once I've got back what I lost."

"My friend and I are going to D'Clet," Cara said. "That happens first. *Then* I'll help you."

"You really think you have room to negotiate? Your friend was one of my guild, remember. He abandoned his contract. By all laws, I could have him strung up."

Cara's heart thudded against her ribs. *Sandu only just recovered.* She started, "You–"

"Fortunately for you, I can get what I want no matter where we go. I travel with you, you help me, and once I have my desire, you will be free to make as many horrible decisions as you please."

As loathe as Cara was to have this stranger join them, she didn't see much of a choice. She said, "Druam won't relinquish me easily."

Laris raised a brow. "I transport in and out of his palace at will, and you're afraid of *him*? I'll help you escape, if that's what worries you."

The thought of his magic made her insides cold, but she saw little choice. Sandu wasn't as quick or capable as her; he needed help to get out. Cara met the sorcerer's eye and nodded. "We have a deal. As soon as Sandu is able, we'll send word."

Something ominous glittered in the sorcerer's eye. He said, "Call my name three times, and I shall come. We have a contract?"

He held out his hand. Cara eyed it distastefully, then took it. As soon as her palm met his, she felt a jolt, as if sparks traveled up her skin. The sorcerer smiled. He released her and stepped backwards. Before his foot hit the ground, he had vanished, leaving a whiff of rosemary in the air. Cara blinked at the empty space, her hand still tingling.

✳

A quinn passed, five days of recovery and plotting. Cara spent most of her time with Sandu as he recovered. With the curates' help, he made rapid progress. He could stand by the end of the first day and walk about the second. They allowed him short trips in the garden on the third, then longer jaunts on the fourth. By the fifth, they released him from their care, pronouncing him as healthy as any other young man.

Cara walked with Sandu back to her rooms. Guards watched them as they passed. The beast shuffled about inside, sensing her excitement. *We're leaving*, she thought. *We'll be gone by nightfall.*

When they reached the junction between her rooms and Alex's, Cara told her friend to go on ahead. She remembered from Druam that Alex had once tried to catalogue all *fampir*. Perhaps his record still existed, and perhaps, while she was at it, she could find more useful things for their journey. Sandu needed money if he wanted to pay off his father's debt, and she needed better traveling clothes.

Alex's rooms were just as she'd remembered, sumptuous and filled with books. His wardrobe was open, and she ran a hand over his clothes. She lifted one of his tunics to her nose. His scent lingered on it, memories of his taste and skin dancing in her head.

Cara pulled away, casting the tunic to the floor. *He's an enemy. You can't daydream about him.* Keeping that thought in the front of her mind, Cara methodically searched Alex's bedroom and antechamber. She found assorted coins and jewels stashed in various hiding spots, collecting each one in a leather purse. Among his clothes, she discovered a light leather cuirass with greaves and bracers. Fortunately, he was a slight man, and, if tied tightly, the armor would fit her well enough.

His library, she found, was not so forthcoming. She searched high and low among his many books of history and science, but not one mentioned the *fampir*. Disappointed, Cara turned to Alex's desk. That too, proved fruitless; the parchments and scrolls on it spoke only of taxes and vassal grievances.

Then her fingers found a small hole on the bottom of the desk. She ducked below to see a little keyhole. Her heart leapt and she set to searching. She tore the desk apart. No keys of any sort were to be found.

Cara slumped in the chair, running her eyes over his room. *It has to be here*, she thought.

A memory drifted up from a cold night when Sandu had made spiced soup. He had said, "There are three things every Valadi child learns: their grandmother's recipes, how to drive a wagon, and to always hide your dearest treasures in your shoes."

When they first met Alex, they had learned that he had been Valadi, though not raised in a caravan. *Maybe he still practiced their customs.* She returned to the wardrobe and pulled out each shoe she could find. With methodical determination, she upended and shook them until, with a tiny clatter, a small key landed on the carpet.

Her hands trembling, Cara grasped the key and went to the desk. It fit perfectly in the lock, and as she turned it, she heard a click. A secret drawer popped out. Inside was a small, indistinct book.

Cara opened it to see Alex's familiar hand: *The Descendants of the* Fampir, *as recorded by Alexandro Strilu.* Thrilled at her victory, Cara opened the book.

Many of the fampir *were eradicated soon after the Dead's War. By my estimates, there are fewer than a hundred at this time in all of D'Ehsen. Most dwell in Dotschar under the sanctuary of Earl Druam Strilu, the eldest known of us. A few make their home in Skålland, away from civilization. If any have crossed the oceans, I am unaware of them.*

As best I can, I've acquired the names and locations of all remaining fampir *and their lineages. I wish to speak with some of the elders in the coming years and add their knowledge to this record.*

Druam Strilu, turned 2E 148. Currently Earl of Seastone. Sired by Galiyar. His offspring: Helene Ishtar, turned 2E 199. Deceased. Master Eigbrett Bogdan, turned 2E 379. Steward of Riverfen. Gerrine Seri, turned 2E 497. Deceased. Marin Kirreth, turned 2E 599. Curate of Riverfen. Alexandro Strilu, turned 2E 672. Lord of Riverfen, Scholar of Mott.

Verdon Strilu, turned 2E 148. Presumed deceased. Sired by

Galiyar. No known offspring.

The record continued like that, page after page. Most of the names were followed by the word 'deceased', but a hundred *fampir* remained, spread out over the River Valley and Skålland. Some lived alone, immortal hermits, while others dwelled in covens of five or ten.

And some on the way to D'Clet. Cara tucked the book into her belt. It would prove useful in her campaign against the *fampir*. She took her new armor and heavy purse back through the servants' passages to her rooms.

Sandu was ready, dressed for the road and with a haversack slipped over one shoulder. He pointed to her new belongings. "Is that...?"

"They were Alex's." She slowed a moment, feeling a sudden weight between them. They hadn't spoken about their friend yet.

"I wonder where he's gone," Sandu said. "I would've liked to see him."

"He's *fampir*. He's not–"

"He was our friend no matter his deceptions. He didn't want to hurt us. He brought you to Riverfen and saved me from the queen's torturer. He's a good man." Sandu sounded so sure that Cara wanted to believe him.

But she couldn't. *Fampir* were evil, and very good at hiding it. Cara didn't meet Sandu's eye. "He's gone now. We don't have to deal with what he is."

She moved to put the armor on a lounge. Sandu caught her arm and said, "Alex was our friend. You forgave me for my betrayals; why can't you forgive him?"

Because he's evil, and that same evil lives in me. Because if I forgive him, it opens my heart to the possibility of loving him. Sandu wouldn't understand such thoughts. He was a good man, but a simple one. What could he know of Autorus or the daily war waged inside of her? *It's better he stay innocent.* So Cara merely shook her head and wrenched her arm away. "It's not the same. You came back for me. He wouldn't do the same."

"But–"

"I don't want to talk about him anymore, Sandu," Cara spat. Sandu recoiled from her, and too late Cara realized that the beast had overcome her, transforming her features. With an effort, she forced it back down, and her face returned to normal.

Sandu shook his head. "I'm not your enemy."

"I know." Remorse immediately filled her, but she still couldn't give in. Sandu was wrong about Alex. Cara gestured vaguely at the room. "I'm sorry. It's just this place. All the death and lies. It's choking me. We need to leave as soon as we can."

"Alright." Sandu didn't come any closer. "Alright."

Cara stepped forward to hug him. He tensed in her arms, and she drew back. "What's wrong?"

"It's nothing." Sandu gathered himself. "I just need some air." He walked to the balcony door and went out without another word. Cara stared after him for a moment before she set to packing.

Once that was done and Sandu had come back inside, Cara asked him to help her with the armor. She strapped on the cuirass, and though it was a little long in the torso, it otherwise fit rather well. The bracers and greaves felt awkward at first, but she soon grew used to their weight.

"You look like a soldier," Sandu commented.

"Good," said Cara. "It's closer to what I am."

Sandu frowned at her. "Remember your promise. My father comes first. Don't get lost in your vengeance."

"I won't." The little book pressed against her hip, and Cara lied easily. *We'll still free his father. He doesn't need to know about the* fampir *I'll kill along the way.*

Abruptly, the door crashed open. Both of them jumped. Cara drew the old sword she carried. A small troop of soldiers filtered into the room, going straight to guard the servants' entrance, balcony, and other doors. Captain Dirgard followed them, his helmet plumes scraping the doorway.

Druam Strilu came next, his dark hair slicked back as always, his hands clasped behind him. He strode slowly in, blue eyes fixed on Cara. "Put the sword away, child. It will do you no good against the men's spears."

Cara's eyes flicked from Druam, to the soldiers, to the now-blocked exits. With careful slowness, she sheathed her sword. "What do you want?"

"It's time for you to face your destiny. You cannot escape it." Druam's expression betrayed nothing: no satisfaction, no anger, no disappointment. It was blank as stone.

Under her breath, Cara spoke the sorcerer's name three times. Her eyes never left Druam's. *I might be able to hurt him before I go.*

The beast rose within Cara, howling for his blood. For once, she agreed with it. It poured hotly up her throat, her skin turning into ridges and hard lines, her teeth growing into fangs. With the beast's sharpened sight, she could see the individual hairs on Druam's arms, the blemishes on his cheek. The lack of pulse in his neck. She focused on that tender skin and lunged.

Laris stepped from an invisible gateway into the center of the room. He held one hand out to Cara, the other pointed at Druam. The guards leveled their spears at him.

A sharp word rang out, a word laced with magic. It shot through the air, halting Cara in her tracks. She pressed against the invisible barrier that held her tight, but it was no use. Laris uttered another spell, and all in the room froze, their eyes the only things that moved. The sorcerer stepped forward, took Cara and Sandu's hands, and growled a third spell. An icy feeling spread over Cara's limbs. She stumbled as the magic suddenly released her. When she righted herself, she hesitated.

Her room at the Cascade Palace, the guards, Druam, all had vanished. In their place was a slimy rock wall and a single torch guttering in the surrounding darkness.

"What in the—" Sandu started before his voice stuttered out.

Cara whirled to the sorcerer, the beast still in her veins. As she tried to claw at him, she found that her limbs wouldn't respond. She growled, low in her throat, as a different cool sensation washed over her, beating the beast down against her will.

When it stopped, she felt like she'd been out in the rain. She reached up to her hair, and was somewhat surprised to find it dry.

With a satisfied smirk, the sorcerer shook his head. "Forgotten our contract already? You called, and I answered. Now, are we ready?"

"Where are we?" Cara asked.

"In the catacombs below the city. If I know the earl, though, these will soon be swarming with guards. We'd better be quick about it."

Sandu's mouth gaped open. He said, "What's going on?"

"Laris is coming with us," Cara said.

"Why?"

"I'll explain later," Cara said. Laris had already started forward, and she hurried after him. She said over her shoulder, "We should go before we waste our chance."

With each step through that dark, damp place, past each grinning skull and cocooned corpse, Cara doubted her arrangement with the sorcerer. *We may have escaped Druam, but what have I gotten myself into?*

CHAPTER FOUR
Mavian

A glass vial shattered against the wall, tinkling as it hit the floor. The delicate copper alembic came next; Mavian flung it away, perversely delighting in its crash against the sculpted cavern wall. Glowing red stones illuminated the space, lending a furious light to Mavian's own anger.

"Vecking hells!" Mavian shouted, throwing a wooden tray. It did not make nearly so good a sound. "Damn Strilu! Vecking damn!" His nervous energy not nearly spent, Mavian paced around the large chamber. Deep in the bowels of the mountain, under the city of D'Clet, he knew that no one would hear his rage. That was as it should be. He didn't want others to stifle him.

This chamber, given to Mavian by Earl Egil Rask, held a plethora of necromantic tools: a table filled with flasks, books, and gems; a desk with papers, more books, and magical artifacts of varying power; a rough-hewn rock formation in the center of the room, unlit candles adorning its surface. Amidst the candles, a woman's stiff body lay in repose, her blonde hair laid in a halo around her head, her hands clasped over her breasts. The red glow cast unearthly shadows over her features, making them appear otherworldly. No breath filled her lungs, no blood flowed in her veins. Beneath her black gown, a fatal wound – now cleaned and packed with herbs – pierced her flesh.

Mavian avoided looking at Maeria's corpse. It had lain there for five days now, a whole quinn of grief, despair, and vengeance that filled Mavian's soul, bursting from him in fits.

Across the room, another man stood silently, arms hanging listlessly. Well, not quite a man. Not anymore. Its skin had a bluish tint, its eyes grey and blank. A dark-bladed greatsword hung at its side. In life, the creature had been Merick Deregard, watchman for the Nellestere family. Now, he was an undead wight, subservient completely to Mavian's whim. Or, supposedly subservient. Flashes of obstinacy emerged now and then.

"What use is necromancy if it brings back mindless constructs?" Mavian asked his creation. "You're nothing but a reminder of what undeath *shouldn't* be."

The wight didn't move.

"There must be something," Mavian muttered to himself. He pulled out books and manuscripts, scrolls and loose paper, and piled them on the desk and table. Some he had stolen from Alex and his Mott scholars, others he'd collected over years of study. All hinted at necromantic powers. It was through these books that Mavian had learned of the *fampir* and wights, both created during the Dead's War. None of the books mentioned prowlers, though it was clear that, like *fampir*, prowlers survived on mortal blood. Why they were feral, he couldn't say, but he didn't much care. The wights, though, had neither a *fampir's* scant humanity, nor a prowler's savagery. They simply obeyed, living as long as their masters did. *Too bad the process for their creation is so intensive. The mages of the Dead's War must have had many more magical resources lost to us today.*

Mavian flipped through a centuries-old tome. One of its spells promised eternity, but the working was badly constructed. Any modern mage would scoff at it. *I have to try.* He found another book, this one even older, and located a similar odd enchantment.

"Bring me two corpses," Mavian ordered his wight. "No more than a quinn old."

The wight began to shuffle off, and Mavian said before it could vanish, "And don't kill anyone to get them."

In the meantime, Mavian worked. He set up candles and

drew runes in circles on the floor, then laid out bowls of incense and herbs. The cloying smell mixed oddly with the stale scent of death that clung to Maeria. Her body would not decompose, for he had found a spell to preserve it, but it still had a faint odor.

When at last the wight returned with the bodies of two rustics – no doubt taken from freshly-dug graves – Mavian's nerves had grown close to shredding. He mumbled to his creature to place the corpses in the circles. *If it works on them, it'll work on her,* Mavian told himself.

Yet he knew, deep down, that such a spell could never succeed. The required magic was far too great.

The first spell took a candle to cast, with oddly specific injunctions to light each wick after certain phrases. By the end, when he doused the body with water, Mavian's hands trembled, his throat raw from chanting.

The body didn't move for a moment. Mavian watched it closely, praying for any hint that his spell had worked.

When the corpse moved, it didn't just twitch a finger. It flailed and moaned, its arms and legs twisting in the circle. To Mavian's horror, its torso ripped open, its muscles and organs squeezing themselves out. He shrieked to his wight, but the body grew still. Blood oozed from its open wounds, its eyes staring blankly upwards.

Mavian didn't try the other working. He knew that it would fail, too. All of them failed. *If a mage of ages past had truly found the secret to resurrection, it would be taught to every curate and hedge witch.*

Around his neck, his white gem pulsed. It was a curious thing, one he'd attained through an unscrupulous trader. That gem was the source of his connection to the Underworld, allowing him to use his dread portals and reanimate Merick's corpse. The process had not been easy, and he often wondered if more such gems had existed when wights had been created by the hundreds.

It would not help him now. The Maeria he would raise with the gem would not be his Maeria. More than likely, since her death had not been caused by the gem's dark magic – as

Merick's had been – she would simply crumble to dust.

Mavian cursed again and slammed his hand on the book. "Useless! A thousand years of knowledge and none of it works." He gripped the gem tightly, its familiar edges hard on his palm. *What is the use of dark power if I cannot wield it for my own gain?*

A clicking sound echoed in the room, followed by light and shadows in a connecting corridor. The shadows coalesced into two shapes, one tall and strong, the other shorter, a cane held in its wavering grip.

The High Earl Egil Rask and his nephew, Sir Chadron Elliot. They hadn't bothered Mavian since the Masque, no doubt handling Chadron's injury; he'd lost his hand in the battle. They entered Mavian's study together, Chadron holding a lantern aloft in his one remaining hand. A silver prosthetic at his side flashed in the red glow. Rask, though in his late winter years, carried himself high, his spidery-veined fingers gripping his wolf's-head cane. He wore a long orange robe lined with fur, a heavy diadem on his brow.

Mavian didn't acknowledge his patrons. Chadron's lip curled at the mess on the floor as Rask stepped around it.

"There is news from Riverfen," Rask said. His voice slithered snakelike from his thin lips. "Earl Stillmeadow is dead."

"The kingdom is splintered and weak," Chadron added. "The king rushes back to Con Salur to meet our friends the Skals on the eastern coast. Hawk and Strilu have yet to gather their armies. If we return through a dread portal now, when they least expect it, we can–"

"No," Mavian said.

Chadron regarded him with open disdain while Rask gave a watery glare.

Rask asked, "Why not?"

"Druam's lapdog, Avallune Martill, constructed magic defenses against my portals. He must have done it right after the Masque. I already probed through the Underworld. We will gain no access to the city, and I doubt we're prepared for a siege."

"What use are you to us now?" Chadron demanded. "Your portals were our greatest advantage."

"Hush, Chadron," said Rask. He still eyed Mavian as if assessing a cut of meat. "How many prowlers survived the attack?"

"A dozen or so." Bitterness tinged his voice at the loss of so many. He'd invaded the Cascade Palace with well over a hundred prowlers.

"Not enough to do more than nip." Rask peered at the undead Merick. "And this one here? How much use would he be in battle?"

"Better than a mortal soldier, as he doesn't feel pain. He'll fight until his limbs are hacked off him. But he's still only one."

"Can you raise more?"

Mavian shook his head. "The spell worked on him because he was killed by the gem's dread magic. Others I've tried it on collapsed into dust. I theorize–"

Rask waved a hand, cutting him off. "So you have few prowlers. Find more; they reproduce like rabbits. If we are to take the River Valley and Stonetree, we must have an army. I have other prospects, but those are unreliable at the moment. No matter the case, we must strike before winter's snows close the passes."

"I have work to do!" Mavian shouted.

"Your woman is dead," Rask said bluntly. "I've lost two wives and many children, and I've survived. You're still alive. Best make use of that while you can. The dead don't always stay dead, and you don't want to be one of the mindless ones."

"There has to be a way. Didn't the necromancers of old create the *fampir*? It *has* to be possible to raise one woman! It has to be." Mavian came beside Rask, his eyes drifting over Maeria's remains. Chadron leaned against the wall, clearly bored.

Rask was silent a moment. "You work on gaining prowlers, Strilu. You don't have long to figure out what to do with her." He gestured vaguely at the corpse before turning to Chadron. "Come. We're needed in council."

The two men departed, leaving Mavian feeling worse than

before. He stared at the corridor long after their light had vanished. Before the Masque, he had thought himself equal with Rask, a co-conspirator. Now, though, he realized the truth: they only tolerated him for his use in their campaigns. They didn't care about him. To them, his ambitions were but a tool.

Mavian slumped beside Maeria and took her cold hand. "What can I do against them? Without Rask's support, I'd lose all I have. Everyone else in Dotschar would sooner see me hanged."

He sighed. "Remember when we met? At the summer festival in Kell. You danced and sang with your townsfolk. I only thought to rest there, but then I saw you, beautiful as the day. I hadn't given much thought to love before you.

"You know that everything I've done, I've done for you? I stole from the scholars for you, I learned the secrets of the gem and Underworld for you, I killed for you. All so that you may have the status and wealth you desired. I gave you a new, high family, and you loved me for it. With every letter we wrote, I fell more in love with you.

"I only wish we'd had more time together. How many kisses have we lost? How many perfect nights? You were taken far too soon from me, before the world could truly be ours." Mavian kissed her hand, holding it tightly. "I won't give up, my love. I promise. Not until you're by my side again. Neither death nor Rask can keep us apart."

She didn't respond. How could she? Maeria was dead.

Yet Mavian was sure that death didn't have to be the end. It wasn't for Druam or Alex, nor for Merick. *You will not remain with Autorus for long. Not as long as I have breath to change my world.*

CHAPTER FIVE
Seanna

As she leaned on the ship's rail, Queen Seanna stared back at the horizon where Riverfen had disappeared from sight. Only blue waves and gulls high overhead met her eyes. Behind her on the deck, men worked, their bare feet slapping the wood. The ship groaned as the wind filled its mainsail, guiding it to the southeast.

I don't deserve this, Seanna thought. *I should be preparing for the Masque and wearing my golden gown, not stuck here on this rotten vecking vessel.* Her husband, King Henrik, had been clear in his verdict: Seanna was no longer to enjoy high society, and all would know of her shame.

Rubbing her pregnant belly ruefully, Seanna turned her back to the rail and watched the helmsman. Beside her, Sir Eric kept a hard eye on the working sailors, his hand resting on the pommel of his sword. Seanna suspected that he didn't trust the group of strange men. She was glad for his sturdy presence beside her, the only friendly face she'd seen in the last few days.

Though friendly may be a bit too poetic for him, she mused. *Dour, maybe. He smiles once a year at most.*

With a sigh, she turned back to stare at the sea. "What went wrong, Sir Eric?"

The knight kept an eye on the sailors. "I don't know how to answer that, Your Grace."

"Yes you do, don't be coy. I want honesty from you if you're to be my only companion in the coming year."

"Blunt or tactful honesty?"

Seanna frowned. Part of her, the trifling part that had gotten her into this mess, wanted only gratifying words. But the part that had felt guilt at Druam's parting words, that wanted to make amends, yearned for the truth. She thought for a moment, dithering between the pettiness she'd indulged for so long and the good woman she'd been before her marriage. "I give you leave to be blunt with me. Speak as if to a friend and not your queen."

"You cannot control the king." Sir Eric didn't meet her eye and spoke in a low tone. "But you can control yourself. Whenever you had an opportunity to make a decision, you always chose the one that would reap benefits for you and you alone. You tore down those who admired you, and you always contradicted the king even when you secretly agreed with him. I cannot fault you for loving the maid, but you treated her sorely after her betrayal. You reached high with *Kair* Aremo and Sir Chadron and didn't think of their motives. Neither saw you as an equal. You rolled dice on a chessboard, yet were still surprised that others called checkmate."

His words stung to her very core. Never before had her knight said more than two sentences strung together, and this small speech was gravely delivered, without malice, without pity. She wanted him to console her, but she had asked for it.

She just hadn't realized how blunt he could be.

Sir Eric said, "I am sorry if I overstepped myself, Madam."

"Enough." Seanna gripped the rail tightly and suppressed the vicious anger that rose within her. The knight remained silent.

An errant wave splashed the ship's side, high enough to sprinkle salt water on her cheeks. Seanna lifted her head to the breeze and breathed deeply of the fresh air. It did little to halt the shame that coursed through her. *He's right, of course. I was blinded by my vanity.* She still resolved not to let Henrik win. Let him try to take their child from her once it was born, for she would fight tooth and nail to keep it. Let him try to keep her from society, and she would find a way to involve herself.

Before she could sink into further self-pity, a shout rang out from the crow's nest. "Sails on the horizon!"

"What flag?" the captain shouted.

"Can't tell yet, sir."

"Stay on course for now. Gelpen, keep an eye on those sails."

"Aye, sir."

Curious, Seanna leaned slightly over the rail, peering at the never-ending seascape of blue. Nearly a quarter of a candle later, she finally spotted the white sails that emerged over the horizon. The captain came up next to her with a spyglass.

"They've changed course to follow us," he said. "No flag flying."

"Let me see," Seanna said.

The captain handed over the instrument and she held it up to her eye. The white sails ballooned in size, and she could see tiny figures scurrying about the other ship. Like the captain, she couldn't see any flag.

"Why no pennant?" she asked. Her ship flew two flags, one that denoted it as belonging to Dotschar's navy, and another to indicate that a member of the royal household was aboard. "And why would they turn to us?"

The captain didn't answer her. He stilled, then roared at his crew, "Take down the royal flag! Take it down, *now!*"

The men scurried to obey, and Seanna grew more worried. "Why must they take it down? Answer me!"

"We can only pray that they haven't seen it," the captain said. His face had turned white above his beard. "They could be scouts from another kingdom, or–"

"Corsairs!" shouted the sailor in the crow's nest. "They've raised the red flag."

The captain swore, "Veck! Sorry, Your Grace. Symbol?"

The sailor called down, "It's Steel-Eyes, sir."

Sir Eric stiffened, his hand going to his sword. The captain swore again, and Seanna's heart dropped to the bilges. Cairn Steel-Eyes was a legend of the seas, appearing at one port and then another on the opposite coast within days of each other. He captained a fast ship with a bloodthirsty crew and was not known for leaving many survivors. Some said the loot he'd stolen rivaled the king's own coffers.

Seanna clung to the rail and prayed for the first time in years. As she prayed, the other ship drew ever nearer.

"Celtu, let there be a reef, let there be great waves, let the winds turn against it," Seanna muttered, her eyes fixed on the red flag. She jumped as a hand gripped her arm, and she turned wide-eyed to Sir Eric.

"We're going below. It'll be safer for you there." Holding onto her as if she may resist, the knight led her past the scrambling sailors and to her cabin. There, he pushed her inside and followed after, closing and locking the door behind them. He stayed there, knuckles white around his sword pommel, shoulders tense.

From above, all Seanna could hear were the slap of men's feet against wood and unintelligible shouts. She peered out the porthole. Another few minutes passed before she could see the corsair's vessel skipping over the waves toward them. It hove alongside their ship as men whooped from the rigging. Seanna's sight was soon blocked by the bulk of the other vessel.

Her small cabin grew dark and still. Sir Eric's eyes were fixed on the ceiling as if he could see through the wood. Like a child afraid of the dark, Seanna eased closer to him. She whispered, "Do you think the same person who wanted me dead...?"

Her voice faded as her throat locked up in remembrance of the hands that had pushed her into soapy water. She listened to the waves against the hull; would the assassin try to drown her again, this time in salty waves? *At least they can't send prowlers on a ship,* she thought with a shiver. Those red eyes and slathering jaws haunted her dreams.

The Realm's Protectors still hadn't caught her would-be assassins. Were they coming now to try again?

Sir Eric grunted, "Steel-Eyes doesn't take jobs like that, far as I know. Likely he wants the ransom money he'd get from you."

The ship shuddered, and Seanna imagined great chained spears thudding into the hull. Yelps of pain and the clanging of metal carried down to her, and she huddled on her bed, grateful for Sir Eric's presence. *Rahska give us the victory!* Seanna appealed to the war goddess whom she had never prayed to before.

All too soon, the deck above went silent save for the sound of feet moving about. Every nerve tight, Seanna waited.

Some minutes later, the door to her cabin jolted as someone jiggled the handle. Something metallic scraped in the lock, and the door opened. Three men stood outside, none familiar. They had mere seconds before Sir Eric barreled into them. He was silent, his breath the only sound above the parrying steel.

In the tight corridors, the corsairs couldn't get around the knight. They growled and swung their short swords. Sir Eric countered the first and punched the second. His gauntleted hand crunched the man's nose and sent his head into the wall. The third stabbed at Sir Eric's stomach, his blade sliding off the mail. He, too, crumbled when the knight's sword met him. The last corsair turned to run, but tripped over his companion's body. He scrabbled over the smooth wood. Sir Eric stabbed downward, and the man lay still.

The corsairs' blood coated the floor. Seanna retched, her tasteless breakfast in her throat.

She shivered as Sir Eric turned back to her. "We must leave. Now. I smell smoke from below; no doubt they've set fire to the hull. When we reach the deck, you will stay behind me. We'll make a run for the nearest longboat. No matter what happens, *do not put yourself in danger.*"

Seanna nodded mutely. Her hands shook. She followed her knight, stepping daintily over the corsairs' bodies and into the corridor. Her panicked breath threatened to overwhelm her. Smoke filled the corridor, and she held a handkerchief over her mouth, trying not to cough.

The dark of the ship's interior gave way to daylight. As she climbed the steps to the deck, Seanna strained to listen, but couldn't hear much. She nearly opened her mouth to ask Sir Eric what he saw, then thought better of it.

At the top, Sir Eric quietly emerged onto the deck. Seanna couldn't see past his bulk. He froze, and she heard a shout, "Loose!"

Sir Eric moaned and pitched forward, a dozen arrows protruding from his chest. Most hadn't penetrated his armor, but one lucky shot stuck in the soft flesh of his neck.

Seanna screamed. She couldn't tear her gaze away from her dead knight. He had always been there, a solid, unstoppable force. The notion that he could be killed had never crossed her mind.

Corsairs leered at her. Seanna tried to retreat down to the cabins. Smoke filled her lungs. Rough hands grabbed her. The ship's crew lay dead on the deck. Seanna struggled and kicked, but there were too many corsairs. They hauled her along the deck and over a heaving gangplank to their vessel.

On the bow of the corsair's ship, a handsome young man leaned with his back against the rail, smugly watching events unfold. When he saw her, the man gave an extravagant bow and flashed white teeth.

"Ah, the honored guest!" he said, his vowels accented and the ends of his words lilting. He swung his dark braid around, nearly whipping her cheek.

Seanna's lips were dry, but she refused to lick them. She would not show fear in front of this corsair.

He smiled broadly. "We are being friends here, no? Let us share names. I am Laaravat Demirka, captain of the Queen's Ruby. Fitting name, I am thinking, for carrying a queen." At that last statement, he lifted a knowing eyebrow.

Seanna stared straight ahead. She would not give in, *she would not*.

"Ah, I am thinking perhaps you are hard of ears?" He began to shout, "I am Laaravat–"

"I heard you," Seanna said sharply, her wounded pride only able to take so much. "Must you speak in such an atrocious accent?"

Laaravat beamed. "I am speaking only how I have learning."

48

"How could you possibly know that I'm the queen? Perhaps I'm a decoy or an imposter."

"One, you are being with child," Laaravat said, pointing to Seanna's belly. Jewelry flashed on his wrists. "Just like queen. Two, I am knowing of all things on my sea."

Raising her chin, Seanna met his eyes. "I know this ship's flag. Where's the real captain? I want to speak to Cairn Steel-Eyes."

The corsairs behind her sniggered. Her cheeks reddened, and she kept her eyes on Laaravat. "If he's here–"

"No King of the Seas here," Laaravat said with a grin. "However, our Queen wants to see you."

Queen? "You mean to say that Steel-Eyes is a woman?" Seanna's head spun. A *woman* leading the most terrible criminals on the seas?

"Now you are understanding. Queen of the Oceans, our Steel-Eyes is."

"Then let me see her." *Woman or man, I will only speak with the true captain.*

"Ah. There is being the rub. She's not here." Laaravat examined his dirty fingernails. "This is being my ship, not hers."

Seanna scoffed. "Which ship, pray tell, is hers? For this one has her flag and her bowsprit."

"And yet her ship is remaining with her, moored at her castle. If you are done asking silly questions, we may be going there now."

Her castle? Seanna had no idea what he meant. Trapped among enemies, she had little choice but to follow along. *I hope this Corsair Queen is not as merciless as her reputation implies.*

The corsair gave her a sweeping bow. "You are traveling in one of two ways: in brig or in comfortable cabin. I allow you to choose."

"And will I be sharing these lodgings?"

Laaravat laughed. "Only if you are wishing it. We are not cowards on the Ruby, no. It takes no guts to force a woman to bed, but great big stones to persuade her."

"If I am to be a prisoner, I will be a prisoner in relative

comfort. Take me to the cabin." Seanna forced her voice to remain calm and commanding, as if she were the captor and not the captive.

She took one last look to the other ship, but couldn't pick out Sir Eric's body among the dead. Well and truly alone for the first time in her life, Seanna followed the corsair captain below, determined not to show her fear.

CHAPTER SIX
Seanna

The cabin on the corsair's ship was small but well-appointed. Tapestries hung from the walls, a rug graced the floor, and the bed had a down pillow and quilted sheets. Seanna could cross the room in only a few paces, and there was no porthole. She sank slowly onto the bed, trying not to let her lip quiver. Laaravat stood on the threshold flanked by two guards.

"Is fit for a queen, no?" Laaravat asked, his smirk taunting. "Is not as nice as my cabin, but is good." He gestured to the two men behind him. "Karl and Lindhoff. They are being your guards for our journey."

"How long will that be?" Seanna asked.

He shrugged. "Not long."

"A day? A few candles? A quinn? Not long could mean anything, depending on one's definition of long." A voice inside her head told Seanna not to goad him, but she'd never been one to curb her sharp tongue.

Laaravat only laughed. "As long as it takes. Are you needing of entertainment? Books, sewing? My men have many clothes to repair."

"I'm not a servant," Seanna said frostily.

"Enjoy the view!" The captain gave a mock bow and sauntered away. The door closed behind him. She heard a key click in the lock, and had no doubt that her two guards were stationed just outside.

Other than the bed, there was no furniture in the room.

There was nothing to turn into a weapon, nothing to bash against the door. The bed was bolted to the wall, the tapestries secured with small nails that she couldn't pry out. Running her hands over the wood, Seanna tried to find some weakness or crack she could exploit, but the walls were well-made. She would find no escape through them.

Tears came to her eyes. Her knight was dead, no one knew she was missing, and she was alone with bloodthirsty corsairs. They had captured her rather than outright killing her, yet for what purpose? What could Cairn Steel-Eyes possibly want with her?

A tidal wave of dark thoughts overcame her. The Corsair Queen cutting the babe from her belly. Being keelhauled, her poor skin scraping over the barnacles under the ship. The men raping her, one by one, until she bled so much she lost her child.

Seanna sobbed, muffling a scream in the pillow. She'd never again see Con Salur, never again see her family or the courtiers. She'd even take Henrik's scorn over this awful fate.

And her son. Would he ever live, ever feel the sea breeze on his cheeks or blow the hunting horn?

Seanna shook herself. She *had* to survive, *had* to ensure her child's life. He would be born, damnit, and he would grow into a strong man!

"We'll find a way out of this," Seanna murmured to her belly. "Every man has his price."

With no light to mark the passing of time, Seanna didn't know how long it had been before the door opened again. She had sat, alone and worrying, for candles. Her stomach gurgled with hunger. When the door opened, her head snapped up. A corsair entered with a tray of food. He set it on her bed, then stood near the door.

Too ravenous to turn her nose up at the meager fare, Seanna snatched at the food. She ate quickly, and when the plate was empty, she was still hungry.

"Is there any more?" she demanded.

The silent corsair merely took her tray and went out the door, locking it behind him. Seanna watched him regretfully. *A braver soul may have tried to fight him and get out.* She caressed her stretched belly. "If I didn't have you, I would have tried it."

In her condition, though, she knew that such attempts could hurt the baby. She had carried him for over six months, and he kept growing ever larger. *Big-boned, like his father.* As she thought it, the baby pressed against her bladder. She quickly found the chamber pot.

When she was done, Seanna heaved herself onto the bed and curled up, her legs pressing gently against her stomach. She closed her eyes, intending just to listen to the water against the ship, but she soon fell asleep.

Candles must have passed, for when the door opened again, she was hungry once more. She accepted the food and tore into it. This time, the corsair leered at her. His teeth were stained yellow, his greasy hair falling over his eyes. Seanna shrank back from him, and he barked a laugh.

"Is it morning?" Seanna asked. The corsair only licked his lips.

While left alone, Seanna plotted. She hadn't the strength or skill to fight her way out; the efficiency with which the corsairs overran her ship was proof of that. Though she loathed the idea, she would have to try and bribe the ship's captain through any means necessary.

After she had practiced her speech a few times, she knocked at the door. One of the guards peered in at her. His black hair dangled around his gaunt cheeks. His arms were coated in black tattoos which depicted various scenes of violence. He said nothing.

Swallowing her fear, Seanna said, "I wish to speak with your captain."

"Captain's busy," grunted the corsair. His breath reeked of onions.

Seanna slid a small gold ring set with an emerald from her finger. Fortunately, it seemed the corsairs had no interest in looting her, for they hadn't stripped her of her jewels and fine clothes. "Perhaps you can convince him?" She dropped the ring into the man's hand. "For your troubles."

The corsair bit into the soft metal with a cracked tooth and grinned. "Aye, I'll see what I can do. Karl, take her to his cabin."

Lindhoff strode away, pocketing the ring, while Karl took Seanna's arm and guided her down the corridor to a gold-painted door. Inside was an opulent cabin. A large four-poster bed took up one corner, with a heavy desk and cushioned chair opposite it. A dining table sat in the middle of the room, laden with exotic foods and wine decanters that sloshed with the ship's movement. Rugs covered the wood floor, and gilded paintings hung on the walls.

Karl hovered nearby while Seanna sat at the table. Her stomach grumbled, and she reached for a piece of fruit, her eye on her guard. When he didn't stop her, she proceeded to fill a plate and gorge herself.

A few minutes later, Laaravat swaggered in, though this time he didn't look very pleased. Lindhoff cowered behind him.

"What is this?" Laaravat demanded, throwing the gold ring at Seanna. "Trying to bribe my men?"

Though Seanna flinched when the jewel smacked into her dress, she composed herself and said smoothly, "I rewarded him for doing as I asked."

The corsair gave her a level stare, and she met it with as much bravado as she could muster. She asked, "Won't you sit?"

"You are eating my food."

"I bear a child, dear captain. Eating is about all I do these days. Now dismiss your men, and let's you and I have a little chat."

The captain frowned, clearly uneasy with her commands. However, after a moment, he waved the men away. He flopped into a chair next to her while the corsairs shut the door behind them.

"Well?" Laaravat asked as Seanna bit into a pastry. "What are you wanting?"

"I want to go home, Captain. You're a smart man, you know that the king has great wealth. If you take me home, here and now, you may walk through my chambers in the Silver Palace and take whatever treasures you desire. And there are many of those, I can assure you. All far grander than the tawdry things you'll find at any coastal manor." Seanna forced herself to smile confidently. Her heart pounded, the baby moved, she felt nauseous and exhilarated all at once. If her plotting in Riverfen had taught her anything, it was to never reveal her true feelings. "You'll be the wealthiest man on the seas. I can write to my father, the Earl Stillmeadow, and have him commission a new ship for you. You could be a privateer for the crown. You would be a hero, returning me home and defying the Corsair Queen." While she spoke, Seanna could see his eyes turning thoughtful. At her last sentence, though, he frowned.

"You are having no idea of my queen's power," he said softly.

"Yet she is only one, and my husband the king commands armies." Seanna leaned forward and placed a hand on Laaravat's knee. "I could do other things for you, too. No man save the king has ever lain with me. You could be the first and only."

Laaravat took her hand, raised it, and kissed her palm. Seanna's heart quickened with hope instead of lust. She didn't want to sleep with him, but if it freed her, she would do it. For her son.

"You are very beautiful woman," Laaravat said, his breath hot on her skin. "Perhaps I will visit you, if my queen allows."

Seanna's hopes sank into her shoes. She said with venom, "You are loyal, aren't you?"

"Unlike some in this room," he shot back. His nails dug into her skin. "I am being Steel-Eyes' most trusted man. And loyal I am, to my death and beyond."

"You realize that it's your head that will roll when the king's navy finds me?"

"Or maybe yours will go first," he said. Malice lit his eyes. "I am not liking prisoners who think to threaten me on my ship."

"And I don't like being held prisoner!" Seanna shouted. "Please, just let me go. If not for my sake, for my child's."

The corsair gave her a terrifying grin. "I would rather be cutting your child from your body than to disobey my mistress."

Fear jolted Seanna to her feet, but the ship rolled

unexpectedly. She crashed to the floor, her hands instinctively cradling her belly as her hip and shoulder struck the hard wood. Pain spiked through her, and she moaned. Through the tears that sprang to her eyes, she could see Laaravat's boot.

"You will be returning to your cabin."

The heavy footsteps of her guards sounded next to her, and rough hands lifted her up. They half-carried, half-dragged her to her cabin. She hung limp in their arms, her hopes dwindling to nothing.

Seanna stayed in her prison while the ship moved and swayed beneath her. The days passed in a blur. When she was tired, she slept. Her guards brought food and water at intervals and always watched her eat. If she didn't have her child, she would have starved herself in protest.

After too long isolated, she heard louder shouts and pounding feet against the deck. She sat on her bed and waited for something new to happen. By and by, Laaravat came to collect her. He led her onto the deck where she relished the sun's warmth and the wind ruffling her hair. From there, he took her to the bow and pointed to the horizon.

"You see it, yes?" he asked.

Oh yes, indeed she could see it. Fog rose before them in a great mass, its tendrils reaching over the waves. Seanna clutched the rail.

"We can't go in there," she said dully. "Ships that go in never come back."

Everyone raised in the coastal towns knew to keep away from the fog in the southern sea. Many a good crew had been lost in its depths.

The corsair said nothing. Seanna thought she saw madness in his eyes. She turned to him, anger bubbling inside her. "We're all going to die in there!"

"You are thinking so?" he said without care. "Watch."

The ship dove into the fog. Moisture clung to the bowsprit and coated Seanna's hair. She shivered, her hands held protectively over her child. No sounds came from the endless white. For a few minutes, nothing happened. Then, through the mist, she saw a glowing golden light.

They passed the light, and another one emerged from the gloom. Then another. *A guide,* she realized. Curious now more than afraid, Seanna kept her eyes on each beacon as it came and went. The corsairs still talked and laughed jovially behind her, and she had a sinking suspicion why no ships ever emerged from here.

The ship came out of the fog, and bright sunlight illuminated a strange sight. In the middle of the ring of mist was a collection of ships, built haphazardly onto each other like a child's construction of sticks and mud. The mass bobbed at its edges like a dock in the bay.

"What is it?" Seanna asked, both awestruck and fearful.

"My queen's castle," Laaravat beamed. "Is beautiful, no? If we need to be growing it, we capture more ships and build them together!"

"It must be a maze," said Seanna.

"Oh, yes."

"But the fog. It can't be natural." She peered past the city to the towering wall of mist.

"Is not. You think your king is only one who is hiring mages?"

Seanna swallowed. "And Steel-Eyes is in that place?"

Laaravat nodded, and she turned her gaze back to the corsair city. Many ships were anchored near the floating city, all with the same flag, same bowsprit, same hull design. Seanna's eyes widened, and her breath caught. *Steel-Eyes herself isn't hitting opposite coasts within days of each other. Her fleet is!* Little wonder the navy couldn't pin down the Corsair Queen. Her fleet could lead the soldiers in a merry dance from one end of the ocean to the other with multiple ships and crews, and the navy would be none the wiser.

Seanna swallowed hard. Steel-Eyes was a woman who commanded hundreds if not thousands of loyal men, had built a floating city, and controlled the ocean without any of the kingdoms knowing the extent of her power. A woman who wanted Seanna and had gone to great lengths to get her.

Queen's Ruby weighed anchor, and Laaravat steered Seanna into a longboat. They lowered into the water and rowed to the city. As they drew closer, Seanna spied many men in windows or small doorways. If they had catapults or other siege machines, they would have quite the defensible position.

Seanna shuffled along the uneven passages and strangely tipped floors, her balance constantly thrown off. The ships that were lashed or nailed together rolled with the ocean's waves. Water splashed through holes, drenching her feet.

From all sides, corsairs came to ogle her, each more horrible than the last. One of them threw something slimy at her; it struck her hair and splattered down her cheek. Seanna bit her lip and held back tears. Laaravat did nothing to stop the corsairs from shouting and leering. They threw rotten food and dung at her. Her fine dress was soon a painting of refuse. A few men pissed on the planks in front of her feet.

The maze wove through what felt like a hundred ships. In the distance, Seanna could hear music and a tavern's roar, along with the clinking of metalworking and the smell of a tannery. This was truly a city unto itself. Yet this city held no wonder for her; she kept her eyes to the floor and flinched whenever a projectile successfully hit her. She didn't try to stop herself from crying now.

They came abruptly to a massive wooden door through which was a long stone tunnel. At the end was another door which the corsairs opened on silent hinges. Seanna gasped at what lay beyond. She expected a massive ship, or perhaps a treasure room, but this was something else entirely.

A dock bobbed beyond the door, where longboats and dinghies lay berthed. The dock stretched out over a quiet, massive lagoon. A rocky crater stretched up from the water and curved around on all sides. Its height would be a treacherous climb, yet the ship city around it was taller, disguising it. On the opposite side was a beach dotted with small boats, and on that, a large manor built from stone, surrounded by trees and verdant flowers.

Laaravat led her to a dinghy. Aloud, Seanna marveled, "A

lagoon, inside a crater, surrounded by ships. Remarkable."

Laaravat tapped the side of his nose. "Our queen is most remarkable. She is designing it herself."

An architect, too. Gods help me.

Still, a part of her admired the corsairs' audacious city. It would be no small feat to conquer it.

The dinghy glided across the lagoon's blue-green waters, clear as glass. Thousands of sparkling fish and a great sea turtle swam beneath them. Seanna wanted to pretend she was on a simple boat trip, a carefree day of sun and laughter, but the stench of the corsairs intruded into her fantasy.

The dinghy slid onto the sandy shore and she was faced once again with the Corsair Queen's power.

Sailors materialized from the manor and lined the shore up to the great double doors. They saluted as Laaravat led the way. Seanna followed, held by two of his men. She quailed under the corsairs' eyes and determinedly stared at Laaravat's back. Enemy or not, he was the only familiar face among the throng.

They entered the manor, which was well-lit and richly decorated. Treasure filled every available spot: Eadron rugs, Dotsch tapestries, Skallish headdresses, Demar chainmail; chests of jewels and gold stood overflowing, and shelves teemed with artifacts and priceless statues. Nothing was placed tastefully. This was a collection not of art, but conquest. The corridor oozed with loot, tantalizingly out in the open. The corsairs didn't even glance at it, and Seanna surmised that it was both a boast and a test. No man would be foolish enough to steal the Corsair Queen's gold.

Doors and halls sprouted off the corridor, but Laaravat strode straight ahead. The roar of shouts and merry howls boomed down the hallway, growing louder with each step. At last, the corridor of treasures ended in a massive oak door. Laaravat swung the door wide and walked in with his head high. One of his men shoved Seanna, and she stumbled into the great hall, barely keeping her feet.

A host of corsairs occupied long tables, some standing, some sitting, some drunken on the floor. The tables groaned with food and drink, and the rafters rattled with the sound of so many raucous voices. Men threw food across the room, spilled goblets, and fought each other over bites of sweetmeats. When the door opened, a few turned, but most ignored the newcomers.

At the head of the table was a golden throne raised on a dais. A handsome woman lounged there, one leg thrown carelessly over the chair's arm like a contented cat. Her hooded eyes lingered on Seanna, and she sipped from the goblet in her hand. When she stood, though, each movement was precise.

Cairn Steel-Eyes, the Corsair Queen, clapped her hands once, and the hall suddenly grew silent, each eye on her.

"Bow to the Queen," Laaravat murmured, sweeping his arm and bending at the waist. Without urging, Seanna dropped into a curtsey, though she didn't lower her eyes.

"Is this her, Laaravat?" Steel-Eyes asked, her words clipped, her tone assured.

"This," Laaravat said, standing proudly, "is being Seanna Bergfalk, Queen of–"

"Queen of Dotschar," Steel-Eyes breathed. Her gaze sharpened, her lips curling at the corners. "Well done, Laaravat. You shall be rewarded." With a snap of her fingers, the Corsair Queen directed two men to bring Seanna forward.

Now that she was closer to the other queen, Seanna could see that Cairn Steel-Eyes was in her middling years. She had wrinkles around her eyes and lips, and her hair was more silver than brown. Still, the corsair carried herself with confidence and authority, and Seanna could see why so many men followed such a woman.

"Well, well," Steel-Eyes said, appraising Seanna. "You are a beauty, aren't you? And well-along, too. You could go into labor here if your body is stressed enough."

"No," Seanna said impulsively. She would not give birth in a den of villains.

Steel-Eyes laughed. "As if you can dictate your child's coming." She drew a thin sword from her hip and laid its steel against Seanna's belly. "I could speed things along, you know.

How long do you think it would survive? A day? Two?"

Seanna quivered with fear and rage. If she didn't have a hundred men at her back, she would have slapped the blade away. "Do it. Or is the Corsair Queen one for idle threats?"

In that moment, Seanna realized why the other queen was called Steel-Eyes. Her glare could melt ice. The blade bit every so slightly into Seanna's skin, a pinprick of pain. The Corsair Queen said in a low, harsh voice, "It's not a good idea to test me, Your Grace."

Seanna's mouth worked, but nothing came out. In a fluid motion, Steel-Eyes sheathed her rapier. As soon as the blade was away, Seanna breathed a sigh of relief.

Steel-Eyes asked her crew, "Now, men, what should we do with our royal prisoner?"

"Send her head to the king!" one man shouted. "Show him we're to be reckoned with!"

"Show no mercy to this Dotsch bitch!" another yelled. More joined the chorus:

"Keep her here until she rots."

"Put her in a longboat out at sea."

"Strand her on an island."

More and more yelled until none of their voices could be heard over the others. After listening a moment, a finger on her chin, Steel-Eyes waved for silence. The corsairs obeyed, dogs hearing their master's whistle.

"All quite amusing," Steel-Eyes said, tapping her lips with a finger. "What do you think, Queen of Dotschar?"

"If you wanted me dead, your men would have done it already," Seanna said. She wanted to sound proud, but feared it came out as more of a squeak.

"An astute observation," the Corsair Queen purred, stepping closer. Too low for others to hear, she whispered in Seanna's ear, "Tell me of Druam's court. Tell me everything that has happened in the last month."

Though she wished to be more mature, more cautious, Seanna was still her petty, proud self. Habits were difficult to break, after all. "And why should I tell you, O Mighty Queen? I have nothing to say to a lowly kidnapper."

"Then rot until your tongue loosens." Steel-Eyes snapped her fingers. "Put her in the cells, strip her of her valuables, clothe her in whatever rags you can find. No man is to touch her. Not yet, at least."

Not yet? Seanna would have liked to resist the men who pulled at her, but she couldn't find the strength. She wondered why this corsair wanted to know of Druam's court. *And what if she slits my throat the moment she learns what she wants to know?*

CHAPTER SEVEN
Gwen

Gwen's body felt weightless, yet nausea filled her stomach as her limbs were pushed and pulled, the Witches' magic calling to her, drawing her out of the Masque and into mystery. Her eyes were closed, an image of the ballroom as she had left it imprinted on her eyelids.

Druam stood to the fore, his hands reaching for her. Pain filled his eyes, so powerful that Gwen's teared up. A collection of people in grotesque masks surrounded them. Light filled all corners of the hall. She heard the last strains of music, but they were tinny in her ears. As she listened, the melodies faded. Slowly, the people swirled into abstract colors and shapes. Druam alone remained clear for a moment before he, too, coalesced into the wash of bright color that burned her eyelids.

Her feet touched solid ground. All her weight slammed back into her so hard it knocked the breath from her lungs, and she fell to her knees. She huddled on the earth for a moment, feeling out her hands and feet, enjoying the solidity of her own body. The weight of her gown pulled at her shoulders, and she tore off her constricting mask.

As she assessed her surroundings, she didn't see the woods from her dreams, nor the three enigmatic women who had summoned her. She was home in Demarren.

The brick-and-wood houses of Lordstown rose tightly around her, the dirt road dusted by sand. Colorful clothing hung from clotheslines, and the tinkling of bells flitted on the air, but the atmosphere was not cheerful. Shutters over empty market stalls rattled in a faint breeze, doors and windows were bolted. Few people dared the streets, and those near Gwen did not notice her as she stood and brushed herself off.

It was the rune of the Witches that had marked her hand, their calling that she'd answered. Did they merely want her to see this? Or had they really brought her home? Nothing for it but to find out.

In the distance, Gwen could hear the roar of a crowd. The few people on the street were inexorably drawn to it. She followed. As she drew closer, the streets filled with more and more people, almost all of them the white-skinned Skals, though she spotted the occasional dark-skinned Demar like herself. Those, she noticed, were grim and wary.

Gwen stumbled into a woman and didn't feel any impact. When she purposefully pushed against a man, her hand went through him, like walking through fog. She spoke aloud, and no one took notice. *I'm not really here*, she thought. Buoyed by this, she walked straight through the crowd, her body traveling like mist around them, until she reached the very front.

She halted, her gaze trapped by the sight above her.

Three Skals, all men dressed in weighty fur-lined robes, stood atop a low retainer wall. Behind them, a gallows with four ropes had been erected. Beside the gallows, four Demar people waited, their hands tied behind their backs. Three were women, and one a boy no older than ten.

Gwen knew them. She wished she didn't, but she knew those Demar. They were her brother's wives and eldest son. Two of the wives wore determined expressions, as if to meet their deaths with dignity. The youngest woman and the boy were both openly frightened. Gwen's mouth was dry, heart hammering against her ribs. She remembered the day her nephew was born and the bells that rang at each wedding.

Of the three Skals, she recognized one: Olfrick Kron, her brother's advisor before his betrayal. Olfrick now wore a crown and the richest robes. He waved his hands for silence.

"My people, this is a glorious day for Demarren! We have

overthrown the wicked Liegelord and brought low the evil magicians that dwelt among us. Now, we sentence to death the wives and oldest child of Wullum Zaman!" At Wullum's name, the crowd booed. When a soldier emerged on the wall, bearing a spike with her brother's head on it, they cheered.

Gwen retched, and nothing came up. *I have to do something.* She ran to her family and tugged at their bindings. Her hands went straight through. Desperately, she called up the Gaiar in her belly, but it was sluggish, refusing to respond.

"Why are you doing this to me?" Gwen yelled at the air, sure that the Witches were there.

No answer came from the sky, and Gwen turned to watch the execution, her stomach churning. Bile caught in her throat as her family was hanged, one by one, from the gallows. The crowd pulsed and shouted, glorifying the senseless violence. Gwen couldn't help herself; she shouted at them, "They did nothing to you! They were innocent! My brother is dead, I've left your country, leave them be!" She turned to Olfrick, pounding at him with her small fists though he was unaffected. "You monster! You did this to us! We did nothing to you!"

When her energy was spent, and still Olfrick beamed and the crowd cheered, Gwen slumped on the wall. The hanging bodies drifted and bumped into each other in the breeze, and she prayed for their souls.

A voice suddenly spoke in her head, a voice she recognized as belonging to a Witch: *Do you feel sorrow for them?*

"Yes. They were my family."

They died, and you live.

"I would be dead, too, if I'd stayed in Demarren."

What will you do to the Skals?

Gwen pondered that a moment. She had once tried to cast a curse against the Skals who killed her brother, but now it seemed too little, too insignificant to assuage her burning heart. "I want them all to die."

Your wish is granted.

Without warning, the world spun around Gwen, faster and faster. Her hair whipped around her head as reality became a vortex of wind and sensation. She smelled tender beef and rotting meat, heard a child's laughter followed by an old man's wracking cough. A buzzing whine filled her ears as the world spun and spun and spun until she thought she'd either faint or vomit.

As suddenly as it started, it stopped. Gwen now sat on a stump instead of a wall, and low hills surrounded her instead of buildings. A brook babbled not far away, and birds flew overhead. In the distance was the same mountain range she had stared at through her childhood window.

Voices drifted to her, and she stood, fumbling with her long skirts. As she crested a hill, she marveled at the sight before her. She knew that river and those peaks. This was where Lordstown should be.

What met her eyes wasn't her ancestral home. A tiny village lay next to the river, with a long, low wooden building surrounded by animal skin huts. Smoke rose from the longhouse roof, and people moved about outside it, some fishing while others prepared meals or cared for their children. All of them were Skals, dressed in leather or linen tunics, their blonde hair braided down their backs. As Gwen descended to the village, she heard them speak to each other in a foreign tongue.

"What is this place?" Gwen asked. "Has Lordstown been torn down?"

Lordstown does not exist yet, the voice answered. *These are the Skals who lived here before your ancestors came.*

These were not the angry Skals of her own time. They were happy, with full stomachs and warm beds to sleep on. A young woman about Gwen's age carried a small child on her shoulders. The child burbled something, and the woman laughed before plucking a doll from her pocket and handing it up.

Gwen watched them, torn. These weren't the people who had killed her brother, yet their descendants had.

A man appeared over the hill. He ran toward the village, legs pumping as he shouted. The people stopped and stared. At his yell, they dashed away, some of them calling out. A child's wail sounded over the din. Gwen stood still in the chaos, confused.

The earth shuddered beneath them as the roar of hundreds of pounding feet split the peaceful day. Gwen turned with the villagers and waited with morbid expectancy.

An army crested the hill, their skin dark beneath their bright helms. The soldiers rushed madly down to the village, yelling war cries and brandishing weapons. Gwen tried to cast a spell to slow them, but as before, her magic failed her. She could do nothing to stop their charge.

The villagers ran, yelling. The young woman held her child against her breast. A soldier's axe buried itself between her shoulders. She fell, the child screaming beneath her. As it struggled to get free, more soldiers flooded the village, hacking apart all those in their way.

Gwen rushed to the child, tried to pull it from under its mother, but her hands found no purchase. She sobbed desperately, the strange magic she was caught in refusing to allow her to help.

The soldiers charged on heedless, intent only on their prey. Cries for help and screams of pain filled the air as blood flowed into the river. Gwen's heart ached for the villagers, though it was her own ancestors who ravaged their tranquility.

Do you still wish all Skals to die?

"Make it stop," Gwen said, burying her head in her knees. "I don't want to see anymore."

When she lifted her head next, she found herself in the Cascade Palace in Riverfen. She knew that bookshelf and fireplace, that grand desk, that view over the city. This was Druam's study. Her husband leaned over the desk, poring intently over a collection of maps and charts.

Already, she missed him. She could smell the soap he'd used that morning and the cologne he'd dabbed on his neck. He smelled like home.

"I'm so sorry!" Gwen blurted as she reached for him. He didn't move. Her arms passed through his; he could see and hear her no more than the other visions. "Please! Let me speak to him!" Her pleas did no good. He still didn't move.

The door opened, and Avallune Martill, the palace mage, stepped into the room. His skin was pallid, his face drawn. He sat heavily in the chair opposite Druam.

"What news?" Druam asked, his voice cracking slightly.

"None," Avallune said, shaking his head. "I've used every spell I know, every scry, everything at my disposal. I can't find Gwen. Not even a trace of her, like she's left Earda entirely."

"So she's dead." Druam's voice was so soft, so despairing, that Gwen longed to comfort him.

Gwen said, "I'm not dead. I'm here with you." She whirled, glaring at the air. "Why must you torture me? What have I done to earn this?" No reply came from the Witches.

"I don't think she's dead," Avallune said, "otherwise my magic would have found her body. She's alive, just...out of reach."

Druam sat down heavily and ran his fingers through his hair. "I don't know what to do, Avallune. Our world is changing, too fast for me to follow. I need to find her. I need at least one thing I can save."

"I will keep searching for her. But you must be strong for the River Valley."

"I know. That doesn't make the grief easier to bear."

Gwen reached out again to Druam, but the vision shimmered and faded, leaving her in blackness. The black suffocated her, and she gasped for breath. Her lungs would not fill. It lasted mere moments, and when the blackness receded, she gasped, clawing at her throat.

Air! Sweet, fresh air. But strange air. She found herself in an unusual forest, unlike anything she'd seen before. Instinctively, she knew this place from her dreams: the Whispering Woods.

Gwen strained her ears but couldn't hear the cries of birds or squirrels, nor the rustling of leaves in a breeze. All was still. All was silent. She shivered as she studied the woods. She had never seen trees like this before. They were twisted and knobbed, with grey-black bark and no leaves. The branches interlocked with each other to form an impenetrable wall around her. Through a small opening above, Gwen could make out a hint of blue. As she watched, branches moved of their own accord and hid the sky from sight. As the trees shifted, they whispered, the scratch of bark against bark sending a wave of soft sound across the glen.

Murmurs came from the branches. The trees stirred and revealed a path into the gloom. Staggering to her feet in her entangling brocade gown, Gwen stepped closer. The trees stilled as if waiting.

Before she went down the path, Gwen hesitated. The visions she'd seen disturbed her. She thought, too, of the Trials. Once before she had fled her old life and those who would condemn her for her magic. That time, her brother fueled her escape, promising her that all would be well. *But now Wullum is dead, and the Inquisition will invade Dotschar if I am not given to them.* If Gwen turned now, perhaps she could return to her second life, the life she had lived with Druam, for he was so distraught at her disappearance. That was a life of splendor, peace, and tranquility.

The splendor hid Mavian's cruelty, the peace foiled by Queen Seanna, the tranquility ruined by my own magic. There was no way to go but forward. Though the queen had offered friendship, it was a false entreaty. Though Mavian had begged for her help, Gwen spurned him. Though Druam had implored her to stay, she left him.

The Whispering Woods beckoned, promising a third life that she could not yet see.

I loved – love – Druam, yet if I stayed with him, I could not practice and grow in my magic. Just as I had to leave Demarren for my safety, so too did I leave Riverfen for my sanity. The Witches brought me here, and so I must follow the path I have chosen. The marking in Gwen's palm, the hint of magic that had granted her access to this place, had vanished, and she somehow knew she would have no second chance.

The Witches can explain those visions to me. Druam will grieve, but he will survive. He has to survive without me.

Her heart sore in her chest, Gwen moved down the path.

As she did, the trees closed behind her. Though she could not see the sky or sun, Gwen's eyes picked out the shadows of the wood, and she had no trouble navigating the gloom. The trees she passed had visages jutting from them, expressions of pain and peace in turn. Some carvings seemed so real, Gwen paused unconsciously, her tender heart yearning to help the poor soul trapped within the bark.

The whispers of the trees grew louder, and Gwen thought she could detect words among the sighs: "Do not leave me here." "I am afraid." "Praise the gods." "Let my body feed the spirits." The words were ancient, spoken in an old tongue understood not through the mind, but the flesh. Her skin tingled. Gwen kept moving, trying not to look at the agonized complexions in the trees.

Even without the guiding sun, Gwen felt the woods grow darker, and still she walked the path with no end in sight. Her feet were sore and protesting from dancing and walking, and she flung her heeled shoes off. Her ears and neck complained at the weight of her earrings and necklace, so she threw her jewels to the ground. Meandering branches tugged at her vast skirts. In a haze, Gwen tore at her dress and sleeves until she was unencumbered.

Grime smearing her cheeks and arms, her once-beautiful intricately embroidered gown ruined, Gwen stumbled down the path. At last, the trees opened to reveal a smoky glen.

In the center, a large bonfire burned with merry flame, popping and cracking against the dark forest. Beyond it, trees melded with civilization, for a strangely proportioned building stood amongst the trunks. It blended into the bark until Gwen couldn't tell where tree ended and home began. She saw no doors or windows, only openings either too large for humans or just the size to squeeze into.

"Greetings, child."

Gwen jumped at the voice. Peering past the smoke, she saw three women clustered between the bonfire and building. Gwen swallowed her fear and approached them.

None of the women appeared young, yet neither were they

old. Their features morphed and twisted on the edge of sight, beautiful yet ghastly, ancient yet youthful, ethereal and fae, utterly unlike anything a mortal would ever understand. One stood tall, another short, and the third in-between. Their hair could have been dark or light, colorful or monochromatic. The shifting firelight gave no hint to the truth.

"Why have you brought me here?" Gwen asked. "Why did you show me those visions?" She knew these women though they had only come to her once in a magic-fevered haze. Who else could have brought her to these Woods?

The tallest Witch inclined her head. When she spoke, her voice was motherly and warm. "The past cycles into the future. You come with vengeance in your heart, yet you do not understand your enemies. You leave behind a man who loves you for the promise of violence."

"The Skals are not evil," said the one who was neither short nor tall. "They are people who have suffered and died at the hands of your ancestors, who in turn suffered and died at the hands of others. So the cycle continues."

The shortest spoke, "Yet the cycle can be altered. We know the way, but cannot walk it. You can."

Gwen shook her head, more confused than before. "I don't understand. You aren't making sense."

"You will learn in time, child," said the first. "You are afraid now, but you will learn to wield power not seen on Earda for far too long."

All three spoke together: "Welcome, Gwendolyn Strilu, Princess of Demarren and Lady of Seastone, born to power of man and fae alike."

Gwen's head reeled, her nostrils filling with smoke and her hands grasping at the air. Falling to the ground, she breathed in deeply as the smoke washed through her lungs. She grew more solidly *there*, as if she had only been a specter before. She saw the Witches more sharply, their features defined, the haze around them clearing.

Still, she didn't close the gap. She didn't edge toward the fire though its warmth beckoned to her. Nothing made sense.

Nothing was right in this place, a place that could not be of Earda.

"You have taken the first steps, child," the tallest one said, coming forward. "An imbalance has come to our world, and though your actions alone cannot right it, you can do the work of many. By coming to us, you have started down a path from which you cannot retreat. Here you shall be tied to magic, inundated as if it were your own blood. Forget the petty squabbles of your world; they matter not here."

In that moment, Gwen thought that the Witch appeared awfully similar to her own deceased mother. "What of Wullum's death, and Druam?"

"Death is merely another stage of life. As for Druam, he has lost many he loves, and will lose many more, before all is done. Be not afraid for him, for he has long walked his path."

Gwen licked her lips and stared at a particularly grotesque tree. "What must I do?"

"I do not know," the woman answered gravely.

"But–"

"If you are successful, your actions shall change Earda irreversibly."

"In a good way?" Gwen asked hopefully.

The Witch regarded her with a blank stare. "In a necessary way."

Shivering again, Gwen hugged herself. "What if I don't want to?"

"That is no longer your choice. You have started down the path."

"And if I leave it?"

"It is possible that straying will cause the very change you seek to avoid."

"Then I have little choice."

"That is correct."

It was not a pleasant thought. However, in this glen, far removed from the pain of Earda, Gwen didn't feel as desperate as she should have. Was it possible the Woods were already in her, changing her?

A glimmer of pride flickered in her. Of all the mages, in all Earda, *she* had been chosen. *She* possessed the power necessary to alter the world.

Taking the Witch's hand, Gwen rose. She didn't know what to expect of this third life, and she still grieved for Wullum and ached for Druam's comfort, but she couldn't go back.

The Whispering Woods had claimed her.

Chapter Eight
Cara

Indistinct lights glittered on the horizon, marking distant Riverfen. Somewhere back there, Druam must be fuming at their escape. Perverse pride filled Cara's breast, and she gave a small salute to those far-off lanterns. *Next time we meet, you bastard.*

She adjusted her pack over her cuirass and turned back to the road. She followed behind Laris and Sandu as they wove through the mass of refugees that crowded the dirt. Nearly all were headed for the safety of Riverfen, fleeing prowlers and the plague. For many, the coming winter would mean death unless they took advantage of their liege's generosity. Cara wanted to scream at them to turn back. No one should accept kindness from that monster, but who would listen to her? These men and women were too tired, too sore, too hungry to listen to the ravings of a stranger.

Once night fell, they set about making camp. The work wasn't as it had been with Alex, all cheery comments and seamless team efforts. Laris had brought small cloth tents, and merely watched as Cara and Sandu set them up. As they started a fire, Laris growled, "Not tonight."

"Why not?" Cara demanded. There was a chill in the air, a taste of winter yet to come, and her aching bones desired warmth.

"We're nice and off the road, and fire'd give away our position. If Druam wants you, he'll send riders to find you. We're not taking that risk tonight."

"Just use your magic to spell us away if they come," Cara said.

"Don't show all your ignorance at once, girl." Laris pointed a thin finger at her. "Magic is far more complex than you could imagine. There are costs to it."

During all this, Sandu remained to one side, head down. Cara turned to him, appealing. "We can escape if we need to, can't we, Sandu? A fire would be nice."

"I don't think so," he replied slowly. "My legs hurt. I don't know if I can run that far. We have blankets, we'll be alright."

Cara glared at him, but he didn't meet her eye. *Since when did he become so pathetic?* she thought, then berated herself. *He's your friend, don't think about him like that.* The battle lost, she stayed quiet for a moment. Laris sprawled in the dirt chewing on dried meat and fruit. In the dimming light, he looked for all the world like a serene old man.

An old man who could stop her in her tracks, should he so choose.

Cara asked him, "What are the costs of magic?"

"Depends," he said.

"On what?"

Laris gave her a quelling glare from beneath his bushy brows. "On whether a sorcerer wants to leave any bits for the soldiers to find in the morning."

"Are you going to threaten me every time I talk to you?" Cara's beast flared inside her, and she stacked her mental walls to keep it away.

"Don't ask anything about me or my magic, and I'll answer your questions."

Doesn't leave much room, does it? Cara's initial dislike of this man seemed wholly justified. She pondered a moment, and asked, "You used magic to help my mother and father conceive a child: me."

"Don't ask how I did it," he warned, and she shook her head.

"I don't care to know. It's not like I plan to bear a *fampir's* child." A memory of Alex intruded, kissing her, his skin hot against hers – she shoved it away mercilessly. "But you can tell me about my father."

"I don't remember him," Laris said.

The beast beat against Cara's walls, and she reinforced them, though she too longed to tear out this man's throat. Sandu sat beside her, lending her his calmness. She simmered down, took a deep breath, and asked, "Why not? Surely you'd remember his name, at least."

Laris shrugged. "Magic of that power has immense costs. I was young and blind to them, and I've learned my lesson now. I barely recall your mother's name. Half my memories are gone, among other things."

"Her conception did all that?" Sandu asked, sounding more awed than annoyed, which in turn irritated Cara. "How?"

"*Fampir* are infertile. They're dead, or their bodies are. Immense magic through Autorus keeps them alive. The magic to counteract that and make them able to conceive is powerful, and it takes from the caster."

"So you don't know what happened to my father?" The little hope Cara held slipped away, leaving only dull loss. Would she have to track down her mother, in all this vast world, to learn the truth?

"Unfortunately not. He could stand before me today and I wouldn't know him." Laris gave her a strange look. "You don't need your parents. You are not their child beyond blood."

"Merick was your true father," Sandu said. "He raised and loved you."

"And now he's a monster, too," Cara said with a shudder. She didn't want to think about the abomination Mavian had made out of her Merick.

The wind whipped through their camp, bringing a hint of frost with it. Reluctantly, Cara followed Sandu into their tent and wrapped herself in warm blankets. She lay awake, wondering whether it would be better to run away and pursue Mavian on her own. *I made Sandu a promise.* She sighed. Sleep came long after the mens' snores filled the night.

Three days passed in much the same manner. Laris had yet

to do anything beyond give orders or complain, and Sandu stopped often to rest his legs. As they drew farther from the city, the river of refugees slowed to a trickle, and they only met a few along the road. The third night, Laris allowed a fire, and Cara relished its flames against the bitter cold.

On the fourth night since their exodus, Cara asked, "What's the nearest village?"

Sandu said, "Yilfer is about a candle's walk away, I'd say. Can't be certain, it's been awhile since I've traveled this road."

"Aye, Yilfer is the next town," Laris agreed. "More of a hamlet, really. Nothing but farms."

Cara ducked inside the tent and consulted Alex's book. A *fampir* lived not too far away, just outside Yilfer. A rush of excitement made her hands tremble, but she waited until Laris and Sandu slept before she left camp.

Cara let her mental walls collapse and accepted the beast. It rushed into her mind, reveling in the night air, making her feel warmer, stronger. With the beast's speed, Cara loped along the road. Trees blurred beside her as she ran.

She stopped to sniff the air and caught a familiar scent, human yet with an undercurrent of mustiness. The same smell that Alex and Druam had. Cara followed the scent, moving carefully and quickly through the forest until she came to a farmhouse. Its lights still shone, its occupant bustling about and tending to his animals.

With her sharpened sight, the man looked human. As she stepped closer and a twig snapped beneath her feet, he whirled, a flash of red entering his eyes.

Cara raised her hands in a gesture of peace and stepped forward. "Thought I smelled kin."

The farmer considered her ridged brow and sharp teeth. He nodded. "Welcome, friend. Need a place to stop and rest?"

With an effort, Cara pushed the beast back down. Her features returned to normal, and she smiled, though she hated the sight of the farmer. *He's* fampir, *no better than a prowler at the end of the day. Both kill innocent people.* She said, "I'd appreciate that."

The farmer moved into his barn and offered her a waterskin. Cara accepted it, but didn't drink. She observed him carefully. He seemed a simple man, tending his cows and puttering about his chores, all the while chattering, "Don't see much of our kind these days. Most are in the city, I think. Or up in the mountains. I never could bring myself to leave the farm. Where are you from?"

"North," Cara said. Her fingers drifted over the pommel of her sword. "I have a thirst. Who's the best around here?"

"Ah." The farmer gave a half-hearted shrug. "Well, see, I don't mind your staying here, but you can't be scaring the villagers. They hardly bother me, and I like to keep it that way."

"Don't they notice when you drink?"

He eyed her suspiciously. "Are you newly turned? Didn't your sire show you tricks not to kill as you feed?"

The beast burned inside Cara, and she gave into it. *No point delaying it anymore.* Even if he'd claimed to only drink from animals, she had had no intentions of leaving him alive.

She snarled and leapt at him. The farmer shouted in alarm, his features warping. He dropped the pitchfork he held as she barreled into him with her shoulder.

The *fampir* stumbled and tried to attack. Cara was faster, more cunning, more sure. She drew her sword and pinned him against the wall.

"Why do you do this?" the *fampir* panted, his hands held up pleadingly. "I've done nothing against our kind!"

"*Your* kind has no place here," Cara growled. She swung her arms. Her sword cut through the man's neck and upheld hands. He collapsed into the straw as his cows grunted in their stalls.

In death, the *fampir* looked like a normal man. Cara knew the truth; he was a menace, just like the prowlers. Yilfer would be far safer with him gone.

Cara wiped her sword clean. She opened each stall door, hoping the animals would leave. They didn't move. She shrugged. With the beast still lending her its strength, she hauled the *fampir* and his separated parts onto the straw. She lit the pile with a candle.

The animals lowed and cowered, but didn't leave. Some part of her regretted their deaths, but she couldn't stay long enough to lead them all to safety. Cara walked away into the forest, apathetic to seeing the place burn down. As she turned away, she felt as if someone were watching her. She peered into the darkness and couldn't see anything. After a moment, the feeling disappeared, and she discounted it as nerves.

On the way back to camp, she washed her face and hands in an icy pond. Blood specked her clothes and armor, and she scrubbed them as best she could. As she cleaned herself, the beast slithered happily back to its lair. A sense of grim pride filled the void it left. *One less monster that lives to harm others*. It was a long road to D'Clet, and she took pleasure in the *fampir* she would end along it.

When she returned to camp, she found it quiet and still. Her contentment soon turned sour as Laris emerged from his tent, rubbing his eyes and scowling.

"Do you smell that?" he asked.

"Smell what?"

"There's a fire burning nearby," he said, peering into the woods. "Though perhaps it's nothing."

"Could just be a nearby farm," Cara suggested.

"Could be," Laris agreed. He pinned her with fierce eyes. "Well, since we're both awake, we might as well get started."

"Started on w–" Cara's question ended abruptly as pain flashed through her, her very blood dragged through her veins. Her stomach seemed to rip up through her.

Cara could only scream.

Laris muttered something, and the pain ended. A different sensation coursed through her. Magic forcibly pulled the beast from its rest. Cara half-stood and half-crouched, her limbs and back convulsing. Her features morphed, but even the beast couldn't control her body. Both of them were caught in Laris's spell.

Sandu burst from the tent, freezing at the sight. Cara craned her head, pleading with her eyes for him to *do something*. He didn't move. Fear filled his expression, and he shut his eyes.

It stopped, and Cara collapsed to the ground. The beast retreated, howling in pain. She glared up at Laris, tears streaking down her cheeks, and managed to spit out, "What...veck...what did you do to me?"

"It didn't work," Laris grumbled. "I'll have to take notes on this."

Cara tried to unsheathe her sword, but her fingers fumbled. Laris only shook his head. "I told you, I need you to help me find something. Though, I may have left out that that something is inside you. I need to find the right spell to bring it out. And it's not your 'beast,' if that's what you were thinking. That's just a part of the puzzle which I must figure out."

A desperate grunt escaped her throat. Laris bent down so he was close to her. He murmured, "If you resist, I'll do much worse. There are spells which would make you weep just from hearing about them. Try and hurt me, and you'll be sorry." With that, he ducked into his tent, and Cara shuddered on the ground, trying to keep her dinner down.

Sandu stared down at her in horror. She didn't feel as friendly to him now. "Why didn't you do something?" She didn't know what he could have done, but surely *something* would have been better than nothing.

"I-I-I..." Sandu's mouth worked, and he merely shook his head. He didn't say anything more.

"Useless coward," Cara growled. She climbed to her feet and pushed past him. He didn't stop her. Even after she'd flung herself into her blankets, he remained outside the tent. Part of Cara felt guilty for snapping at him, but the rest of her trembled with the echoes of pain. The beast, strong though it was, whimpered after Laris's magical torture.

Perhaps this is my punishment for killing the fampir, Cara thought. She discarded the notion as soon as it came into her head. *He deserved to die. Laris is a bully and a liar. He'll get what's coming to him.*

Sandu came into the tent after a long time, mumbling an apology. Cara rolled over, pretending to be asleep. She sensed him standing over her for a moment before he retreated to his own blankets. *Good. Let him feel bad for not helping me.*

When she woke, regret seeped into Cara's leftover aches, and she resolved to apologize to her friend. He was all she had left.

CHAPTER NINE
Mavian

In the darkest part of the night, Mavian waited for the prowlers. He loathed this task, but it was necessary. Rask held no goodwill for those who failed him, and Mavian disliked thinking what would happen without his patronage. He imagined being back in the warmth of his workroom, but even that thought held little comfort. His research to raise Maeria had come to a thorough dead end.

An autumn chill descended on the forest, making his breath fog. He shivered in his furs, envying Merick its lack of feeling. The wight stood behind him, silent and ready, an ever-present shadow. Out in the clearing, a calf whined. Its legs had been broken, its skin cut just enough to bleed. It had stopped struggling a while ago, but it still huffed and turned at each sound. Safe behind a sound-muffling spell, Mavian mused aloud.

"Think any will come?" Mavian asked though he knew the wight wouldn't reply. The only time it had ever spoken was during the Masque to taunt Cara. No matter what he did, it refused to respond to him. Despite this, Mavian kept on talking. "I once caught twenty prowlers in a night with this trap. Once their pack leader submitted, the rest followed easily."

Mavian watched the calf without pity. He said softly, "Months and months of work, catching and taming, and they all died in one night. And it'll all just happen again. Once I have more prowlers, Rask will send them into war, and they'll die.

Just like that. If I made more wights, he'd ask the same of them, too. Is that wrong, you think?"

The wight didn't move or speak. Mavian continued, "I've often wondered if the prowlers have any emotion in them. They can communicate with each other, that I know, yet once they're under the gem's power, I can't help but feel that they act differently. Docile, obedient, single-minded. Perhaps in the wild they have their own sort of families and fears. I have often wondered if I should try to speak with them, but I've seen what they can do. They ripped my own father apart, did you know that? I saw it happen. No doubt they'd do the same to me given half a chance."

The calf whined as a dark shape sprinted from the dark trees. Three more joined it, a pack of prowlers descending on the helpless animal. Their long talons ripped at the calf's flesh. They crawled on all fours, tatters of clothes hanging over their thin bodies.

Mavian drew out his white gem and spoke in the tongue of the dead, "*I draw you and bind you to me. You will obey me and bring no harm to man unless I will it. By Autorus below and the gods above, I bind you.*" As he spoke, he moved his hand through the air, drawing out complex runes. The shapes hung in the night, glowing a soft orange. His last words blew into the runes, carrying them to the creatures. The binding was complete.

The prowlers stilled, their red eyes flashing in the moonlight. They waited warily as Mavian emerged from the trees, Merick behind him.

"*Eat your fill,*" Mavian allowed. As one, the prowlers fell to, sucking the calf's blood and chewing its tender meat. When they finished, Mavian commanded them to follow, and they did.

He led them to a low-ceilinged cave, then a tunnel beyond it, and up through the mountain until he reached the large cavern he had found to keep his prowlers. It was far below D'Clet, farther even than his workshop, where no innocents would wander. No matter his feelings for the nobles, Mavian would not allow his prowlers to kill rustics.

The nightly feeding had already occurred, for two cow

skeletons lay picked clean in the center of the room. Since his return to D'Clet, Mavian had found another thirty prowlers to add to his numbers. The four new ones easily joined the pack, sniffing each other and trilling in their strange tongue. Some were restless, but none would leave the cavern without his permission. The magic on them was too strong.

Assured of the prowlers' behavior, Mavian wearily climbed the stone steps to a heavy wooden door. He knocked thrice upon it and heard the distinct sound of multiple bolts drawing free. The door opened. Five soldiers waited on the other side, their swords partly drawn.

"None came up with you?" one asked.

"Of course not. They never have," Mavian said, pushing him aside. He went to a ledge overlooking the lair as the door was closed and locked behind Merick, and Mavian rolled his eyes. No matter how many times they'd seen him walk among the beasts, the soldiers had no confidence in his ability to keep them calm.

Mavian examined his creatures below. He asked, "How long did it take them to eat their dinner?"

The same soldier replied, "A few minutes."

"Three cows tomorrow night. They need to be kept well-fed."

"Understood, my lord."

Mavian nodded, then followed the carved tunnels up and up until he finally reached his workshop. The red lanterns glowed softly, illuminating Maeria's white skin. As Merick went to stand in his usual spot, Mavian checked his beloved. The spell to preserve her still worked, keeping her as fresh as the day she died. If he were to touch her cheek, he might swear there was still some warmth in it.

Mavian didn't touch her. Not now, while she lay lifeless.

As he turned from the rock, he realized he wasn't alone. Rask and Chadron lurked in the shadows, waiting for him.

"You're late," Rask said.

"I didn't realize we had an appointment."

"Did you gain more for the army?"

"I did."

"That, at least, is satisfactory." Rask pushed himself forward, his watery eyes gleaming. "I have need of you tonight. Take us to the coast."

"Why?" Mavian clutched his white gem protectively. "I'm tired, I want to sleep."

"Because I said so, boy. Take us to the coast."

"It's not as easy as–"

Rask's cane whipped up, catching Mavian's ear and knocking into his head. Mavian reeled as Chadron laughed. Rask said, dangerously soft, "You will do as I tell you, Strilu, or I'll feed you to your own prowlers."

They won't obey you, Mavian thought, but didn't dare voice. He glared at his patron. *I could crush you if I wanted.* The only thing that stayed his hand was the knowledge that no one else would accept his dark magic. He gritted out, "Where on the coast?"

Chadron stepped forward and gave Mavian a piece of paper. He studied it, unable to read the Elvish written there.

"Your magic will find the elf who wrote that, yes?" Rask asked. Mavian nodded. It was how he'd located Alex's caravan. "Take us there."

"I have to go with you," Mavian said, half hoping that Rask would change his mind. He hated being a mere tool to the earl, yet he also knew there was little choice but to obey. *Someday, I'll set my prowlers on you.*

"I'm aware. Just do it."

Mavian glared at his wight, which hadn't moved as Rask assaulted him. *Some help you are.* He gestured to the two men. "Not here. I don't want my work disturbed."

With Rask and Chadron in tow, Mavian walked to a nearby empty room. There, he gripped the gem and began the incantation to open the dread portal. His skin crawled as he drew different runes into the air, these ones darker, more sinister. Each one hovered like a terrible wraith until he finished his spell.

The purple-and-black void opened with a crackle, its edges

reaching for the walls, blurring vision. The floor shook, then stilled. Mavian held the paper and stepped through.

Darkness closed in around him. He shivered at the screams and wails of unknown souls pleading for help. There was nothing he could do for them. Slimy tentacles reached for him, and he brushed them off brusquely. He took another step and emerged from the void, leaving its suffering behind him. The trip had lasted no longer than a heartbeat, yet he swallowed in relief. Traveling through the Underworld always had its risks, and he wondered if it might someday claim him. The thought made his stomach queasy.

Rask and Chadron stepped out behind him, and Mavian closed the void with a word. As it popped into nonexistence, a wave of dizziness overcame him, and he had to put his hands on his knees. He closed his eyes, images of the dead pressing on his eyelids, close yet far, figures swimming in the edges of his vision.

Bringing others through with him was always more difficult than going by himself. On the night of the Masque, when he'd opened multiple dread portals and sent his army of prowlers through, he hadn't felt the effects during the battle. Somehow, it was easier to bear the portals while they remained open. Once they had closed, debilitating sickness had overcome him, emptying his stomach and bowels, making his head pound with a thousand different pains, turning his limbs into jelly. The dead were loud the night of the Masque, screaming into his ears until he shrieked from the noise.

Rask and Chadron, less affected, regained themselves quickly. Mavian saw, with some shred of delight, that Chadron shuddered, and hoped the man had seen particularly gruesome images.

"Are you ready, Strilu?" Rask demanded.

Mavian gathered himself and pushed aside the voices in his head. He straightened as the other two men moved off. Able to focus now, he realized that they were on a rocky beach dotted with boulders. In the dim light Mavian could just see a stone hut built above the shoreline. Trees grew right up to the shore, their branches creaking in the night wind. A longboat was drawn up and anchored.

As they strode up to the hut, the door opened, and an elf clad in armor demanded to know their identities. Rask answered, and they were allowed inside. The hut had only two rooms and was clearly long abandoned. Furniture lay broken and dusty, the fireplace empty and cold. Three elven soldiers crowded inside, and a driftwood door blocked the view of the next room.

"Wait here," Rask said. Mavian eyed the soldiers and obeyed. Chadron moved to join his uncle, but the earl waved him off, too. Alone, Rask walked through the driftwood door and shut it behind him. Chadron frowned, crossing his arms.

"Not as trusted as you'd like to think, are you?" Mavian said. He leaned against a stone wall, ignoring the soldiers. "Do you know who he's meeting in there?"

"Of course I do." Chadron gave him a withering look. "Mind your tongue, Strilu. You're only as useful as your beasts, and once they're dead..."

"You forget the powers I hold at my fingertips," Mavian said, opening his shirt for the gem to poke out. He had never liked Chadron, but the cur was part and parcel of Rask's patronage. That didn't mean he couldn't taunt the blowhard, though. "I could drag you into the Underworld before you could screech for your uncle's help."

"*If* you have a tongue left to chant your little spells," Chadron spat back.

"At least I still have both hands. Bested by a 700-year-old, not what I'd call worthy of legends."

Chadron's nostrils flared, and he drew his sword. The elves watched him, but did nothing as he stepped forward, his steel waving beneath Mavian's nose. "Give me one reason not to cut you down now."

"You have to get back home somehow," Mavian drawled. "I don't think your dear uncle would be happy to hear he has to walk all the way back to D'Clet."

"My uncle may have promised you land or power, but he

won't be around to protect you forever. You'll be ousted as soon–"

"As soon as I'm dead and you have my seat?" Rask's voice slithered across the room. Mavian and Chadron both jumped like boys caught misbehaving by their tutor. Chadron sheathed his sword, smart enough to look ashamed.

"Uncle, that's not–"

"That's precisely what you vecking well meant." Rask glared at him. "You may be my heir now, but I can grant it to someone else. Don't tempt me, boy." Seemingly satisfied with his nephew's shame, Rask said, "Come on, both of you. It's time you learned your part in this."

He turned, and they followed him into the other room. It was just as small as the first, crowded with a large desk that clearly had not been there before the elves arrived. It held a parchment map marked with lines and symbols. On the other side of the desk, *Kair* Aremo Teru waited, long fingertips tapping the desk impatiently.

"These are your lieutenants, Rask? A one-handed man and a Strilu?" The elf prince's eyes were hard on Mavian. "You're sure he won't betray us to Seastone?"

"My nephew is capable of his task. As for Strilu, he was willing to disgrace himself in Seastone's eyes and led the attack on the Cascade Palace. Surely you were present?"

"I had other concerns rather than attending a party." The elf sat with a flourish. "So, Strilu, you can control the prowlers?"

"Yes," Mavian replied. He disliked the way the elf studied him as though he were a cut of meat.

"They shall be our frontlines for our attack on Seastone."

"No!" Mavian said impulsively. He wished he could swallow his tongue when the other three regarded him with immense disdain. Shaking his head, he tried again. "There aren't enough of them to be on any frontlines, not in a real war. They wouldn't last a minute against armored opponents."

"Rask." The elf nodded to the earl. "Keep your men in line."

For the second time that day, Rask swung his cane at Mavian, this time catching his elbow. The earl snapped, "Do as you're told, Strilu. This is no time for objections. You will send your prowlers where we tell them to go. Is that understood?"

Mavian nodded, not trusting his tongue. He rubbed his elbow and glared resentfully as the elf and earl turned to Chadron.

"Nephew, you're to hold D'Clet while I lead our armies against Seastone. You will have a skeleton force of men, but our walls are strong. Defend my city against all who may take it."

"What of the king and his army?" Chadron asked. "They won't let you attack another earl."

The elf gave a sly grin. "My allies in Demarren have promised a delightful distraction while my forces move into position. Henrik will not be a worry for much longer."

"You're attacking the king *and* Seastone?" Mavian asked. "With what armies? I doubt Dedaria has–"

"Dedaria has powerful friends," the prince purred. "We have the men necessary. Well, Rask, we have a treaty. My generals will meet you in a month's time."

"Excellent." Rask clasped the elf's hand. "I look forward to the fruits of our arrangement."

Once they left the hut, both Chadron and Mavian asked questions about the imminent invasion. Rask waved them off. "Our army, with the Lofalins, will attack where Seastone least expects it. When we arrive, Mavian will bring his prowlers to join us. We needn't worry about Henrik; the *kair* and his allies will take him down."

"And you trust these elves?" Mavian pressed. "If their army is as great as they promise, they could easily dispose of us."

"I trust them as far as you trust me," Rask returned. "Enough to attain our goals, and no farther."

"But–"

"Enough, Strilu." Rask stopped short. "You needn't trust them, but I will not lead you astray. In fact, I have found a solution to your plight. Take us back to D'Clet, and I will show you what I've discovered in bringing your beloved back."

Mavian paused, his fingers twitching. He didn't trust the high earl, but had he any choice? If the man spoke true, Maeria could be alive and in his arms again soon. *I'll even work with elves if it brings her back.*

"As soon as we return," Mavian said.

"She'll be with you again before we leave for war," the earl promised. Something deceptive gleamed in his eyes, but Mavian didn't care to question it. He was too full of excitement and nervousness and hope.

As he opened the dread portal, Mavian imagined hearing Maeria's voice again, and the thought of her drove the dead from his mind.

CHAPTER TEN
Seanna

Don't make this worse on yourself, Seanna thought, but she still glared distastefully at the colorful pile of clothes. Near the door, Captain Laaravat waited with mocking eyes.

Through a tiny window, she could still see traces of sunset, a marker of the day she'd passed in the small cell. Only a day, yet it felt like quinns. The moment she'd left the hall, the corsairs stripped off her jewels and fine clothes, leaving her a sack-like dress which she pulled on as they laughed.

Now, it seemed, they wanted her to rejoin the festivities.

"Is belonging to the queen's fool," Laaravat said, gesturing to the gaudy clothes on the straw. "Is fat man, should be fitting you."

"And this is what your queen wants of me?" Seanna asked.

"Yes."

Just do as she says and perhaps you'll live to bear your child, Seanna reminded herself. With a sigh, she bent awkwardly to the straw and picked up the breeches and shirt. They were festooned with colorful ribbons and odd patches, clearly a court fool's garb. Thankfully, the fool took care of his belongings, keeping them clean if threadbare.

Not wanting to change in front of Laaravat again, Seanna slipped it on over her rags. The shirt hung past her hips and the breeches were loose at her knees. There wasn't much to do about her hair; it hung lank and oily around her face, and she hadn't the pins or ties to contain it. Her feet were bare.

"Are there shoes to match?" Seanna asked, not a little sarcastically. To her chagrin, Laaravat produced a pair of red-and-orange boots that laced up past the ankles.

Seanna tried to put them on and found that she couldn't reach past her large stomach. She sighed again. "If you want me to wear these, you'll have to help me." Laaravat didn't object, and with his assistance, she soon had the ridiculous shoes laced on over her swollen feet.

The child moved about as Seanna and Laaravat left her cell. It had been doing that a lot lately, and she could only pray that it would wait to come. *Too early, my love.*

Once again, Laaravat led her up through the manor and past the ostentatious loot-filled corridor to the rowdy main hall. Steel-Eyes sat on her throne, sharp eyes watching her men. That gaze fixed on Seanna as she and Laaravat entered, remaining there as they made their way around the tables.

"You look like a fool," Steel-Eyes said.

"Even the greatest ruler can be a fool," Seanna replied, pleased with herself. It was wit without offense, something she had yet to fully master. "And this is my time."

Steel-Eyes tilted her head, a smile touching her lips. "Good. My men are hungry and thirsty; serve them."

Seanna nearly laughed. "Do I look like a common wench to you?" Her indignant remark came without thinking. Before she could react, the Corsair Queen stood and slapped her cheek, leaving a stinging mark. Seanna staggered, her hand going to her face. Henrik, despite his threats, had never laid a finger to her.

"I do not abide insolence in my court," said the Corsair Queen, smile gone. "My men are hungry and thirsty. Serve them."

Another biting remark rose to Seanna's lips, and she quelled it with difficulty. She glared at the woman, resentment seething inside her. A corsair held out his mug, shouting for more. Steel-Eyes inclined her head, her message clear: do it, or else.

Her pride quickly dissipating, Seanna obeyed. She moved

as quickly as she could from man to man, carrying their mugs to the barrels to refill them or bringing another plate of meat to their table. A servant shoved a heavy tray into her arms without a care for her condition. Seanna struggled under the weight of so many mugs. The corsairs leered and spat at her, laughing as she cringed away from them. Some gave her lewd remarks, though not one of them touched her.

"Always wanted to fuck a queen," one said, his toothless smile revolting.

Another stared at her belly. "D'ya think the baby'd feel my big cock inside ya?" She glared at him, but he only jeered at her.

"C'mon, lovely, give an old man a kiss." That one pursed his lips, and his buddies all laughed.

Seanna had never been so humiliated before. Even in the depths of her shame at court, none of the courtiers would dare speak so crassly to her. Her eyes sparkled with tears, and she stumbled with drinks in hand, nearly falling into a corsair's lap. His hands grasped at her waist, and she reeled away. Without thinking, she threw a mug at him, spilling ale over his stringy beard. Surprise crossed his face, then he stood, a knife appearing in his hands. He loomed over her, his breath rotten. She shrank back, afraid yet defiant. What right had he to lay hands on her?

"What d'ya think–" he started, but stopped short, staring over Seanna's shoulder. She turned to see Steel-Eyes, arms crossed, eyes murderous. Seanna backed away.

"What was the one rule, Graff?" the Corsair Queen asked softly.

"D-don' touch 'er," he replied, quickly sheathing his knife. He raised his hands, pleading. Despite her anger, a small pity stirred in Seanna.

"What do I do with rats who disobey me?" Steel-Eyes took a mug from the table though her eyes never left the corsair.

"Please, I didn' mean it, she fell–"

"And you grabbed her. What should a gentleman do, Graff?" Her voice was low, dangerously soft. Seanna couldn't tear her eyes away. The child squirmed inside her, and both nausea and fear warred in her throat.

"I d-don' know," he said, falling to his knees. "Please, I didn't–"

"A gentleman helps a lady back to her feet," said Steel-Eyes. With one graceful movement, she drew the blade at her hip and swept it across the man's throat, her expression never changing. He gurgled and grasped at his neck, his hands coming away bloody. With a *thump*, he fell to the floor, eyes staring widely at nothing.

Seanna's hands went to her mouth. She gagged – barely holding it down – and stared at the corpse, not quite knowing how to feel. She asked, "Did he deserve death?"

"He disobeyed," Steel-Eyes said, stepping around the body with practiced ease. "All my men know the price." She came to stand in front of Seanna, taller by half a foot. She said, "Don't displease me, Your Grace. Until you tell me what I wish, you will serve my men. Each one who touches you – even by accident – will see the same fate."

"But–"

"Let it haunt you, and know that I will not falter." Steel-Eyes swept away, glaring from one side of the room to the other as if to dare any man to object. None did. As her profile turned for a moment, Seanna thought it seemed oddly familiar, like she'd seen the woman before.

Drums sounded throughout the manor. Steel-Eyes paused, half-turning to the door. She waited a moment, listening to the pounding, before striding to her throne. She announced as she sat, "Our guest has arrived."

The men put down their mugs and meat and turned to the door, expectant. Forgotten for the moment, Seanna crept to an alcove that lay partly in shadows, grateful for the relief.

The doors opened and a troop of elven soldiers marched inside. At their head a tall elf with shoulder-length black hair stalked into the room, his dark eyes glittering above his thin mustache. His sleeveless robe was embroidered with snakes, and his shaved chest gleamed in the torchlight. Once, Seanna had thought him magnificent.

Now, she shrank into the shadows as he came closer to the

throne. The last time they'd met, he had said her head would adorn a pike. Thankfully, he only had eyes for the Corsair Queen.

"*Kair* Aremo Teru," Steel-Eyes said. "Welcome to my fortress."

"Queen Steel-Eyes," he replied, bowing though his black eyes never left hers. "I am honored to be welcomed here. I bring gifts for your treasury." A troop of elven servants entered, carrying nine heavy chests between them. They laid them in a row before the throne and opened the lids.

The first held silver coins in great heaping piles, the second precious furs, the third elaborate metal-worked sculptures, and so on, each filled with a different treasure. From her alcove, Seanna watched the Corsair Queen, who didn't smile or frown, her expression patient and calm.

"Are they not pleasing to you?" Aremo asked. He wore that same confident, sardonic look Seanna had seen before. She shivered, grateful that he hadn't noticed her.

Steel-Eyes pierced him with her harsh gaze. "Let us not be coy, *Kair*. You would not journey this far, nor bring such wealth, without reason. What do you want?"

"Always the shrewd woman. Very well, I have a request to make. I am expecting ships within the quinn and I want them to be left alone. No harrying, no looting. Completely free and safe passage."

"To Dedaria?"

"Some, yes. Others will travel farther north."

"How many ships?"

"Sixty."

A wave of surprise traveled around the room. Men muttered to each other as Steel-Eyes' face darkened. Seanna glanced from Corsair Queen to elven prince, waiting. Aremo still had that awful smile.

"I have fifty-five ships in my fleet," Steel-Eyes said quietly, "with a good crew for each. And yet, I have less than three thousand men under my command. How many elves are you bringing to D'Ehsi shores, Aremo Teru? How many spears do they bear?"

"An army greater than any human has known," Aremo replied. "I know your tactics, corsair, and I know your capabilities. I would rather us not be sunk from afar before we can reach Dedaria."

"Dedaria and farther north, you said. What is that other landing?"

"The River Valley."

The Corsair Queen's shoulders stiffened, and the tension dropped to an icy temperature. Even Aremo's smile slipped.

Steel-Eyes stood, coming to stand in front of the elf prince. She was of a height with him.

"No," she said.

"So you will not give us safe passage?"

"Not to the River Valley. I have an accord with the earl which I will not break."

"Tell me your price. Whatever he has given, I will pay thrice over." He leaned forward, voice low. "Be reasonable, Cairn. You would not want us seeking you after our prize has been won."

"You bring an invasion to my home and expect me to be grateful? I can gain these treasures tenfold in one year *without* betraying my country." Her eyes bored into him. "What else can you offer?"

"A fleet of the fastest ships we elves can make." The corsairs murmured appreciatively at the prince's words.

Steel-Eyes tilted her head again. "Intriguing. Tell me, what is your prize?"

"I knew you'd come around. We take Con Salur and Riverfen first, and then all of Dotschar and Rengu."

Seanna couldn't help herself. She gasped, uttering a cry of "No!" Immediately, she clamped her hands over her mouth, but Aremo had heard her. His black eyes gleamed when they saw her. He stalked over and pulled her from the safety of the alcove.

"My, how far you have fallen, Your Grace," he said, circling her like a shark. "From the Cascade Palace in your silks and jewels, to a corsair's lair in fool's clothes. They are better fitting, methinks. You are a greater idiot than you realized."

Seanna trembled, anger building in her breast. Sir Eric wasn't there to help her this time. With his cool fingers, Aremo cupped her chin, staring into her eyes. "What are you doing here, little Seanna?"

"She is my guest, Aremo," Steel-Eyes said. "Release her."

Aremo did no such thing. His fingers gripped harder, and Seanna's eyes watered. He said, "No words of defiance? Have you finally learned your lesson? Did Henrik beat it into you? You poor, pathetic creature, you truly thought you could gain me as an ally and have the elves at your beck and call. Your reckoning has come, and you will be the first to feel its pain." He turned to the Corsair Queen, one hand latching around Seanna's wrist. "I will pay for her. As much as you want, every coin in my treasury if need be. Give her to me!"

"Why so desperate, Aremo? She can do you no harm."

Desperately, Seanna tried to meet Steel-Eyes' gaze, but the other woman only looked to the prince.

"Because it would amuse me," Aremo said, a manic pitch to his voice. "Because I want her to watch her people burn!"

Seanna tried to pull away, but his grip was iron. Steel-Eyes spared her not a glance.

"The king will pay a mighty ransom for her," the corsair said.

"I will pay more!"

"And what if your army loses? Then where shall my head be?"

"We will not lose."

"You–"

Seanna cut her off. She remembered now where she recognized the Corsair Queen's profile, the shape of her lips and eyes, the curve of her nose. "Wait! I'll tell you about Druam and his court. I'll tell you about Maid Gellder."

Aremo turned to her with a befuddled expression, but Steel-Eyes had frozen, her hazel eyes fixed on Seanna. Seanna stamped on Aremo's foot and broke free. "Let me speak, please."

"You can't be–" Aremo started, and Steel-Eyes interrupted,

"I will consider your proposals, elf. Now I will speak with the queen – alone."

Aremo's eyes flashed. He raised a hand, and the elven soldiers about the room drew their spears, pointing at the corsairs. To their credit, the corsairs didn't flinch. They all waited for their queen's word, hands straying to the blades at their hips.

"You think you can threaten me, in my own fortress, surrounded by my own men?" Steel-Eyes said.

Aremo hesitated. Seanna shrank fearfully away from him.

"Even if you manage to strike me down, you will never leave this fortress alive," Steel-Eyes continued in a stony voice. "Leave us for the moment, elf, or I will make it my personal mission to sink every one of your ships. I said that I will consider your proposal, and my word is not given lightly. Go."

With a final threatening glare at Seanna, the elven prince turned on his heel and left the hall. His soldiers followed and the corsairs rushed behind them. The massive doors shut, and Seanna was alone with the Corsair Queen.

"How do you know that name?" Steel-Eyes demanded immediately.

"I've met her," Seanna said. Her pithiness was gone; she would have to be honest now if she wanted to remain out of Aremo's clutches. "She came to us as the *sulpari*, brought by Lord Strilu. She saved my life when prowlers attacked me."

"So Druam has her," Steel-Eyes breathed. "What else do you know?"

"She told us of her education and her training, and the disappearance of her lady. She came to Riverfen to seek Maid Nellestere." Speaking the name sent a lump into Seanna's throat. *Don't think of Maeria now. She's dead, and you can't have her again.*

"What did she look like?"

"Beautiful. Confident. Just like her mother," Seanna said, observing the Corsair Queen carefully. Steel-Eyes' expression slipped into something like pride before it hardened once more.

"I don't know what you're talking about."

"No one knows about her mother, Sura Gellder, or how

such a woman could have attained the wealth to pay for her daughter's intense education. Well, now I know." Seanna dared to take the other woman's hand. "Your secret is safe with me."

"There is no secret. Cara–"

"I never mentioned her name."

Steel-Eyes paused. Vulnerability and desire warred on her features. She tore her hand away. The Corsair Queen smoothed her hair and straightened her tunic. She said, "I killed the last person who discovered this."

"I hope you will make a different decision this time."

Steel-Eyes was already moving toward the door, her back to Seanna. The Corsair Queen allowed Aremo back in and said, "What purpose does your invasion serve?"

Aremo gave a hungry look at Seanna, then turned to Steel-Eyes. "My cousin in Lofaliri wishes to expand his religion. I wish to expand my territory. You should know why wars are waged."

Steel-Eyes's lips tightened, and she sighed. She said loudly, "I will allow your ships to pass, but if they come within ten leagues of Riverfen, I will sink them. My guest remains with me."

The elf shot another glare at Seanna, a strange malice gleaming in his eyes. He licked his lips and hesitated. After a moment, he said, "A disappointing decision, but I will not argue it. Queen Seanna and I will meet again, I am sure. When she will have no one to protect her. However, you must not release her until my ships have landed. We have an accord?"

"We have an accord."

The elven prince left as suddenly as he'd come, and the corsairs made their way back into the hall. Once they'd regained their seats, Steel-Eyes said, "Laaravat, prepare your ship. You're to waylay the king's barge and bring him to the spit for a prisoner exchange."

Laaravat saluted and hurried off as Seanna sank into a chair in relief. "So I'm to be freed?"

"You're to be ransomed. A queen and an heir are worth a pretty coin, so I hear." Steel-Eyes lowered her voice so only Seanna could hear. "Tell your king of Aremo's armies. Sixty ships with hundreds of men on each. War is coming, Seanna. Try to survive it."

"Why allow us this chance?"

Steel-Eyes shrugged. "There's no fun if there are no odds, is there?"

There was something in the woman's eyes, something that Seanna couldn't read, that told her the Corsair Queen had other reasons for going against her agreement with the elven prince.

CHAPTER ELEVEN
Seanna

The Corsair Queen's ship appeared the same as all the rest of her fleet, down to the writhing mermaid bowsprit. The cabins below told a different story. Each was large and well decorated, boasting comforts most minor lords would envy. Seanna's quarters held a large silver mirror that was finer than any she'd seen before.

After Aremo's visit, Seanna had spent three days in relative ease in the corsair manor. She was given hot meals and allowed to keep to herself. Though she never regained her jewelry, she was at least allowed to dress in a wool gown that buttoned up to her throat. Cairn Steel-Eyes hadn't spoken to her since that day, and Seanna didn't seek her out. Her ransom was coming, and she would have to be patient.

The fourth day, the corsairs prepared their queen's ship for departure. It was almost two days to the meeting point, and Steel-Eyes wouldn't want to be late. Seanna didn't protest as she was pulled hither and thither. Great relief rushed through her the moment the ship left the floating wooden city.

It was in the evening, after Seanna had eaten and washed, that the Corsair Queen came to her chambers. Seanna glanced up from the porthole and tensed. The other woman had her hair down for once, though the loose strands did nothing to soften her roughness. She had removed her bodice and various belts and weapons, wearing only a linen shirt and breeches. Like her sailors, her feet were bare and callused. She shifted her weight easily to match the ship's rolling.

Seanna rose as the door closed behind the corsair and managed a small curtsey. With the motion of the ship and growing child, she doubted she could bend any more without falling. "Steel-Eyes. What brings you here tonight?"

Somewhere in the last few days, Seanna had developed a sort of kindness toward the Corsair Queen. The other woman had kept her from harassment, but more importantly, she was a mother. Each time Seanna caught a glimpse of Steel-Eyes, she longed to know more about her. How had this woman come to be the greatest threat on the seas? Why have a child, yet abandon it? Why give her daughter a lord's education?

Even more than that, Seanna desired to know how she could be more like the Corsair Queen. A woman who was equally respected and feared, who wielded power like a farmer his scythe, separating the wheat from the chaff with ease. What Seanna would give to be seen in such a light.

"Your Grace." Steel-Eyes raised a bottle to her lips and drank with loud gulps, then wiped her mouth. She held out the bottle for Seanna, who declined. Steel-Eyes shrugged and lowered herself into a chair. She didn't speak.

Sinking back onto the bed, Seanna watched the other woman carefully. Though Steel-Eyes drank heavily, she didn't appear drunk or even somewhat out-of-sorts. There was a guardedness in her every movement.

"What was your daughter like as a child?" Seanna finally asked. She dearly hoped it was a safe question.

A faraway look came into the other queen's eyes. "Shy and quiet. I never could stay in one place for long; it was hard for her to make friends every time we moved."

"I imagine it was difficult for you to leave her."

"Aye."

The Corsair Queen didn't seem too angry, so Seanna broached, "Who else knows that you're her mother?"

Steel-Eyes took another large swallow and said, "Just Strilu."

"Not even her father?"

"Her father's dead."

Once, Seanna had wished that Henrik was dead so that she could raise their child as she wanted. Now, after her ordeals at sea, she wasn't so sure. She asked, "Why did you have your men kidnap me?"

"Because it was an easy job, easier than taking one of the other lords who saw her in Druam's court."

It was a blow to Seanna's pride – the woman had only wanted her knowledge of Cara – but she swept aside her ill feelings. When would she ever have another chance to speak candidly with the Corsair Queen?

"You said to Aremo that you're allied with Druam. Why not go there yourself and see her?"

"Rumors can be false, spies misled. I've heard that she's already departed his court." There was a hesitancy in her tone, as if Steel-Eyes wanted to say more but couldn't.

Seanna took a risk, scooting closer and leaning forward. "There's more to it than that."

"She's a grown woman now, she can make her own decisions. And, if she's anything like me, she's already decided that she hates me." Steel-Eyes swept an arm around to indicate her point. "In the years since she was born, I attained all this. That power came with a cost. I'm paying for it now, and I can't say what I'd do if I could go back and stay with her instead."

"She could have grown up on the sea, learned–"

"To kill and steal? Likely been raped several times over then murdered and thrown into the water? I survived because I clung on after a lifetime of close calls. Neither of us would have made it if I'd had to care for a child at the same time."

Seanna held her belly, not quite comprehending. "Why not stay with her? She was your child, and you left her."

"Aye, and I regret it every damn day. Her father and I thought he'd raise her, and I could sail. But he's gone. I tried, you know. Until she was four or so, I tried to be a good mother. The sea always called to me, and I was worn down with caring for a child." Steel-Eyes drained her bottle. She gave Seanna a hard look. "I was selfish, and it's good that she'll always hate me."

Even in her vulnerability, Steel-Eyes carried an aura of such command and anger that Seanna couldn't understand why she had been allowed into the corsair's confidence. She blurted, "Why tell me all this? Why not just sell me back and be done with me?"

"Because you're about to be a mother and you'll make the same mistakes. How many noble women are present in their children's lives? Actually present? Few, if any. They send their children off to nursemaids and tutors and coo over them once a day before going back to their politicking games." Steel-Eyes pointed at Seanna's belly. "Whether you're carrying an heir or a girl, you'll be tempted once it's born to the pursuit of power. You've tried it already, so I've heard. You failed. Don't try again. It needs a mother more than it needs a queen."

"A life at court isn't the same as a life at sea," Seanna said. The part of her that wanted to acknowledge her past wrongdoings clung to the Corsair Queen's words, but the part that still resisted refused to listen. "I can be a mother and a queen."

"War is coming, Queen Seanna. Take your child and run. What are you leaving behind? A husband you hate, a court full of backstabbers and sycophants? Be selfish, for the both of you."

"If I have a son, it is my duty to the kingdom–"

"Veck the kingdom!" Steel-Eyes rose, looming over Seanna. Her breath stank of ale. "Listen to me, you foolish bitch. Either the elves will kill you or the loneliness of court will drown you. Take your child and escape it all. What's a crown to your child's happiness?"

"Why should I listen to a woman whose only control is through fear?" Defiance heated Seanna's breast, and she stood, forcing the other woman back. "You know *nothing* of court life. There will always be sacrifices, but they must be made for the sake of the kingdom. If not me, some other poor woman would have to give her joy to gain stability."

Seanna decided that she didn't, after all, want to become more like this jaded woman. Her men respected her, true, but it was a respect born of fear. They would remain loyal because any other course would be met with death.

Yet I tried to gain respect through bribery and the promise of power, Seanna realized. *Is that any better than her? She sees her men as tools and no more, yet I did the same with the courtiers.* She wasn't sure *how*, exactly, she should view those beneath her, but at least she knew now that there was a different way, perhaps a better way.

"Go to your daughter," Seanna said, a sudden spark. "Perhaps you'll find you hate yourself more than she does."

Steel-Eyes slowly shook her head. "Isn't that more selfish than staying away? I'll only leave again. It'll hurt her more to have hope and lose it, than to have none at all." She put a hand to her waist and drew out a small leather pouch. From inside, she withdrew a simple brooch of filigree silver and black onyx. She rubbed it between her fingers, her eyes distant in thought. After a moment, she said, "This was her father's. I always said I'd give it to her when she's old enough."

"You still can."

"Can I?" Steel-Eyes gave a wry smile. "I won't go to her. If we meet again, it'll be her choice, not mine." She clutched her fingers around the brooch for a moment, then dropped it back into the pouch. For a moment, sadness flitted across her expression. "I cannot control you, but if I could, I would have you run away and leave this country forever."

Seanna began to respond, but the Corsair Queen strode from the room, slamming the door behind her. The baby moved, and Seanna soothed it with a murmur. *I don't believe I've ever met someone as sad as Cairn Steel-Eyes.* She looked ruefully down at her hands. *And will I end up just like her? Lonely and aloof?* As she contemplated it, Seanna decided that she would do whatever it took to end up happier. Even if it meant being a little kinder to Henrik and a little less proud.

✳

The rocky island was barely more than a spit of land without a tree in sight. Water crashed against the boulders, and the corsairs expertly maneuvered their small craft ashore. Steel-Eyes, accompanied by seven corsairs and Seanna, climbed onto the rocks, somehow not slipping on the wet surfaces.

Henrik stood at the other end of the spit with his guards and advisers, his stern countenance unchanged by the spray misting his beard. Strangely, the sight of him brought a surge of joy into Seanna. Perhaps it was the danger and loss she had experienced in her journey, or perhaps the knowledge that she could soon speak to another about the elves' invasion. Whatever the case, she actually smiled at him as her party approached.

Arrayed with King Henrik were various advisors, including Dyle Belrose, the court's Grand Wizard. Only he smiled back at Seanna, the others focusing only on Steel-Eyes.

Halting thirty feet from the king, Steel-Eyes called out, "I trust your winds were fair?"

"What's your price, corsair?" Henrik spat back. Seanna frowned at his tone.

"Straight to business? As you can see, the queen is unharmed, if bereft of her worldly goods." Gesturing to Seanna, Steel-Eyes continued, "I would think ten thousand gold marks to be a fair price for her."

"I will not believe her to be unharmed until our Grand Wizard may inspect her," Henrik said, though he flinched at the Corsair Queen's price.

"Very well. Let him come forward and cast his spells from a distance. My men and myself are warded by our own caster; you cannot harm us."

"Is this really necessary, Henrik?" Seanna shouted. She didn't like the idea of a magical inspection. "I'm perfectly alright."

Henrik nodded to Belrose, and the wizard entered the no-man's-land between the groups. Holding out his hands, fingers pointed at Seanna, he muttered a series of incantations. The air shimmered between them, and a slimy magical film settled on Seanna's skin. It entered her, making her shudder. After a few moments, the feeling dissipated, and Belrose retreated to the king's side. His words were lost in the wind.

"Is everything to your satisfaction?" Steel-Eyes called.

"Indeed. But we don't agree to your price. We will pay no more than three thousand gold marks for the queen," said Henrik. It was an abominably low price, stinging Seanna's remaining pride.

"Not just the queen you're paying for, is it?" The Corsair Queen smirked. "How much is the heir worth to you?"

If he could only pay for the child, he would.

"Five thousand, then." Henrik's frown deepened.

"Nine."

All the while, Seanna stood still, willing herself not to cry. She felt like a piece of meat at the market, or worse, a slave in a barbaric land. *Just let me go home!* she wanted to scream.

An advisor leaned over and whispered into Henrik's ear. With a sigh, Henrik said, "Seven and a half, and no higher."

"Got to save money for your parties somehow, don't you?" Steel-Eyes laughed. "I suppose the life of your queen is worth little to you."

Henrik's lips tightened. "Seven and a half is what we will offer, along with safe passage out of our waters."

"You think you could stop our ships even if you wanted?"

"We haven't all day, corsair. Take the gold or take the queen." Henrik's grey eyes met Seanna's, and she saw no pity in them. Her breath caught in her throat.

Steel-Eyes nodded. "Seven and a half. Gold can buy more than a pregnant woman. Release her."

Seanna walked slowly towards Henrik as a knight carried a large chest to the corsairs. The exchange done – and the gold all there – Steel-Eyes made a sweeping bow. "Pleasure to make your acquaintance. Our ship would always be keen to host another royal, if ever you wish to pay ransom again. Men, to the boat."

As the corsairs departed, Henrik stared at a spot in the sky past Seanna. "Let's go. Belrose, care for the queen."

With Belrose's help, Seanna stepped into the longboat. Now that she was no longer a prisoner, there was a lightness in her limbs as if she were floating. Breathing deeply of free air, she imagined the hot bath and clean clothes which awaited her on the king's ship.

A hot bath and clean clothes which would be tainted by her knowledge of the Lofalin fleet. As the free air turned bitter in her mouth, she studied the king. His hair had greyed even more, his beard flecked with white. Jaw tight, he watched the waves, not joining in any conversations. *Does he already know?*

At the king's ship, Seanna grabbed Henrik's arm. "I need to speak with you."

"It can wait," he said, shoving her off. He vanished below before she could stop him. Seanna bit her lip and allowed herself to be escorted to a cabin where a tub of steaming water awaited her. She bathed quickly, hardly noticing the filth accumulating in the water. After she dressed and went to the door, she found Belrose waiting for her.

"Your Grace," Belrose said, bowing. "You are to remain in your cabin for the duration of the voyage, by the king's orders."

"I need to see Henrik," Seanna said. She resisted the urge to stamp her foot. "It's urgent."

Belrose frowned. "Perhaps I could relay your words."

"No, Belrose. This is important."

Belrose nodded and led the way to the king's quarters. He raised his hand to knock, but Seanna pushed past him and opened the door into the king's dining room. Signaling Belrose to wait, Seanna went straight to the study. When she didn't find Henrik there, she continued on to the bedroom. From inside, she heard a low moan. She didn't stop to think before throwing open the door.

Henrik lay on the bed, head thrown back into the pillows. He wasn't alone. His personal steward, Jacobi, crouched at the king's hips, head bobbing back and forth. He stopped short and stared at Seanna, eyes wide.

"Wh–" Henrik startled, opened his eyes, and saw his queen. Standing quickly, Henrik rasped, "I thought I ordered you to stay in your cabin!"

"And I thought you were a loyal husband," Seanna said as

Jacobi scrambled to his feet. "Leave us, Jacobi."

The air grew tense between queen and king, and the steward scurried away, shutting the door behind him.

"You have no right to order about *my* steward," Henrik said, his voice rumbling. "And you have no claims to loyalty yourself, whore."

This isn't important right now! shouted the sensible part of Seanna, but her petty side lashed out instead, "How long has he shared your bed? Hm?"

"What right have you to question me?"

"Did you ever care for me or Fleta? Perhaps this was never my fault, perhaps you drove me away so that *men* could lay with you instead!" Seanna laughed at the irony.

"I am the king, I may do as I please! You are mine, to obey me as I please! You–" Henrik angrily wrapped a robe around himself, his neck turning red as he whirled on her. "If I had a *wife* who preferred her husband over her handmaids, I would never need–"

"Well, I suppose a woman's mouth on your cock feels the same as a man's."

Henrik turned his back to her, and Seanna wanted dearly to do the same. Yet as she glared at his broad shoulders, she realized the absurdity of the situation. *It's a wonder I never saw it.* Giggles burst from her, and Seanna laughed in earnest. *The gods must have had a lark when they joined us together.* Between her chuckles, she managed to say, "You with men, and I with women. It's a miracle we ever conceived!"

Henrik turned with a confused expression. He finally cracked a small smile. "Perhaps we should have commissioned a larger bed to fit all four of us."

"You'd have gone mad with jealousy."

Their laughter died out, and they regarded each other with new curiosity. Henrik asked, "Why are you here, Seanna? I would have thought you'd want peace by yourself after your ordeal. You've never made it a secret that you hate being around me."

Oh. Right. In that moment, Seanna wished that shared

infidelity was the greatest of their issues. She levered herself onto a chair, stared at the table, and said, "While Steel-Eyes held me captive, Aremo Teru came to the fortress. He said that Lofalin ships are sailing for our shores. Sixty of them, to Dedaria and the River Valley. They'll be ready to attack within months."

Henrik sat slowly on the bed. "You're sure?"

"Yes," Seanna said. "Aremo wanted me kept captive until the invasion began."

She shivered at how close she had come to being his prisoner. And she trembled, too, at the thought of so many ships landing on her kingdom's shores. No one had seen true war in a hundred years, and she doubted the old ballads told the truth of battle.

Henrik rubbed his eyes. "Gods. First the Skals, and now this."

"The Skals?" Seanna asked. "What happened while I was imprisoned?"

Playing with his hands in his lap, Henrik said, "A Skallish-Demar force landed on our eastern shores. We've tried mustering our forces to meet them, but with Strilu and Hawk marching on Rask, we haven't had the men yet. The Skals run wild through our lands."

"Strilu marches on Rask? They dare a civil war while–"

"I gave them my blessing before I left Riverfen," Henrik said. "After the Masque."

"The Masque?"

His eyes dropped. In a rush of words, he told her about the revelations made, the battle, the aftermath. "We lost many a good man and woman," he finished. His hesitance shook her. *He's hiding something from me.*

"Anyone we know?" she said in an attempt at brevity. Henrik sighed deeply and didn't meet her eye. His silence was worse than words. Seanna's pulse rushed in her ears. She tried to think whose death would affect him so.

At last Henrik met her gaze and said, "Your father didn't survive."

Seanna fell back in her chair, too shocked to cry. Her throat constricted. She tried to remember the last conversation she had with her father, but it eluded her. Henrik's words couldn't be true. Once they landed, she'd rush to her father's city and see him there, laughing and drinking with his arm around her mother's waist.

Henrik left the room, then returned after a few minutes.

"I've sent word to Udolf to gather our forces at Con Salur. With luck, the Lofalins will wait to attack until spring, and we may bolster our defenses before they lay siege." Laying a hand on Seanna's shoulder, Henrik said softly, "I am sorry for your loss. Your father was a good man, despite our disagreements."

"Did he die bravely?" Seanna whispered. Her mouth resisted the movement.

"Yes."

"And my brother will be earl now." It was all she could think to say. Her mind still hadn't quite understood the reality that lay before her.

"Yes. We may have to delay his ceremony until after the war."

"Of course." Clutching the armrests, Seanna still didn't move. Her father's round face, his jovial guffaws, his warm hands, all were cold and gone. Forever.

Henrik stood up, and Seanna grasped at his arm. "Please stay with me."

He hesitated, then nodded. Seanna held his hand, and though she had never loved the man, she couldn't imagine being alone in that moment.

CHAPTER TWELVE

Gwen

The fire, high and wide, roared as Gwen sat in a circle with the Witches. Its din had a strange musical quality to it, as if the flames sang a melody she couldn't understand. Around the grove, birds filled the branches of the trees: crows and ravens, songbirds and hummingbirds, hawks and falcons. They stared at Gwen with jewel-like eyes, eerily silent. The trees groaned, bare branches waving with no wind.

The tallest sister took Gwen's hand. "I am Una, the one who hears the music of nature."

The sister of middling height took Gwen's other hand. "I am Dona, the one who hears the music of humanity."

The shortest, who sat across from her, leaned forward and cupped Gwen's chin. "And I am Tresa, the one who hears the music of the dead."

Gwen blinked in confusion. "The music?"

"Close your eyes," Una instructed. The other sisters released Gwen as she obeyed. "Listen."

Gwen heard the rustling of the trees, the crackling of the fire. A bird chirped and another clacked its beak. She told the sisters what she gleaned.

"No. Listen deeper, beneath those sounds. Listen with your breath and your skin, hear with your tongue and your eyes. Watch the fire."

Gwen opened her eyes. The three Witches were gone. Feeling uneasy with a thousand birds' eyes on her back, Gwen studied the fire. It spat and popped merrily, but gave no sound otherwise.

Still, Gwen stared into it. She observed its whorls and tendrils, the ebb and flow of flame. Unconsciously, her hand drifted to the dirt beside her. She pressed her palm into the cool earth, playing with the specks on her fingers. A warm breeze kissed her cheek and ruffled her hair, bringing with it strange smells.

Yet Gwen couldn't hear the Witches' music.

For candle upon candle, she sat entranced by the fire. Her belly rumbled with hunger, her heart aching for home. Her back grew sore from sitting in one position for so long. Just as she was about to stand and seek the Witches, something changed.

The fire *snapped*, but with that sound came another. A single note, quick and high, like a bell's chime. It rang in her head, echoed through her bones, lingered in her breath. It was euphoric and exhilarating, and in its sound, Gwen could *feel* fire rather than see it.

She waited, breath held, for another note. None came from the fire. When the wind blew past her, it brought a chorus of music, pipes in the air that held a low steady note and a higher melody cavorting about. The music felt East going West, storm into calm, hints of sea and grass. *Wind from the Cascade Palace*, Gwen thought.

Then all was quiet again, and she lost the music. Another candle passed, and again Gwen became aware of her aching muscles, until a bird hopped onto the ground near her, pecking at the dirt. She moved her hand through the earth, closer and closer. The bird tentatively stepped onto her palm. It stayed there a moment, its beady eyes fixed on her.

The bird's music was more complex than fire or wind. It flew high and low, twisting and turning. Somehow, in the melody, Gwen caught a sense of family and fright; the chicks the bird had raised, the snake that had taken them. All the bird's little history rang throughout its music, along with its physiology: feathers and sinew, wings and beak.

With wonder, Gwen held the bird as long as it allowed

while its music sang to her. She would have held it forever, but it flew away, seeking the refuge of the trees once more.

"Do you hear it?" Una asked, materializing into the glen. Gwen nodded. The Witch's eyes were brown and warm, a mother's eyes. "Your first step is complete. The Songs have accepted you."

"The Songs?" Somehow, this word weighed heavier than the music of mortals, unending, unyielding. These were no mere melodies.

"They are the source of all magic," Dona said, her voice deep as dirt. Her face reminded Gwen of a leather-skinned matriarch. "They formed Earda and the Cythra, they created life and death. The Songs run through all, *are* all. When the world began, every creature could hear them. When once sorcerers roamed, the Songs could be rewritten, molded, undone, done again. But no more."

"What happened?"

"Men forgot how to hear them," Tresa said in a tone light as air. The vigors of girlhood shone through her cheeks. "Their hubris blocked their ears. The mages crafted their Principles and their spells, not one of them hearing the music threading through all their workings. You must hear the Songs and bring their knowledge back to Earda."

The birds on the branches trembled and chittered to each other, the fire roared with a great flame, the wind howled through the trees. All grew calm once more, and the Witches stood together. They spoke with one voice, faces glowing in the firelight. "Master the Songs of Nature, Humanity, and Death. Become one with them, and you will find what you are meant to do."

Gwen shivered despite the fire, her skin pricking at the terrible words. They rang through the glen, a cage closing in around her. She suddenly wanted no part in it, wanted nothing but to be home with Druam, safe and away from these strange women.

However, she had come here, and she couldn't go back. Pulling together her resolve, Gwen said, "You brought me here by promising me vengeance. When will you teach me the spells to kill the Skals who murdered my family?"

"Still so petty," said Tresa.

"So spiteful," said Dona.

"So young," said Una. She regarded Gwen for a moment. "She doesn't yet know the Songs. They will encompass her, renew her. If she still yearns for vengeance afterwards, we will have lost."

Gwen was discomfited by this. She didn't want to be renewed, she wanted their promises to be kept. She stood her ground. "You made a vow–"

"Your journey has begun," the sisters spoke together.

"Journey?" Gwen asked. "But I've barely–"

"You will learn," they said. "Use the Songs or die."

"How will I know when I've succeeded?" Gwen clutched at Una, but the Witch gently pushed her away.

The Witches' voices rang out. "When the Songs are in your breath and your heartbeat, one with your soul, your journey will take you back to Earda. If you fail, there shall be no return."

The birds in the trees screeched and cawed, and all took flight as one, whirling around Gwen, their wings beating at her. She covered her face, crying out, as the mass grew tighter and tighter around her. Flashes of brown and green and blue and black filled her vision. Futilely, Gwen tried to run, but the birds converged, a tornado of wings, and kept her in place.

As quickly as it started, it ended. The birds flew off into the sky, leaving Gwen disoriented and scratched. She righted herself, ready to attack the Witches, but they had vanished. The fire was gone, and so too was the strange building in the trees.

Gwen had been spirited to a different part of the Woods. This glen held a stream, a copse of small trees with purple leaves, and red grass underfoot. As Gwen got her bearings, she realized there were no paths out. The grey-barked goliaths barred her passage, their branches whispering in a strange chant. Remembering how they had once opened for her, Gwen strode to the trees. She commanded them to move, but they held firm. She kicked and slapped at the bark, and only heard faint laughter. A branch descended in front of her, and, with a flick, cut a small scratch on her cheek.

More branches joined the first, their twigs reaching for her. Gwen backed away, sure that there was no way out.

The sky darkened, and the air grew cold enough to blacken fingers. Gwen quickly gathered wood into a pile and squatted beside it. Whisper-singing, she cast a spell of flame – one she'd learned with Mavian a lifetime ago – and tried to ignite the wood. Nothing caught. Frustrated, she remembered the Witches' words: *use the Songs or die.*

Shivering now, her teeth chattering, Gwen tried to remember the note she'd heard in the flames. It would not come. As the night grew deeper, her desperation heightened. *I'm going to die in the Whispering Woods and no one will know what happened to me*, she thought, heart racing. *Druam will die wondering.*

Perhaps she should have stayed with him in that gilded palace above the sea. True, she would have had to sacrifice her magic to do so, but she missed the warmth of Druam's arms, his honey-mead voice, his breath against her skin.

Gwen shook herself, realizing that she had almost fallen asleep. *A fatal act.* She wouldn't die. Not yet. Not before she learned the Witches' secrets.

Instead of thinking of the particular note, Gwen thought about fire, what it was, what it meant. Fire was heat and flame, coal and embers. It was home and comfort, but also dangerous and unpredictable. It was large and small, wild and tamed, a dichotomy of life and death. As she contemplated fire, she hummed quietly at first, then with greater strength, the feeling of fire pouring into her song. She held out her hand.

Heat coursed through her fingers, and the wood ignited.

The rest of that night, Gwen huddled next to her fire, wishing she were back in her large bed in the Cascade Palace. She imagined Druam with her, his hand resting gently on her leg as he snored. Angry at the Witches, Gwen threw a stick into the fire. Flurries of sparks flew out.

When night finally gave way to day, Gwen gratefully welcomed the meager sunshine. She had slept very little, only in brief spurts of restless dozing. Her stomach rumbled with hunger, and her stiff limbs protested with every movement.

There was still no way out of the glen. Gwen shouted and cajoled and pleaded with the trees, but they made no response.

A twig snapped behind her, and Gwen whirled to see a mighty ëlg, a large hoofed creature. It stood over nine feet tall at the shoulder, with giant antlers extending far above its head. It regarded her for a moment, then bent its head to graze.

Gwen stood frozen, watching the creature. Her stomach groaned, and she licked her lips at the thought of its meat. Except she had never killed an animal before, much less done so without a weapon.

Listen, she thought. *Listen and learn*. Gently, ever so gently, Gwen walked to the ëlg. She moved cautiously, her eyes never leaving the animal's. It didn't move. She hesitated before placing a hand on its shoulder. It didn't protest. She took a deep breath and listened.

The creature's music moved slowly and steadily, coursing with caution and instinct. There was pride, too, for this ëlg had the largest antlers of its herd. Digging deeply, Gwen found the strains to its muscles, its nerves, its organs, and its heart. Not quite sure what she was doing, Gwen focused on the heart and softly sang a harmony.

When she felt brave enough, Gwen cut into the ëlg's Song, creating a discordant melody, cutting off its heart's music.

The creature keened, a low cry, before falling to its knees. Its large brown eye fixed on her. It died without a visible wound.

With no knife or tool to aid her, Gwen tried to use spells to skin the beast. Candles passed, and her hunger filled her head before she found one that worked. She didn't know the name of the Song, but it skinned and gutted the creature to reveal red meat that glistened in the sunlight.

Too ravenous to care, Gwen dug into the meat with her bare hands. She thought of cooking it over her fire, but that would take too long. Already her head spun with hunger. She slurped at the blood and sucked the marrow from the small bones she was able to crack. She ate until she was sick, and curled up in the grass trying not to vomit.

How long will they expect me to survive? She had hoped it would be only for the night, yet there was no sign of the Witches. Yet in her despair, Gwen nursed a small sense of pride. She had discovered the ëlg's Song, and so been able to eat. Fire's melody still smoked on her tongue.

Gwen imagined an Earda with the Songs, their music strong and capable. What feats of magic could be done? What new mages would emerge? *This is why I'm here,* she reminded herself. *I have to survive and bring the Songs home. First I have to make it through this journey.*

She had no inkling how long such an endeavor would take.

CHAPTER THIRTEEN
Cara

The mountains of the Selldar Range grew in the distance. They filled the horizon, grey-and-green with white peaks that rose jagged into the sky. Hills and forests blossomed at their base. Hamlets and villages sprang up on the road and faded behind Cara's little group, the denizens assessing the travelers with wary eyes. Here in the wilds, each day brought the threat of plague and prowlers, and the villagers had no patience for strangers.

For Cara, this was only a relief. She didn't want to answer questions about where they were going or why she was armed and armored. Sandu purchased rations and gear for them when necessary. Still they pushed forward at a grueling pace. Each night, Cara feared more of Laris's magic. He spent his evenings engrossed in thought, mumbling to himself about theories and enchantments. Many times she considered trying to run, but the memory of his magic torture swept through her, and she abandoned the idea as folly.

The road wove through the hills and forests, and the mountains towered over them. As they walked one day, a sensation tingled on the back of Cara's neck. It was the strange feeling of being watched that she'd experienced after she killed the *fampir* farmer. She paused and swept her eyes over the road and saw nothing. When the feeling remained after another mile, she called to the men, "I need to check something. How about you two take a rest?"

Laris grumbled and Sandu dropped his haversack and sat down, stretching out his legs. Cara ducked into the woods, letting the beast ease into her without overwhelming her. It lent its sense of smell, and she followed her nose deeper into the forest. Dappled sunlight filtered through the branches. A doe sprang away into the undergrowth, and Cara ducked away from it. When the branches settled, she moved onward. Nothing save trees and shrubs greeted her.

She nearly turned back when a metallic flash caught her eye. Drawing aside a low-hanging branch, Cara saw its source. A knapsack decorated with metal buttons leaned against a tree, glinting in a single ray of light. Cautiously, Cara edged forward, fingers on her sword hilt. She pushed the beast back to its resting place, sure that whoever was there would not take kindly to seeing her with its horrid features.

"Care to join me for tea?" A voice came from her left, and Cara whirled to face it. A man sat cross-legged on the moss. It was hard to tell his age, for his pale skin was untouched by blemishes. He held a wooden cane in one hand, and his brown locks fell into his eyes.

Those eyes, though, made her skin prickle. The iris and pupils were both cloudy grey like the sky after a storm. She had only ever seen such eyes on a blind beggar in Kell. Cara stayed back, cautious of this strange man in the woods.

He didn't move, and she scanned him for weapons. The man was dressed simply in a long tunic with a brown shirt underneath, and his breeches and boots were travel-worn.

"Who are you?" Cara asked.

"I am a man who waits." The blind man smiled pleasantly.

"Who are you waiting for?"

"A warrior. Do you know where I might find such a person?"

"No," Cara said immediately. Every moment she grew more wary of this man whose blank eyes bored through her. She backed away.

"How disappointing." The blind man looked cheerful enough at her words. "But I think you lie."

"You couldn't possibly know that."

The blind man said gently, "Oh I do, Caralyn Gellder, *sulpari*."

Her mouth went dry, and she nervously licked her lips. "How do you know that name?"

"I know all entwined with the Song of Death."

Cara didn't wait for him to say anything more. She ran back to the road. First Druam, then Laris, and now this blind man who somehow followed her and saw her without seeing. *I won't play anyone else's game*, she thought. She was determined not to let the blind man interfere with her mission against Mavian and the *fampir*, and in their brief encounter, she was sure that he would somehow get in the way.

Cara burst from the woods and raced to her companions. "We need to move. *Now*."

"What–" Sandu started, but she dragged him to his feet and started walking. Sandu fumbled for his pack while Laris grunted and stood.

"What did you see?" Sandu asked, hurrying to catch up with Cara.

"Nothing."

"Lot of commotion for nothing," Laris muttered.

"The days are growing shorter. We need to move quickly." That was all the answer Cara would give them, at least for now. Her spine tingled as she remembered the man's words: *I know all entwined in the Song of Death*. Something about those words made her feel naked, as if everything she'd ever done was exposed for all to see.

That evening, Cara thought she sensed the blind man's presence, but again she saw nothing. She stared out into the woods, sure she'd see a glint of metal or those milky eyes.

As she twitched and turned, Laris sat beside her. Something in his attitude made her pause.

"What do you want?" she asked harshly.

"You stole twenty years of youth and magic from me," Laris said. "The magic I used to create you forged a bond between us. Through that bond, I intend to regain what I've lost."

"I don't understand," Cara said. She pulled back from him. "You have magic, you've been using it."

Laris spit on the ground. "Pah! Cantrips and simple things, not the complex workings I cast in my youth. You are a conduit to what I seek. Now, sit still so–"

"No! Not if you're going to cause me pain again."

Laris ignored her. He pulled at her arm, implacable to her pleas. When she resisted, he sent a rush of magic through her that forced her to be still. Cara tried to catch Sandu's eye, but he focused on the ground. She wanted to scream at him, tell him to help her, and he wouldn't risk it. *Coward.*

The sorcerer chanted an unfamiliar language, his words resonating with power. The expected pain did not come; instead, a flood of emotions rampaged through Cara, from soaring ecstasy to encompassing fury to hollow melancholy. With each emotion came an image, either memory or imagined, to match. She saw Renna and Merick, happy and alive once more; Sandu, strung up on a beam and whipped; the streets of Riverfen running with blood. Gaping wordlessly, too absorbed to scream or cry, she sat motionless while Laris's magic worked through her.

When at last he stopped, Cara collapsed to the ground, a void of a human. The beast's wrath was swathed with a haze of emotions. From the corner of her eye, she saw Laris examining his hands and tutting in frustration. "Mm, progress, but it shall take too long. No, this spell was not enough."

"What more can you do to me?" Cara mumbled. The beast slumped under the weight of what she'd seen.

"Oh, sweet child." Laris's smile disconcerted her. He left to get his dinner, murmuring to himself, while Sandu crouched beside Cara.

"Are you alright?" he asked. Cara shook her head, wanting to retch but unable to force her body to do it.

"We should find a healer, see if..." Sandu trailed off. His soft brown eyes held an enormous amount of guilt. "I'm sorry Cara, but I can't do anything. What do you expect of me? Laris tolerates me because of you. If I interfere, he'll kill me. You know he will."

"I'll kill him first," Cara said. They were empty words. *He can stop me with a thought. What more magic could he possibly want?*

Sandu looked at her sadly. "I'm not going to kill him, and neither will you. You don't want to become the monster you hate. Just stay with me and stay yourself. We need to support each other. Da might not have much time left, so we just have to get to D'Clet as quickly as we can."

"You don't know how this feels," Cara said, a surge of anger popping in the pit of her stomach. "You don't know what I'm going through."

"Every night, I have nightmares–"

"Nightmares?" Cara laughed bitterly. "A child's pain." She shrugged him off and hugged her arms around herself. Sandu's shoulders slumped. He stood and left their campsite, murmuring something about finding more firewood.

Let him go, Cara thought. *He's not the true friend you once thought he was.* Dimly, Cara wondered if she would even reach D'Clet after Laris was done with her. She decided that she'd dispose of him, no matter their agreement, if he prevented her from reaching Mavian.

Laris chewed slowly. "What did he say about a healer?"

"Just that I'd need one before you're done with me," Cara spat.

"Have you ever been healed by a curate?"

"Yes." Regret filled her as soon as she said it. A gleam entered Laris's eye as a slow smile spread across his thin lips.

"Curious," he said. "Most rustics would never receive such treatment. I never expected *you* to have had it."

"Why does it matter?" Cara edged away from him. "My leg's healed now, there's–"

"Oh hush, child," Laris said. His expression took on a strange delight and he set aside his bowl. Cara tried to scoot away from him, but he uttered a word, and her limbs refused to budge no matter how she fought against the magic.

Laris peeled the greaves from her legs and rolled up her breeches, feeling her calves with his rough hands. There was nothing loving or romantic in his merciless touch. He peered at the leg which had been broken during Mavian's attack on the caravan.

"Yes, I think this will do," Laris said. "If I use the Gidlark Binding and the Trior Summoning..."

Cara forced her mouth to move. "What are you doing?"

"Using the healing spell to create a conduit into the magic deep within you. With that, I should be able to retrieve what I've lost." His grin held no sympathy. "You should survive."

Dread seeped into her bones as Laris began a new working. Her leg burned beneath his hands. A reddish light glowed beneath his fingers, making his bony hands translucent, the blood beneath his skin showing in stark relief.

To Cara's horror, the veins in her leg turned green and black, her skin taking on a sickly hue. The burning turned to an ache, then a greater and greater pain, until–

Crack! The bone snapped. Light ran up Laris's arms to his chest. Cara screamed, her leg quivering despite the magic holding it in place. Tides of agony swelled in her calf and traveled up her knee and to her hips, as if she had never been healed, as if the break had worsened and grown infected in the intervening deshes. Tears streamed down her face, and she hiccuped and gasped.

Laris released her, staring at his hands. His skin became tighter and pinker, moles and spots disappearing. His white hair turned brown, his beard now patches of blonde and red instead of pure snow. Wrinkles lessened around his eyes and mouth, and he grew taller. Instead of a man of sixty or seventy, he looked no older than his mid-forties.

"It worked!" Laris gasped, flexing his younger fingers.

The magic holding Cara released, and she fell to the moss, avoiding the sight of her ruined leg.

"What did you do?" she demanded. "What did you do to me?"

Laris ignored her. With a laugh, he called lightning from the sky. It flashed in Cara's vision, crackling through the air and sending all her hairs on edge. It gathered around Laris, brighter than the sun, before he sent it thundering back to the clouds, where it rattled the air and exploded with a noise that made her ears pop.

"My magic! My youth!" Laris cried, his hands raised into the air.

Cara tried to summon the beast, but it quailed in her breast, disoriented by her pain and confusion. It would not help her even though she desperately wanted to lunge at the sorcerer and sink her teeth into his throat.

"You bastard," she said.

Laris's bright eyes were manic. He stooped to her, disconcertingly different in his regained youth. "I was twenty-five years old when I lost my magic. Your conception stole it and my youth from me. And now, I have them back."

"Let me go. You got what you wanted," Cara said, though she had no intentions of letting *him* go. Not while she still drew breath. Mavian, Druam, and Laris. Another one added to her list.

"Oh no, not yet, sweet child. I must test my power, ensure that it won't suck me dry. Wait here as I measure the limits of my success." He chuckled. "What am I saying, of course you have to wait here. Can't move with that, can you?" He whacked her broken leg, and she bit her lip to keep from crying out.

His smile turned taunting, and he grasped her chin in his hand. "I regained more than my power. I remember your father's name now. I may even tell it to you, if I decide you've earned it."

Cara wrestled her chin from his hand and spat at him. Laris only chuckled. He rose and shouted a spell. Wind gusted through the trees, and he half-walked, half-glided from their camp, laughing all the while.

Alone by the fire, Cara tried to summon her beast, but it remained out of reach. Her leg twinged and burned, and she refused to look at it.

Movement beyond the fire caught her eye, and she groaned as the blind man emerged from the trees.

"Veck off," she growled. He came toward her anyway, his

cane clicking against the stony ground. With the firelight behind him, she couldn't see his expression. She tried to retreat, but her leg burned with agony when it scraped against the dirt. She stopped, heart hammering, as the blind man reached down to her.

"Be calm. We are here to help you."

"We?" Cara managed. Any more protests died in her throat as a tall, tall man materialized from the forest, his blonde hair hanging around his gaunt cheeks. His blue eyes, rimmed with gold, held a haunted cast to them. Knives upon knives were strapped to his large frame, and when he moved, it was with an assassin's grace.

"He's dead," Cara said as Jagger Cross moved forward. "This isn't real, he's dead."

"And the dead always remain so?" Amusement filled the blind man's tone.

Jagger advanced, drawing a knife. Cara couldn't move. She opened her mouth to scream for help, but the blind man clamped a hand over her lips.

"Hush now. Don't be frightened."

The fire dimmed as the assassin's body blocked its light. He leaned over Cara, silent and terrible.

I don't want to die like this, Cara thought before her every nerve inflamed in torment.

CHAPTER FOURTEEN
Sandu

The trees closed around him, the cold air both invigorating and harsh. Sandu fled deeper into them, his mind overcome with memory. He had told Cara he would get firewood, but truly he ran from the monster in her eyes. Her anger awoke a deep fear that dwelled in his breast, a fear he had hoped would only haunt his dreams.

He was not dreaming now.

Sandu fell to his knees beside a birch whose branches were nearly bare. His breath hitched in his throat, and though he desperately sucked it in, he couldn't get enough. In and out, in and out, faster and faster, the staccato of his heart thundering in his ears as his breath made him dizzy. His hands curled into fists, then released, over and over, muscles moving faster, fingers flying with the speed of his breath.

In Cara's fury, red had flashed in her eyes, the ghost of fangs on her lips. Now he saw prowlers all around him, their claws digging into him with phantom pain. He imagined the tinkling of glass chandeliers and the screams as men and women died. Within the quiet forest, he was caught in a storm of wails and piercing teeth.

The queen appeared, her laughter ringing throughout the trees, jarring and terrible. Her hands grabbed his face, her lips forced onto his. When she pulled back, it was a prowler's countenance he saw, blood dripping on its lips.

He wanted to scream, but his breath came too short to allow

it. He wanted to run, but his legs shook beneath him. *It's not real,* he told himself, but gods, it all seemed so real, Cara and the prowlers and the queen whirling around him. His head pounded with them, a chorus together of misery that sank into his soul and wouldn't release him.

Another scream ripped through the forest, and in his haze, Sandu couldn't tell if it was real or imagined. He cowered, hands drawn over his ears, rocking back and forth as he sobbed. "G-g-g-g–" He tried to form words, and they wouldn't come. His lips betrayed him.

In the throes of his fear, a bluejay alighted on a nearby branch, its bright colors stark against the dark brush. It tilted its head, regarding him with a beady eye. An eye shot through with green flecks. A human eye.

Sandu stilled for a moment, entranced by the bird. The longer he remained thus, the easier his breath came, the slower his heart. Eventually, he tried speaking again. "P-p-p-"

The bird opened its beak, and a man's voice came out. "You are unwell."

Sandu shook his head, too emotionally overdrawn to be surprised that the bird spoke. He'd seen enough magic to not be overly concerned. "Just a-a-" He had no words to describe the panic that had rushed through him, the phantom kisses and bites, the figures who had hurt him materializing as if really there. *Is this magic?* he thought. *Is Laris doing this to me?*

"Can you speak?" the bird asked.

"I-I w-" Even past the worst of it, Sandu couldn't force his tongue to obey. He dropped his eyes, ashamed of himself.

The bird cocked its head, uttering a few singsong words in another language. A warm glow pooled at Sandu's feet before traveling up his body. He watched, fascinated, momentarily distracted from his fright. The golden light sank into his chest, and his heart slowed. His lungs filled with air. Though his head was light, the horror that had filled it dissipated.

Vaguely, Sandu remembered a young noblewoman performing a similar spell back in the Cascade Palace. Yet the bird spoke with a man's voice, not a girl's.

"Who are you?" Sandu finally managed. His limbs shook from his exertions, and his head cleared by the moment. "How did you lift the spell on me?"

"It was no spell that caused your fear," said the bird. "I have seen it before in men who live through terrible things. I simply allowed your mind to let go of what haunted it – though only temporarily."

Sandu shivered. "Then it could happen again."

"Yes." The bird clacked its beak. "Now, to business. Have you passed into the mountains yet?"

For some reason, Sandu felt compelled to answer. His mouth formed the words, "Not yet, though we're close. Near to Dunfrey, I would say."

The realization shook him. Dunfrey was where he had left his wife and twins and abandoned his old life. *But I can't go back there. Not while Da's still in prison.*

"Good. And the sorcerer, Stanthorpe? He still travels with you?"

"Yes."

Sandu started to ask how the bird knew so much, but it opened its wings and took off, disappearing into the gloom. The moment the last of its feathers vanished into the night, Sandu forgot he had ever seen it.

After another long breath, Sandu staggered to his feet. He couldn't tell how far he'd come from the camp, but he followed his path back through the woods as best he could. The memories slowly receded, leaving doubt and confusion in their wake. Though his dreams had often been plagued by those figures, this was the first time they had ever intruded in his waking hours. Somewhere deep in his head, he knew that this was no magical attack, but his own mind betraying itself.

One foot in front of the other, that's all that matters now. Cara would be there for him, she'd help him understand. *Except she hasn't helped lately. She only cares for herself these days.* The thought was so despondent that Sandu rejected it immediately. *Once you tell her what's happening, she'll listen. She'll help.*

At last, after an eternity of walking, a flicker in the woods showed him where the camp lay. He stumbled toward it with relief. As he came closer, he heard an unfamiliar voice. He slowed and crept through the trees on his belly until he could see.

Two men crouched over Cara, one with a hand on her mouth, the other holding a knife. Sandu reached for the axe on his hip as Cara struggled. The man with the knife lowered it to her leg, pressing the blade into her flesh. She writhed as the first man kept hold of her.

Sandu sprang to his feet and burst from the trees, hollering wordlessly as he raised his axe. The man who held Cara didn't even glance up, but the knife-wielder stood, his bulk large against the fire. Sandu skidded to a halt, not quite believing his eyes.

"What in the vecking hells?" Sandu said aloud, his hands sweating on his axe.

The man with the knife shrugged and bent back down to Cara's leg. He shouldn't have been there. He had been murdered by the mist-folk. Jagger Cross, no matter what Sandu's eyes told him, had died.

His eyes had already lied once that night.

"Stop!" Sandu shouted. He lifted his axe. "Don't you touch her!"

"Easy, friend," said the first man, lifting his hand from Cara's mouth. "We're here to help her."

"And who the veck are you?" Sandu demanded. "What are you doing with *him*?"

Cara wriggled. "Run, Sandu! Don't let Jagger get you!"

"Be calm," the first man said, though he nudged the giant of a man beside him. "Hold for a moment, friend." His head lifted, milky eyes turning in Sandu's direction. "You must have many questions."

Sandu didn't want to acknowledge the should-be-dead-assassin, so he asked the simplest question that came to mind. "Who are you?"

"Darian."

"Your surname?"

"Does it matter?"

"I suppose not." Sandu paused. "What are you doing to her?"

"Her leg is broken and infected. We're draining the pus before we bandage it, to give her a chance to heal." Darian patted Cara's shoulder. "Not that she'd listen to us."

"You ambushed me, held me down, and now claim to be helping me?" Cara glared at him.

"You didn't listen earlier, so why would I believe you'd listen now?" The blind man quirked a brow at Sandu. "Why don't you help Master Cross with her leg?"

"I'm not going near him."

"Even to help your friend?"

"He'll kill me first chance he gets."

"Oh, I doubt that. He's not here to kill."

"You don't know him like I do. He's killed men, women, and children, whoever gets in his way. You're safer far away from him."

Throughout the argument, Sandu's eyes flitted to Jagger. The assassin sat back on his haunches, watching with silent amusement. His fingers played with the knife, twirling it over his knuckles. He appeared much the same as Sandu remembered: extraordinarily tall and lithe, with a gaunt face and blonde hair that swung around his cheeks. Scars roped across his flesh, white and hard at the stumps where his pinkies should have been. There were deep circles under his eyes, and even in the firelight, his skin had a bluish tint.

Darian sighed. "He is not here to murder, torture, or extort. He is here as my guest."

"What do you mean?"

"The mist-folk killed him. I heard his soul cry out for help, and I aided him."

"You brought him back?" Sandu took a step away from the blind man. "You resurrected him?"

"In a way, yes."

"*How*?"

"By listening."

Sandu waited, but it seemed no further answer was forthcoming. So, he looked directly at Jagger and asked, "Are you going to try and kill me?"

"He can't speak," Darian said. "That was the price he paid to rejoin the living."

Just as another question came to his lips, Cara moaned and arched her back, her leg twitching. The blind man took hold of her once more as Jagger bent with his knife. Sandu slowly put away his axe. He crouched across from Jagger, glancing now and then at the gleaming blade.

"Same incision point. Press until the pus turns red," Darian instructed. "Sandu, hold her hips steady."

Sandu did as he was told as Jagger once more put his knife to Cara's leg. Green-and-black pus, unnatural colors, oozed out along its length. Turning his head, Sandu tried not to gag.

"How did this happen?" he asked. "I thought you were healed?"

"I was," Cara gritted out. "Until Laris stole the curate's magic from me."

"Bastard. Where'd he go?"

"Don't cross him, Sandu. He's stronger now. He disappeared to play with his newfound powers." She cut off with a hissing breath as the pus turned red. Swiftly, Jagger withdrew his knife as Darian put a cloth over the cut.

"Jagger, bring my satchel. Sandu, hold her leg steady. Cara, bite down on this," Darian said, handing her a stick. Her eyes burned, but she obeyed. Sandu moved down to her foot. When Jagger returned with the satchel, Darian moved to Cara's calf. He poked and prodded at her skin, then dug his fingers beside the break. He worked the bones back together as Cara writhed, held only by Jagger's large hands.

"The bone is set," Darian said, pulling out linen, felt, and a series of splints from his satchel. He set them aside and removed a jar of strange black ointment. This he rubbed on the cut before he wrapped the cloth around her calf and arranged the finger-width splints. He secured it all with three lengths of flax rope, one above, below, and right on the break. Cara whined, and

Sandu watched with fascination.

"How long will it take to heal?" he asked as Darian rocked back on his heels. By his care and precision, Sandu would never have suspected the man to be blind.

"In about a deshe, I will create a wax plaster to hold it firm while the bone strengthens. If all goes well, she will be able to walk in five deshes."

"That's too long," Cara said, pushing herself to her elbows. "I can't wait that long."

"You'll have to."

"I'll kill Laris," Cara muttered.

"How do you know all this?" Sandu asked, disregarding her comment. "About Cara, and healing?"

"A man learns a great many things through listening and experimentation. As for Cara, I've heard a great deal about her." Darian's strange white eyes were red in the firelight. "The dead speak of much lately."

"The dead...speak?"

"To me, yes."

"He's mad, Sandu," Cara said. "They're both mad."

Sandu didn't listen to her. A spark of hope flared inside him, and he sat beside Darian. "Do you...can you...has my father spoken to you? Is he dead?"

"No. He's alive."

Sandu hesitated, but he had to know. "My wife and children?"

"They still live, too."

Sandu hoped the man told the truth. That hope overpowered his common sense and suspicion, and he found he truly believed Darian's words. Relief washed through him, and he stood, giddy. He glanced at Jagger, whose blue-gold eyes held none of the fury they once did. Sorrow and regret lived there instead.

"Oh." Sandu inspected his feet. "I'm sorry, Jagger."

Jagger shrugged, digging his knifepoint into the dirt. Feeling immensely awkward, Sandu sat beside the fire. Darian went to Cara and spoke to her in a low voice. She protested, but he spoke again, and she went quiet. He put his shoulder under her arm, and together they limped slowly to her tent.

Alone with Jagger, Sandu stared up at the night sky. The stars twinkled in their blue blanket, so distant yet intangibly close. After a moment, Sandu sighed.

"We didn't part so well, did we?" he asked.

Jagger stilled, eyes flicking up. Beneath the sorrow, resentment flared.

Nothing for it but honesty.

"I'm glad you're alive. Well...you know what I mean. Even though you've tried to kill me the last few times we met, I'm glad to see you." Sandu twiddled his thumbs, knowing that he had to say more, but finding it difficult to do so. Finally, he said, "It hurt me to the core to betray you and Raven. I never thought it'd be hard to turn in Fauste's Shiv, but after you treated me so warmly, I couldn't do it myself. So I went the cowardly route and told the Realm's Protectors about you.

"It was all for my father. I didn't want him to die in debtors' prison. I still don't want him to die. But I betrayed you and caused Raven's death, even if it was the right thing to do in the eyes of the kingdom. For that, I'm sorry. I was plagued for months with doubt and regret, and then I saw you driven mad by grief, and I had to face myself. I came clean to Cara, and she accepted me for all my flaws. When she did that, I had to face that I'd been a coward all my life." Sandu continued, both awkward and relieved at his confession, "I never forgot you, nor the kindness you showed me. You may have been a paid assassin, but you were a good man under it all, and I took the only precious thing in your life from you. I'm sorry."

Sandu stopped, acutely aware of his rambling. He met Jagger's oddly lovely eyes and held his breath.

"He wants to know what's wrong with you," Darian said, emerging from Cara's tent.

"How do you...?"

"We are bonded, him and I. He is my eyes, and I his tongue." Darian sat beside Jagger, dwarfed by the man's height. "He wants to know what's wrong with you, that you'd place your family over his. Why that's right, and his cause was wrong."

Sandu mulled it over. What answer could he give? "I can't tell him why. If I hadn't caused Raven's death, then I wouldn't be in a place now to save my father. I regret it, every day, but I can't say I'm sorry to have this chance now."

Jagger held Sandu's eyes and nodded once. Darian said, "He doesn't forgive you yet, but he understands. He will help you find your father."

"Thank you." Sandu hoped that Jagger knew the regret, hope, and trust he laid into those words.

For a while, the three men were quiet, watching the fire slowly die down. As he stared into its depths, Sandu thought about the night's events. First Laris's magic, then his own panic in the woods, then the arrival of a dead man and a strange one. Sandu couldn't quite wrap his head around it all. *I don't know what's happening to me, but this stranger might.* When Sandu tried to tell them of his fear, though, he found that his tongue wouldn't work. He closed his mouth over the words he wanted to speak and resolved to try again in the morning.

The blind man faced the sky, humming. After a moment he fell silent, and deep pain crossed his face.

"The dead are loud tonight," Darian said. "I can even hear the dying. Your wife is among them, Sandu. Go to her now, before it's too late."

Sandu leapt to his feet. "But you said–"

"Death moves quickly. You, of all people, should know that, Bartholomew Barrow."

The blind man's eyes held eons within them. Sandu's knees buckled, and he leaned on Jagger for support, barely noticing what he was doing. *He knows my real name,* he thought. Then, *Tambrey. Tambrey is dying.*

"I need to find her," he said through numb lips.

"I know." Darian rose, putting a finger to Sandu's chest. "You are touched by Death. Listen, and you will find your wife before Autorus takes her."

"But Cara–"

"Will be safe with me. Jagger will go with you. You cannot delay. Her voice is faint, but her time will come. Go."

Sandu just stared at him. Jagger put his large, callused hand on top of Sandu's. That simple touch conveyed such brotherhood and warmth that Sandu almost thought it was someone else, and not a legendary murderer, who he leaned against. But that murderer carried strength, and Sandu needed him now.

"Do you know what we'll face when we find her?" he asked.

Darian's eyes were morose. "Life succumbing to death. *Go*."

With Jagger to help push him along, Sandu stumbled from the camp and into the night, driven only by the thought of seeing his wife. Perhaps, if he got there in time, she would make it. He could do something to help her. It couldn't be the end, not after so many years of separation and despair and secret hoping. Not when he was so close to freeing his father and proving himself worthy of her again.

There has to be a way to save her, Sandu thought. *We're going to find a way*. Whether because of that thought, or Jagger's strangely comforting presence, Sandu's tired limbs became rejuvenated, and he knew he would not rest until he saw his wife.

CHAPTER FIFTEEN
The Monsters in the Night

"Did you make contact with Master Crin?" Druam asked. He pressed his knuckles into the desktop, focusing on the pressure to keep himself calm. Constant emotion roiled through him: anger, grief, hope, each a tidal wave that crashed against his tender skin. He kept his face carefully neutral, not daring to let others see.

So it had been since his turning, growing worse with each passing century.

The others stood patiently around him. None knew his inner battles. None of the other *fampir* he knew experienced such emotional symptoms. Perhaps because they were so relatively young, or perhaps...

Perhaps it is a weakness in myself. Druam had always been far more emotional than his brothers, and his passions followed him into his undeath. And the more memories that faded, the more each emotion came anew, as if he were a child experiencing them for the first time. *No one should live this long.*

Avallune Martill, the resident wizard and alchemist, cleared his throat. "I have contacted Crin twice now. Cara is still traveling east and nears the passes to D'Clet."

"Was it wise to let her go?" said Edsel Hawk, the Earl of Stonetree. Of all the earls, he most resembled a soldier, with short grey hair, trimmed beard, and a stout bearing. "When she harbors such hatred for you?"

"If she had stayed, she would have started killing us."

Druam rubbed his temples. Regret beat through his blood, yet he had made the decision to allow Cara's escape. The sorcerer had been an unexpected surprise, but it all ended the same. She was gone, and he would not yet pursue her. "Right now she has her eyes on Mavian. If she kills him, that is one less enemy for us to contend with."

"And what if her power grows under the sorcerer's tutelage? She may become too much for you to deal with." Edsel leaned forward in his seat.

"I have everything in hand." Druam hated lying to his old friend, but he didn't have much choice. Everything the man said was true, however it wouldn't do to admit weakness. Though he had had every intention of keeping Cara until she agreed to ally herself with him, he had dreamt of Alex and Gwen and woke weighed with guilt. Would they want him to imprison the girl, a slave in all but name?

"If that's all?" Druam nodded to the others. "Edsel, you and I will inspect the troops tomorrow. Avallune, search your books again. Find my wife."

Avallune bowed as Druam and Edsel departed. Edsel murmured a goodnight and left for his rooms. Druam strode down the hall, too aware of the eyes on his back. The palace had grown quiet since the Masque. Only a few nobles and their entourages remained, curious to see what the undead earl would do.

Druam opened the door to his study, eager for the wine that awaited him. But there was someone inside, sitting in his chair, her legs thrown over its arm with a carefree disregard.

After closing the door behind him, Druam turned to Cairn Steel-Eyes.

"Usually my guests come in through the front door and announce their presence." Druam came around the desk and perched on a rounded corner.

Steel-Eyes shrugged. "It was faster this way."

"I assume you know of our plans with Rask."

"I'm aware." She adjusted her seat and leaned toward him. "Where's my daughter?"

Druam quelled the guilt that rose within him. "She's gone."

"Where?"

"To D'Clet, I imagine, to kill my cousin."

"And you just *let her go*?" Steel-Eyes the corsair was gone, replaced by Sura Gellder, the seething mother.

"Would you rather I keep her under lock and key?" Druam allowed a flash of humor to cross his face. "I seem to recall you threatening me should I ever come near the girl."

"I haven't forgotten. Your brother brought her here against the terms of our agreement."

"She was headed here anyway to seek her kidnapped lady. Xandro simply gave her access to the palace which she would never have achieved otherwise." Druam stood and went to the window. The lanterns below were just being lit, the wave of light spreading through the city. "If you wish to breach our agreement, do not expect free passage back to your ship."

Sura joined him, the fingers of one hand playing with a dagger at her hip. It was always this way when the two of them met. She would threaten him, and the reverse, until they reached a terse compromise.

"War is coming, Druam," Sura said.

"Rask? The campaign won't start until after winter."

"Not just Rask." For once, her confidence cracked, and she showed fear. "Lofalins. Sixty ships are landing now, some in Dedaria, others farther north. They'll siege Con Salur before the month is out. Riverfen is a target as well."

Druam swallowed as fear writhed within him. It tugged against his lips and eyes, urging him to show it. He pushed it back, his hands clenching.

"How do you know?"

"Aremo Teru came to me with a request that my men not harry the ships. I agreed."

"If your goal was to alleviate the suffering of war, I fear your actions will do the opposite."

Sura gripped his arm. Druam stared down at her, surprised to see her deep concern. She said, "I had no choice, Druam. The storms this summer were heavy and half of my ships are under repair. Teru came to my fortress without invitation. He *found* me, and if he wanted, he could bring all sixty of his ships to bear on my men. How long would I last against such a force? A floating island of wood against fire and armies?"

"How long until they reach Riverfen?" Druam asked. He stared out over his city, imagining warships on the horizon, black and ominous.

"They won't come by sea. I told Aremo these waters are mine. My ships are already forming a blockade to protect these shores. But I can't promise the safety of the northern River Valley."

Druam suppressed a sigh of relief. He gripped Sura's hand and nodded to her. "We will work together to keep this city standing."

"If she does return, you will keep Cara away from battle, you understand?" Sura's fingers dug into him.

"She is a woman grown, Sura. I will do what I can, but she must be allowed to make her own decisions." Druam carefully pried her fingers from his arm. "And I don't believe she will listen much to me if she does return."

"We share that in common." Sura gave another nod and headed for the door, but Druam called for her to wait. She stopped and gave him a curious look. "What else?"

"Cara asked about her father. I had no answer for her."

Sura hesitated. "You wouldn't know him anyway."

She was gone before Druam could question her further.

The next morning, Druam rode into the troops' camp. It smelled like an army: refuse from the outhouses, grease and stew from the cooking stations, sweat from thousands of unwashed men, the stink of horse and cattle, the scent of polish to shine armor and weapons, the melting metal and burning wood from the smithies. The harvested fields had been trampled into mud. Unlike some armies, this one was orderly and divided into sections for each troop. The commander's tent lay in the center of the neat rows, the heavy canvas held up by stakes and painted with Seastone colors.

A wave of nausea churned in Druam's stomach as he rode

through the camp. How many times had he seen such war camps, in how many different places and eras? He had been at the Siege of Brin and the Battle of Forle, marched in the dark to reach Darmon and wept at the sight of his dead brother at the Belleslye Massacre. The armor and weapons had grown more sophisticated over the centuries, each new generation creating ways to kill each other or avert their own deaths. During his first war, Druam had worn boiled leather and carried an iron sword, the pinnacle of technology of the time. Now, men had mail and scaled armor, with steel weapons forged with folded metal. *What will the fields be like in another hundred years? Another thousand?*

On the eve of battle – whenever it might come – these men, some no older than fifteen, would be praying, pissing themselves, or drinking to avoid the terror of death, but Druam would have no room left for fear. No, his emotions, as battering as they may be, did not contain fear for himself. He had been stabbed, hanged, and poisoned by many different hands, and none of them succeeded in killing him for good. He had always returned.

As Druam reflected on the many wars he'd fought in, he realized he could barely remember the first from so many long years ago. The war that he'd joined as a boy and departed immortal. Images fluttered in his head, but he couldn't recall whether they truly belonged to that event. He knew – from the history books, from his own knowledge – the places and the knights, yet his own memories had faded.

Gripping his horse's reins, Druam tried desperately to pull up the memory of his elder brother donning his armor in the dawn before their first battle. He thought he knew what his brother's face should look like, except the pictures were blurry and fleeting, melded with the ones Druam had seen over so many centuries, mixing with men he had never loved.

Even his own, true, birth-given name eluded him. Over the years, to keep up the facade with each new generation, Druam had given himself many different names, reusing some and discarding others that he found didn't suit him.

He hadn't used his real name since his turning.

Our brother fell in battle, and we buried him in a field of flowers. Father called us home, for monsters in the night plagued the caravan. Druam told himself the memory, holding onto it as best he could. *Verdon wore his new armor, and I carried an axe. Or was it a hammer? We returned to our family, but we found them dead, murdered by the* fampir. *We chased the monsters until our sire forced pain and undeath on us.*

Druam shook himself. *It doesn't matter now. My sire has gone back to Autorus, and there shall I go someday, too. I have reflected too long on the past when it is the future I must look to.* Again he thought of Gwen, where she was, what had happened to her. He didn't allow himself to dwell too long on her, for a council of war must be held.

Druam entered the commander's tent to find Edsel and Commander Rutki poring over a map, conversing between themselves.

"The Lofalins–" Druam began, but Edsel interrupted:

"Rask is on the move."

"Coming here?" Druam asked.

Edsel shook his head. He was deathly pale. "North. He's going north to Stonetree."

For once, Druam didn't stop his dread from reflecting in his eyes. "The Lofalins are going to meet him there."

"The Lofalins?"

"Sixty ships, some landing in Dedaria, others on our shores here. I thought they would move to Con Salur and Riverfen, but–"

"But they're joining Rask." Edsel shook his head. "The snows should have come by now. With the passes so dry..."

"Damn." Druam ran his fingers through his hair.

"I must take my men and defend Stonetree."

"Of course you must."

"I cannot do it alone."

Druam hesitated, thinking. "Riverfen would be left nearly defenseless–"

"Damn it, Strilu! Stonetree is a fortress, yes, but it cannot hold a siege forever. And if the Lofalins and Rask take it without resistance, they will have a stronghold from which to lead a campaign through the River Valley." Fire in his voice, Edsel said, "I need you with me, Druam. I cannot hold Stonetree alone. Leave men here to defend the city and take the rest with us. If we are fortunate, the winter will be harsh and the siege will break on its own. While the elves and Rask starve and freeze, we will be warm and well-fed, our men happy. Then, when they're weak, we shall strike and break their lines, leaving them no opportunities to march on Riverfen. The war in the River Valley can end before their forces even set foot here."

"It could be a trap," Druam said. "They may aim to have us stuck in Stonetree while their forces pull back to engage Riverfen."

"That is the risk we must take." Edsel's tone turned into pleading. "My wife and children have returned home, Druam. Lead your army north with mine. If we move quickly, we can fortify Stonetree before the enemy arrives."

Druam tore his eyes away from his old friend's, his heart heavy. "Two-thirds of my men and I will march north with you. Commander Rutki, I shall leave you to defend Riverfen with the remaining men. You're right, of course. Stonetree must stand if Riverfen is to have a chance in this war. Steel-Eyes is already preparing to protect our waters."

The earls held each other's arms and nodded.

"To war, then," Edsel said, his smile not touching his eyes.

"To war, my friend." *And the terrors of an unknown dawn.*

✳

His hood drawn over his head, Alex pushed through his fatigue and sun-weakness. Up in the high mountains, the snows should already have begun. But it was unseasonably warm, the retreating sun still a threat to his humors. On his journey with Cara, Alex had been able to drink the blood of animals and the occasional nearby human and so regained the strength the light had leached from him. Now he refused even though his instincts screamed at him to tear the throat from every living being he saw.

I will not give in, he told himself as his stomach cramped. The garlic-infused wound in his side festered horribly, smelling each time he changed the bandages, but he refused to drink. *I will not give into that evil.*

Few people roamed these roads, which was all for the better. Fewer to tempt him, fewer to see his weakness. Those kind, simple souls would try to help, and he didn't trust himself not to betray them. Half the time now, his *fampir* side leaked into his features, giving him long fangs or a wrinkled forehead that he hid with his hood. He'd never gone this long without drinking, but he knew the symptoms: first, his *fampir* instincts would drive him to drink unless he resisted with all he had; second, he would begin to feel the mortal frailties he had so long ignored, such as the cold and the numbness of tired legs; and finally, if he still did not drink, he would slow and slow until, at last, his body would dry out, frozen in position, his soul still trapped inside. Unless someone destroyed that husk, Alex would be trapped for eternity in his own body. *I will be cured before it comes to that.*

Alex traveled as far as he could each night, but though he tried to hide from the sun's heat, it scorched his skin and made him dizzy and faint. His throat was parched no matter the water he poured down it.

He was in the high mountains now, far from civilization. For the better. He couldn't be around living creatures. They were too soft. Too tempting. Their pulses throbbing in their necks, sweet and clear, whispering of the blood held inside.

Alex beat a hand against his forehead to drive out the horrible thoughts. The bushes beside him shook, and a rabbit leapt into his path, nose twitching. Before he could stop himself, Alex's *fampir* side reared up, instincts flaring deep within. He lunged at the rabbit and grabbed it with his long, starved fingers.

It shrieked and jumped in his hands, and he held it to his lips, his fangs already seeking the succulent blood, his tongue lapping against his teeth, his wound throbbing–

"No!" Alex shouted. He flung the poor creature into the woods. It bounded away, and he pulled his hood over his eyes, desperate not to see anything else. He couldn't bear the thought of his own thirst.

That night, he tried to climb to his feet, but they failed him. He lay and convulsed on the loam, his empty stomach sore and twisting, his wound burning, his body hot to the touch. He thought he could feel the change in his skin, turning into a husk that would lie forgotten forever.

"No," he said. "No, not yet, damn it!"

Alex struggled to his sore feet. He stumbled through the forest, his destination clear but his path uncertain.

Ancient scrolls spoke of a cure for the *fampir*. Most scholars discounted them as fae tales, yet if the undead were real, then a legend could be, too. From his many years of study, Alex had found a few scrolls, each from a different author, that hinted at the same cure. None of them gave a route or location, though each had a similar cryptic hint:

"Seek your loss and your desire," Alex mumbled, eyes straining in the darkness. "The Whispering Woods will find you."

CHAPTER SIXTEEN
Gwen

When the Witches failed to come for her that day, Gwen once again used the Song she learned from fire to keep herself warm. The second morning came with dewdrops that coated her skin. She still wore the remnants of her Masque gown, its silk providing little warmth or protection.

They want me to survive, Gwen thought. *So survive I will.* She appraised the ëlg corpse which still lay in the grass. Its skin, if treated properly, would make a warm dress or cloak. But how to do it? The Songs she had used flitted in her head, but she couldn't quite grasp them. Instead, she rooted in the grass until she found a large stone.

Stone would be easier to alter.

The stone's Song was not nearly as complex as the creature's, and Gwen shaped it until it was long and sharp like a spearhead of ancient times. With her new tool, she skinned the remainder of the ëlg's hide and laid it out. She cut up its meat and organs and spread the pieces to dry. As she worked, a flock of large brown birds with leaf-like wings gathered around her. They stole the meat and fought over the organs. She tried to drive them away, and they snapped at her and pierced her skin. She threw rocks at them, and still they pilfered her food undeterred. After a few pitiful swings with a branch, Gwen sat on the ground not far away, her head on her knees, and watched the flock destroy her hard work.

Not as if she could have made proper use of the animal

anyway. Her education had lacked how hunters might use stomachs to create waterskins or how to properly cure meat. *I was a princess, not a ranger,* she thought sourly. *They should teach princesses these things, too. We shouldn't rely on others to clothe and feed us.*

Her stomach grumbled again, but no ëlg conveniently wandered into her path. She again tried to enter the trees, pushing the branches with her hands and kicking at the roots. They didn't budge. Gwen slammed her fists against a trunk with a cry of frustration.

Hunger followed her for three more days. Her stomach stretched with emptiness. Her hands shook. Gwen thought longingly of the grand feasts at the Cascade Palace, with fruits and bread and pastries and tender meat perfectly cooked. She could almost taste the honeyed wine on her tongue. The thought of such things tortured her.

As evening turned to night and frost gathered on the tree branches, Gwen collapsed into the red grass and stared unseeing at the Woods. Her belly ached, and she reached for the grass, yanking it up. She had tried it before, and it did little to appease her hunger, but the pain in her belly demanded to be satiated. She put a handful into her mouth. Each strand of grass took forever to chew, and their bitter taste tainted her saliva. She swallowed with effort and could feel the meager fare sliding down to her stomach.

A rustling in the Woods caught her attention, and she weakly turned her head to see. Another strange creature, the size of a pony with spindly insect-like legs and a triangular head, lumbered into the clearing. Its pincers chittered together, making a humming sound. As the creature grew closer, the humming grew louder. It thrummed through the air and into the ground.

Try as she might, Gwen could not hear this creature's Song. It was simply too strange. It moved like an insect, but it had tufts of fur on its back and peculiar eyes. Instead, Gwen listened to the humming. The sound pulled at her, and she realized that it was a Song. As the creature hummed, the ground at its feet rumbled and moved, the dirt piling itself up to expose a strange tuber. The creature ate the tuber and moved on, bringing more roots to the surface.

Gwen wanted to hum the same music. She could feel it inside her, warming her cold skin, like a beacon she should follow. When she tried to hum it, though, the melody changed on her tongue. However the creature was making the noise, Gwen couldn't imitate it easily. She tried whistling and singing, yet the Song eluded her.

The creature continued its circuitous path, still humming its food-giving Song. Gwen observed it jealously, her own stomach hurting so badly she thought she might vomit. *Perhaps I could steal its food.* If the birds had done it to her, she could do it to others.

Just then, the creature turned its oddly-shaped head. It looked at her with strange blue eyes that had no whites nor irises. Its humming continued, but instead of tubers, a fruit fell from a too-high branch. *The Song changed slightly,* Gwen realized. She listened to this new iteration, a similar melody that felt more comfortable to her.

Gwen hummed with the creature. One of the trees near her shook. An unfamiliar fruit, fully grown and ripe, fell from its branches to land at her feet. Gwen snatched it up and tore into it. Juices coursed down her chin.

Nothing had ever tasted so delicious.

Gwen sang the Song again, and again, until multiple fruits lay on the ground in front of her. She ate and ate until she threw up, the sudden fullness in her stomach too much to bear.

Armed with a new Song, Gwen experimented with notes and harmonies. She brought tubers and roots from the earth, different fruits and berries from the trees and bushes. Some were sour or underripe, while others tasted so poorly she spit them out. She Sang a fire into existence and roasted her bounty over its flames.

The chill that night dispelled even that small victory. Frost crept over the Woods, freezing the water and extinguishing her fire. No matter how Gwen tried to reignite it, it only flared briefly before frost killed it. Through blue lips, Gwen tried to augment the Song to make her fire larger and stronger. The flames leapt over the cold wood.

A harsh wind blew the fire out. Its Song carried a note of warning. The Whispering Woods, it seemed, wanted no fire that night. Gwen didn't know what else she could do, for the wind's Song was far more powerful than hers.

Gwen shivered, her teeth clacking. She dragged the ëlg skin over her shoulders, but it wasn't cured properly. It provided bare warmth and stank of blood and innards. Her breath steamed in the frigid air, her fingers turned blue. She stuffed them into her armpits, and the rest of her trembled with the extreme cold. Even her thoughts chattered.

The cold deepened and deepened. As it grew deathly chill, Gwen became warm. No, not just warm, *hot*, as if her whole body was about to burn. She shed the hide and threw off her clothes, feverishly hot. Hot, and so very sleepy. She curled up on the ground, ready to fall asleep, to embrace that deepest dream that led to death.

Something huge and warm curled around her. Gwen opened her eyes to a large green-golden iris staring back at her. She twisted around to see what lay against her, and would have gasped had she had any breath remaining.

A nightcat of enormous proportions huddled against her, holding her against its belly. It was lithe as a panther, with long red-black fur and paws the size of her head. At the end of its tail was a scorpion-like stinger. A smaller nightcat – a cub – curled at Gwen's feet, safe within his mother's warmth. Gwen thought she should be afraid, but something in the animal's gaze comforted her.

The beast purred, a rumbling sound that shook Gwen's body with its force. A Song filled the purr. It caressed her with a mother's love for her cub, and in its melody rang intelligence and empathy. The melody held the same feeling as a blanket laid over a child, or the comfort of laying next to a loved one after a nightmare. Gwen listened as heat coursed through her, infusing her skin and warming her bones. Real heat, not the heat of her delusions.

Grateful, Gwen curled up against the nightcat and slept.

In the morning, she woke to find the nightcat gone. She straightened, shivering in her nakedness, and surveyed the glen. The creature hadn't gone far; it crouched beside the stream, its tail flitting to and fro. Gwen came up beside it, entangling a hand in its fur. It turned one large eye to her before returning its attention to the stream.

Listen, Gwen thought it said. The nightcat no longer purred, yet in the way it moved, she heard a melody that spoke of the hunt and the need for food, for the life given to sustain another. Just as with the other Songs, Gwen heard it not with her ears, but deep within her bones. She reached a hand into the water and waited for the Song to tell her when to close her fist.

When she did, she held a wriggling fish between her fingers.

The nightcat pushed its head against her before walking away. She followed it, but stopped short. The nightcat cub lay in the grass watching them. His back legs were shriveled and useless, the stinger on his tail not yet functional. The cub mewed, and his mother nuzzled him before peering at Gwen.

Carefully, Gwen sat down beside the cub. With her stone tool, she cut the fish into small pieces and fed them to the cub as her soul listened to the Songs.

In the cub's Song, she heard love and comfort, pain and desperation. Like all living creatures, he wanted to survive, except he had been born deformed. His mother provided for him as long as she could, but at his age, he should be hunting for himself. Winter was near, even in the Whispering Woods, and the mother couldn't feed them both.

Gwen reached deeper, listening to the buried Song within the cub. What she heard both excited and frightened her.

"He can be healed," she murmured, stroking the cub's head. "But not without sacrifice."

The nightcat mother lay beside her and blinked a slow golden-green eye. Gwen heard its Song too, and the creature's desire to live. Greater than that was the desire for its offspring to grow and prosper.

Gwen scratched the nightcat's ears. "I heard that your kind are nearly as intelligent as humans. Perhaps it's true."

The nightcat licked her hand and prodded the cub with her nose.

"Are you sure? The Songs must be balanced."

Gwen could swear she saw tears in the nightcat's eye. It lay its head on top of its cub and began to purr. Twining her hands in both the mother and cub's fur, Gwen listened carefully, sensed their melodies, pieced them together with the Songs around her: nature and healing, life and death.

This is what the Witches meant by sorcerers making Songs their own, Gwen thought. *They don't change the essence of the Songs, but adapt a note here or there, add a harmony or dissent.* It seemed to her similar to embroidery, the needle moving differently to accommodate new stitches. Just the same, she must place each stitch carefully and build to the final picture.

Candles, perhaps longer, passed before Gwen started her new Song. Her voice carried high and low, quick then steady, joy and grief pouring into her melody. As she Sang, magic formed around her, coalescing between the cub and his mother. Tendrils of the Songs came into being and wove into glowing fur.

As the Song went on, the mother twitched and growled low in its throat. It didn't move, its eyes trusting on Gwen. The cub's ruined legs spasmed, then grew longer, heavier, stronger.

The Songs took from the mother and gave to the cub. The cub whined and purred. His mother gave him one final lick before pressing its nose to Gwen's chest. Its head fell into her lap, heavy with death.

Gwen ended her Song. The last notes faded into the still air. She stroked the mother's head, saddened that she had been the one to kill such a magnificent creature. The cub climbed to his feet, unsteady at first, and tested his newfound legs. He ran across the glen and pounced in the grass, his tail whipping to and fro. The cub raced and bounded before returning to Gwen and his mother. He sniffed at his mother and keened, and his trust for Gwen echoed loudly in his Song.

"I'm so sorry, little one," Gwen said, reaching to the cub. He leaned into her hand and curled beside her to press his head against his mother. "She did what any mother would. Grieve, but the pain will pass in time. I know; my mother died when I was young. Then my father, a few years later. And my brother. But I persist because I must. They wouldn't want me to give up. Neither would your mother."

The thought of her brother's death rammed into her, fresh pain that dug into her spirit. Gwen pushed back her tears. *I can't think of him now. I have to survive.*

The cub purred. Gwen said, "I don't know what I'm doing here, nor what the Witches want of me. I can hear the Songs, and I think you can, too. We're both alone, but we don't have to be. We can stay and survive the Woods together. What do you think of that?"

A happy mew came from the cub, and Gwen smiled. "I'm Gwen. How about I call you Lintem? It means 'brave' in my forefathers' tongue."

Lintem mewed again, and Gwen felt a surge of joy. At least she wouldn't have to be alone.

With Lintem beside her, Gwen experimented with her magic. Though she regretted doing so, she skinned the mother nightcat. As she laid the fur to dry, the brown leaf-birds returned to scavenge. Lintem pounced at them and drove them off. As he did, Gwen lay in the sun. Its warmth dried her hands, a Song drifting in its rays. This she adapted to quicken the process of drying the hide and meat. She wept when it worked.

With this new Song, Gwen preserved the meat in the river, wrapped in organs and plastered with tree resin. Lintem swatted at curious fish, and in his throat she heard a growling Song. Carefully, Gwen repeated the Song and wrapped it around their food to keep the fish from eating it. This worked for a time, but she found she had to do it again later in the day. The fish were particularly persistent.

Her successes gave her newfound energy. With Lintem by her side, Gwen explored the glen to hear all the Songs that lay within it. The threads of so many Songs gave her a headache until she learned to pull at just one at a time.

Over the next few days, She Sang the trees into a shelter, though her first attempt was more of a woebegone nest. Just like her sewing, she unpicked the melodies and notes that didn't work, revising the Song until it did as she pleased. Once she and Lintem had a place to rest, Gwen made a cellar for her food and an oven to heat it.

Lintem went everywhere with her, a constant shadow that helped her to hunt and cuddled with her at night. With fresh skins and greater knowledge of the Songs, Gwen made more clothes and added to her shelter. More than once, she grew frustrated with a failure and would scream at the sky. Lintem always comforted her, and in due course she found a new way to work the Songs.

Days melted into deshes. At first, Gwen kept track of time with notches on a tree trunk. One day, she forgot to make a mark, and then the next, and so on until she had completely forgotten her calendar.

The glen became more than home for Gwen and Lintem. It was, at first, a playground, a treasure trove of new Songs and interesting creations. Yet as time passed, Gwen heard fewer and fewer unfamiliar melodies. At last, she had heard nothing new for days.

When that happened, Gwen went to the trees that blocked her way from the glen. She sank her toes into the ground and Sang. She urged the earth to tremble and riot, to throw up the roots of the grey-branched trees.

The whispers of the trees grew to shouts, and they withdrew their branches from each other. The path opened up, and Gwen halted her Song. She smiled in satisfaction.

She and Lintem wandered into the Woods. They slept in hollows or meadows, sometimes wandering down paths the trees showed and sometimes forcing their own way. In their travels, they saw fantastic beasts with skin of bark or stone and impossible plants of dirt and flesh. Gwen heard the murmurs of the trees and began to understand them. She spoke with creatures and shrubs, learning their languages through their Songs. And, every day, she created new spell-Songs to suit her needs and whims, so comfortable with the connection that she hummed, if not Sang, nearly every waking moment.

Deshes, months, perhaps years might have passed. Her grief was buried deep inside her, a raw wound that she ignored until she forgot it was there. The Woods were her identity now, her soul and her ambition, her hope and despair. She stopped trying to bend them, and instead let them guide her wherever they would.

If Druam could see her, he would not recognize the forest witch that stood before him.

CHAPTER SEVENTEEN
Sandu

Bright moonlight illuminated the forest, trees casting shadows over the road. A bridge spanned a sluggish stream in front of them with a crossroads right after it. Sandu paused to inspect his surroundings and realized that he knew this place. He knew the marks on the sign and the missing rail posts on the bridge, the old stump and the fallen tree that dangled into the stream.

"That road leads to Dunfrey," he said to Jagger. The town where he and his father lived after their caravan's massacre was only a league or so away, snug in a vale between two large hills. He hadn't traveled there since Tambrey threw him out.

Somewhere within his chest, a tug pulled him toward home. *You are touched by Death,* Darian had said. *Listen, and you will find your wife.* Sandu took a deep breath, crossed the bridge, and headed down the side road. He didn't need to read the weathered sign. His feet knew the grooves left by wagon wheels, his ears recognized the nightingale's song.

This was home.

His steps quickened, his earlier fatigue and worry forgotten. He passed Hafton's farmhouse and Jiller's mill, tapped a hand on the oak tree which had split and grown over an old axe, stepped over the crossing-stones of Lewton's Creek, knowing each one even in the dark. Dawn was close, and he imagined the bustle of the waking village. He would see Clifton working the millstone on the edge of town, and Lirette collecting laundry from each house.

Sandu came up over the hill just as the sun's pale light filtered into the valley. Cascading emotions flooded through him: joy at returning home, hope that he would make it to Tambrey in time, dread at how she would look at him. And the children! How he longed to hear their laughter and answer their many questions, hold them in his arms and marvel at their growth.

As he stared down at Dunfrey, an uneasy foreboding settled in his guts.

No smoke rose from the homes. No dogs barked, no cooking scented the air. No one moved amid the buildings. From that distance, Sandu couldn't see the shapes around the houses, for they were too dark in the pre-dawn light.

Sandu moved toward the village, but Jagger's large hand stopped him. The giant man held Sandu's shoulder and shook his head, his eyes suspicious.

"You think it's a trap?" Sandu asked. Jagger narrowed his eyes and shook his head again. "What then?"

Jagger shrugged, releasing Sandu. His gaze was still sharp and scrutinizing as he followed Sandu down the hill. As they drew closer to the village, a horrible smell assaulted them. Sandu gagged. Jagger frowned, covering his nose and mouth with his sleeve. *Tambrey is there somewhere*, Sandu thought. The pull in his chest grew stronger, and he followed it into the village.

The sun rose over the hills, revealing the dark shapes around the buildings. Each was a corpse, strewn where the villager had died, their flesh rotting as their blank eyes stared unseeing into the dirt. Sandu kept his distance from them, shielding his face with a kerchief.

"What do you think?" he asked Jagger. He tried not to examine the dead too closely, afraid he'd know each one of them. "Bandits? Prowlers?"

Jagger stepped near one of the bodies and turned it over with his foot. His body language indicated that Sandu's guesses were wrong.

"Plague," Sandu realized. "Gods, how many did it take?"

156

Dunfrey had been home to a few hundred souls. There were bodies in doorways and alleys draped where they fell, and horses and dogs lying in the streets. Now that Sandu knew what he was seeing, he noticed the burst pustules and pale white tumors that sprouted from the deceased.

The smell grew worse nearer the town green. Rows upon rows of bodies lined the once-healthy grass, older than those scattered around town, rotted to the bone or ripped to shreds by opportunistic animals. Those same animals lay dead nearby. Behind the novum, piles of churned earth showed a multitude of fresh graves, dug before the plague had overwhelmed the town.

"Nearly all of Dunfrey is here," Sandu said, voice muffled by his kerchief. "Gods, did any of them escape?" *Did my family escape?* The tug in his chest was persistent now. Sandu stepped past the bodies and headed to the smithy. After Tambrey had told everyone Sandu was dead, she had remarried the blacksmith. Her new home was the best place to start his search.

The forge lay cold and unused, tools scattered about the workshop. The door to the house was open, the interior beyond dark and quiet. Sandu hesitated before stepping inside, careful not to disturb the dust that had collected.

The kitchen and living space were well-kept and organized – Tambrey's handiwork – if a little sparse. Some pots and pans, as well as other goods, had been taken from their places, leaving the spots conspicuously empty. No one was there. *She must be upstairs.*

Quietly, Sandu crept up the stairs, ears straining for any whisper of noise. All was silent and deathly still. He came to the first bedroom and cracked open the door. Toys lay in their little chest, and small clothes had been thrown about the two beds. Sandu let out a breath; the beds were empty. If his children were dead, they hadn't died here.

He moved to the master bedroom. Its carved door was partly open, and he creaked it further, wincing. Nothing came leaping from the shadows, no screams rent the air. With Jagger following, Sandu crept into the room, his gaze on the large bed on the far wall. This room, too, had been ransacked for goods and left in a hurry.

The tug inside his chest told Sandu that Tambrey was here. He paused and took a candle from its shelf. Though he fumbled with his flint, he managed to light it. The small flame barely pierced the gloom.

Something shifted in the bed. It moaned, holding out a pale, thin arm with bloating pustules. Sandu swallowed and moved closer, staying out of the occupant's reach.

"Frederick?" A voice, papery and low, so faint that it was barely audible in the silence. "Is that you?"

Sandu brought the candle up to reveal his wife. She appeared a ghost, her fair skin deathly pale, her flesh corrupted with boils and scabbing wounds. Her beautiful yellow hair, once thick and shining, was translucent and falling out in clumps. Her eyes were crusted and only barely opened, fluttering at the light.

"Freddy? Freddy, go back to Bluston. The children aren't safe here."

"It's me, Tambrey," Sandu said, kneeling beside her. *This isn't how it should go*, his denying mind said. *She should be lovely and laughing, like I remember her.* But the specter before him was woefully real. "It's Sa—Barty. Your Barty."

"Barty?" Tambrey tried to open her eyes further and winced with the effort. Disregarding the danger in his actions, Sandu removed his kerchief and soaked it in water from the skin at his hip. He tenderly wiped her eyes, cheeks, nose, and mouth. She lay there, allowing him to work. When he finished, she managed to open her eyes slightly more.

"Gods, Barty. It is you."

Though tears pricked at his eyes, Sandu held them back. *I must be strong for her*, he thought. He took her thin hand and held it close. "I came back, Tambrey. After all these years, I'm finally home." His voice cracked, and he looked away from her. "I didn't think I'd come back to this."

"Why are you here, Barty?" Tambrey's voice was too frail to hold any malice or anger. Still, Sandu thought he could hear accusations and years of repressed fury deep inside her. *How can she forgive me, if I never have?*

"I came for you. I had to see you again." Sandu held her hand with both of his, savoring her touch, slight though it may be. Her hand remained limp, her gaze soft.

"Oh, Barty. You're late again."

Just like before: late for dinner, late for the children's bedtime, late for everything. And she resented me for it. Sandu hung his head, giving into the tears that flowed into his beard.

"I didn't ever want to see you again," Tambrey said. Her quiet voice was worse than screaming or shouting. *How many condemnations are still held within her breast? How many nights wishing I were truly dead so she'd never have to worry about my striding into town and ruining her life again? How—*

"But I'm glad you're here now," she said. Sandu couldn't believe his ears. He gripped her hand and leaned forward, stroking her face.

"I'm so sorry, Tambrey. I'm so sorry for all I did to you and the children, that I drove you away, that I was a vecking horrible husband. I wanted to be better for you, but I didn't know how. Every single day I've thought about how much I hurt you. Every day I've thought about returning and earning back your love. I thought I could do it if I tried hard enough, if I became a better man. But I failed. I'm not a better man. I'm still just a coward who's always too late." He grasped at her, staring into her bloodshot eyes. "I can't forgive myself, Tambrey. I just can't. I've done too much bad in this world. I've done too much bad to you."

She took a breath, and Sandu strained, hoping against hope that her next words would be ones of forgiveness, that she might do what he could not. She had always been stronger than him.

Then her breath leaked out, and with it her soul.

Sandu stared at her, not comprehending. He clutched at her, muttering her name over and over, his vision blurred with tears. But she didn't move, didn't speak. A corpse could give no forgiveness.

Jagger pulled at Sandu's shoulder, and Sandu fought back. He threw himself over Tambrey, protecting her. From what, he didn't know, but he couldn't let anything happen to her. He had to preserve her somehow, get her to Darian so he could resurrect her. He snarled at Jagger, "We can take her with us!"

Jagger shook his head, pity in his eyes.

"He brought you back, he can do it for her!"

Again Jagger pulled at Sandu. The larger man's greater strength won out. Against his wishes, Sandu was dragged from the bedside, down the stairs, out the door, and back through the streets. By the time they reached the edge of the village, Sandu only fought weakly against Jagger, Tambrey's name still on his lips.

Jagger dumped Sandu beside a still-green pine. Immediately, Sandu struggled to his feet. "You bastard, you're just jealous that she's not gone forever! Let me go back, let me bring her to Darian."

Though his lips thinned into a line, Jagger didn't fight back as Sandu railed, his fists beating against the taller man's chest. Eventually, Sandu gave up. He tried to go around Jagger, but was blocked. As a last resort, Sandu clutched at Jagger's tunic. "Please. I have to go back to her. I can help her."

She's gone. Sandu didn't know whether he read the words in Jagger's expression, or if they had welled up from his own heart. He shook his head. "Darian brought you back."

He can't bring back everyone. Tambrey is in Autorus's domain now. She may have gone on to Lyael. She's gone forever.

Sandu shook his head, his hands entwined in Jagger's shirt. He stood mutely, denying the truth that lay in his chest. *Even if she did return, she'd only go back to Frederick. She doesn't want you.*

A tear splashed onto his hand.

She's safer in death than she would be in life.

Gently, Jagger helped Sandu to sit back on the grass. Sandu shook as he sobbed.

You have to look to the future. Da's in jail, and the children need to be found. There's no more you can do for her.

Jagger pointed to the grass, his glare clear: *Stay here.* Too much in grief to disobey, Sandu watched through watery eyes as Jagger went back to the town. Thoughts ran wild in his head, but always came back to one thing. *She never forgave you. You have to find Da and the children before it's too late for them, too.*

One by one, Jagger set the buildings alight. The black smoke carried the smell of death with it. Sandu did nothing, his heart crying out for those whose homes were being destroyed.

Doesn't matter. They're dead now. Everyone is dead.

The fire licked at the village, cleansing the plague. When every last home burned, Jagger came back. He looked neither pleased nor sorrowful, just a man who had done what needed to be done.

"Tambrey was in there," Sandu mumbled. "We should have buried her."

Jagger laid a hand to Sandu's shoulder, and in the gesture Sandu knew his companion's pity.

This is how he lost his wife, too. Fire and smoke.

Together, they watched Dunfrey burn.

CHAPTER EIGHTEEN
Cara

The sun had yet to rise, the forest grey and haunting. Cara forced herself to move. She carefully eased out from her tent and crawled to the fire, her injured leg dragging uselessly behind her. Whatever draughts had lessened the pain had faded, and agony lanced up her calf.

Much of the night had passed slowly, her dreams full of dread. Her wound woke her often, and she tossed and turned to get comfortable with the splint. Somehow, this time was worse than when it first broke. Of course, after the attack on the caravan, Alex had been there to hold her at night.

For once, Cara let herself imagine what it would be like if Alex were with her again. He would stroke her hair and murmur tender words, and his laughter would help her forget her pain. Druam had said that Alex had gone on a fool's quest. She wondered where he was and whether he still thought of her.

Darian emerged from the other tent, making his tentative way to the fire, and Cara abandoned her thoughts of Alex. *There's nothing I can do about him now.*

"Here," Darian said as he joined her by the fire. "Take this." He held out a small flask filled with a dark blue, molasses-like liquid.

"What is it?"

"Something to help with the pain."

Though still suspicious of him, Cara took the flask and swallowed its contents in two gulps. It slid down her throat and into her empty belly, making her slightly sick. As she sat there, a numbness entered her leg, mercifully cutting short the fire from her wound.

Cara asked, "Is Sandu still asleep?"

"He went to see his wife."

"Did he now?" Venom tainted her voice. *What right has Sandu to abandon me, after all I've been through?* The beast stirred, agreeing with her.

"Had he not gone, he would have lost the chance forever." Sadness filled Darian's voice. "She died in the night. One of many."

"He left without a word. That's not what friends do," Cara said stubbornly. At Darian's chiding expression, she amended, "But I see why he did."

The blind man nodded, and Cara watched him closely. "How do you know she died?"

"I heard her Song."

"I don't know what that means."

Darian laid his cane in his lap, his strange eyes piercing. "The Song of Death. All are beholden to it. The Songs are the threads of our world. Few can hear them, and fewer still can hear each Song in its entirety. I know not the Song of Man or the Song of Nature, but the Song of Death...*that* I hear thrumming in my mind, waking and sleeping, continually flowing. I can hear it carrying each soul to Autorus's domain, and their agony in his purgatories or joy in his heavens. I know those who seek the unknowable Lyael, a death beyond the Underworld, and I hear their Songs end as they enter it."

Cara tried to fathom his words. Had he heard the moment of Merick's death, when he begged silently for release? Did he know if her mentor's soul was at rest while his body still roamed? *To know when each person dies. What an awful thing.* "Doesn't it drive you mad?"

"Sometimes. I have long grown used to it, and I mourn no longer for those who pass. It is a fate we must all encounter, and I have heard the Songs of countless people, young and old, married, rich, poor. Though I have sympathy, I know that there is little I can do." Darian stoked the fire with his cane. A log cracked into ashes. "I have heard your Song of Death for many years now, always in the background. In recent deshes, though, it has grown stronger, encompassing all around it, tying together so many threads. So I decided to find you, and help you, as I have helped so many others."

My Song? Cara wondered how it sounded. *Does my beast have a Song, too?*

"Do you know of the *fampir*?" Cara asked.

"Of course. Their Songs are louder than a mortal's, but I have learned to ignore them. They are not helpless like those who simply pass on, nor those who turn prowler." He frowned, turning the cane over in his hands. "The prowlers are an abomination in the Song, a new mutant, unexpected in the weaving. I cannot help all those poor souls who wander Earda, untethered from their bodies, lost and unseen."

Cara was silent a moment, absorbing all this information. She wasn't quite sure if she trusted this man or believed his every word. He certainly seemed convinced, but it could be the ramblings of a lunatic.

Darian's white eyes pulled her gaze. "I heard a *fampir*'s Song end the other night, not far from here."

Cara rubbed her arms. Her leg throbbed. "I don't know what you're talking about."

"Lie to yourself if you must. Your Song has become discordant, confused. It knows not what it wants or what is best." He reached out to her shoulder, and she froze. One hand moved lightly to touch the left side of her chest. "Here is your heart, where Caralyn Gellder lives." His fingers trailed to her stomach. "And here is that part which both fascinates and frightens you: the *sulpari*, that foul creature within. She is that side of you which is tied to the Underworld, and from which you derive all your power. When the *sulpari* rises," he said, moving his hand up the center of her chest to her collarbone, "she overpowers you. Sometimes she obeys you, but other times you are at her mercy. This is not the way of the *fampir*, for they never lose themselves as you do, nor of the prowlers, for they are wholly lost."

His touch tingled against her skin. Cara contemplated his words. When the beast first rose within her as a child, it had frightened her. As she used it more and more in battle, with its speed and sharp eyes, she had grown used to it. Yet Darian was right; sometimes, she did feel lost in the beast's hunger. In her worst dreams, it overpowered her and shoved her deep down into her own belly, roaming the world in her place.

Could this stranger help her? Cara had once sought the scholars of Mott for a cure. Even after everything she'd experienced, some part of her longed for the simplicity of a life without the beast.

Darian continued, "How can we unite your two halves? Cara and *sulpari*, maid and beast. One cannot exist without the other, yet your mortal side will always fear the undead half. Always, until you listen to what the Song is telling you, and allow yourself to be both at once, holding each equally, centered–" he pushed at a point in the center of her chest "–here. It is only when you are whole, and truly what you are meant to be, that you will find peace. Not through the wanton murder of Autorus's creatures."

Doubt and anger flared suddenly within Cara, fueled by the beast. *He doesn't know what I've been through.* She spat, "You don't know why I'm doing this."

"Perhaps it is not the *sulpari* which is the source of the darkness within," Darian said.

"Perhaps you don't know all there is to vecking know," Cara shot back. She tried to scoot away, but her leg twinged, and she winced. "I'm grateful for your assistance, but I don't need you, or anyone else, to tell me what to do."

His expression was unreadable. "You hear without listening, judge without knowing. What, other than your blood, makes you the arbiter of death's court? Have you years within the judiciary? Have you studied the books of law or listened to the masters of philosophy?"

If Cara had two whole legs, she would have stood and walked away. Instead, she turned her back on the blind man and focused on watching the forest for signs of Sandu's return. When she didn't respond to him, Darian sighed and said softly, "Perhaps I have come too late."

He's a madman, Cara thought. *He's not to be trusted.*

Yet his words ate at her. Did she have the right to kill the *fampir* farmer? Once her leg healed, was it her duty to destroy Mavian and Druam for all they had done? She could see the smugness in Mavian's lips as he summoned Merick's corpse to taunt her, the fury of Druam's primal eyes as he drove the sword through Renna's tender flesh. *Darian knows nothing about me.* If he truly heard the Songs of all the dead, then he knew how Merick had died, not with a sword in his hand, brave to the end, but in the infernal agony of dark magic. Darian would have known when Renna's heart stopped beating, so soon after Cara had found her again.

Maybe Darian is as corrupt as the rest of us, as close to Death as he is.

In the growing light, two figures emerged from the woods. Their movements were slow and weary, their postures defeated. As they came to the edge of camp, they stilled. Sandu's face was gaunt, his eyes bloodshot. He held his hands under his armpits and didn't look at Cara.

Darian stood behind her. "Don't come closer. The plague is on you; we mustn't let it taint us."

Cara observed sullenly as the blind man directed the other two to undress and burn their clothes. He handed them a foul-smelling concoction to scrub over their skin and forced them to wash thrice in the cold stream.

"Sandu, you will touch nothing before we touch it," Darian said as Sandu and Jagger pulled on new clothes. "You will sleep in a tent away from us, and always sit across the fire. You will not tend to Cara. After five days, the infection will either show itself or you will be deemed safe once more. Jagger will not carry the disease, but should still wash after touching you or handling your possessions."

Serves him right, Cara thought. *Leaving without a word and bringing the plague back to us.* Across the fire, Sandu plopped wearily to the ground, limbs dragging, all cheer gone from him.

Cara asked, "Did you find her?"

"Yes." Sandu stared away from her.

"And?"

Sandu's red eyes told the story, yet still Cara goaded him. "Did you speak with her?"

"I don't want to talk about it yet, Cara." Sandu stared at his wringing hands. "I just need to rest."

"You could have told me you were leaving."

"And what would you have done? Sometimes I have to care for myself. You're not the only woman in my life." Sandu glared at her. Somehow, his temper satisfied her.

"You left them long ago. What's important now–"

"Is that you're hurt, you're angry, and you want a scapegoat?" Sandu rose and turned away. "Don't forget my father. Or will you be as selfish when I find him as you are now? My children are missing, my wife is dead, my entire village was consumed by the plague. Everyone I knew is gone. Perhaps you should consider your words more carefully before you speak." He marched away into the woods before Cara could respond.

Jagger and Darian just sat there, quietly observing. Cara glared at them. "This doesn't concern either of you. Leave. I don't want you here anyway."

"That's no longer your choice," Darian said. "Jagger is here for Sandu, not you."

"And what about you?"

"I'm here with Jagger."

Cara's anger and helplessness was matched by the beast's. She drew into herself, speaking no more. If she did, she knew that the beast would rise, and she would gladly welcome it.

Though Sandu returned soon after, he didn't say anything to Cara. He, Darian, and Jagger spoke together in low tones. Cara watched them resentfully, wanting to be included but also despising all three of them. Sandu was *her* friend, he should be there for *her*, not those two strangers, one of whom had tried to kill them in the past.

As the day slowly passed, guilt ate into her. Sandu curled

by the fire and stared into nothing. He didn't respond when Darian spoke to him. Unbidden, a memory came into Cara's head of the days after Merick's death. She had grieved and despaired in turn, and Sandu had been there for her. He had cooked his grandmother's soup, providing a warm relief from her mourning. He had listened to her when she needed to talk.

His loss is as great as mine, Cara thought. When she gained the courage, she said to Sandu, "I'm sorry." He only rolled over and turned his back to her. Though she longed to speak with him, Cara left him alone.

That night, Darian gave her another dose to relieve her pain. Feeling lonely and hurt, Cara crawled into her tent and tried to sleep.

Renna filled her dreams. Sometimes Cara would sit and talk with her friend, other times she would be unable to find her and run around screaming Renna's name. Then came an awful dream where she pinned Renna down and gave into the beast. It tore at Renna's skin, drinking her hot blood, reveling in it.

In the dream, Cara's leg healed. She stared at it, her face coated with blood, and wondered.

Cara woke from the dream still tasting the imaginary blood. She grimaced, swallowed, and lay back down on the blankets. Sleep wouldn't come again. Her leg throbbed as pain shot through her, and she thought again of Sandu's grief.

Cara crawled out of the tent and away from the fire. Her shame awoke the beast. It rose within her, its hot emotions coursing through her limbs. Her sharpened vision showed her the tracks of a small creature. The hard ground pushed against her leg as she crawled, sending spikes of hot pain. Every few feet, she paused to breathe deeply and push down the vomit. She followed the animal's scent until she found a rabbit caught in some hunter's snare. It squeaked and thrashed, its veins pumping with its heightened heartbeat.

Cocking her head, Cara studied the helpless thing. Its large brown eye stared up at her, pleading. She reached a hand down and caught it in her strong fingers. Carefully, she removed it from the trap. It quivered between her fingers, and she thought she could smell its blood through its fur.

This is wrong, Cara thought. She hesitated, caught between desire and morality. She so, so wanted to be healed and whole once more. Yet a life had to be snuffed out to do it.

The beast urged her to drink. Cara wavered, and her fingers loosened just a touch. The rabbit twisted, and its small claw scratched her. Drops of ruby blood puddled on her skin.

The beast encouraged her, and Cara bent down. With one easy motion, she twisted the rabbit's head around, not killing it, merely exposing the largest vein on its neck. Her *sulpari* fang pierced its flesh, and hot blood pumped out. It touched her tongue –

And, oh, such ecstasy. Cara gave in and ripped further into the rabbit, its blood soaking her skin and gliding down her throat, coppery and bitter and all the best flavors she never knew she wanted, perfect and divine in a way nothing else was.

Her calf began to warm, and she could feel it healing. Not enough to mend fully, but the remaining infection died down, and the muscle began to work its way back to normal. It twinged, but oh, it was so good.

Cara tossed the rabbit aside, desperate for more. No matter how she searched, she couldn't find another creature, and her leg, though slightly healed, was still too hurt to walk on. Despondent now after the blood ecstasy, Cara crawled back to the camp, the beast still strong within her.

She could hear Sandu's heartbeat and smell the blood in his veins. She stopped beside his tent, warring with herself. A man was different from a rabbit; she couldn't harm him.

The beast purred, *What if? Think of what his blood could do, what a mere rabbit's could not.*

Cara listened to Sandu's blood pumping through him, so tantalizingly close. She reached out to the tent fabric.

She stopped herself. *He might have the plague. He's your friend.* With a great effort, Cara forced the beast down into her belly. As she had when she was younger, she built mental walls to keep it in place. She shivered, aghast at herself for even contemplating such a deed.

As she retreated to her tent, Cara thought she heard the faint strains of music on the wind. *The Song of Death?* she wondered. When she tried to listen closer, the melody faded away.

The taste of blood was still cloying on her tongue, and when she slept, she dreamt of the hunt. This time, it was victorious instead of frightening.

CHAPTER NINETEEN
Mavian

As soon as the dread portal closed behind them, Mavian turned to Rask. "How can I raise her?"

The old man coughed, holding a kerchief to his mouth. He took a deep breath, then began to speak. Mavian listened intently, hanging on the earl's every word.

"There are dark powers below this city, lingering since the Dead's War. It was here that the *fampir* were first created, a secret kept within the Rask family for generations. It was here, too, that the last of the original *fampir* was killed. The creature's sarcophagus remains, built by its long-dead followers. Stories within my family tell of a way to resurrect the creature, a spell enshrined there that will defeat even Autorus. Perhaps–"

"Perhaps it can be used for Maeria instead," Mavian said. "Take me to this place."

"I know not where it lies," Rask said, "only the stories. These tunnels are vast and ancient. Search them. If you need labor, send for men from the mines."

Giddiness filled Mavian, but his suspicions had to be voiced. "Why didn't you tell me sooner?"

Rask shrugged. "I've always believed it to be a legend. But your persistence is admirable, if foolhardy. *If* the legends are true, and *if* the sarcophagus could be found, why not give you the chance?"

"What of the prowlers and the attack on Seastone?" Chadron asked. "Shouldn't he be focused on that? We don't have time for tales and legends."

"My army will be on the move come morning," Rask replied. "If Strilu can find a way to capture more prowlers for battle, I see no reason to keep him from his wishes."

Already, Mavian gathered parchment and ink, preparing to chart the tunnels. He asked Rask, "Will you be traveling with the army?"

"Do I look like a common soldier to you?" Rask sneered. "Once they've arrived, you and I will take the dread portals to meet them. You have as long as an army takes to march, Strilu. Better use your time wisely."

✳

Mavian wiped dust from his eyes and squinted at the tunnel. Four laborers gathered behind him and stared at their fallen comrade on the floor. In front of the body was a door made of stone which the laborers had been working to uncover. At its center, a series of runes glowed faintly in a circular design.

"What happened?" Mavian asked.

"He touched the markings," one of the men said. "And he screamed, and collapsed."

Mavian bent to the fallen laborer and whispered a spell. A wisp of magic curled around the man and flowed into Mavian's hand. He focused for a second before dispelling it. "A protection rune. Meant to kill whoever would trespass here. We're close."

For fifteen days Mavian had worked, exploring the tunnels and piecing together clues from all the old texts Rask had given him. He labored all day and into the night, only stopping to spell any prowlers the soldiers had captured, and sleeping only a few candles at a time. Every time they met, Chadron sneered at his efforts, but Mavian persevered. His time, he knew, ran short.

At last, he had come to runes carved in the wall and the door mostly buried under stone and dirt. The laborers had dug and hauled away the stones for the better part of the day.

After stepping aside for them to move the body, Mavian

peered closely at the door. The runes, though ancient, were still quite clear. Their thin lines had been carved neatly into the rock, the ends of the characters curving into points. They were written in High D'Ehsi, the language spoken by the peoples of the far past. In his studies into the Underworld and its magic, Mavian had learned to decipher the old tongue. He read the runes, carefully keeping his fingers from touching them.

Let Death come to those who would harm our master, and Death be the key to witnessing glory. Mavian contemplated the riddle.

"Clear away the rest of the rubble," Mavian said to the workers. "Be careful not to touch the runes. Call for me when it's done."

The laborers gave each other frightened looks, but didn't dare disobey. They had heard the stories of Mavian's prowlers, and none wanted to find out if they were true.

As they went back to work, Mavian followed the red orbs back up the tunnel. Multiple pathways veered off from this one, all of which were marked with an 'X' after he had found nothing inside. The tunnels twisted and turned back on themselves, many seemingly having no purpose. His lungs burned by the time he exited the warren.

In his workshop, he pored once more over all the tomes that spoke of the original *fampir*. Few were more than stories or whispers of legends. Yet one, written by a man named Oroth, spoke at great length of the ten Lofalin and ten Rengu elves who had been experimented upon. Some died immediately while some lived for mere candles. Others survived and sired offspring. The author didn't know what happened to most of those *fampir*, but he did speak of the chambers in which King Landin's sorcerers worked, as well as the cults which sprang up around the most powerful of the monsters. These cults, he claimed, worked to bring immortality for themselves after witnessing the might of the *fampir*.

It was this tome that Mavian consulted again, searching for a hint. His head ached, and his eyes burned with exhaustion. How many days had he gone with little sleep? Too many, and the army's arrival drew ever nearer. Yet he was so close now, he couldn't give up.

His eyes glazed over, and he stared at the page without seeing. His thoughts moved like molasses, his feet sore from so much walking.

"My Lord?" One of the laborers stepped into the room.

Mavian shook himself. "Yes?"

"The door is clear."

"That was quick."

"It's nearly midnight."

Surely not? Mavian's eyes tracked blearily around the room. Of course, no light could penetrate that deeply. Had that many candles really passed since he'd inspected the door?

"Go home." Mavian wished he could do the same, but he was too close. "I'll send for you and your men if I need anything else."

The laborer bowed and hurried away. Mavian rubbed his temples and tried to focus again on the page. The words melded together, swirling around, inky fish in a white ocean.

His eyes closed before he realized it, and he fell into a deep sleep, there in the hard wooden chair, while the undead Merick stood silent watch over him.

Crack!

A sharp pain roused Mavian, and he fell to the floor, dazed and still half-asleep. He mumbled and rubbed his head where a sizable lump was already forming. He groaned when he saw Chadron standing over him, his silver hand raised for another blow.

A grunt was all Mavian could manage.

"Wake up!" Chadron said, kicking him in the side. "Dawn approaches, and there are prowlers to be brought in."

Mavian wheezed, his breath knocked out of him. Chadron pulled his foot back, and Mavian rolled out of the way just in time. The knight sneered at him. "Get to work, Strilu. I've reports of a dozen prowlers caught in your little traps. Uncle would be furious if any of them were lost to the sun."

Mavian coughed, fumbling to his hands and knees. His ribs hurt now, too, along with his head and feet. He managed to climb up and glared at Chadron. "I'm not your servant."

"The army is less than a deshe away from Stonetree, and yet you dither about with your misguided notions. You have one duty, and that's to the war effort." Chadron moved to hit Mavian again, but froze. For a moment, Mavian was confused. Then he grinned.

Merick had the upstart knight in its grasp, one hand around the man's throat, the other gripping his prosthetic hand.

"Release me!" Chadron demanded. He gulped as the wight's blue fingers tightened. "Mavian..."

"Why should I?" Mavian asked. For once, he had the upper hand. "You're a reckless man. You could easily have died from a hunting accident, or fallen into the ravine after a drunken night. Your uncle wouldn't question it."

Chadron gurgled, unable to speak. His face slowly turned white, his feet scrambling at the floor as the wight lifted him from the ground. Mavian relished the sight.

His gaze flickered to Maeria's corpse. He sighed and said, "Release him."

The wight let go and stepped back, as still as stone once more. Chadron choked and tried to swallow, pawing at his throat. He panted and spluttered, fear in his eyes.

"Don't...you *dare*...ever set...your monster...on me again," Chadron finally managed.

"I didn't. He did it himself," Mavian said. It seemed that his wight had some loyalty after all. *Though why it waited so long*...Perhaps there was something deeper to the wight's mind than simple obedience. *A puzzle for another day.* "Don't strike me again."

"Just do your damn duty. The army is close, and your prowlers will be needed in the attack," Chadron said before slinking out of the chamber. He gave the wight a wide berth.

Though he resented the man, and quite enjoyed Merick's display, Mavian did proceed down through the tunnels and out into the woods. He followed the white gem's steady pull to three of his traps where soldiers watched the prowlers with wide eyes. Once he was done and the prowlers spelled, his new additions to the pack followed him to the cavern. The strength he had felt at Chadron's humiliation was leeched away by his magic, and when he reentered his workshop, he was as exhausted as he had been that night.

A little sleep can't hurt, he thought, but he didn't sit down. He stood by the altar and gazed at Maeria. *Except my time is running out.*

Instead of sitting, he picked up the book and paced while he read to keep himself awake. When his eyes watered, he went to a natural wellspring and dunked his head under the cool stream to force himself to remain alert.

Still, he had to reread passages when he caught himself with wandering thoughts. Over and over, random words would jump out at him, none of which made sense.

Death...death...leagues of death...the Unmaker...bodies piled...midnight strikes...call upon him...leagues to march...Valder calls, many answer, many die...

Mavian paused, something clicking in his overly tired head. He returned to the passage which mentioned something called the Unmaker: *...and in his foresight, the Unmaker hath given them a great jewel with which to call upon him. His name is too precious to be tainted with mortal tongues, yet they may seek his favor when they hath found the blood necessary for the ritual. Yet, Valder's ruse hath killed the very ones needed for the cultists to bring back their beloved...*

Mavian stopped, piecing together the clues in his mind. The Unmaker...an archaic term for Autorus, used by men too afraid to call upon him directly. And Valder was the one who destroyed much of the *fampir* population, though even Oroth didn't know how it was done. *Who did Valder kill? Whose blood was necessary?*

His pacing grew into walking. His feet carried him back to the accursed door which had already killed one man. Mavian approached the door and reread the runes. Their glow had faded, leaving only the carving in the stone.

"Let Death be the key to witnessing glory," Mavian murmured. Pressing a hand to the door, careful not to touch the runes, Mavian whispered in High D'Ehsi, "*I follow the Unmaker, may his glory bring back the beloved."*

The gem throbbed against his chest, its light pulsing with a faint blue. The runes on the door glowed to match. With a shuddering of walls and cracking of stone, the door pulled back and down into the ground, moving through some magical means.

There was darkness beyond. Mavian summoned a red orb above his palm and peered through. He stepped over the threshold and into a passageway. The air was musty and old, trapped for centuries. It pressed in on him, tightening his chest, his breath growing shallow. Only the sound of his shuffling feet disturbed the overbearing silence.

The passageway opened into an unnatural cavern, its walls created by long-dead men. The floor sloped slightly, as if the center of the room pulled everything into it. Torch sconces lined the walls, with shelves below them cramped with bowls and other assorted objects. Yet Mavian's eyes were instantly drawn to the huge sarcophagus which dominated the center of the cavern.

A circular dais lay beneath the sarcophagus. The tomb was constructed of pure black stone that radiated menace. It was as high as Mavian's chest, longer than a bed, and wider than the great stone door which had allowed him through. Statues decorated each of its four corners, depicting beasts of the wild with dripping fangs. Runes and pictures ran along each side and the top of the lid, the words in circular patterns much like the door's riddle. In the darkness, Mavian could barely make them out.

With a word, he lit the torch sconces. A warm yellow light filled the room, though it glowed faintly compared to the overpowering blackness of the sarcophagus. Mavian examined each of the four sides and the lid, translating the runes and writing down the instructions given. When he had finished, he reeled, exhilarated and fatigued, overwhelmed yet wanting to start immediately.

His Maeria was in reach once more.

*

"Why do we have to be here?" Chadron complained, hovering at the tomb's entrance.

"Because there must be two witnesses," Mavian said calmly. He had slept for many candles and awoken with fresh insight and determination. After carefully going over the sarcophagus's spell, he had spent much of the day collecting components and preparing the chamber for the working. Then, he'd summoned Chadron and Rask, requesting they bring an elderly hound from the kennels.

Rask sat on a bench by the wall, his hands shaking around his cane, the journey into the bowels of the mountain tiring for him. He looked at the sarcophagus, awe in his eyes. "I'm surprised you found it, Strilu."

Chadron wasn't listening to him. "And you need us as witnesses? We're not warlocks, we can't help with any spell–"

"You won't be doing any magic." Mavian's patience was surprisingly vast as he explained the working, yet again, to the knight. "You must sit there, and your uncle there, and watch me perform it. When the time comes, one of you must bring me the *sulpari*'s blood while the other slaughters the hound. That's all. However, the runes are very clear that both of you must remain for the entirety of the working."

"But–"

"Shut up," Rask growled. "Do as he says."

This surprised both Mavian and Chadron. The former grinned while the latter lapsed into petulant silence.

Mavian set to work. He lit candles and incense in the bowls on the shelves. Maeria's body lay on top of the sarcophagus, as gentle in repose as ever, small and delicate against its black malevolence. Mavian paused to touch her cheek, a soft prayer on his lips. Hope and excitement thrilled through him, and fear, too. *Let it work.*

He began.

First, he placed a finger over the flame of each candle. With an incantation, he turned the fire from orange to green. Each candle took a few minutes, for the working was long and complicated. By the time he was done with the candles, the room had an eerie tint to it, and sweat ran down his temples.

Mavian went to the sarcophagus. He walked around it fifteen times, touching the statues on each corner and chanting. The gem on his chest pulsed and lent him strength, for each of the fifteen chants drained him further.

Mavian paused and gestured to Rask and Chadron. Rask bent to the hound and slit its throat, letting its blood flow into a bowl. Chadron brought the vial of Cara's blood to Mavian, then stepped away with disgust.

Nearly shuddering himself, Mavian poured the *sulpari*'s blood into Maeria's mouth. He took the bowl of hound's blood and dabbed a finger into it. He traced the finger on Maeria's forehead, followed by his own. He did the same for each wrist, the cheeks, the chin, and finally the eyelids. His mouth was dry as he sang the final part of the working.

"Unmaker, grant us this remaking. Grant us the soul of our Maeria, that our lives may be blessed by her returning." He replaced the word *Beloved* with Maeria, hoping that it would call her soul back. The chant went on from there, nearly twenty lines of verse that he must repeat ten times.

After the first, the chamber remained silent. Mavian kept chanting.

The second, and wind howled from nowhere, blowing at the green candlelight. Shadows danced ominously around the room.

The third, and Mavian swore he heard drumbeats in the darkness. The pulsing rhythm echoed in his heartbeats, growing into a fevered pitch until it went suddenly silent.

His hands shook, and he wet his lips. The fourth chanting brought the echoes of a dog's lonely howl, a creature abandoned in the wilderness without knowing why. Mavian thought of the poor hound whose blood dried on his skin. Shame filled him. *Gods, let this work. Let it all be worth it.*

During the fifth repetition, the smoke from the candles and incense coalesced around the sarcophagus, whirling above the shiny black. Figures and shapes danced inside, too vague to be seen clearly.

The sixth. The smoke spun faster, green above their heads.

At the seventh repetition, the smoke floated down to Maeria's corpse and sank into her pale skin. Green worms wriggled underneath her flesh.

On the eighth, the sarcophagus shook with a deep rumble. Sweat gathered on Mavian's brow. He doubted himself suddenly. He had been so tired as he translated the texts, perhaps he had rushed into it.

The ninth, and the room went dark, as if the black stone had expelled all its color. In the hush, Mavian heard sharp intakes of breath from the other two. He wondered if they would still be standing when the darkness lifted.

The tenth and final repetition. Light grew steadily as the blackness seeped into Maeria. It showed under her skin for a moment before her pallor returned to normal. Mavian's eyes darted over her, and it took him a moment to notice that the sarcophagus had turned white.

Mumbling now, Mavian ended the working, his lips dry. His knees trembled, his arms rattling in their sockets. He sank to the floor, staring at his love. Behind him, Rask and Chadron coughed and spluttered as if the very air had been stolen from their lungs.

A heartbeat passed.

"It cannot be easy, returning from death after so long," Rask muttered hoarsely.

Another heartbeat. *What if it went wrong?* Mavian clasped at Maeria's hands, willing it to work. *What if replacing the* fampir's *name wasn't enough?*

Maeria shuddered and took a long, slow, deep breath.

It was the sweetest sound Mavian had ever heard.

Chapter Twenty
Seanna

Two quinns passed after arriving home in the capital, and still her father's letter lay undisturbed on her bedside table. Confined to her vast rooms in the Silver Keep, Seanna had done everything possible to avoid that letter. She'd embroidered, practiced playing the harp she hadn't touched in years, wandered her small gardens to pick and arrange flowers. For candles on end, she told stories to her unborn child of her father's life.

"...and the water closed over my head," Seanna murmured as she stroked her belly. "I felt his arms around me, and he pulled me out. He'd ruined his best clothes to go in after me."

Tears dripped onto her hands, and she blinked them away. She had been six when she'd fallen into the fast-moving stream outside her home. Afterwards, she and her father had cuddled together in front of the fire to dry off, his beard tickling the top of her head. It was one of her fondest memories.

"Seanna?" Henrik stood at her sitting room door, shoulders slumped under his heavy robes. He entered when she gestured and sat across from her. Dark bags clouded under his eyes, and his hair had grown grayer. Though they didn't speak much, he came each day to sit with her, a quiet moment for the both of them.

"I was just telling the child about my father," Seanna said. "How he saved me from drowning."

Henrik gave a small smile. "My father taught me to burn

ants with a hand mirror. I was the scourge of the gardens."

"If only armies could be defeated with a hand mirror," Seanna said. She asked, "Any news?"

With a heavy sigh, Henrik rubbed his eyes. "The Lofalins proceed without much resistance across the plains. They've laid siege to Brin, and we expect them to break through within a deshe. The Skals are setting fire to any of the eastern villages they find. Refugees pour into Seawind, but it won't be long before we must close our gates to them."

Though Con Salur was a vast city, even its four districts could not hold all the people of Dotschar. Seanna set aside her embroidery hoop though she hadn't made any progress on it that day. Grim thoughts gripped her. Her mother and brother were in Brin, and if the city fell, they might not escape. *And then Con Salur will stand alone against the tide.*

Seanna asked, "Will you ride to meet the Lofalins?"

"No. If the scouts' reports are accurate, their force is far greater than ours. We wouldn't last a day against them."

Seanna nodded. The baby moved inside her, and she suppressed the nausea that accompanied it. *I don't want my son born into a world of suffering and death.* She said, "Meeting the Lofalins on the open field would destroy our forces. Holding the city will starve us sooner or later. There is no right answer."

"Indeed."

Seanna said hopefully, "Our walls are strong. No army has ever breached them. And once Darkroad's doors are closed, nothing will reach the Silver Keep."

"Many of our people in Seawind and Dockside will die."

They sat in silence for a few minutes, the weight of war settling on their shoulders.

Outside, a soft rain pattered against the windows. Despite the grey light, the room felt warm with the glow from the candelabras.

Seanna took a deep breath and said, "Henrik, I need...could you...? My father's letter."

He gave her a confused look, but retrieved the parchment from her bedroom. As he slid his thumb under the seal, he said,

"If we have a daughter, she will learn to read. She can't have stewards altering letters unbeknownst to her."

Unfolding the parchment, he read, "*My dearest Seanna, I hope that this letter finds you in good health. I wish I could see you tonight at the Masque, but I understand Henrik's motivations. You haven't acted in a proper manner, though I believe his punishment to be too harsh. When we return to the plains, I will write to him and ask him to reconsider. Every mother should be allowed to see her child, no matter the circumstances.*"

Henrik hesitated, then continued, "*Last time I saw you, Henrik mistreated you. I pray that you two may find forgiveness and become friendly to one another. Having a child will help, but you must work hard to overcome your differences. Your mother and I saw our fair share of fights, and we always resolved them in the end. I pray the same for you.*"

As Henrik read, Seanna sank deeper and deeper into the cushions, her tears staining the fabric. She imagined her father's mellow baritone speaking the words, with him sitting at a small desk in the Cascade Palace, staring out over the city as he wrote.

"*Now I must be fatherly, and you must forgive my chiding. When you married him, you swore to be faithful, obedient, and compassionate. He swore the same. You have broken your promises in retaliation for him breaking his. This is not how I raised you. I taught you to turn the other cheek, rise above, be the better. You have lost your way. You must find it again.*

"*I am getting old, Seanna. I feel it with every step I take. This will be my last journey, I think. Take care of yourself, my child. You are the light of my life, even if you vex me. Next we meet, I shall bounce my grandchild on my knee.*

"*With greatest regard and love,*

"*Ulmer Aylmer, Earl of Stillmeadow.*"

Seanna cried quietly as Henrik finished reading. Sniffling softly, she wiped her eyes. "Thank you. I appreciate this, more than you can imagine." She took the letter back and pressed it to her bosom. "He never got to meet his grandchild."

"He will see the child from beyond. Have faith in that."

Seanna thought of her father's booming laugh and her

mother's smile. *Will I see Mother and Halmer again?* "I miss him."

"Then we can't disappoint him."

The rain splattered against the windows, its persistent *tap-tapping* matching the staccato of Seanna's heartbeat.

"I'm sorry," Seanna said after a heavy silence.

Henrik glanced at her. "Seanna..."

"Just listen." In her many days of contemplation, Seanna had tried to form the words she needed to say to him. Some days, she wanted to feel that old resentfulness and spite toward her husband, but grief made her empathetic to him.

Focusing on the streaks of rain on the glass, Seanna said, "I wish I could have been loyal to you. I wish I could have loved you deeply and been the queen you wanted. I never could force myself to it. When I lay with my handmaids or ladies, it wasn't to spite you. Not entirely, at least. I found comfort and joy in their arms. I felt like I belonged. I am sorry, though, for the scandal and humiliation I brought to you. For a long time, I justified my actions, claiming to myself that you deserved betrayal. But you didn't really. I know that now."

Though it stung to speak the words aloud, a weight lifted from her chest once she was done. *There. I've done it. I've apologized, and been honest in it.* The child settled, mirroring its mother's relief, as she slumped in her seat. Through the glass, small rays of light peppered through the clouds. Flowers by an open pane perked up, their fresh scent drifting across the room.

To her surprise, Henrik reached out and took her hand. His large fingers engulfed hers, white skin against brown. He didn't speak.

Swallowing her fear, Seanna ventured, "As for Jacobi, I'm not jealous. How can I be? Seeing him with you wounded my pride, but not my heart. If he brings you joy, be with him. I won't tell a soul. On my father's grave, I promise it."

"How can I trust you?" Henrik said, still holding her hand. "I've lost count of the lies you've told."

"Because we're the same, you and I. Condemned to love those we cannot have. If we had trusted each other from the start, perhaps we both could have found happiness much sooner."

"I loved Fleta, you know. I'd been raised with the knowledge that my marriages would always be chosen for me, that I would have to forge love with my wife. When I saw her, I knew that I loved her." Henrik squeezed Seanna's hand.

Shame settled on her. *If he loved her, why couldn't he love me?* It was a childish thought, but one she couldn't suppress. It was far easier to accept his affection for men, and know that to be the reason for his coldness to her, than to know that he was also capable of romantic love for women.

Henrik took her cheek in his other hand, forcing her to meet his eye. "You were beautiful the day we married. I mourned for Fleta and the child that died with her. When I saw you, I thought perhaps the gods had twice blessed me. I lay awake many nights after wondering why my heart didn't yearn for you as it did for her. I think some part of me blamed you for her death, or resented that I allowed myself to remarry. I'm still not sure."

His words comforted her, a balm to truth's sting. Too full of emotion to sit still, Seanna went to the flowers. She inhaled deeply, letting the crisp smells calm her. With a gentle hand, she plucked a kingcup from the arrangement. The bright yellow shone in the growing light from the window.

Turning back to him, Seanna said, "When all this is over, Henrik, and the war is won, can we start anew? Can we be in our child's life as more than unseen parents and show him the respect that is possible between unloving spouses?" When she had spoken of starting anew, so many months before in Riverfen, it had been a ploy. A means to her ends. Now, though, she desperately wanted it.

Henrik nodded slowly. He took the flower from her hand, twirling it between his fingers. "I have been thinking. If we have a daughter, I want her to take the crown. It would require some work with the magistrates, but it is allowed. Udolf is too hot-headed, he shouldn't take the throne." He met her eyes. "I don't know if either of us will survive this war. All I know is that I want my child to inherit my kingdom no matter the costs."

Seanna was too stunned to speak. All this time, she had worried and fussed over bearing a male child, seeking power to protect herself in case she produced the wrong gender. She instinctively placed a hand over her belly, rubbing the stretched skin.

"What do you think?" Henrik asked.

"Udolf won't like it. Neither will many others."

"They don't vecking matter."

Seanna laughed. "You've changed since last we met. Softened, dare I say, and grown stronger at the same time."

"So have you."

"Being kidnapped, humiliated, and sold like a pig will do that." Seanna's smile faltered.

Henrik held out his hand. "Come to court with me today."

"Why?"

"Because I want my queen by my side. She is the mother to my heir, after all."

"Let me dress; I'm not presentable right now."

"Of course."

As Henrik moved to leave, Seanna asked, "Who else knows? About your plans for our child?"

"Belrose and my closest advisors. We will present it to the magistrates tomorrow." With that, Henrik swept from the room.

As Seanna dressed in a finer gown, she contemplated their conversation. Never would she have expected him to be so warm to her, nor herself so kind to him. It was a giddy feeling, almost like being young and in first love again. Did she love her husband? *No*, she decided, *but I do like him again.*

Strange, how much can change in so little time.

When Seanna moved back to the sitting room, another man waited for her. She sighed, and he turned to her, flashing a bright smile.

Prince Udolf. Though only seventeen, he carried himself with swagger and excessive confidence, utterly sure that he would take his uncle's throne. He was bedecked with jewels at his throat and hands, his robes embroidered to a tawdry extent.

"Dear Aunt!" he proclaimed, sweeping a mock bow. "Has

my uncle come again to shame you? Your red eyes speak of yet another humiliation."

His presence – especially without announcement – surprised Seanna, and she didn't have a retort for him. She was in no mood for the barbed words she and Udolf had so often spat at each other.

"What? No rejoinder? I am disappointed, *Your Grace*." Udolf spoke the title sarcastically. "Here I came for some entertainment, and you promise only to be boring."

"I am in mourning," Seanna said.

"My parents both died years ago. You don't see me moping about."

"You were barely more than a child," Seanna said without the fierceness of days past. "You didn't know them."

"Ah, there she is. Tell me, Madam, were you confined to quarters because of your spread legs or your pitiful politics? I have been *so* interested in the rumors from Riverfen."

As if you haven't bedded every maid from Seawind to Dockside. Seanna shook her head. "I made mistakes, Udolf. Something you will learn as you grow older."

"Ever humble now, aren't we?" Throwing himself onto a chair, legs splayed over the sides, Udolf gave her a taunting smile. "When I'm king, I'll throw you into the dungeons for the rest of your life. Oh! Perhaps I could dress you as a servant and parade you around the palace?"

"Curb your tongue," Seanna said. She bit back the words, *Perhaps time in a cell will humble you a touch.*

The prince continued heedlessly, "I quite like that thought. Queen Seanna, mother of stillborns, reduced to a mere servant. Maybe even a slave."

Before her humiliation in Riverfen and her time with the corsairs, Seanna might have risen to the bait and said something equally as awful. She wanted to say, *You're as fit for the crown as a slug, and dress worse than a jester.* Now, she only said, "Be careful what you wish for, Udolf. Life does not go as expected."

"What *did* my uncle say to you? A bitch made into a mewling pup? Where's the Seanna I could insult without guilt?"

Getting to his feet, Udolf said, "You're not nearly as fun anymore."

Seanna opened her mouth to say something witty – she was sure it would come out so – but the palace shuddered under their feet, sending goblets tumbling to the floor. Seanna and Udolf clutched at the furniture. The flowers by the window crashed down, the vase shattering into a thousand ceramic pieces.

As soon as it started, it ended, though the chandeliers still bounced and reeled with a tinkling noise.

"We're under attack!" Udolf shouted, springing for the door.

Seanna followed him as fast as she could, though it was more of a waddle than a dignified run. Courtiers and stewards dashed along the halls, all heading to the throne room. When the crowd grew too large, Udolf shouted for room, and the others scrambled to leave space for the royal family.

Seanna raced into the throne room and halted, aghast. The baby moved, and she instinctively covered her belly.

Four of the king's soldiers lay sprawled dead on the floor, their blue cloaks stained red.

A small man crouched in the center of the room. Lightning sizzled in a ring around him, a perverse halo of energy. It kept back the soldiers, though they pressed as close to him as they could. The man's eyes darted around, seeking a route to escape.

Nobles screamed and held each other, staring wide-eyed at the throne.

And there, on the throne, sitting as if holding court, was Henrik. But his head was pushed back against the chair, blood leaking from his nose and ears. A dark spot in the middle of his forehead, like a bruise, crackled with spent energy. Henrik's eyes stared fixedly forward, blank and glassy.

Seanna's hands flew to her mouth. The baby kicked. Her stomach threatened to purge itself, she was dizzy and nauseous and terrified. As she watched, the crouching man uttered something in a strange tongue, pointing at one of the soldiers. Lightning struck out from the circle at the poor fellow, and he shuddered before screaming and falling prone, blood leaking from under his armor.

One of Henrik's council members raced to Seanna, urging her to leave. She shoved him away.

Udolf sprang forward with his sword drawn, but his blade couldn't penetrate the assassin's lightning. The assassin turned and locked eyes with Seanna. He grinned.

With both hands, the assassin sent a bolt straight at her heart. Seanna screamed.

An orb of fire materialized in front of her, absorbing the lightning strike. Seanna turned to see the court mage, Dyle Belrose, sweat streaming down his forehead, his mouth in a snarl. He muttered something, and the orb began to inch toward the assassin.

The assassin grimaced, arcing more of his lightning at the mage. Their magic collided, sending sparks of energy in all directions. The assassin drew from the lightning around him, for as he sent more and more bolts at Belrose, his circle grew smaller. Gaps appeared in the crackling halo.

Udolf danced around the lightning. His sword edged through a gap, and the assassin dodged the sharp blade. With a flick of his wrist, the assassin sent lightning at the prince. Udolf cursed as he tried to move away. The attack caught his side, ripping his tunic and bruising his skin.

The prince hefted his sword. Though Belrose's fire still burned, the mage's hands shook with effort. The assassin smiled grimly, his lightning still strong enough to keep out the soldiers. *There has to be something I can do!* Seanna cast about her for inspiration, but all she saw were terrified nobles and sweating soldiers.

Her eye caught on a hand mirror hanging from a noblewoman's belt. Sun rays came in through a multitude of skylights. Seanna remembered Henrik's story of burning ants with a mirror. *I can't burn him, but I can blind him.* She pushed through to the noblewoman, yanked the mirror, and turned to a particularly strong ray.

"Murderer!" Seanna shouted. The assassin's eyes turned to her. She flashed the mirror, sending the ray across his eyes. He yelled, raising a hand to block the blinding light.

With the assassin distracted, Udolf stepped through a gap into the circle of lightning. Too late, the assassin turned to face him. With a clean sweep, Udolf separated the man's head from his body.

The lightning flashed out, leaving spots in Seanna's vision. Slowly, Belrose lowered his hands, his cheeks pale. The nobles murmured in fear as the soldiers prodded the assassin's corpse.

After inspecting the body more closely, one of the soldiers whispered to Udolf, then ran to Seanna.

"Your Grace, this was a Lofalin plot. His ears were cut off to make him look human."

"Dear gods," Seanna gasped.

"We must get you to safety," the soldier said.

"But Henrik..." Seanna stared at her husband, not quite believing her eyes. "Is he...?"

"It's too late, Madam. Please, come with me. We'll keep you safe."

How can I be safe if the king is dead? What will happen to me and my child now? Shivering, Seanna followed the soldier. Knights formed a cordon around her as the courtiers whispered and glanced fearfully about themselves. Belrose joined Seanna, eyes darting about as if searching for more enemies.

"The king is dead," Seanna said to Belrose, still in shock, as if he hadn't witnessed it.

The mage nodded, pale and shaken. "You are regent now, Your Grace. The kingdom is in your hands."

Seanna lurched toward a nearby pot and vomited everything from her stomach.

PART TWO

CHAPTER TWENTY-ONE
Cara

In the morning, Cara's lips cracked with dried blood. She rubbed it away and stared at the red-brown on her hand. *It wasn't a dream,* she thought. *I killed a rabbit, I drank its blood.* Tearing the blankets from her leg, she prodded at her flesh and winced. It still hurt, but not as badly as before.

The beast purred contentedly inside her. It gave a constant warmth now, like it belonged. Cara placed a hand over her stomach, wondering at the new sensation. Was it the blood? The hunt? Something else, something far more sinister?

As she washed, her limbs didn't feel like hers. They moved in a disconnected way as if separate from her mind entirely. When she pinched her arm, the sensation was muted, cloudy. As she moved her fingers, she thought she saw them through new eyes. Eyes tainted by the beast.

Though the beast itself stayed in place, tendrils of it roamed her veins, moving her arms for her. She tried to force it down, but those tendrils clung on, ghosts that could not be removed. They haunted her flesh, danced in her head. Now that she was up and moving, her head pounded, with soreness in her eyes and temples, pain in her forehead and ears.

Then she heard it. *Thump-thump, thump-thump,* steady and strong, from outside the tent.

Sandu's heartbeat.

She heard Darian's, too, lower and slower, and a wisp only from Jagger, as if he needed little blood flow to survive. The men's blood pumped through their veins, louder than wind. Constant and so, so tempting. It was a golden sound, intoxicating as wine and the headier drink by far. For once, Cara was grateful for the injury Laris had imparted on her. If she had the ability to move more easily, she feared that she would already have leapt at her companions and rent skin from bone to revel in the fall of crimson life.

Reaching to her face, Cara felt for the telltale ridges and longer fangs. Surely, surely the beast must be showing on her face if it was so strong in her? But no, her cheeks were smooth, her brow normal.

Moving with her phantom limbs, Cara slowly crawled from her tent to the fire. Jagger didn't look to her, and neither did Sandu, both sitting on the fire's far side. Darian acknowledged her with a nod and held out another vial of blue liquid. She drank it quickly, hiding the shaking of her hands with the movement.

"Let me see your leg," Darian said.

Cara spluttered and deflected. "Why?"

"It may be time to change the poultice."

"Oh." Her cheeks burned. How could he know what she'd done in the night?

The same way he knew about the fampir *you killed. He hears when things die.* Yet surely he wouldn't have marked a rabbit's passing?

Darian, with his gentle hands, peeled away the sticks and linens and changed them out for fresh ones. His fingers prodded at the break, and he said nothing. Cara held her breath, sure that he would accuse her of blood-drinking. But he didn't, and he wrapped the limb up again quickly.

"You should speak to him," Darian said, too low for the other two to hear.

Cara played with a blade of grass. "No."

Even if I stay distant, will the beast spur me to attack? A shiver passed through her. *If he has the plague, would it pass through me by his blood?*

"He needs his friends now more than ever. The mind is a

delicate thing, and his has been set upon by so much."

Cara scoffed, "He hasn't had a monster living inside him since girlhood."

"This isn't a tourney to see who has the greater pain. Give him peace as best you can, and receive peace from him."

"No." Rather than her own heart pounding in her ears, she heard Sandu's. It had grown faster, and his head was in his hands. Jagger laid a hand to his shoulder, and he shrugged it off with a wordless cry. She could see the vein in Sandu's neck, enticing and strong. *Would the beast know that he's infected before I bite?*

"You won't hurt him," Darian said as if reading her mind.

"You don't know that," Cara replied. She stared at the dirt. "He'd be safer away from me. Renna and Merick are dead because I didn't do enough to stop Mavian, and Sandu's fate could be worse than theirs. It almost was."

"Yet from the ashes rises greener life."

"Is that all you do? Spout meaningless words?"

His blank eyes fixed on her. "And listen. I listen more than most, and what I hear–"

"I don't care what you hear," Cara spat. Before he could continue, she crawled away to a spot distant from all the men where she remained the rest of the day in a black mood. Sandu tried to meet her eye a few times, but she ignored him. *Let him make the first apology.*

As day drew to a close, Cara retreated to her tent. Her headache had worsened, the heartbeats in her ears louder by the candle. She couldn't stand it anymore. When she curled on the blankets, she took wax and rubbed it between her fingers until it was soft enough to plug her ears. Only then, finally, did the sound of blood fade.

With a sigh of relief, Cara fell asleep.

Cara searches for Renna but can't find her. Grey walls rise around her, and no matter where she turns, she is met with unyielding stone. She hears Renna's voice, faint and alarmed.

Cara beats her fists against the walls. They melt away, sending her down, down into darkness. She lands on her feet, and finds herself in a cavern lit by glowing red orbs. In the center of the room is an empty slab. She walks toward it, running her hands along its cool granite surface. Behind her, something clatters to the floor. She turns and comes face-to-face with Mavian. He is much as she remembers: cool and aloof, green eyes blazing in a pale face.

He backs away from her, raising his hands to summon his dread portal. She lunges at him, pinning him to the floor. He raises his hands, and she tears them from his face. Slowly, like a lover savoring her first kiss, Cara bends to his lips.

She bites him, drawing blood from the pink tulips of his mouth. Mavian whines and struggles, but he can't stop her. Licking the liquid from his skin, Cara savors the moment. She has won; he's in her grasp, helpless.

"Cara!"

Renna is there at last, her golden hair spread over her shoulders, her blue eyes wide in horror. She wears a white gown tied with a golden cord. Cara tries to cover her own blood-splattered collar.

"How could you?" Renna cries, falling to her knees beside Mavian. "He loved me!"

"Not as I love you," Cara growls, her voice guttural with the beast's tones. "He stole you away, changed you—"

"Oh, dear Cari," Renna says, stroking her cheek. "Nothing he did was against my wishes. If only you could know the lengths he went to for me. He would even breach the Underworld if it meant he could have me back."

"It's not possible," Cara says. Mavian twitches beneath her knees, and she presses down harder. "You're dead, I watched you die."

Renna holds her, gazing into her eyes. "I walk again, my old friend. You'll see. Death doesn't last forever, especially not for one with my power."

"Your power?"

Renna nods gravely. "When Mavian called, with his incense and spells, I rose. I returned to the living at his bidding, and now I hold greater power than he could ever know. But I don't want to share it with him. He is weak, beholden to the wishes of those more powerful than him. Not you, though. You are strength incarnate. I need you with me, Cari. I need you to help me free those in the Ossuary."

Caught in Renna's hands, savoring the feel of her fingers, Cara can't think straight. "Isn't this just a dream?"

"Death and dreams walk side-by-side, and you tread both, one foot in the water, one on sand." *Renna's eyes are warm, but something lurks beneath them. Something Cara can't read.*

"What is the Ossuary?"

"A place only the dead know. I have been there. I can return again, with you by my side."

The dream fades around Cara. Mavian vanishes and Renna turns to mist, her last words echoing in the darkness.

Cara opened her eyes, the taste of blood lingering on her lips. She raised a hand to her mouth, and it came away clean. *It was just a dream. Nothing more.* Yet her cheeks were still warm where Renna had touched her.

In the darkness, she lay awake and thought about the dream. Killing Mavian and drinking his blood had brought satisfaction like none other. She longed for it to be real, to know the taste of his death.

Her leg ached, and again she left the tent. Moving slightly faster than the night before, Cara hunted slowly in the woods, dragging her leg with deliberate carefulness. Silvery moonlight cast shadows through the trees, but her vision was true, her nose sharp. The beast filled her limbs, lending her its strength. It hungered, too, famished by her dreams.

She came upon a fawn and paused. Its mother was nowhere in sight. It trembled in the loam, trusting to its spots to hide it. Its large, liquid eye stared up at her, pleading with her.

Better you than Sandu. Cara grabbed the fawn's forelegs. It jerked and struggled, but she held firm. With one hand, she held its legs. With the other, she traced along its flesh until she found a suitable vein. Her talon pierced through its fur. She raised her hand and licked the blood off, then fell to, drinking in the fawn's life essence.

As she drank, she shuddered and moaned. She could feel the bone in her leg mending, the muscle around it finding its place. In the span of a few minutes, quinns of healing had occurred.

Cara sat back and wiped the blood from her chin. The fawn twitched on the ground, the last ebbs of its breath steaming onto the forest floor. Pity stirred in her, and disgust. She hadn't even hesitated as she had with the rabbit. Yet the strength that coursed through her was so incredible.

A worthy sacrifice.

When she undid the bandages around her leg, she found that the flesh was still mottled and bruised, the muscle thinner than her other calf. Healing was not complete, but she could walk once more.

The fawn gasped its final breath and went still. Cara silently thanked it for its gift.

"Your Song is loud tonight."

Cara jumped at Darian's voice. He stood a few feet away, cane in hand. In the moonlight, his white eyes were brighter than usual.

"For a blind man, you have an uncanny knack for sneaking up on people," Cara said, turning away from him to desperately wipe herself off. Even though he couldn't see, she pondered if he could smell the blood on her.

"I know what you did here, Cara," Darian said.

"Of course you do," she muttered. Using a tree to help, she clambered to her feet, putting some of her weight on her injured leg. It twinged, but held her. She turned to Darian. "What do you want?"

"To help you."

"All you've done so far is some healing and cryptic words. If that's all–"

"The blood thirst will grow worse the more you drink," Darian said. He sat cross-legged on the moss and rested his cane on his knees. "It will taint your tongue, clog your ears. Every person you meet, you will be tempted to drain. Each time you give in, you will lose more of yourself to the *sulpari*. You are not *fampir*, you cannot control yourself as they do. They came to Autorus later in life, but you were born with his darkness inside you. It will haunt you, goad you, encourage you."

"You said I and the beast should become equals," Cara said.

"How, if not through blood?"

"Through your Song."

"But the blood healed me," Cara said. "Look at my leg."

"Yes, and your power will grow with the blood of greater animals. It is a dangerous path to walk. The *sulpari* should not–"

Cara remembered her dream and Renna's mention of the Ossuary. Tired of Darian's warnings, she interrupted him, "What's the Ossuary?"

He grew still, his milk-white eyes staring at the sky. "How do you know of that?"

"So it's real?"

He sighed. "Yes, it's real."

"What is it?"

"A tomb for the victims of Valder Riesk's power. The souls of thousands are locked inside, eager to go to Autorus, but trapped."

How does Renna know about it? "Do you know where it is?"

"None have set foot inside the Ossuary in nearly eight hundred years. Few who know its location survived to tell of it. I could not tell you where it lies."

"Would Druam know?" Perhaps she would torture the answer out of him before she killed him.

"No. His sire died inside the Ossuary soon after turning Druam. The earl was still a young *fampir,* too wrapped up in his own misery to join the attack on it. It was sealed before he ever left his homeland."

"So you can't help me find it."

"I cannot."

Cara stared up at the sky, her mind full of questions. In her deepest heart, she hoped that Renna had spoken true, that she had truly come back from the dead. If Cara could find her, she might learn more of the Ossuary.

"The Ossuary is a place of old magic," Darian said. Again, his uncanny ability to guess her thoughts disturbed her. "If you go there, you will find what you seek and more. But, like everything with magic and Autorus, your desires will come at a cost."

"You don't know what I seek."

"Don't I? It is written plainly on your heart. You don't wish to be connected to Autorus anymore. You want to be a normal woman. You want the *fampir* and prowlers, reminders of your inner beast, to be gone. The Ossuary is what you seek."

Cara shivered, rubbing her arms. She hated how well he knew her. "How do you know so much about it?"

"Sometimes I hear their voices. Those trapped inside, desperate for eternity. They tell me the story." His face was guarded, unreadable. Cara thought he lied, but she couldn't tell about what. Perhaps it was all a lie and he was a madman. Except he'd shown her too well how much of the truth he could weasel out.

"Come on," she said, stepping past him. "It's almost dawn. We should return to camp."

He turned, grasping her arm. She halted.

"Remember what I said of the blood thirst. Don't let it overcome your love for your friend."

"I won't."

"Take care, *sulpari*." He didn't follow her.

Cara paused. "Aren't you coming with me?"

"Even the lowest life deserves sanctity in death. I will follow when my work is done."

Discomfited, the taste of blood now sour in her mouth, Cara meandered back to their camp. *I won't let myself harm any innocents*, she thought. *The blood thirst won't be too strong for me.*

*Though if I see Mavian...*she grinned at the memory of her dream. He was one she would have no qualms in killing. *Then Renna and I can find the Ossuary. Together.*

CHAPTER TWENTY-TWO
The Forest Witch

Lean and lithe, the Forest Witch darted through the branches of the grey-barked trees. The faces within the trunks Sang to her as she passed by, whispering their secrets or making promises they couldn't keep. It was a game they liked to play with her. They knew she would ignore them, and she knew that they would not stop.

Below her, an adult nightcat ran along the undergrowth, eerily silent despite his immense size. His red-and-black coat somehow blended with the brush around him. The stinger at the end of his tail twitched when the Forest Witch paused, and the nightcat stopped without prompting.

The tree beside hers leaned hard to one side, its great roots pulled from the ground. The face within it held an expression of agony. With careful steps, the Forest Witch descended to the mossy floor. She put a hand to the trunk of the listing tree and listened to its Song.

It wanted to move, she hummed low in her throat.

The nightcat, Lintem, licked his paws. He hummed back, *Too weak.* They communicated solely through the Songs. What use was speaking in the Whispering Woods when they could convey thought and emotion with the ease of breathing?

The Forest Witch ran her hands up and down the fallen tree. In its Song she heard grief and shame. *It wants to be strong.* She had encountered many such trees. The younger ones especially wanted to uproot themselves and move from place to place, eager to see the many sights of the Woods. By the time they grew older, they had learned the wisdom of finding a sturdy patch to root themselves in. This tree was very young.

Be at peace until you're ready, the Forest Witch hummed. The tree shook its branches; the face in it morphed to one of consternation. She hummed a Song that shifted the dirt by its roots. At first, the tree resisted. Then, with a sigh of its leaves, its roots dug back into the earth. Bit by bit, it righted itself. Soon its crown joined its brothers in the sky, and the Forest Witch smiled. *When you are ready, I will help you move.*

The tree's Song flowed with gratitude. Deep in its melody, though, came a hint of discord. Not from the tree itself, but from its many brethren. Every so often, the Forest Witch heard this disharmony, its message clear: *You don't belong here.*

She only shrugged and climbed into the tree to continue her patrol. *I am the Woods, and they are me.* Her skin was mottled, grey and brown and black and green, covered with moss and dirt. Beneath the grime, she knew she had once had smooth skin that smelled pleasantly of flowers and soap. That time had long passed, centuries away. She couldn't recall the languages she had spoken or the places she had lived. How old had she grown in the Woods? It didn't truly matter, for years or decades or centuries had no meaning within the Songs. They sustained her, gave her a longer life than others could know.

The Forest Witch didn't often think about such things for there was too much to do in the Woods. She had creatures to care for, gardens to tend, trees to nurture when supernatural storms made of pure elemental energy ravaged them. Lintem accompanied her, and he was all she needed now.

She knew, of course, of the other Witches who lived elsewhere, but she couldn't recall their purpose or connection to her. They didn't bother her, and she didn't care to find them.

The discord faded away, and the many Songs of the Woods thrummed around her. In the corner of her eye, the Forest Witch could see their notes and threads, vivid and many-colored, as they flowed in the air and beneath the bark of the trees. Each one she knew well. Their melodies were like childhood rhymes, familiar and easy to recall.

The Forest Witch leapt to the next tree and the next. As she went, birds with jeweled eyes flew alongside her. Their Songs darted high and low, quick and urgent, though she knew that this was simply the way of such creatures. Everything was urgent to them. She nodded and hummed to their Song, and they twittered in reply.

Until the birds Sang of a new tree in the Woods. That made the Forest Witch pause. She stood on a branch of a tall tree and surveyed the sea of leaves. Yes, there it was. A Song that was unfamiliar to her.

The Forest Witch took off toward the unknown Song. She tried to glean its melody, but it escaped her, as if it wasn't wholly tied to Nature.

From her perch in the trees, the Forest Witch peered down into a glen filled with trees the shape of boulders and stones the shape of trees, with tall wildflowers bending in the breeze and grass the color of the sunset waving between.

A voice rose from within the wildflowers. It cracked among the Songs, discordant and oddly loud.

"Help!" It was deep and low – a man's, said her distant recollection of humanity.

The Forest Witch moved carefully through the trees until she came to an unusual sight. There, on the edge of the trees, stood a young man in rusted armor. A blood-streaked tabard hung torn and limp from his shoulders, its coat of arms hidden beneath the grime. The man's feet were rooted to the ground, grey roots twisting up around his ankles.

"Please, someone help me!" the man shouted again. Beneath his helm, his cheeks had a boyish roundness with no beard to disguise his youth.

From her perch, the Forest Witch assessed this man, intrigued. She knew that all trees had once been human, though like her, they had lost their memories of Earda and become wholly part of the Woods. Yet in all her years there, she had never seen a new tree take root.

Sobs punctuated the man's pleas. He pulled at his boots,

desperate to free his feet. They would not budge. The man twisted and turned, his cries loud in the calm meadow.

Lintem prowled back and forth, tail flicking, concern and curiosity in his growl. *What is this thing? What is it doing here?*

Human, the Forest Witch hummed in return. *Like I used to be. His Song is weak.*

I agree.

Shall I kill him?

No. The Forest Witch cocked her head, curious. *He is a ghost, and I want to Sing with him.*

Leave him, Lintem growled. *The trees have all earned their fate.*

Look at him, the Forest Witch said. *He's so young. How did he come here?*

Does it matter?

Yes, she decided. She sprang down from her tree, leapt to a stone-branch, and onto a wooden boulder before slipping to the knee-high grass, red blades against the ambiguity of her skin.

The Forest Witch crept closer to the man while Lintem remained hidden. Something itched inside her breast. This man smelled of humanity, sweat and blood and skin and clothes, a scent she hadn't met in a very long time.

The man twisted and saw her. His hands trembled, and he renewed his efforts to escape. "Who are you? What do you want?"

Tilting her head, the Forest Witch regarded him. Had she ever known him?

Her voice, so attuned to conversing only through the Songs, sounded hoarse speaking aloud. She tried several languages – the names of which she had forgotten – before the man understood her.

"You do not belong here," the Forest Witch said. The threads of Songs grew clear in her sight, ready for her to pull on should he try to attack.

"I don't know where I am," he pleaded.

"The Whispering Woods."

His eyes widened. "I-I thought it was only a fae tale. A myth. My mother used to tell me stories of the Woods."

"Many have forgotten the truths of such tales." The Forest Witch peered closely at him, from his mud-scuffed boots to the damp hair that plastered his cheeks. A boy, barely out of his home. A soldier?

She came closer, and the boy trembled. He shivered as she pressed cool fingers to his skin. How many times had the Forest Witch heard the Songs of animals and trees and stone? A man was no different, flesh and blood and hopes and failures. Here in the Woods, with the closeness of his frightened breath on her cheek, his Song blared with a hunting horn's clear call.

The surface of his Song gave away his pattering heartbeat, tremulous as a rabbit's. He hadn't eaten in over a day, his stomach moaning for sustenance. Cuts and bruises lined the sorry skin beneath his armor, evidence of a recent battle.

The Forest Witch dug deeper, her Songs interlacing with his, like reaching to like. Part of her recoiled – *I am of the Woods, I am no human* – but an ingrained instinct pushed her forward. His most recent memories leapt to the fore of his mind, his Song echoing with their terror.

A battlefield, screaming Skals with their long braided hair, axes in tattooed hands. The boy stands with his fellows, his spear shaking as he lowers it. His breeches are warm with his fear trickling down. The Skals' high cries sound like eagles rending the air. A wildness is in their eyes.

The Forest Witch took a deep breath. She had seen Skals before, many lifetimes ago. She recalled torches and spears seeking out mages, and her own pounding heart in the bottom of a merchant's wagon.

Though he shouts a battlecry, wordless in the seconds before they collide, the boy is terrified. He wants to go home. He wants to be with his sweetheart and his mother and his brothers and sisters, safe in their hovel. The Skals ram into the lines, their spit flying into his face. One, with swirling black-and-blue marks on his face, is face to face with the boy. The Skal grins, yellow teeth bared in a feral smile. The boy screams and tries to pull away, but the press of soldiers behind him blocks his escape.

He doesn't feel the axe blade in his side. Blood coats his tabard.

His fingers are slick with it. The Skal pushes past him, and the boy falls to his knees. Turmoil is all around him. No matter where he looks, he sees blades and armor and limbs and death. So much death.

The Forest Witch drew back a little, allowing his Song to fade. She glanced down at his soaked tabard and what she assumed was someone else's blood. Pity stirred within her. *He's just a child.* Another memory came to her of a skirmish in a palace, an enemy with dark magic and her husband's sword skewering a blonde-haired woman.

Husband? The Forest Witch wrinkled her nose. *I have no husband.*

She returned to her task, somewhat discomfited at the thoughts that sprang unwillingly to her mind. She didn't wish to remember a life before the Woods. She was the Forest Witch, her duty was to the creatures and their Songs. Yet somewhere, buried deep, deep within her, there stirred a terrible knowledge that threatened to burst forth. As she had for many years now, she forced it down. *I will not remember what never happened.*

The soldier's Song rang clearly now, a dam that burst forth into their collective music. The Forest Witch concentrated on the melodies, intent on forgetting her own past.

The battle has moved on, the dirt churned into dust that chokes lungs. The boy lies where he fell, one hand clutched to his side. He doesn't want to move. He doesn't want to die. His cracked lips move, whispering a silent prayer to whatever beings might hear him. "Please don't let me die. I want to go home. I want to be better."

Tears trickle onto the ground. The boy coughs, and his side flares with pain. He is in a haze, not even sure what he's saying. "Take me to the Woods. Anywhere but here."

He hadn't known that the Woods would listen to him. They took him, and now he stood with his feet rooted in the strange earth, far from home and far from relief. The Forest Witch shook her head. *Humans don't know what they really want.* The boy's tears washed through the grime on his face. He had relived that awful scene as the Forest Witch listened to his Song.

"I want to go home," he said.

"This is home now," the Forest Witch replied. At his

stricken expression, she amended, "Not all the trees are unhappy. Some have found peace."

She tilted her head, regarding him sympathetically. *I am a custodian of these Woods, am I not? I will help him find peace.* She said, "I will help you."

"You'll take me home?"

"No. I will make sure your Song is calmed before the bark claims you."

The boy whimpered, and the Forest Witch ignored him. She settled into the red grass at his roots. The bark had already started to climb past his knees. She took a deep breath, reaching for the Songs of Humanity she had long forgotten.

With tender care, the Forest Witch listened to the boy's Song, parsing out the threads of the greater Songs that tied men together. The Song of War and the Song of Regret, the Song of Fear and the Song of Bravery. These were the loudest, but beneath them she detected other Songs: Family, Love, Duty, Service. A hundred Songs wove into this boy's tapestry, some repeated often, others touching only briefly.

The Songs tugged at the Forest Witch's heart. She knew the Song of Regret and the Song of Fear, for she had lived them often before she came to the Woods. In her own Song, Love mixed with a Grief so loud that she covered her ears. That deep part of her responded to her Grief, and she mercilessly shoved it away.

With the various threads of his Songs laid bare, the Forest Witch began her work. She examined his past to find the things that comforted him. Family around the hearth, a warm meal in his belly, and the hope for a brighter day all Sang the loudest, so she drew upon them.

The Forest Witch labored for much of the day on a Song to heal this boy. Lintem curled up beside her, and the boy watched, his face a mask of fright and pain. If she were to leave him, the bark would solidify over him in that state, and he would forever be a tree that suffered.

At last, as the bark grew over his shoulders, the Forest Witch laid a hand to his forehead. She Sang of long nights of stories around the fire. She Sang of play-fighting in the snow and kissing a girl in the winter moonlight. She Sang of his favorite meals and the drinks that made his head dizzy with delight. Her Song would not make him forget the battle, but it would allow him to focus on his happiest memories.

As she Sang, his lips turned up in a smile. The tears dried on his cheeks. His eyes closed in peaceful remembrance as the bark finally closed around him. Moments later, the tree formed its branches and wide trunk, and only his face could be seen, happy at last.

The Forest Witch smiled. She hummed to Lintem, *I had forgotten all the various Songs of being human. So much pain, but so much joy, too.*

He whined and pressed his head into her hand. *You won't go back there and leave me?*

Never. Her fingers trailed through his fur. *This is my home now.*

As she trotted back into the Woods, that discordant harmony buzzed through the Songs: *You don't belong here. You never belonged here.*

The Forest Witch ignored the harmony. Her human memories were already fading back into their obscurity, her attention on the Songs around her. She paused as she entered the trees, for another new Song echoed through the threads.

It's at the edge of the Woods, she hummed.

What could it be? Lintem growled back.

I don't know. The Forest Witch pulled herself up into the branches and loped through the trees. *But we'll find out.*

CHAPTER TWENTY-THREE
Mavian

Mavian tried to read to distract himself. He perched beside the great opening in the wall that served as a window. A chill wind seeped into the room, curling around his hands and brushing Maeria's hair from her pillow. The book Mavian held – *A Treatise on Valder Riesk* – was dry and dull, concerned mostly with the ancient king's politics rather than his magic. After reading a full page for the third time, he shut the book and stared at the bed.

Twelve candles had passed since Maeria's first breath, yet she had not woken. She slumbered peacefully, her chest rising and falling in a shallow rhythm. Though Mavian knew he had succeeded, he needed her to hold him, kiss him, speak his name, in order to truly believe her return.

Setting the book aside, Mavian stood and paced. Like all rooms in the castle of D'Clet, his chambers were sparsely decorated with granite furniture. The beds, chairs, couches, all were carved from the rock itself, and layered with cushions, blankets, and other such comforts. A rug covered the floor, deep enough for feet to sink into. As Mavian strode the rug, he found himself missing the idle beauty of the Cascade Palace: the carved wooden chairs, the marble tables, the tapestries and mosaics.

Not for the first time, Mavian wondered how things may have been different had he put blind faith in Druam. He would never have discovered the secrets of necromancy, never met Maeria or learned to control the prowlers. Perhaps, in time,

Druam would have told him of the *fampir* and entrusted Mavian with immortality.

Don't dwell on what ifs, Mavian reminded himself. *You made your choice, you accepted Rask's patronage. Druam is too old for our world, too stuck in his ways to see the importance of change.* True, Rask was old and stubborn, but his death was inevitable.

Mavian's thoughts were interrupted by a rustling from the bed. He rushed to Maeria's side and grasped her thin hand. She rolled her head from side to side, moaning.

"I'm here, my love," Mavian said. "I'm here."

Maeria's eyes flitted open, coming to rest on him. They widened, and she struggled to sit up.

"Easy, love. It's alright. I'm here." Mavian helped her, pushing pillows to support her back.

Her tongue darted out, wetting her lips. "Where...?"

"You're safe here in D'Clet. How do you feel?"

"Sore, like I haven't moved in days. Mavian, what happened?"

Mavian caressed her cheek, still scarcely believing his eyes. "What do you remember?"

"Lady Seastone was in our chambers." Maeria shook her head, her blue eyes filled with tears. "You were trying to make her help us. Earl Seastone came, and...I think he wounded me? I don't remember anything after that. And in my dreams, I was in this cold, dark place. I screamed, but no one would help me. There were others there, trapped like I was." She shuddered. "It was horrible."

"Shhh, love. You're safe now. It was all a dream." Mavian's heart ached for her. He couldn't stomach telling her that she had been in the bowels of Autorus's realm.

"I never want nightmares like that again." She curled into his arms, her head fitting into the nook of his shoulder.

Mavian caressed her hair and murmured, "You won't. I promise."

With Mavian's help, she stood from the bed. She touched the puckered flesh where Druam's sword had entered her.

"Incredible," she breathed, "that such a thing did not kill

me."

"Rask's curates are wondrous," Mavian said, coming up behind her and placing his hands on her hips. Even with her new scars – one in her belly, and one on her back, showing the path of the blade – he found her the most beautiful thing he had ever seen. *She's with me again, and she's mine.* His victory made him heady.

As Maeria dressed, she asked, "The Masque? Were you victorious?"

"Nearly. I exposed Druam for the monster he is, but they had powerful magic that drove us back. Many of the prowlers died, and Chadron lost a hand. Though he did wound Alex Strilu."

"What will we do now?"

"Rask's armies head north to Stonetree as we speak. A Lofalin force will join us there. Our scouts report that Druam and Edsel will arrive before us, but they will fall. After that, Riverfen is ours for the taking."

"Oh, Mavian," Maeria purred, stroking his cheek. "You always were so clever."

Hearing her voice, feeling her touch again, was a dream. He leaned into her hand, breathing in her scent. *I will never leave you again*, he thought.

"Maeria, when the armies are in Stonetree, I must go with them and aid the attack with my prowlers. Before I go, I want us to marry. We are unhindered at last. And, should I die, I want my lands to be in your possession so you never want for safety." He tilted his head against hers. "Please, my love. Marry me tonight."

He stared down into those perfect blue eyes. For a moment, he thought he saw a ring of black in her irises, but he blinked, and they vanished.

Maeria cupped his face with both hands. "Tonight, my love, we will finally be together."

Mavian treasured the love in her gaze. However, guilt pressured him, and he said, "There's something I must tell you first."

"What?"

"The whole court now knows that the real Maeria Westerburg is dead. If you wish, I will still call you by her name, but the world sees you as Renna Nellestere again."

"It was such a pretty scheme, too," she sighed. "If the truth is revealed, we won't speak of Maeria again. I will wed you as Renna, as I was and will be again."

Renna kissed him. He held her, savoring the fullness of her lips, basking in the feel of her soft skin against his.

His body yearned for hers, as great a yearning as anyone who has lost their love can feel.

Mavian kissed her fiercely. He pulled her to the bed, drawing off her silk, his hands knowing their favorite places on her body. She moaned and gasped, her fingers grasping at his back and hair, her legs trembling around his waist.

Afterwards, laying on the bed beside her, sweaty and musky, Mavian thought that he must be dreaming. Here was Renna, whole once more, smiling up at him.

"What are you thinking?" she asked.

"Just how much I missed you." He kissed her forehead. "I have been waiting for this moment for so long."

She laughed. "I was only ill, my love."

"I know. But I worried for you."

"Come," she said, standing and redressing. "Show me the castle. I've always longed to see D'Clet."

Mavian and Renna wandered the corridors. He pointed out tapestries and paintings, explaining their history while she hung on his arm. They had done this in Riverfen, whiling away the candles exploring the vast palace. Now, though, Mavian jumped at every sudden movement, fearful that a hidden blade would steal her away once more. There was no hidden blade and nothing to fear. Rask's castle was a fortress unto itself, and no harm would find them there.

Even so, Mavian summoned Merick to guard them. He felt safer with the wight at their backs despite Renna's complaints.

"He's too eerie," she said. "I don't like seeing him like this."

"He is more loyal than any soldier," Mavian assured her.

"He won't let harm befall us."

"You said yourself that we're safe here."

"I know. But Druam is wily, and Cara clever."

"Well, I'd rather that I don't have to look at him. I never liked Merick, not really. Too coarse and rude; he never understood how to speak to a lady." She cast a disdainful eye on the wight. "You and Cara should have stayed home. I don't regret what I did at all, and it's your own fault this happened to you."

The wight didn't speak, but Mavian thought he saw it frown.

As they walked, they spoke of many things. Of course, Renna wanted most to know about the court: what happened to the queen and Lady Seastone, the latest gossip with this lady or that maid. For most of it, Mavian had no answer. He never cared for courtly politics. For the rest, he answered as best he could.

"Lady Seastone vanished the night of the Masque. I don't know the magic she used, but whatever it was, it was powerful. I could feel it in the air, even in the middle of battle. She's strong. I wish she had seen reason."

"She was always a ninny."

"Renna..."

"It's true. I don't know why you ever spent time with her."

"She was intelligent and kind, something I can't say for much of the court. And she was eager to learn. Having a student to work with was–"

Renna yawned loudly. "I'm bored of talking about Lady Seastone. What about Cara?"

"She fought on Druam's side," Mavian said. He decided not to mention stealing her blood. "I don't know what happened to her after. I know that the king and queen spoke with her after she saved the queen from my prowlers."

"Too bad Chadron didn't manage to kill her as she bathed. I don't know why there was a Protector in her rooms that night; Seanna always told me how she hated a man's touch."

"I couldn't say." Mavian still disliked the manner Rask and Chadron had approached him after Chadron's attempted assassination of the queen. She was a mere nuisance to them, no one to be concerned with, yet they wanted him to use his prowlers and prove his strength. *A silly idea, and it failed, too. The queen was too low a target to care about.*

Finally, they reached the novum built into the castle and there found a curate. As the sun sank in the sky, they spoke their vows to one another. Though wrapped up in joy, Mavian couldn't help but notice Renna's scowl as she promised to obey him and be a faithful wife. The scowl vanished, as quickly as it had come, and she beamed up at him.

Tricks of the light, he thought to himself. *That's all. I've had little sleep in the last deshes and spent too much energy on the ritual to bring her back.*

On their way back to their chamber, they encountered Rask and Chadron. The knight swept a bow, smiling for once.

"My lady, I am pleased to see you again." He kissed her palm, and Mavian wanted Merick to choke him again. Chadron continued, "I'm sure you've tried extracting gossip from Mavian, but he's useless when it comes to court. Come to my solar tomorrow, and we may share wine and stories."

"I would like that, Sir Chadron," Renna said. Her smile was altogether too eager for Mavian's liking. "And my dear Earl Hjalder, I am honored to be allowed to stay in your fine castle. Its ancient walls tell many stories."

"That they do." Rask's eyes gleamed. "My lady, I would like to speak with you as well when you are able."

"What about?" Mavian interjected. Though Chadron and Renna had often shared gossip, Rask had never shown an interest in her.

"She was close with the queen, and with Maid Gellder," Rask said, his watery eye turning on Mavian. "She has information that could help us."

"I've told you all she told me," Mavian said.

"Be that as it may, I would like to speak with her." Rask extended a thin hand to Renna. "I would like to know more about the *sulpari.*"

Renna stiffened, eyes sharp on the old man's. There was a

faint frown on her lips. "Of course, Your Distinction. I can meet you tomorrow for breakfast."

"Excellent. 'Til then, sweet lady."

The earl and his nephew departed, leaving Mavian decidedly unhappy. He glared after them. "What was that about?"

"Nothing," she said quickly – too quickly. Before he could ask, she drew him down for a kiss and whispered about their marriage bed. She kissed and kissed him until he was assured. He even forgot the strange behaviors he had witnessed.

That night, Mavian was woken by his wife's screams. She thrashed in her sleep, her sweat soaking the bed. He shook her awake, and she stared at him with wide eyes.

"I was trapped there again," she said, trembling in his arms. "I couldn't escape. There was this other woman. She laughed at me and said she would always be with me. She looked just like me, my own face taunting me."

"Who was it?" Mavian asked. He wished he could dry her tears and scrape the echoes of Autorus from her mind, but he had no such power. All he could do was comfort her.

"I don't know," she sobbed. "I don't know, but I'm afraid of her, Mavian. More afraid than I've been of anyone."

"It's alright, my love. It was merely a dream. Dreams have no power to hurt us."

Yet as he spoke, Mavian remembered words written in that ancient tome: *Dreams are the bridge between life and death. The dead touch us through dreams, and sometimes their pull is stronger than the waking world.*

Chapter Twenty-Four
Seanna

"How many are outside the gates?" Seanna asked. She sat in Henrik's chair in the council chambers, a selection of powerful lords arrayed before her. Udolf, of course, leaned back in his seat, smirking at her.

Before them on the table, two maps had been arranged. One showed Dotschar and its neighbors, the other a map of Seawind and the surrounding plains. Markers had been placed showing the Lofalin and Skallish armies which drew ever closer to the city.

Three days had passed since Henrik's murder. Three days of war councils and arguments, three days of little sleep and an irritable stomach. Seanna's head hurt, yet she had little choice but to remain alert. The kingdom was in her hands now.

One of the councillors coughed, drawing her eyes. "Seawind is full of refugees, Madam. It cannot hold any more."

"How many are outside the gates?" Seanna insisted. The men all glanced at each other – *Silly woman*, they must be thinking, though they dare not say it – then at the table.

The mage, Belrose, said, "By my count, there are still over five hundred refugees on the plains. More come by the day, ever since..." He paused.

Seanna held back the tears, forging onward. *I am Regent, I must be strong.* "Since Brin fell and my family were killed."

The reports of the city's destruction had reached them a day after Henrik's death.

216

As Brin fell, Seanna's brother had led a futile charge against the Lofalin siege. His head now adorned a pike; her mother, gods bless her soul, had drunk poison rather than face the axe. Seanna mourned them now, too, as she did her husband and her father.

"The Lofalins have reached the river," Belrose said, moving the pieces on the map to match his words. "Once they cross, the bulk of their forces will arrive within a quinn. Their fleet is on the move, too. They'll be in our harbor in days."

"Have any of the refugees come into Darkroad or Midtown?" Seanna asked.

One of the lords spoke, "We didn't think it wise to allow–"

"Bring in as many as can be held. I want Dockside emptied of all except soldiers, too. Fill the novums, quarter the refugees in the homes of the wealthy if we must. Women and children first. Men of fighting age should be kept in Seawind and trained as much as possible."

"But the nobles–"

"Open the Silver Keep as well," Seanna plowed on, her eyes hard on the offending lord. "Are these people not of Dotschar? Are they not worthy of safety and hope? If any man shall protest the opening of his manor, he may come to me. This is war, my lords. We cannot allow any of our people to die outside the gates when we have roofs to put over their heads."

"Why should we obey you?" Udolf's whine floated up the table. The lords shifted in their seats. Udolf stood, gesturing at the markers. "As the Lofalins cross the river, they will be divided. I say we lead our army to meet them before they ever reach Con Salur. No noble should give up their home to filthy rustics."

Murmurs of approval swept the table. Seanna met Belrose's eye. He quirked a brow. *This is your kingdom now. Prove it to them.*

Seanna didn't stand; bodily intimidation was a tool for men.

"How many men and horses do the Lofalins have?" she asked softly.

"By the scout reports, half their army is here while half marches to Stonetree. Eight thousand spearmen, three thousand horsemen, and three hundred knights," Belrose said.

"So only half that attacking us?" Udolf laughed. "That's–"

"Those numbers *are* the half marching toward us," Belrose said over him.

"We can still face them if we have the advantage!" Udolf insisted. "We have the same number of spears, more horsemen, and twice as many knights!"

The lords muttered, but Seanna smiled, as a mother would at her precocious child. She asked, "How many Skals are with them?"

Belrose grimaced. "Six thousand axemen and four thousand horses. And gods know how many northern wildmen."

"So, Prince Udolf," Seanna said, indicating Belrose to move the map markers, "Your proposal is to meet the Lofalins at the river with all our men. You do realize that that would leave the city undefended? And the Lofalins would cross no matter what we do. If you cut down each elf as he wades from the water, two would rise in his place.

"And what of the Skals? They could circle from the north, attack your rear, and slaughter your men. You'd be caught in a trap. Or they may attack the city. With so few men at the walls, they would breach before you could return. What then? The Lofalins would still be crossing, and you would have no safe haven to return to. The late king knew the folly of meeting them on the open field. I will not allow so many lives to be thrown away for nothing."

Udolf gaped at her, and the lords looked impressed. Seanna smiled, though inwardly she felt sick. *Was this what Henrik would do, day after day? Scarce wonder he turned gray so young.* She continued, "Now, my lords, we must think of supplies. Wagon trains have been coming from the smaller towns along with their refugees, yes?"

At a lord's nod, she said, "Stockpile everything in storehouses. I want it divided evenly between Midtown, Darkroad, and Seawind. We must begin rationing our food or risk starvation. Yes, even the nobles.We can't dine upon smoked pork while the rustics eat hard tack and dried meat. Lord

Chastain, I delegate this task to you. You may have whatever men you need. Sir Dirk, you must send men to open space for the refugees. Go through each room of every inn and manor if you must to determine how many will fit inside, but get it done. I want every refugee inside these walls before the Lofalins tramp over the horizon. Is that understood?"

"Yes, Madam," the men said. Sir Dirk saluted with grim approval.

"I understand how difficult this will be," Seanna said to the lords who still frowned at her. "The time has come where we must stand together, lord and farmer, curate and tavern wench. Any lord who is heard speaking against this will be brought before the justiciars for treason." She glared at Udolf. "Even those within the royal family."

Though they muttered, the lords bowed as they scraped their chairs back. They departed, whispering among themselves, as Seanna surveyed the map. Only Belrose remained behind, his deft hands moving markers to and fro.

"Was I wise, Belrose?" Seanna asked.

The mage's hawkish eyes studied her. "You were firm, Madam. We cannot know whether or not any course is wise until we see its results."

"You're a clever man, are you not?"

He shrugged. "Some would say that."

"Your task is to find a way out of this. If diplomacy fails, there must be a way to avert as many lives lost as possible. Can you do that?"

"I can try."

"Good." Seanna rubbed her pounding temples, desperate for a few minutes to relax. But her duty was never done, and there were yet more important men to speak to. "The predicants failed to elect an Exalt, correct?"

"Correct."

"It was a vote split between Ropaz and Manderly?"

"Indeed."

"I wish to speak with both. Where may I find them?"

"Manderly is within the Grand Novum," Belrose said.

"Ropaz, I believe, is outside the city."

That surprised her. "Doing what?"

"Helping the refugees, if I am told correctly. Many have come who are sick or wounded. Shall I summon the predicants?"

"No," Seanna said. She needed to get out of the keep, see her city and people. And perhaps a visit to the refugees would quell any stirrings of discontent. A riot would not do, not when the Lofalins were so close. "I will go to them."

"As you will it." Belrose hesitated, then said, "Beware Udolf. He wants the kingdom; he'll stoop to great lows to get it."

"I understand." *Yet another problem I must contend with.*

Though she loathed forcing men to carry her in a silk cushioned chair when there were so many hungry and sick, Seanna saw no other way to travel. Her belly was too large, her feet too sore, and it was such a long way to Seawind and the Grand Novum. She settled into the chair and was lifted by four servants. Eight soldiers guarded her, eyes shifting among the people as she was carried through Midtown.

Women and children crowded the streets and alleys of Seawind, begging for scraps and trying to sell whatever small luxuries they possessed to buy more food. Whenever Seanna saw a family with multiple children, she threw a small pouch of coins to them. It was the least she could do. The chairmen met no resistance as they carted her through the streets, and the people bowed or gave shouts of "Long life to Queen Seanna!"

Despite their strong words, their eyes showed their fear and resignation. *This is the last bastion of hope, and I its captain,* Seanna thought as the chairmen took her to the Grand Novum. *Will my decisions lead us to victory?*

The Grand Novum was crowded with citizens, each holding their prayer beads or bending with their foreheads to the floor, muttering for guidance and miracles. Clothmen, curates, and predicants circulated among them, offering wine, water, and food. The lofty ceilings and painted arches echoed with the whispers of prayers. Each pillar had supplicants leaning against it, each candle on every altar lit. Though the space was huge, it felt small and hot and crowded with so many bodies.

At Seanna's entrance, a curate hurried over and bowed. "Your Grace, do you request a private alcove for worship?"

"Not today," Seanna said. "I would speak with Predicant Manderly."

"Ah." The curate shifted his feet. "He is not here, Madam."

"When will he return?"

"I don't believe he will. His rooms were found emptied of their possessions this morning."

"He fled the city?" Seanna reeled. Manderly, the man whom she had claimed spoke for the rustics, who stood against the face of evil...gone?

"Yes, Madam."

"Damn his cowardice," she muttered, turning back to the door. *It seems I misjudged the man.*

Seanna returned to her chair lost in gloomy thoughts. She watched the people around her, all of whom had the same tight fear. It was plain in how they moved quickly, not lingering to chat, or how they held their children close, eyes darting about as if more elven assassins would appear to destroy their loved ones. When they glanced at Seanna, they looked to see if she was afraid, too.

I mustn't show them, she thought, straightening in her chair and smiling down at them. *These are my children, and I must be strong for them.*

Her chair wound through the masses to the gates. Little camps had popped up outside the city walls. Rustics shouted at one another, cook fires smoked, and the people inspected her warily, not trusting her to help them. These were the people who had seen firsthand the Lofalin army, witnessed the destruction of their homes and livelihoods.

An idea struck her. Seanna leaned over her chair, calling to a man, "Which people have traveled the farthest?"

He pointed to the back of the camp. "Those from Jintor, Your Grace."

"Is their steward with them?"

"They have no steward, only elders."

"Thank you." Seanna directed her soldiers to take her there. Their captain protested, but acquiesced at her insistence. Soon, the city walls were small behind them as they reached the edge of the sprawling camp.

At her arrival, a few men came from their ragged tents and bowed, their expressions hard and suspicious. One among them, a man in his prime, hung back. He wore similar simple clothes that weren't nearly as road-wearied or grimy as the others.

"Your Grace," one of the men said, straightening. Seanna climbed from her chair to meet them.

"What your names, Masters?" she asked.

"I'm Master Huxton," the man said. "These are Masters Rielow and Brai."

Seanna nodded to them. "And you are the elders of Jintor?"

"Aye, Madam."

"When did you arrive?"

"Just yesterday."

"How many women and children with you?" Seanna noted the men's pained frowns.

"Too few," said Huxton. "Jintor was one of the first attacked. Most didn't escape."

"I am sorry for your losses," Seanna said. She wanted to add that she, too, had lost family in this war, but these men didn't seem like they'd want to hear her own sad tale. After all, she had a crown and a warm bed to sleep in while they huddled in wretched tents in the rain.

The men shifted, glancing at each other. One of the others, Brai, spoke up, "We are pleased to be worth speaking to, Your Grace, but why us?"

"I want your advice," Seanna said. The men looked taken aback. "My council is filled with lords who have barely had to wipe their own arses." Her coarse language stunned them. "I want you to assemble all the stewards and elders within this camp and elect among yourselves three to be represented within the keep. My men work even now to find shelter for you within the city, but I want your voices. You may see something that I have missed."

"We're honored, Madam," Huxton managed to say. Seanna suppressed a smirk. *They never expected such a thing from a royal, let alone a woman.*

"I want your three men in the Silver Keep by tomorrow, as well as the women and children of Jintor. They will be kept in the keep until the war is won."

The men shuffled their feet. One of them finally said, "Thank you."

Seanna was absurdly pleased with herself. Before all the commotion in Riverfen, she would never have even visited the refugees, much less spoken to them. She felt a small pleasure in imagining the lords' faces when three rustic men joined their numbers.

"Your Grace." The man in cleaner clothes came forward. The three elders deferentially made way for him.

"And who are you?" Seanna asked. This man carried himself with quiet authority; surely he wasn't from some backwater hamlet? His tunic and breeches were fine linen, if not new, and his brown hair greyed at the temples. His eyes were hooded and cunning, though not unfriendly.

"I am Predicant Gavriel Ropaz," the man said, sweeping a bow. "We have met once, Madam, though in the finery of the Grand Novum. I'm afraid I am rendered unrecognizable today."

His ruse delighted her. Seanna smiled. "Predicant Ropaz, I am pleased to see you. Come; I wish to speak with you."

With her soldiers around her, Seanna and Ropaz began the long walk back to the city gates. No doubt she would need the chair before they reached Seawind, but for now she enjoyed the small exercise.

"You aren't the first nobleman I have seen dressed as a rustic," Seanna said. She examined Ropaz out of the corner of her eye. She hadn't supported him in his bid for Exalt, but she had been very foolish in many things. Perhaps this man who hid among refugees was just who she needed after all.

"Oh?" Ropaz tilted his head. "Am I to guess the man you saw thus?"

"It was Earl Seastone, gardening in his grand palace,"

Seanna said. The memory was bittersweet. Druam had sent her away, yet she had been truly humbled in his presence. She admired him for knowing himself so well. "We did not part well, but he showed me his true measure that day."

"I assume you are judging my measure now?"

"Of course. Is that not the game we play? Lords and earls, queens and predicants, constantly assessing each other for weaknesses or strengths to exploit."

"What would you say my weaknesses are?" Ropaz asked.

Seanna stopped, studying him with a thorough eye. "You are guarded. You listen rather than speak, and you remember."

"Those sound like strengths."

"It depends on who wields them." Seanna turned, her feet pressing into the mud. "What of me, Predicant? What judgements have you made?"

"You are impulsive," Ropaz said without hesitation. "You are proud, and think yourself more clever than you are."

Aremo said those same words to me in Riverfen. Why did they sting then, and not now? Seanna laughed softly. "Yet I am Queen Regent. Don't the divines bless the crown with absolute wisdom?"

Ropaz gave her sly smile. "Of course. Sometimes, that wisdom is to allow their kingdom to be run by their advisors."

"I believe that to be my wisdom as well." Seanna amended, "In some matters, at least. Did you know, Ropaz, I despised you for many months? You stood in the way of my wishes. I didn't know you nor your deeds very well, and still I hated you."

"Mm." He looked at her sideways.

"I have acquired new wisdom these last deshes. If I had become Queen Regent even three months ago, I would have surrounded myself with sycophants and fools who only catered to my whims."

"And now?"

"I want wise men around me, to challenge me but also acknowledge when my thoughts bear fruit. Do you know of such men?"

Ropaz's hooded eyes were bright. "Possibly. Tell me,

Madam, why did you ask for three elders from these refugees?"

"I have never known want or hunger," Seanna replied. "I know that all folk need shelter and food, but what else? What if feuding families are placed into the same houses? What if fights break out in the grain lines? I know not how to handle such matters. These elders do."

"And beyond that?"

A clever man indeed. "If they believe me to be on their side, they will support me. My nephew wants the throne, and I fear for mine and my child's safety. If I am killed, and not by the Lofalins..."

"You want the people to rise up in support of your child."

"You understand well the game we play." The gates loomed closer now, and Seanna stopped. "I don't yet trust you, and I doubt you harbor any good feeling toward me, but I need you. It is within the power of the crown to elevate a predicant in circumstances such as these."

Ropaz gave her a tight-lipped smile. "I am at your call, Madam. You cannot make me Exalt, but High Predicant does have a satisfying sound to it."

"So we are in agreement?" Seanna held out her hand. He took it, pressing his lips to her palm.

"I am your loyal servant, Queen Seanna. Long may you reign."

Seanna stepped into the lowered chair, savoring her victory. Belrose, Ropaz, and the rustics supported her. Now she would just have to convince the other lords.

When they reached the Silver Keep, Seanna noted the tension in the guards. Belrose waited for her on the bottom step, his hands balled into fists.

"What is it?" Seanna demanded. "What's wrong?"

Belrose grimaced, "*Kair* Aremo Teru has arrived to speak with you."

Seanna's heart plummeted. She stared at the mage. "Where is he?"

"He awaits you in the throne room."

Seanna considered her dress, coated in grime from the

journey to Seawind and back. *Let him see me as I am,* she decided. "I will see him at once."

CHAPTER TWENTY-FIVE
Sandu

Though he once heard that eternity could not be measured, Sandu knew the truth. Eternity was each breath, each slow candle, each sunset, after the death of one's love. They passed in a haze, moving slow and quick in turn, and he was incapable of counting them.

Three nights since Tambrey's death, yet he had lived for three eternities.

Cara would not speak to him, and Jagger could not. Darian's words were cryptic and hollow. Sandu felt utterly alone in his grief.

Surely, he thought, *I will die in the night, and it will all be over.* Alas, he woke with each dawn, and pulled himself from his tent to face the sun. *I hope the plague takes me.*

He knew that Darian had tried convincing Cara to speak to him, but nothing had come of it. Jagger hovered nearby, the only one who knew what Sandu was going through. Yet how could Sandu commiserate with him when Darian had to speak Jagger's words for him?

Then there were the waking nightmares. Someone would say something, or he'd feel a twig pressing on his skin, or any number of things, and the memories would invade his head, drowning out all reasonable thought. His hands shook, unable to still. His breath and heartbeat came too fast, as if he'd run all day and couldn't stop. His skin crawled with a thousand phantom bites and claws and kisses that pressed in on him until he thought he would be crushed into a tiny ball. The attacks came more frequently now, each worse than the last. The one from last night hadn't ended for over a candle.

This dawn, Sandu woke again wishing he had died. The plague didn't scare him anymore.

He heard voices from outside and listened half-heartedly.

"I can walk!" Cara said in that tone she had acquired in recent deshes, that tone that said she would brook no arguments.

"For a day straight? For two days in a row? Three? It is many days to D'Clet, and you are still regaining your strength," Darian said.

"You know as well as I that I'll be healed soon."

"I would not–"

"Not your issue, though, is it? Therefore, not your choice. I say we pack up and leave today."

Sandu struggled to dress, his heavy limbs uncooperative. His head was foggy, his eyes crusted with old tears. He stumbled from the tent. "What's going on?"

Cara turned up her lip at the sight of him. Sandu wasn't bothered anymore by her derision; what did it matter?

"We're leaving," Cara said. She walked about with a distinct limp, though only the day before her leg had still been far too injured to put weight on. She met Sandu's eye as if daring him to question her rapid progress.

He didn't care to ask. She'd just lie, anyway. Instead, he shrugged and strode to the fire. "Alright by me. What's for breakfast?"

Jagger sat next to him and handed over eggs on flatbread. Sandu ate without tasting. Jagger made a strange sign with his hand and gave him a questioning look.

"Huh?" Sandu asked Darian. "What's this?"

"I won't be around forever," Darian said. He scooped another egg into his wooden bowl and sat down a safe distance away. "Jagger and I have been working to develop a way for him to speak, if crudely. That sign means 'good'."

Cara sat apart from the men, her expression suspicious as

she ate. Sandu turned back to Darian. "How many signs are there?"

"We've developed about thirty so far. Perhaps we can teach it to you?"

Sandu thought of Tambrey, of how she would often punctuate her words with hand movements. His egg caught in his throat, and he swallowed with effort. "I don't know."

Jagger made a few more signs, and Darian translated, "*Easy. Good. Distracting.*"

"You think I need distracting?" Sandu asked. Jagger nodded. His eyes were soft.

Darian said, "He wants you to know that he understands. He dealt with his wife's death by murdering people. He hopes you won't do the same."

"Not necessary to kill people when Cara does it for me," Sandu said without thinking. He froze, daring a glance at Cara. She stared at her food, her fingers stilled.

"I don't kill innocents," she said. She met Sandu's eye with a hard look. "You know that."

"I'm sorry," he said quickly. She softened, and he gave her a small smile. "So you're feeling well?"

"Yeah." Her eyes darted away. "I'm better now."

"I'm glad to hear it." Sandu finished his food. Though his words were empty, he supposed he felt a tiny bit less awful. It was a lot harder to deal with Tambrey's death and the waking nightmares while his friend despised him.

Turning back to Darian and Jagger, Sandu said, "I want to learn these gestures."

Jagger smiled, and Darian nodded. "Excellent. We'll work as we travel. Provided, of course, that you agree with Cara's plan to continue today."

If I stay here too long, I'll go mad, Sandu decided. *Bluston, where Tambrey believes my children are, is on the road to D'Clet. I can find them and my father. I can make her memory matter.*

Sandu said, "I do. Do we still need to keep our distance?"

Darian nodded. "Two more nights to be certain."

Though he kept a few paces apart, Sandu walked to Cara's

tent as she worked to break it down. She stayed quiet as she removed her haversack and blankets. Sandu said as she worked, "You don't have to come with us."

"What?"

"I have Jagger with me now. If you don't want to come with us, I can help you get a horse and you can go your own way." It pained Sandu to say it, but he had to make sure that she stayed because she wanted to, not because of pity or obligation to him.

"Do you want me gone?" she asked.

"No." Sandu nudged a rock with his foot. "There's something going on with you, and I thought I'd offer. You don't want to tell me everything, and that's fine, but for awhile now it's felt like you're only here because Laris forced you to be. Now that he's gone, you're free. I'm going to find my children and free my da, and if that's not what you want to do, you don't have to stay."

"I'm still going to D'Clet," Cara said.

"I know. But you'd be faster without us. A blind man, a mute, and a widower. We're not the quickest of groups."

"I won't lie, I've thought about it," Cara said. She pulled the tent fabric into a tight roll. "After Laris's spell, I resented you for abandoning me. I was in pain, yet you weren't there to comfort me."

Sandu thought about the waking nightmares, the longing for death, but held his tongue. Would she reject him again, tell him his pain couldn't compare to hers? He thought a moment, then said, "I had to return to my wife in her dying moments. If I hadn't, I would have lived the rest of my life in regret. I wouldn't know where my children are now."

The tent lay packed, ready for travel. Now Sandu worked on his gear while Cara watched. Sweat rolled down his back as he labored, the sun hot for the autumn season. He relished the work. It distracted his fevered mind, made sense to his tired hands.

Cara said, "I remember searching for Renna, hoping each night that I would find her safe and bring her home. When I lost Merick, I lost hope. You helped me regain it. I suppose I came to depend on you to keep me well."

"And I'm happy to do so. Except you have to return the favor," Sandu pointed out. "I am sorry that Renna and Merick are gone, but there's still a chance for my family." He pulled the strings tight to secure his blankets. "I want to help you, I do, but I'm struggling as well. We have to help each other."

"I don't know if I can," Cara said. "But I'll try."

Their labor finished, they began to walk. Jagger took Darian's arm at the front, leaving Cara and Sandu room to talk as they began the day's hike. The road was wide enough for Cara and Sandu to walk apace, leaving the height of a man separating them. Even with the gulf of physical distance, Sandu thought that maybe their emotional chasm had lessened.

Cara chewed her lip, her eyes on the ground. Sandu waited for her to speak, unsure himself how to tell her about his mind's rebellion.

At last, Cara said, "I've done things that I regret. Things that feel good and help me. But I fear them all the same."

"I don't suppose you'll tell me what these things are?"

"If I do, you'll despise me." She flashed him a worried look. "I'm working through it, and Darian knows what's happening. I'm not alone in this."

"Does it have to do with your leg?"

She nodded, but Sandu didn't press her. After so many days of not speaking to him, he didn't want to risk her wrath. He did ask, "What can I do to help?"

"I don't know. Just be with me, I suppose."

Sandu grinned. "That I can do." He wanted desperately to tell her about the waking nightmares and his grief, but somehow the words wouldn't come. He made a strangled noise, frustrated. Each time he tried to give it voice, his mind fought back, preventing him from speaking. Cara either didn't notice or didn't care to ask, for she kept walking.

Over two days, they traveled higher and higher, from still-green meadows and just-turned trees to browning grasses and fading crowns. Dead leaves crackled underfoot, reds and yellows and oranges, dried from the heat.

Some hamlets were marked with red X's painted on the walls and doors, bright enough to see from a distance. These they gave a wide berth, for the signs could only mean one thing: plague. It had struck most of the villages. They passed the occasional town filled with the living, people with pale faces and worried eyes. Mothers held their children close, townsmen shut their windows and locked their doors.

"They're terrified," Sandu commented.

"Why shouldn't they be?" Darian said. "They have thus far escaped the ravages of disease, yet each new visitor could bring death with them."

Visitors like me. Sandu examined his hands, wondering if he carried the disease.

"They could flee," Cara said.

"To where?" Darian gave a tight-lipped smile. "Most have never traveled farther than ten miles from their homes. They will not leave unless they are forced to."

Sandu's heart went out to these strangers, and he prayed for each town marked with red. He had seen the horrors of the plague. Yet as they traveled closer to the passes, he feared the worst for Dunston. Had the plague preceded them? Would he find his children dead in their stepfather's arms?

Sometimes, the thoughts became overbearing. They brought the waking nightmares, and he struggled to keep walking as his mind caved in on itself. His hands shook on his pack straps, his feet stumbled. Though the air was crisp and clean, his breath came stale and tight.

Most often, Sandu hid these fits from the others. He poured water over his head or focused on putting one step in front of the other. Sometimes, Jagger would notice and walk beside him, lending a calm strength.

Yet Sandu still could not find a way to tell Cara.

In the evenings and mornings, and as they rested during the day, Darian, Sandu, and Jagger would create more hand signs to practice. They had many signs for words, as well as a gesture for each letter so that Jagger could spell if need be. Sandu found these routines wonderfully distracting. Though he ached every moment for Tambrey, the pain grew easier to manage once he had something to focus on.

He and Cara spoke now, but some underlying tension had tainted their relationship. Gone were the carefree days where they laughed easily together. Sandu thought that maybe it was his own hesitation to be honest with her, but he realized that she had yet to reveal her own secrets. *We're back to the times before Merick's death: secrets, lies, and suspicion.* The revelation brought new heartache that piled atop all the rest within his soul.

They came into a low valley spotted with copses of trees and a wandering stream. Tents and campfires lay strewn across the vale, stretching to all sides. Among the canvas and wooden wagons were Valadi caravans and ramshackle huts, the roots of a new village.

"What are they all doing here?" Sandu reflected aloud.

"Fleeing," was all Darian said.

Sandu started the descent, but a firm hand gripped his shoulder. Jagger shook his head, his eyes on Sandu's hand. Sandu's soul dropped into his boots.

A white spot with a grey center, larger than a coin, tainted the back of his hand.

Just when he had started living again, started to feel like he could survive with the knowledge of Tambrey's death.

"Is it?" Sandu whispered, too afraid to speak it out loud.

"Plague," Darian said. He shook his head. "We need to move off the road and erect barriers to keep others away."

Sandu shuffled after him, holding his hand to his chest as if it were broken. He thought of Tambrey, so weak and alone in her final moments. Would he succumb like her, leaving their children orphans? *Not truly orphans; they have Frederick. If the plague hasn't reached him, too.* Dread filled him at the thought of slowly withering away as the pustules ate at his humors until there was nothing of him left.

They walked for a long time until Darian was satisfied that they were adequately far from the road and ramshackle village. As they started to set up their camp, Cara hung back.

"What if I get infected?" she asked. "Or you. You can't

expect us to stay near Sandu."

"You've been around me for days," Sandu said.

"I didn't realize you were really infected," Cara said. "I hoped that Darian was being overly cautious."

Though her callous words stung, Sandu heard the fear in them. And the truth.

"Jagger will not be harmed," Darian said calmly. "And neither will I. The Song of Death has said that plague is not what will kill me."

Still Cara stayed away. Darian said to her, "If you are afraid, go stay in the village until one of us comes for you. If you wish to stay, keep always on the opposite side of the fire and touch nothing that is not yours. We will do the same."

Her fearful expression tore at Sandu. He said, "It's alright, Cara. I understand. I saw my tribe's symbol painted on a circle of wagons below, a sparrow with a flower in its beak. They'll let you stay with them if you reply 'I want to share stories by the fire' when they offer to share their meal. Tell them you know Gerda Skyweaver's son."

Some small part of him hoped she would stay, but it was a selfish wish. Cara would be safer far from him. After a moment's pause, she nodded and said, "Do your best to live, Sandu. I'll wait there until you send word."

Word of my death, most likely.

After Cara disappeared back through the trees, Sandu helped the other men to make camp. None of them spoke; a somber mood pervaded the evening.

"How long do I have?" Sandu asked as they ate supper.

Darian shook his head. "It's not as simple as that. If my treatments work, you'll be well again within a quinn. If they don't, we'll try our last resort."

Another eternity of days. Sandu shivered. "What's that?"

"We burn it out of you."

CHAPTER TWENTY-SIX
The Men Who Once Were Dead

Druam stood atop the crenellated ramparts of Stonetree's fortress and watched the army slowly filter in. The men, tired after days of hard marching, all looked to the keep with relief. They would sleep in a warm barracks tonight instead of on the cold, hard ground.

Along with the men came villagers and supply wagons, some from Riverfen, most gathered along the winding mountain roads to Stonetree. The rustics carried sacks of clothes and food, even the smallest child helping to lug the family's worldly goods into the keep. The column pushed slowly but inexorably forward, each person no doubt wondering when they could go home.

Of course, Druam could not read their minds. He couldn't truly know the thoughts of the soldiers and families below. Yet war was the same no matter who lived it. How many foot soldiers had he spoken to, how many grieving mothers and worried wives? All said the same thing, again and again, throughout the centuries of countless battles: *When will it be over? Will he come home? Will my home be there when I return?*

Druam leaned on the stone, staring forward without seeing. Concern burned inside him, each face below stamped with Autorus's mark. *They are going to die,* he thought. *And they know it.* With deliberate breaths, he forced himself into calm. As his breath normalized and the tics in his muscles relaxed, he radiated his peaceful emotion outward, using his *fampir* ability to influence the minds of those within and outside the keep. He imagined he could hear the reassured sighs.

Were it not for the thunder of a thousand marching feet, it would have been a beautiful day. Situated in a vale below four mighty peaks, Stonetree was surrounded by beauty: tall pines, high mountain lakes and streams, and a quaint town below the fortress hilltop where villagers had lived for centuries.

But the village had emptied, and the hill fortified as much as possible in the short time allotted to them. Druam had not slept the past two nights, worry gnawing at him, a feral dog crunching at a bone that had long ago lost its hearty marrow. His thoughts turned ever toward those he had lost: his parents and sisters, Gwen, Alex, and Verdon, the brother who had walked beside him for centuries before vanishing without a trace. How long would it be before Druam joined them, his soul peaceful at last?

Heavy footsteps sounded on the steps behind him accompanied by weary breathing. *Edsel.* Druam inclined his head without turning.

"Scout reports?" Druam asked.

"Rask and the Lofalins are in the foothills. Their forward forces are two days away." Edsel came to stand beside him. His breath fogged in the air.

Druam shut his eyes, uttering a quick prayer for snow. *Not as if the gods have ever answered my prayers.* "How many more of ours on the road?"

"They should be in by nightfall. The lower barracks are full, same with the auxiliary. They'll have to camp in the courtyard. All the women and children are in the Great Hall or squeezed into bedrooms."

"Good." Druam watched a rustic family, the father and teenage son leading two women. "Will you conscript the rustics?"

"Any who can wield a spear. I'll take strong women, too, if they want to fight."

Druam thought of Cara, a whirlwind of death on the battlefield. She would have done well fighting by his side, but wishes would not win a war. He asked Edsel, "Our stores?"

"Enough rations to last through winter if we all tighten our belts. We've torched each field and emptied the granaries between here and Depmark; the enemy will find nothing to fill their bellies in our lands. When the snows come, they will have no choice but to retreat or starve."

"And what if the snows don't come?" Druam asked. The column of soldiers wound continuously into the vale. "How long can we last?"

"As long as we need to." Edsel sighed, laying a hand to the stone. "I had hoped to die before the next war. I dreamed my children would never see it, either."

"It's not too late–" Druam started, but Edsel interrupted him.

"We'll not be like you. An eternity is too long to live with one's mistakes. I'd rather Autorus take me when it's my time."

Druam nodded. A preemptive grief threatened to burst from him – he did not want to see another friend die while he lived on – but he pressed it down. His face betrayed nothing.

For the next two days, Stonetree prepared for siege. Soldiers readied tar and oil and stacked stones and piles of javelins and spears to hurl onto the enemy. Women labored, too, barricading the gates with stone, dirt, and debris, and slicking the outer walls with oil to keep hooks and ladders from finding purchase. Children, their chubby cheeks taut with seriousness, worked alongside their mothers while their older brothers took a spear in hand for the first time. Many a young woman, too, either too young to be married or already widowed, stepped forward to take up arms. Druam allowed all save the mothers to serve. *Your children will need you in the days to come*, he told them. *Your duty is to protect them until your last breath.*

True to Edsel's estimate, the first signs of the enemy came two days after the last of the column made it to Stonetree. Lofalin soldiers in shining armor accompanied Rask's men, making trenches around the abandoned village and setting up camp. They swarmed like ants over the terrain below, going into the forest to cut down trees.

With each passing candle, night and day, greater numbers of elves and Rask's men flooded into the valley.

Some days later, Rask's emissary and an elven ambassador rode beyond their camp's boundaries to the hill. They flew the grey banner of parlay.

As they came beneath the gates, the emissary bellowed, "We wish to speak with the Earls Stonetree and Seastone."

Druam shouted back, "We're here. Say your piece."

"We bring treatises of surrender. If you lay down your arms, we will spare you and your people."

The usual parlances of war. Druam said, "You must return disappointed. We will not give in so easily."

"So be it. You have declared your lives forfeit. May Amnah have mercy on your soul." With that, the riders departed, banners flying out behind them.

"Amnah? Since when do Rask's men invoke the elven god?" Edsel asked.

"Perhaps it was a sacrifice for their alliance," Druam said. "Whatever the case, we must prepare for the morrow. Sleep well tonight, my friend."

Edsel departed, but Druam watched the enemy camp. Far out behind their lines, elves and men worked tirelessly, building something large. Larger than a catapult or battering ram. A chill ran through Druam's bones. What new contraption had war discovered this time?

✳

Sandu thrashed and panted, his eyes seeing things that weren't there. Though it wouldn't do much good, Jagger put a cool cloth to his friend's forehead. He was rewarded by Sandu gripping his wrist with unusual strength. Jagger simply waited until Sandu released him. He rocked back on his heels, unsure what else he could do.

Nearby, Darian crouched by the fire, running his fingers through the flames. *Preparing*, Darian had said, *for what we must do next.*

The first three days, Darian had tried many different medicines to stave off Sandu's condition from growing worse. Darian gave him potions and poultices, lanced his boils, spoke spells that made Sandu shudder and scream.

None had worked.

All Jagger could do was help as best he could, and pray. He'd never been the praying sort before, but now he sent his hopes to as many gods as he could remember the names of. *Don't let him die now,* he prayed. *He don't deserve it.*

At last, Sandu calmed enough to fall into a fitful sleep. Jagger changed out the cloth for a fresh one.

Darian's eyes were closed, and his lips moved as he whispered to himself. After a moment, Darian said, "Go to the people below. Find Cara and tell her that we are making our last effort tonight. Bring back as much firewood as you can gather."

Don't you know death inside and out? Jagger thought at him. *So you know if it'll work?*

"There are some things that are not clear. Not everyone's Song is as defined as yours and mine. Sandu could either live or die. Go quickly. I must keep preparing myself."

As Jagger descended into the valley, he heard greetings and friendly conversation. These people, it seemed, had no fear of strangers. Some called to him and asked where he was headed. Others asked where he was from. Jagger ignored them until he came to the Sarga tribe.

He paused outside the half-circle of wagons. The symbol painted on the side of a bird with a flower was all too familiar to him. The last time he'd seen it, he'd slaughtered everyone in that caravan save one girl.

Regret weighted his steps. Jagger remembered his knives plunging into the sleeping Valadi, the utter thoughtlessness with which he ended their lives. The girl's terrified brown eyes.

The Valadi past the wagons were alive, but did they know of their kin's downfall? Did they know who had done it? Bells tinkled off their hems and collars, a merry sound that belied the remorse inside him. He didn't belong in such a place.

Movement in the corner of his eye distracted him. He

almost drew his knives, but resisted. *These are good folk*, he told himself. He turned to see Cara. She watched him warily.

"Is he dead?" she asked.

Jagger shook his head. He started to sign, then stopped. She had never learned their new language. Instead, he dug with a knife in the dirt, "*Maybe tonight.*"

Cara nodded, her lips tight. She stalked away before he could do more. Jagger shrugged and turned to leave.

A scream rent the air, echoing through the valley. Jagger halted, his spine tingling. Slowly, he rotated back to face the wagons. Guilt and fear washed over him, drowning all other thoughts.

Dilara, the girl he'd kidnapped, whose entire family he'd murdered, stood on a wagon step. She pointed at him and shrieked, "It's him! The man who killed my family!"

Other Valadi hurried to her. Jagger retreated, his mind frozen. He let his long legs carry him up through the trees and away from the commotion, his head reeling with remorse. The fear in Dilara's eyes as she saw him, the grief and horror that had welled within her, shadowed his steps.

He sank onto a stump and buried his head in his hands. Vecking hells, why couldn't anything go right? Darian had promised him redemption, yet now he faced the worst of his recent crimes. If Dilara wanted him dead, he couldn't blame her. After all, he'd told her as much when he'd left her. *Watching me die won't help your problems, lass,* he'd said to her in that clearing in the woods, *And you've got plenty of 'em now, widout a family to help you.*

When he'd killed her Valadi caravan, her father and mother and brother and cousins and uncles and aunts and friends, he hadn't cared. They were Sandu's family, and he'd wanted to hurt that bastard to the core. *Don' change the truth of it,* he thought. *You wanted revenge, and you got it. Made you happy as could be.*

Well, not happy as could be. He couldn't kill her, even with the knife poised in his hand. Stayed by a guilt he couldn't name.

I didn't do the proper thing and finish the job, he thought. *She would've been better off dead. Now I'm here, hauntin' her, and she'll hold onto it all her life.*

He had claimed to her that he never felt guilt. It was a lie, to himself mostly, to stave away the demons in his head.

Then I died, and Darian brought me back. I didn' kill Sandu, and I know that was the right thing. When I came back, I thought thing's'd be easier. I've died once, can't be too hard to do it again.

Footsteps crunched the fallen leaves, and Jagger peered over his shoulder. Valadi men circled him holding daggers and pitchforks. One had a bow, the string pulled back to his cheek though his arms shook with the effort. Dilara clung to a woman behind them, her dark eyes hard and unforgiving.

"That's him," she said again.

The bowman let loose his arrow. It flew wide, striking the tree next to Jagger. Before he knew it, Jagger was on his feet, a knife in each hand. His instincts screamed for him to fight back. With great effort, he loosened his fingers and let the knives fall to the ground. He averted his eyes from Dilara's.

One of the men holding a pitchfork inched forward. "Is it true? Are you the madman who slaughtered our kin?"

Jagger opened his mouth, closed it. He couldn't meet Dilara's eyes. His throat tight, he finally nodded.

"Any last words afore we kill you?"

I can't die, Jagger thought. He stood patiently, waiting for the blow to come. His silence and stillness were disconcerting; the Valadi murmured and shifted. None of them approached him.

Jagger turned away. He couldn't wait around for them to gather their courage. Two steps into his escape, the bowstring twanged again. A hard metal point sunk into his side. It stung like a bee's prick. Jagger stumbled. The arrow stuck out at an awkward angle. He reached down and pulled it out, somewhat confused.

Usually there's blood when things like this happen. Both the wound and the arrow point were clean. He looked back at the Valadi, shrugged, and threw away the arrow. They stared at him, bewildered and frightened. For a moment, Jagger met Dilara's tearful gaze.

I'm sorry, child. I took from you what I had no right to take. With no one there to translate his words, Jagger didn't know what else to do. He walked away, expecting another arrow. None came. When he peeked over his shoulder, the Valadi still stood there.

As he trudged through the trees back to their camp, idly gathering firewood, Jagger thought about the poor girl. Would it have been best for her to see him fall? Should he have pretended to die?

Won't bring back her family.

When he finally emerged from the trees, he found Darian and Sandu much as he'd left them. He dumped the wood by the fire, then sat at Sandu's side. His friend was no better, the pustules on his skin grown even larger.

"You saw the girl," Darian said, reading Jagger's thoughts.

Aye.

"How did it feel to look in your victim's eyes?"

Awful. What I did to her might have been the worst thing I've ever done. Jagger cradled his head in his hands. *Would it have been better to have let them stabbed me?*

"No. Death does little to bring peace for those seeking vengeance."

It was a lesson Jagger had learned far too late. *Even if I could've spoken to her, it would have done no good. I brought nothing but nightmares for her.*

"Perhaps. Perhaps not. You didn't expect to find her again, but you did. And your actions proved that you are learning. Next time, you will do better."

Jagger shuddered. *I hope I never meet one of my victims again.*

Darian's smile was sympathetic. "Oh, you will, over many years while you atone. Until then, wallow in your guilt. That is good."

It's all for you, Raven, Jagger reminded himself. *I'm doing this to see you again.*

✳

Not long now, Alex thought. *Please, gods, not long now.* His hands trembled, his skin burning even from the moon's gentle glow. His stomach ached with a hunger no mortal could ever know. His features contorted with his *fampir* heritage, stretching over his skull, making him more of a monster.

He stumbled and caught himself. In the high mountains he couldn't escape from the sun, the wind, the cold, the unforgiving wealth of life around him. Each time he saw a bird, or squirrel, or any creature whose blood sang to him, he wanted so to drink.

The wound in his chest had grown too festered to ignore. He tried to clean it, but the infection grew back within seconds. It burned, a constant heat beneath his shirt. It sent a shrieking pain throughout his torso with each movement.

Oh gods, just let me turn into a husk. End this. The gods didn't listen, and Alex continued on.

How long since he'd left Riverfen? He couldn't fathom. It could have been a quinn or a hundred years. All he knew now was pain and incomparable thirst.

Cresting a high pass, Alex saw a valley not far below, tucked into the mountains like a babe in a cradle. The road he walked was the only one in or out of the valley, and nothing but trees nestled there. As he stared down, though, he noticed an oddity in the forest below. These trees appeared like none other: grey-black bark and no leaves, their branches intertwined in an impermeable mass. The normal trees on the edges of the valley leaned away from those in the center as if wary of touching roots.

Something in Alex told him that he had reached the Whispering Woods. As he descended into the valley, he heard sounds drifting on the wind, sounds that could have been the murmuring of gentlefolk, the hushed song of a mother to her child, the chitter of squirrels in the trees.

Alex walked all around the forest, searching for a way in. The mass of branches brooked no entrance, and he walked fully around it three times before his wound throbbed so painfully, his legs so sore, that he collapsed in front of the trees. Clutching at his side, he whispered a prayer, "Please, ye fae of this forest, let me in. I will give anything, *anything*, to be mortal once more. I have come so far, and I cannot go further. Please."

The branches twisted and moved, revealing a path that hadn't been there before. Hope springing anew, its warmth allowing him to ignore his hurts for a little longer, Alex pushed to his feet and stumbled onto the path. The trees closed behind him, and he knew that the Woods truly had him at their mercy. Even the air smelled different here, as if he'd left Earda entirely and come to a new world.

The path ran straight, its dirt free of stones and tripping roots. Alex couldn't see to the end, for a thick fog shrouded the forest. It clung to his clothes and hair, misting his skin. The fog didn't intimidate Alex, and he pressed resolutely onwards, one hand clinging to his side.

The fog dissipated, and Alex came into a glen that held a bonfire, a strange shelter, and three women dressed in rustic garb. Falling to his knees in front of them, Alex drew in a ragged breath, unable to speak for a moment. The Witches regarded him without emotion.

After a long time, the shortest of the three spoke, "What is it you seek, Alexandro Strilu, he who has lived many long years?"

Regaining his breath, Alex said, "I want to be mortal again."

The Witch merely nodded. "A worthy task, if not a wise one. Why do you wish to be mortal?"

"I cannot bear the loneliness and cruelty of being *fampir*. I am not deserving of love."

"Not all mortal men are worthy."

"Each of them is more deserving than me. Please, I beg you, I will do anything."

"It can be done," the Witch said, taking his chin in her warm hand. "But there is a price."

"I'll gladly pay it." Alex trembled at her touch.

"Without knowing what it is?"

"No price is too great."

"Then come with us." After helping him to his feet, the Witch led Alex into the shelter, her silent sisters following. Inside, he saw a table with leather straps, and beside it, another table filled with a strange contraption: vials, glasses, and flasks connected by tubing and filled with strange bubbling mixtures.

"I must prepare," the Witch said, directing Alex to sit on a low chair. "Eat and take water, for you will need strength."

Alex didn't protest. He grabbed the platter of food and gulped the water, not minding the juices running down his chin. To his surprise, his *fampir* instincts had little effect here in these Woods, and the Witches' food gave him as much vigor as blood.

When he'd finished his meal, the Witch pointed to the table. Laying down on it, Alex watched warily as one of the other Witches strapped down his limbs and head. "What's this for?" he asked.

"It is a long, painful process," said the Witch. "You will hurt yourself if you try to move. We will do no harm to you, Alexandro Strilu."

Swallowing hard, Alex winced as the Witch inserted a long needle into each of his arms. The needles were connected to different ends of the strange contraption. As she worked, the Witch explained, "I must draw your tainted blood from your left arm. It will travel through the filters and purify with the help of the Songs, and return to your body through the right arm."

"And I'll be mortal after that?"

"Not yet. There is yet another Song before the process is complete. I would offer you something to stymy the pain, but it would not be effective for one such as you. Now, close your eyes, and try to dream of pleasant things."

Alex obeyed, his nerves as worn through as old linen. As the Witch began to sing, his blood drizzled from his body. A few moments later, he twitched as it reentered his right arm, singeing his veins. Holding as still as he could, Alex grunted. The burning grew and grew as the spell continued, his whole body on fire. He had never before realized how *hot* human blood was compared to that of the *fampir*.

One of Alex's legs shook and thumped against the table. Soon, all of his limbs and head rattled around no matter how he tried to quell them. The other two Witches held him down while the third continued her Song. Daring a peek, Alex saw that no more blood was being drawn from his left arm, and felt dizzy with relief.

Before he could relax, though, the Witch began a new Song. The shelter shook around them, the earth trembled beneath their feet. Thunder cracked in the sky, and the trees outside creaked their branches as if to object.

As the world turned to chaos around him, Alex screamed. Pain such as he had never known before consumed him, ice-cold and magma-hot all at once, pain that reached to his marrow, that flashed every emotion from him in a burst of energy. He screamed and screamed, his fingernails tearing into the table, his toes curling as if that would fend off the immeasurable torment. The Song continued, dark and horrible, and reached inside him, locking his throat, stopping his heart, freezing his organs.

In that moment of being and not-being, Alex's soul shredded inside him. The Song pulled back, and he cried out with shattered agony. His heart restarted, his lungs drawing in air. It felt as if thousands of glass shards had embedded themselves within him.

The Witch drew her spell-Song to an end. Alex screamed until his throat could bear no more, and his cries became ugly sobs. Tears streamed down his cheeks.

A moment later, he realized that he was, indeed, crying. His tears turned to ones of joy, for he had not been able to cry since he'd been turned *fampir*.

"I'm mortal," he whispered as the Witches pulled the needles from his arms and removed the straps. When his arms were free, he lifted his hands to his cheeks to feel the moisture. "I can cry again."

"And you survived," the Witch remarked. "Though the price nearly killed you."

Shuddering at the memory of such suffering, Alex asked, "What was the price?"

"The wholeness of your soul. Even as *fampir*, you retained all of your soul. To break free, it had to be torn apart, discarding that which connected you to the Underworld. You are mortal, yes, but your soul can never be stitched back together."

"It was a sacrifice worth making." Alex sat up cautiously, still reeling from the torturous process. "Thank you."

Bowing her head, the Witch said, "Be careful now, Alexandro Strilu. You are mortal again, and therefore fragile. What would not have harmed you before can now be fatal."

"I understand." Looking down at the wound in his side, Alex was surprised to see it closed. "You healed me as well?"

"It was part of the spell. Rest now, and we shall send you back to the world once you are recovered."

Lumbering off the table, Alex immediately collapsed onto the straw mat they gave him to sleep. His last thought before drifting into unconsciousness was, *At last I am free.*

CHAPTER TWENTY-SEVEN
The Forest Witch

Sunlight shone from beyond the Woods, tantalizingly bright and beautiful. The Forest Witch shaded her eyes as she peered out from between the branches. High mountains covered half the sky, their peaks glistening with the promise of snow. Feathered birds wheeled across the clouds, their eyes black and beady.

What is that place? Lintem asked. He cowered against the tree trunk, his ears flat against his skull.

Earda, the Forest Witch said. She smelled the fresh breeze, sweet and clear with a kiss of coming winter. The Woods were not musty, but neither did they have the freshness of these mountains. Some part of her yearned to leave the Woods and bound through the rocks and green grass, to see pines with green boughs and white-barked birches. Yet she hesitated, her heart torn in two.

Is that where you came from? Lintem chirped.

Yes. When she had first come to the Woods, they had astounded her with their strange, ethereal beauty and creatures that she had never seen before. Now, gazing out from a home she'd known for innumerable years, she longed to experience anew a world that had been lost to her for so long.

You promised you wouldn't go back.

And I won't. The Forest Witch sent a note of reassurance through the Songs. *This is my home now. But I can gaze a little longer at Earda. There's a clarity to it that I never realized before.*

An eagle's cry pierced the Woods, and the Forest Witch

shook herself. A new Song had beckoned to her, and she searched for its source.

A man stumbled along the Woods' boundary, his face twisted with odd features: ridged forehead and gaunt cheeks, red eyes and long white fangs. His fingers ended in talons. A deep-rooted horror threatened to choke the Forest Witch. She had seen creatures like this before, once known them as prowlers. A hiss escaped through her teeth, her back arching as she drew on the Songs around her. Lintem bared his own fangs and dug his claws into the loam, ready to face this monster.

A tremulous note in the creature's Song made her pause. The Forest Witch cocked her head, listening. The man had the face of a monster, but his Song was not feral or animal. Raw humanity danced in his soul, grief and love and pain and desire. Despair and hope warred equally within him. When the trees failed to give way, the man fell onto the hard dirt, his despair nearly winning out. His whispered words carried to the Forest Witch, "Please, ye fae of this forest, let me in."

Something about him called to the Forest Witch. She drew his Song to her, its threads shimmering in the air. His scent was oddly familiar to her, a dream she had forgotten upon waking. Without really knowing why, she hummed to the trees.

Allow him in, she said. *Guide him to the other Witches.*

The trees obeyed her, and the man stumbled into the Woods, his Song echoing with regained hope. As the forest closed around him, the Forest Witch took one final look at the mountains and soaring birds. She repressed her longing and turned away. She knew that the Woods would not stay there for long, and she would not allow herself to grieve over a missed opportunity.

As the Woods detached from Earda, a dense fog pervaded the trees. With the Songs to guide her, the Forest Witch moved confidently from branch to branch, never far from the strange man. She poked and prodded at his Song, its music confusing to her. How could he be both monster and human? His melody said he had lived for over a century, yet how could that be possible? And why did his Song beckon the subdued memories of her soul?

The Woods did not lead him astray, and the man came to the Witches' grove. Their bonfire burned ever-hot, and the Witches greeted him. The Forest Witch hung back, observing from the safety of the trees. Lintem lay down, his head stretched over his enormous paws.

As the Witches led the man inside, one turned to the trees. Her eyes pierced the darkness, and she nodded to the Forest Witch before she disappeared inside.

Songs rose from the Witches' hut, their power sending waves through the trees. The Forest Witch clung to her branch, awed by the complexity of the magic. As she listened, she realized what the Witches were doing to the man. They removed blood tainted by the Underworld and the Song of Death, and cleansed it before returning it to his body. Except the Songs went deeper than that. She examined them, fascinated by what she saw.

The process took a long time, and by its end, the Forest Witch had come to understand *fampir* and prowlers, their Songs tainted not only by lust, but necessity for blood. She couldn't understand why Autorus would allow such a degradation of the Song of Death.

Before she could contemplate it more, the Witches' Song changed, and the Forest Witch recognized this as the Song of Unmaking, powerful music that she had only begun to explore. The Woods went into a tumult around her, objecting to the very use of the Song. The trees moaned and cracked their branches, the skies darkened and thundered, the creatures growled and roared. Lintem rumbled from his loamy bed, his eyes wild in his head.

The Song of Unmaking dug into the man's connection to the Underworld and ripped apart the tendrils of his soul, leaving part of him to rot forever in Autorus's domain. The Forest Witch's own heart trembled at this, the horror of the act dawning within her. Part of her wished to stop the Witches, but she knew that she could not interrupt the Song at its height. Doing so might destroy the man's very essence.

So she waited as the Song raged around her, brutal and terrible. It scorched her skin and made her wish for the simplicity of the Songs she had first learned.

After the final notes boomed through the Woods, the Forest Witch climbed carefully down from her perch. She wrapped her arms around Lintem and shook.

Why would he do that to himself? she asked the nightcat.

Lintem licked her and rested his large head against her. *I don't know.*

An eerie quiet settled over the glen. The creatures of the Woods retreated to their homes, their calls and chitters muted. The trees leaned toward each other, seeking comfort in proximity. Each of them had been an elf or human once, known the trials of life and the jubilations of success. They all still had complete souls. Marred and scarred, trapped within grey bark, but complete souls nonetheless. None of them could imagine the horrific agony of shredding one's own being.

When her legs were steady beneath her, the Forest Witch stood and strode through the glen. The fire beckoned to her, remembering the Song she had learned from it. She did not waver. When she came to the shelter, she hesitated for only a moment before going inside.

The Witches will know why this was done.

For the first time since they had sent her away, the Forest Witch stood in front of Una, Dona, and Tresa. The shortest Witch, Tresa, caressed the unconscious man's hair with a soothing touch. Dona, the one neither tall nor short, tidied up a strange contraption, while the tallest, Una, prepared a sleeping mat for their visitor. All of them continued their work, though their eyes were all fixed on the Forest Witch.

"You listened to the Song of Unmaking," Una said, a storm in her eyes.

The Forest Witch nodded. "I have heard strains of it before. I never thought it would be so frightening."

"It is good to be frightened," said Dona. The ground quaked at her voice.

"The Song of Unmaking has toppled kingdoms and

destroyed forests," said Tresa, the strength of wind in her words. "It is not to be used lightly."

"Why use it at all?" asked the Forest Witch. She regarded the sleeping man. "Why on him?"

"Because you were listening," said Una.

"Because you are learning," said Dona.

"Because you will use it yourself," said Tresa.

Lintem growled, his ears flat, teeth bared. The Forest Witch calmed him with a touch and a soothing Song. Somewhere in the recesses of her mind, she recalled the last time she had spoken with the Witches. She had been so young then, so naïve and thoughtless. When they spoke in riddles, she had been frustrated.

How much I have changed. Instead of railing against them, she tuned her ears to their Songs. Truth resounded in their music, harsh and bright, yet not cruel. The Witches did what they must for the Woods and the Songs. In their music came mutual recognition.

Yet as she explored the Songs of these three powerful women, the Forest Witch perceived a slight difference in their melodies compared to hers or the man's. Both she and the sleeping monster-turned-man had lived far past their normal lifespans, yet these Witches had existed for eons. With a jolt, the Forest Witch saw that the Witches' Songs did not simply harmonize with the rest of the melodies; the Witches *were* the Songs, magic brought to corporeal life. Una's soul was that of Nature, Dona's of Humanity, and Tresa's of Death.

"You're not mere sorceresses," the Forest Witch said.

"No," Una agreed. "We were born with the Songs, our roots as deep as Earda's."

They are Cythra, just like Autorus, the Forest Witch realized. *Forgotten by man, tucked away in the Woods where their worshippers can no longer find them.*

"Are you afraid?" Dona asked.

The Forest Witch shook her head. "Why should I fear truth?"

"Good," said Tresa. "You have come far indeed."

"Yet you have forgotten your humanity," said Dona. "You have lost yourself in the Woods."

That cavernous hole within her yawned open, desperate to draw her into her grief. The Forest Witch gripped Lintem's fur and quelled that ineradicable memory.

Dona took the Forest Witch's face in her hands. "You are not yet prepared to face yourself, dear child. The memories will come when you are ready."

A cool sensation washed over the Forest Witch, freezing that entrenched part of her so that it would not rise again. The Forest Witch nodded her gratitude and said, "I helped one of the trees. He was terrified."

"That is good." Dona took her hand and led her to the sleeping man. "This is Alexandro Strilu. He was *fampir*, and you gave him entrance to the Woods. You allowed his deepest desire to be fulfilled."

Strilu. The name rattled the Forest Witch's mind, thoughts exploding into her of a faraway palace with green gardens and glowing lanterns.

"Reach into his Songs. Find the music which has been lost to you." Dona slipped away, and all three Witches disappeared from the hut.

The Forest Witch knelt beside Alexandro, her hands sweating. She knew that she would not expose the memories embedded at her very core, but what would she find? Would it make her heart yearn even more for Earda?

In her youth, the Forest Witch may have turned away. Now, she laid a hand to the man's forehead and listened to his Song.

He is young and brash and clever. He loves books and knowledge, and misses his brother Verdon, a fellow scholar. He has fallen in love with a woman born of both fampir *and mortal, and given up his gifts in order to prove his worth.*

The Forest Witch paused, her soul already thrumming with the Songs that reverberated through this man's every humor. The Songs of Curiosity and Knowledge, the Songs of Love and Longing, the Songs of Death and Life, a hurricane of music and emotion that threatened to drown her.

Her own memories welled inside her, echoing Alex's Songs. Remembrances of a childhood with a beloved tutor, and the research into magic that made her feel alive. A longing for friendship and acceptance when spurned by a petty queen. Death...but those thoughts were frozen now, out of her reach, and she thanked Dona for her kindness.

The Song of Love intrigued her the most. She loved Lintem with every fiber of her being, yet now she remembered an encompassing love that fulfilled her physically, spiritually, emotionally. An echo of her own Song flitted against Alex's, calling to her.

Without questioning herself, the Forest Witch dove into the Songs, seeking out that remnant that only briefly connected with Alex's. His Song of Love connected to a woman, but there was another – a brother, she realized – who had spoken with him about a deep love. A love for her.

Through a hazy view, she saw the man to whom the connecting Song belonged. He was tall and proud, his dark hair slicked back, his blue eyes piercing and achingly sad. His form blurred and wavered, seen only through a Song within a Song. The Forest Witch scrutinized him, searching for his name.

It came to her suddenly, a beautiful name that thudded into her: Druam.

My husband. I remember gentle kisses and purity lost in heat and watching eyes on our wedding night. I remember the gardens we walked together and the ecstasy of a stolen night in a rowdy tavern.

The Songs pulled her back into herself, the image of Druam lost. The Forest Witch wiped her eyes. She hummed to Lintem, *I loved him with every breath. But my magic there was hollow, without music. He was a cage around me. He kept me from the Woods.*

Lintem gently licked her hand. *You are allowed to miss him.*

I know. The Forest Witch took a calming breath, then another. She brushed Alex's hair from his face. *I'm glad I helped Druam's brother.*

She could not stay for much longer in that bittersweet place. Much of her was still locked away, but her Song sighed with the new music that churned within her. The Forest Witch was slowly regaining her humanity, yet she wasn't quite ready to let go of the Woods.

Birds and blue skies filled her dreams that night, and she woke with an ache for Earda that could not be suppressed.

CHAPTER TWENTY-EIGHT
Sandu

Every movement took gargantuan effort. With all his strength, Sandu reached out and gripped Jagger's hand. His lips moved, but nothing came out.

The pain he expected had not come. Cold gripped him with an iron touch. He barely noticed the pustules on his skin through the deathly chill that pervaded every thought. Vaguely, he wondered if Tambrey had been so cold.

"Sandu." Darian's face drifted into his sight. It wavered in and out of focus. "The time has come."

I'm dying, Sandu realized. He tried to look at Jagger's face, but his vision blurred. Everything faded around him, and the world went black.

✳

"Don't scream," came a honeyed voice. It was low and sweet, a mother's voice.

Sandu lay still, blissfully at peace. The sun warmed his skin, and a smooth hand brushed his hair from his face. He thought he should be cold, remembering his illness. With his eyes still closed, he asked, "Am I dead?"

"No, dear one," the woman said. "But you are close to it."

"Why don't I feel cold?"

"Because you're dreaming."

"Oh." If this were a dream, Sandu could enjoy it. He basked

in the warm rays, soothed by the woman's gentle touch. At last, he opened his eyes, expecting to see Tambrey above him.

The woman wasn't Tambrey, nor any person he had ever met. She had dark, unruly hair that tumbled to her waist, and held centuries in her gaze. Her feet were bare in the grass. Grass, to Sandu's surprise, that was red.

He carefully sat up. The meadow in which he lay was full of the long, waving strands of oddly colored grass. Here and there, boulders dotted the landscape. As Sandu peered closer, he realized that the boulders were actually trees in the shape of rocks, their branches rounding to the earth. In the sky, birds with gemstone wings wheeled on a breeze. A breeze carried music, soft and unearthly, the most beautiful sound Sandu had ever heard.

"Listen," the woman said. "You recognize the Song?"

"Song?"

"Hush and listen."

Sandu obeyed. He closed his eyes, letting the silvery music drift through his ears. It was unintelligible to him, nice but no more. He wrinkled his nose in consternation. "I don't understand it."

"You will when it's time."

"Is it my time?" Tears pricked Sandu's eyes. *I thought I'd become a better man. I never did.*

The woman spoke, "You were not a terrible man."

"I broke Tambrey's heart," Sandu said. "I abandoned the children, and people died because of me. Da wasted years in prison. I should have done better."

"Yes," the woman said gravely. "And you still can."

"I'm dying," Sandu said. "There's no more chances for me. I doubt Darian would bring me back."

"You're right about that. Darian can only do so much, and Jagger is the man he chose to resurrect at great cost to the Songs. He has never done it before, and will never do it again."

"Will I be able to go to Lyael?"

"You have a choice before you," the woman replied. "I believe I can help you make it."

"What–" he started, but words failed him.

There, running across the red grass, were his children. They had grown so much since last he saw them years ago. Their golden hair – just like their mother's – flowed behind them, their smiles brighter than the sun. They held hands as they raced across the meadow, laughing with that pure innocence only found in the very young.

Sandu couldn't move. He sat frozen with overwhelming joy and shame. Eaton and Elvy were just as he had imagined they would grow to be.

"They're six now," he whispered to the woman.

"Yes."

"Can I...?"

The woman nodded. With unsure feet, Sandu moved toward his children. They had clambered on a tree-boulder and giggled together as they played. As Sandu grew closer, they quieted. They watched him with a child's curiosity.

"Who are you?" Eaton asked. His boyish curls bounced around his round cheeks. Elvy clung to his hand, her blue eyes shy.

"I–" Sandu didn't know how to respond. He had left so long ago. Would they even remember him?

Does it matter? This is only a dream.

"I'm your Da," he managed. How he longed to sweep them up into his arms, feel their tiny fingers grip him in a hug, hear their laughter ringing in his ear.

"I don't remember you," Eaton said. "And Mumma said our real Da died."

Sandu's throat closed over his words. Tambrey hadn't lied, not exactly. The man who was their father *had* died, in a way, when he willingly abandoned them for his vices. After a moment, he said, "It won't be long until I really am dead."

"Da?" Elvy's small voice piped. Sandu's knees weakened. He had only ever dreamed of hearing their voices again. *In this dream, all things are possible.*

"It's me, lovey," he said. "My Elva-loo."

Though her brother held back, Elvy jumped from the tree

and into Sandu's waiting arms. He clutched her, kissing her cheeks and the top of her head, feeling as if he might crumble from joy. After a minute, Eaton followed his sister. Both children wriggled in his arms and asked a million questions without ever waiting for an answer.

"Are you going to stay here with us?" Eaton asked.

"I'm afraid I must wake up sometime," Sandu said.

Elvy shook her head. "We eat and sleep here."

Sandu didn't quite know what to make of that. Ultimately, he decided it didn't matter. He cooed and laughed with the children until the sun dipped below the trees.

As night grew on, another woman came into the meadow. She, too, was barefooted. Though Sandu protested, she gathered the children into her arms.

"I haven't had enough time!" Sandu said. "Let me spend one more candle with them."

"If you choose to live, you will find them again," the red-haired woman said.

The dark-haired woman took Sandu's hand. "They are safe here with us."

"But this is only a dream."

"For you."

Sandu pulled away, consternation growing in his heart. He shouted at the woman who held his children, "Eaton! Elvy! Bring them back!"

"You will see them again when you find the sorceress of Songs."

Then pain, such as he had never experienced, flared through his whole body. Fire consumed him. He screamed.

✳

Darian's face flitted in and out of view. Sandu saw him, then the meadow, then Jagger, all flashing in and out as darkness and bright light warred in his head. Sandu screamed again, his throat raw. His limbs were too heavy to move.

His blood was on fire, he was sure of it. The chill that had descended on him retreated, but he panted from the torment of the fire chasing it out. The pustules popped on his skin, pus oozing out with flaming heat. Desperately, Sandu sought Jagger's face.

Red fire took over his vision. All he saw were flames as heat tortured his body. It grew too much for him to bear. He shut his eyes.

At last, cool water doused him. The flames retreated, leaving his skin damp.

Sandu opened his eyes. He blinked once, confused.

He wasn't in the camp with Jagger and Darian. A different fire crackled in the stones, and the sky held no stars. Across the flames, he saw Mumma and Nan seated on comfortable logs. Though he had no recollection of standing, he was on his feet.

"Foolish child," Nan said. She raised her switch. "I told you not to come back until you're old and grey!"

"Barty, you must turn back," Mumma urged. True fear tainted her words. "Go back before it's too late!"

Sandu wavered. He longed to sit down, just to rest for a moment. His body ached, his skin remembering the chill and the fire.

"If you sit down, you won't stand up ever again," warned Nan. "You still have to take care of those children of yours!"

"Frederick will raise them," Sandu said vaguely. His legs threatened to give out from under him. *Just a moment's rest. That's all I need.*

"They've gone where he can't follow," Mumma pleaded. "You have to go back, Barty."

In the distance, carried on the wind, Sandu heard Darian's voice, "Hold on, Sandu. It's almost over. Just hold on."

Sandu's knees buckled. He moved to sit–

Nan's switch whipped through the air. It struck him, and he leapt up.

"No you don't!" she said. In that moment, Sandu feared her fury more than returning to the fire.

Darian's voice had grown fainter. "His heart is slowing. Jagger, help me!"

A phantom hand latched onto Sandu's. He saw nothing, but he could *feel* the calluses on Jagger's fingers, the stumps where his pinkies should be. The hand gripped him hard, squeezing with all the strength it had.

"Go back," Mumma pleaded. "Please, Barty. I'm not ready for you to join us yet."

Her pleas tore at Sandu's apathy. He straightened his back, determined not to let go of the phantom hand. He said to his mother, "I wish I could stay."

"I know, lovey. I wish it, too, but it's not time."

Nan huffed. "We'd better not see you a third time, not until you've grown older than me."

"I'll try."

As Sandu spoke, he heard Darian's voice again, stronger still. He turned his face into the wind and shut his eyes.

✳

The phantom hand held on, even into the blackness of Sandu's unconsciousness. He clung to it, a lifeline in a dark river. He felt as if he would drown, but the hand pulled him, up and up, until he no longer gasped for air.

When Sandu emerged, he opened his eyes. His limbs were sore from the lingering fire. Slowly, Sandu wiggled his fingers and toes. Everything right there, except he couldn't feel his left arm. He looked down at it, but there was nothing there.

Am I on top of it? Sandu tried to shift, but he could barely move. His vision focused on the faces above him, pale faces filled with concern.

Darian put a hand to Sandu's chest. "Easy, now. Take it gently."

Jagger took Sandu's right hand and held it in his lap. He signed, *You survived.*

"I dreamt of a meadow," Sandu said. His voice was raw. "And my children. I saw Mumma, and Nan, same as when–"

"When you almost died after the Masque," Darian said gravely. "Twice now you've nearly crossed into death. It was a close thing."

"It was my choice," Sandu mumbled. "I could go back."

"Few are offered such a choice. If your soul had given in, there would be nothing I could do to arrest it."

Jagger signed, *I'm glad you're awake.*

Sandu remembered the thing that had worried him. He looked again where his arm should be. He noticed a bandage on his shoulder covering a strange knobby thing. "My arm..."

"A sacrifice had to be made to burn out the disease," Darian said. "I had to isolate every bit of the plague in one part of your body and reduce it to ashes so it would never return."

"It's...gone?" Sandu had trouble understanding what Darian meant. He tried to lift his left arm, but the knob only wiggled a little. He stared at Jagger, denying the evidence of his eyes. "Where'd it go? I want it back!"

"There is nothing left of your arm," Darian said patiently.

Jagger signed, *I felt the same after I lost my pinkies. Kept trying to use them.*

Sandu didn't want to believe them. "But I'll still be able to...to..."

Reality crashed in on him. He stared morosely at the space where his arm should have been and watched the stump as he moved his shoulder. Even though his eyes told him it was true, he wished that he were dreaming.

"I'm sorry, my friend." Darian laid a hand to the stump. He whispered a spell, and a numbness crept over Sandu's shoulder. "This will help ease the pain until it heals."

Sandu stared at the stump. At last, he tore his eyes away and assessed the rest of his body. The pustules had gone, leaving small round scars in their place. Nothing else remained of the plague.

"Can I still spread it?" Sandu asked softly.

"No. It is gone entirely."

"Good." Sandu turned his head away from the others and let himself cry. After everything, the dreams and the near-death, he should have been relieved at being alive. Instead, he grieved the loss of his arm. He thought of the dream in the meadow, and the tears came faster, leaving salty tracks down his cheeks.

Now I can't ever hold both my children at once.

✷

Cara came back with the dawn. Sandu had slept deeply through the night, exhausted by his ordeal, but he woke as soon as the sun's tendrils touched the gray sky. He rolled over, oddly light without his left arm, and saw her.

She stood at the edge of camp, her pack strapped to her shoulders, her eyes fixed on the stump of his arm. When she saw that he was awake, she walked slowly toward him. Sandu said nothing.

She can't claim the worse injury now, he thought.

Cara sat heavily beside him. Tentatively, she reached out to touch him. He nodded, and she laid a hand to his shoulder. For a moment, they sat in silence.

"I'm sorry," Cara said at last. "I should have stayed with you."

"Unless Darian would have taken your arm instead, I don't think there's much you could have done." Sandu surprised himself with the dry humor. He laughed a little. "You were right to stay away."

Cara shook her head. "Gods, what a terrible thing. Sandu, I'm so sorry."

"Nothing you could have done," Sandu repeated.

"That's not true," Cara said. "Sandu, I thought you would die last night. Do you understand that? And it wasn't the same as the Masque. At least there, if you'd died, I'd know I'd been a good friend. That I'd tried to save you. But this...I didn't sleep at all for guilt. Your wife died, and what did I do? Act like a self-righteous jackass. You needed me, and I've avoided you."

"Cara–"

"You *could have died*," Cara said. She seemed the same as she had when she'd lost Merick, the scared little girl who didn't know what to do with all her emotions. "I'm sorry, Sandu. I've behaved horribly to you. And it's because I'm afraid of what I might do to you."

"I don't–"

"I thought if I avoided you I'd keep you safe. I've only made things worse."

Her apology comforted him, but her self-pity irritated him. Sandu pushed her hand away. "Yeah. You've been a right bastard. I forgive you, just stop making this about you, alright? Can you just listen for a bit?"

Cara bit her lip and nodded. Sandu slowly sat up. His bones ached, his muscles throbbed. The many round scars on his skin made him ashamed to look at himself.

"You know why my Da's in prison," Sandu started. "And you know why Tambrey threw me out. But let me tell you what you *don't* know. When Darian says we can go, you'll help me find my children and release my Da. No matter if Laris comes back. No matter the things you're doing that you're too afraid to tell me. Understood?"

Cara nodded again.

"Right." Sandu took a deep breath. He started, "Ever since I was trapped in that dungeon, I've had these...waking nightmares."

For a long time, as the sun rose and Darian and Jagger prepared their camp for travel, Sandu talked. A great plug had been loosened in his heart, and now he let it pour out: the dreams, the waking nightmares, Tambrey's death.

No more hiding.

CHAPTER TWENTY-NINE
Cara

Before she found Sandu alive, if forever changed, Cara had been hiding in the forest. The first few nights in the Valadi caravan had passed relatively peacefully. She avoided the eyes of the matrons and spoke little to the uncles of the tribe. The beast's thirst whispered in her ear of the delights of their blood. She resisted, but only through desperate will. The wax she stuffed nightly in her ears blocked little of the lust.

It grew too great to bear when Jagger led a mob from the camp. A mouse darted across Cara's foot, and she grabbed it before she knew what she was doing. Its blood was in her mouth, pure and perfect.

What am I doing? Cara threw the mouse away and quickly wiped her lips. She glanced about, but no one had seen. All the Valadi had retreated into their wagons when the hunt for Jagger began.

Yet the blood-song pounded through her veins. The beast called for more. Her leg twitched, close to whole, but not quite there. *I can't stay here any longer.* Cara hurriedly packed her blankets and rushed from the camp. Heartbeats of sleeping people sounded like waves on the shore, persistent in their tug. Cara clamped her hands over her ears and pushed onward until only trees enveloped her.

Silence at last. Cara leaned against a trunk, her pulse rushing in her neck. *Too close.* She shut her eyes. *I have to keep control.*

The beast roared through her blood. It demanded its thirst be satisfied.

Cara weakened. She, too, wanted the power that rushed under her skin, the feeling of being more alive than she'd ever been. With a shudder, she allowed the beast in. Her eyes sharpened, the night forest clear around her. Her nails grew into talons.

From behind, she heard again the heartbeats of the rustics. *Innocents*, she thought. With great effort, she turned her attention to the forest. *We cannot kill innocents.* Though the beast urged her back to the wagons, Cara loped deeper into the forest. She hunted now for greater prey than rabbits or birds or even the fawn. She wanted something stronger. Moonlight cast shadows over the still trees. Birds winged silently overhead, mice ducked into holes to hide. Somewhere, deep in the forest at the foot of the hills, Cara could smell something large. Something fierce. Its musky scent pervaded the trees, its grunts loud in the air.

Cara stopped suddenly. The creature was close. It snuffled through the underbrush, moving nearer to her. With catlike grace, Cara climbed into the lower branches of a tree and stowed her pack until the hunt was over. She crouched there, watching and waiting.

Soon enough, a boar trundled through the trees. Its large humped back swayed as it searched for food. Its tusks gleamed. Cara tracked its movements, her veins singing for blood but her wisdom holding her back. Many a hunter had been killed by a wild boar. Most who were successful in bringing one down had men with spears and dogs to harry the creature. This was a powerful foe indeed.

Yet what delight its blood would bring! The beast purred, its nighttime eyes eager on its prey. It, too, knew to be cautious. If Cara wanted to survive the encounter, she and the beast would have to be intelligent. *We must slow time if we want to win.*

Even with that power at her call, Cara waited for the boar to draw closer. A thrill rushed through her at the thought of slaughtering such a creature. *Caution, caution.* A lucky slice could sever her skin, and she would not walk away alive.

When the boar came under her tree, Cara leapt. As she fell, the beast beating through her body, the world slowed. The boar moved at a snail's pace, its piggy eyes swiveling up to see her. Cara dropped onto its back. With one hand, she pulled at the creature's head. With the other, she reached around to its throat.

A scream sounded through the woods, the cry of a man in such intense pain that even the beast stopped short. In their time-sedated world, the scream sounded for what felt like many minutes though it truly lasted mere seconds. Cara halted with her claw by the boar's throat.

She knew that voice which screamed with such agony. *Sandu!*

In her distraction, the boar bucked wildly. It threw her off and turned more swiftly than she could have imagined. Time jarred back to normal. Desperately, Cara scooted away from the boar's seeking tusks. Its small eyes shone red with fury. It squealed and grunted, shoving its head back and forth.

One of its tusks grazed her leg. The cut was not deep, but blood spilled from it. The boar charged at her. No matter her beast's speed, Cara only just escaped another strike. She rolled into the brush, cursing her mistake.

Prowlers would not seek prey too strong for them. In her arrogance, Cara had assumed she could destroy anything in her path. She smiled grimly. It was a mistake she wouldn't make again.

The boar wheeled and charged again. With a great leap, Cara caught hold of a branch above her head. It took all the beast's strength to haul herself up out of the path of danger. She lay on the branch, panting, as the boar grunted below her. The beast, though its bloodlust was not satiated, didn't protest when Cara gave up the fight. She watched the boar warily. It sniffed at the base of the tree and struck out with its tusks at the brush.

After a time, it tired of its search. It trotted away, disappearing into the darkness.

Cara leaned against the trunk of the tree. The cut in her leg throbbed. She tore a strip from her tunic and wrapped it around the oozing wound. After awhile, the bleeding stopped. *Lucky.* If she had been just a bit slower the boar would have killed her.

*And Sandu...*Guilt clogged her throat. He could already be dead. Instead of staying by his side, she'd been galavanting through the forest after a creature she had no right to hunt.

No more blood, she told herself. *The leg which Laris injured is whole enough to walk on, if still a bit weak. Darian can bandage this cut.*

The blind man was right. Blood was a gift but also a curse. It only caused her strife. Cara pushed the beast back into her stomach, building up the walls she had neglected.

After retrieving her pack, she slowly walked through the forest, following the glow of a fire on a distant hill. She could only hope that Sandu would still be alive.

✳

"We have to get to D'Clet," Sandu said stubbornly. He kept crossing his arm over his chest, but the movement always brought a frown. He turned to Cara. "I feel fine."

"It's only been a day," Cara said. "We can rest awhile longer." Since her return, she'd barely left Sandu's side. She brought his food, helped him dress, and took over his small tasks. She even started to learn the curious hand language Jagger used, if only to communicate with him about Sandu's wellbeing.

It was evening the day after Sandu's recovery. Darian murmured chants over a vial to prepare healing ointments while Jagger and Cara made supper. Sandu sat irritably nearby.

"You're doing it wrong," Sandu said. "Here, let me do the cooking."

Cara tried to wave him off. "Rest, Sandu. You–"

"First you pretend I don't exist, and now you treat me like an invalid!" Sandu pushed himself between her and Jagger. "I can still use one arm. Let me help with the chores."

At first, Cara wanted to insist that he rest. She stood back at the look in his eyes. Sandu had always been helpful in camp:

cooking, mending, gathering firewood. *It must be awful to feel useless.*

Deep in her belly, the beast howled against the walls she'd built. It raged and tore at her insides, desperate to be released. It heard the pulse in Sandu's neck and wailed at how she was letting such easy prey go. Cara grimaced and held it down.

Sandu stirred the pot and said again, "If it snows, the passes will be shut for months. We have to go now, while we can still get over them."

And because you have to find your children. Sandu had said that Bluston, a town about five days from D'Clet, would be the first place to search. He'd told her everything. His story had solidified her guilt, creating an encompassing shame in her.

Laris hurt me, but so many others have hurt Sandu. She couldn't imagine the terror of his waking nightmares, nor did she know how to stop them. At the least she could put aside her own selfishness and help him find what remained of his family. *And Laris hasn't returned. Maybe he'll be gone forever now, content with what he stole from me.*

Though all of them tried to convince him otherwise, Sandu still insisted that he was ready to travel. At last, as she cleaned the pans from supper, Cara said to Darian and Jagger, "Sandu won't get better by staying here. He needs to move. I understand that. Each day that I drew closer to Renna, I felt better. He's the same way. I say we pack up tomorrow."

It took more arguing until at last even Jagger gave in.

Over the next few days, they reached the mountains proper. They climbed slowly up the foothills. Cara and Jagger took turns walking with Sandu, there to support him in case he slipped on the rocky terrain. He still wavered now and then, off-balance without his arm.

Their travel was slow. Darian also needed help to navigate the rough trail, and Sandu needed to rest often. Sometimes his waking nightmares forced them to stop until the panic receded. Cara shouldered his pack without complaint, and tried to help him when his eyes saw things that weren't there.

The higher they climbed, the harsher the winds that blew

over the road. Trees grew short and stunted, and there were often no good places to make camp. At first, they tried using both tents, but the chill at night proved too much. They started sleeping altogether in one tent, huddling for warmth. Their fires blew out unless they were constantly tended.

Every night, with Sandu's heartbeat thundering in her ears, Cara had to force the beast behind her crumbling walls. She slept with Darian and Jagger separating her and her friend, and still she drowned under the weight of temptation. She didn't know why the other two held no desire for her, but she was grateful for the small respite.

They finally crested the pass and started down the other side. As they came into the foothills, Darian said to Cara, "I am proud of you."

"For what?" Cara grumbled. Her legs throbbed after the steep climb. Both were adequately healed by now, but every once in a while the congealed cut stung. The beast had been particularly vicious the night before, and Cara had had little sleep.

"You've stopped drinking." His voice was pitched low so that Jagger and Sandu, who hiked ahead of them, couldn't hear it. "The beast howls, but you resist."

"Is that all?" Cara didn't think it a great accomplishment to not be slaughtering her way over the mountains.

"It's a greater deed than you think. Other *sulpari* were not so strong."

That made her pause. "Other *sulpari*? What do you know of them?"

"They lived a long, long time ago. Some years after the Dead's War." Darian used his cane to stop himself sliding down the rocky path. "You are the fifth ever born. Three gave into their beast and had to be killed before they became worse than the *fampir*. One helped Valder Riesk to stop the tide of undead from sweeping over the land."

"In the Ossuary."

"Yes. She gave her life for it."

Cara walked a few paces in silence, thinking over his

words. *Four others like me, but most gave into their beasts. What did the last one do to resist?* She asked, "How did the fourth, the one who helped Valder, reconcile the beast and herself?"

"She heard her Song," Darian said. "Not only listened to it, but understood it and her beast."

"I don't understand."

"Think of your beast as a dog. Some are vicious creatures who listen to no one. Some appear tame, but when given the opportunity rip out their master's throat. Others are perfectly loyal and obedient. They can read their master's intentions and act with blinding love. The third is what you should strive for with your beast."

"Then tell me how to hear my Song."

Darian smiled at her. "We shall start tonight."

As they set up their camp, relieved to be out of the harsh winds and not far from Bluston, a storm cloud gathered. It was a strange storm, moving against the wind, with flashes of lightning that struck down with rhythmic regularity. Jagger watched the storm with a frown. Cara turned her gaze toward it, too.

"What is it?" she asked.

Darian's easy smile turned to a frown. He said, "I'm afraid that your sorcerer has returned."

The storm moved closer. Lightning struck the ground at the edge of their camp with a horrid, crashing noise. The light blinded them.

When their ears and eyes cleared, Laris Stanthorpe stood among them.

CHAPTER THIRTY
Seanna

Seanna entered the throne room uneasily. She had avoided entering it since Henrik's assassination, preferring to conduct business in the council rooms instead. Yet Aremo awaited her, and she must not show weakness. She entered with her head high, as if she always had mud on her shoes and grime on her hem. Belrose stayed just behind her, a steadying presence.

Aremo stood in front of the throne, his back to her. He placed one slender hand on the arm of the chair. "Empty without your husband to fill it, isn't it?"

Grief roiled again inside her, but she suppressed it. Seanna smiled, playing the gracious host. *No matter what he says, I will be courteous. That is my shield against his wiles.* "Would you like to sit and speak, *Kair*? We have wine and food; I'm sure your journey has been long."

"Thank you." He followed her to an attached room and sat with a flourish at the table. She seated herself across from him and did not reach for the wine. She watched him warily, all too aware of their last two meetings. *He would have me at his mercy were it not for the Corsair Queen,* she thought. *He must know it, too.*

Aremo bit into a pear, the juices squirting out the sides of his mouth. He regarded her with amusement. "We could be having such fun now, you and I, were it not for that bitch's interference."

"She left your ships unhindered, did she not?" Seanna asked.

"Indeed. Yet she betrayed me and gave you back to the king far too early." His black eyes narrowed. "When I've conquered this city, I shall raze her ships, burn her city, and take her as a whore."

She'd die first. Aloud, Seanna said, "You do speak with confidence. But I must ask why you are here, *Kair.* Surely you have other priorities?"

Aremo ignored her. He leaned back, eyes drifting over the room. When he focused on her again, he asked, "What was it like when Henrik died? I heard his head shattered on the throne, though I must say your servants did an exceptional job of cleaning it up."

Seanna blinked back sudden tears and smiled despite the ire in her chest. "He died nobly, as a king should."

"What of your brother, hm? His head made a pretty decoration for Brin's walls. Though we found your mother dead, we cut off hers, too, and made them a pair atop the spikes. Last I saw, the crows were pecking out their eyes. The most tender part, you know." Aremo watched her, and she knew he waited to see her break.

Seanna glanced at Belrose and took a steadying breath. *Don't let him provoke you,* she told herself. *Don't let him win this battle.*

"You have invaded our lands and slaughtered our people, Aremo," she said quietly. "I cannot say that your words don't bring me pain. I have welcomed you into my home, given you food and drink. You will repay my kindness while surrounded by my soldiers, else I will have no qualms taking you hostage."

His fingers, which had been tapping the table, stilled. "You dare to threaten me when my armies are so close?"

"Close, yet not quite here. I'd imagine we could do many things to you before your elves march over the horizon." Seanna raised her brows. "If you continue to goad me, I will react in kind. We aren't in the corsair court or Cascade Palace anymore, where you had power while I had none. We are in the ancestral home of my husband the king, and I won't abide your indiscretions. Tell me why you came or leave."

"So the cat has claws," Aremo purred. He appeared almost pleased at her words. "Very well. I came to tell you to surrender. You are outnumbered and will be surrounded within a quinn."

"Have you not an ambassador to negotiate terms?" Seanna asked. She tutted, "I may be a woman, but my father versed me in the affairs of war. It is not for you, the commander of the army, to come by yourself. Send an ambassador, and we shall see if surrender can be negotiated."

"What if I am the ambassador?"

"Then your army is doomed indeed." Seanna made to rise, but Aremo shook his head.

"Very well," he said, and she resumed her seat. He continued, "I will send the Lofaliri ambassador to you as soon as they arrive."

"Excellent." Seanna took a piece of sweetbread. "If that's all?"

"You're going to die, Seanna," Aremo said, all playfulness gone. "You and everyone in this city. As much as I may dislike you personally, I hold no offense over the rustics of this country. They should not pay the price for your pride."

"Why are you here, Aremo?" Seanna asked. "Why bring your armies to invade our lands? What purpose does it serve?"

He contemplated a moment, his black eyes unreadable. At last, he said, "Your ancestors enslaved my kind, forcing us from our home and over the sea. For too long, we bent our backs as your laborers and farmers, your washerwomen and servants."

"You were freed centuries ago, when King Mather allowed you to make Dedaria your own. Elves may live some decades longer than men, but none alive today remember your slavery."

"True. Yet the lands granted us have grown infertile and hostile. We need resources to survive."

"Why not bargain and trade for them? Surely a war–"

"My ally is a religious zealot," Aremo said, speaking over her. "He wants all the world to worship Amnah. And I want power. I want Dotschar – all of it – to rule over. As I said, I hold no ill will to your rustics. They will tend the lands if they are mine as well as they tend them now."

"Religion and power," Seanna murmured. "The most ancient of bedmates. If your ally is so fervent in his beliefs, might not his religion undermine the power you may have gained? Even our king has had to balance the Exalt's wishes, and weaker kings in the past have been ruled by the novums."

Aremo tilted his head, perhaps thinking on her words. Then he smiled. A cunning, ruthless smile. "Rest assured, Seanna, once I have my kingdom, I will not abide the temples to run amuck. You need not fear for a future you will never see."

Seanna bowed her head and stood. *I was never going to convince him, anyway.* She gestured to the door. "You will be escorted to the gates. Tell the Lofaliri Ambassador that we will hold negotiations in the Grand Novum once he has arrived."

Before either could step out of the antechamber, Udolf barged inside. He held his longsword in one hand, armor strapped to his chest. Seanna commanded, "Step aside, Udolf. This elf has come peacefully and will depart thus."

"I will not," Udolf said, sparing only a withering glance for Seanna before turning his attention to Aremo. "I issue a challenge to the pointy-eared bastard. If he loses, his armies turn around and go home."

"And you'll surrender if I win?" Aremo scoffed. "I doubt the Queen Regent will allow such a course."

"Stand aside, Udolf," Seanna said. "Don't act the idiot."

Udolf shouted and ran at the elf. Aremo stood still until the last moment, then moved aside and punched Udolf's sword arm. The prince dropped his weapon. Still running headlong, Udolf smashed into the table and fell to the floor, winded. Aremo looked to Seanna. "I see this as an act of aggression against a peaceful envoy."

"You're already marching on the city, Aremo," Seanna said as Udolf groaned. "Send your ambassador, as we agreed. The boy is rash and does not speak for the crown."

Aremo hesitated, as if he wished to say more. He nodded and departed, escorted by four soldiers. Seanna released her breath and said to her nephew, "You foolish brat! You know what you have done?"

"You weak woman!" Udolf spat, regaining his feet. "I did only what Henrik would–"

"Henrik is dead," Seanna said coldly. "What he may or may not have done is irrelevant. I am your Queen Regent, and if you defy me again, I *will* have you imprisoned as a traitor. Do you understand me?"

Udolf glared from Seanna to Belrose, cursed, and left the room, his sword forgotten on the floor. Seanna sighed and asked, "Should I keep him under house arrest?"

Belrose said, "He's not your only concern." He pointed out the door to the throne room where an assortment of nobles had gathered. As Seanna entered, they frowned and turned away.

"What is this?" Seanna asked, coming to stand in front of the throne. Most of the nobles didn't meet her eye, but one man, Lord Neverly, stood forward.

"We support Udolf as our sovereign," he announced to a murmur of approval. "We'll not have our homes requisitioned and our food divided to care for the rustics."

Seanna cast an eye over the crowd of at least twenty nobles. She would have to think quickly. She took a breath and said, "King Henrik, the gods rest his soul, did not want Udolf to take the throne. It matters not whether I birth a boy or a girl; my child will wear the crown. If you continue to support my treasonous nephew, all your lands and titles shall be revoked. You will be marked a traitor to the crown and executed forthwith." She nodded to Belrose, who called for the royal guard. Within minutes, the nobles were surrounded by a force of armed men.

"What is your choice?" Seanna asked the crowd.

They glanced at each other, shifting their feet and whispering. Lord Neverly didn't stand down. He said, "What proof do we have of the king's wishes? The word of his whore wife?"

Belrose cleared his throat. "I am a witness to the king's commands, and have already made preparations with the magistrates should the Queen Regent bear a female child."

The other men murmured. Belrose was a respected mage

and lord; most of them would not defy him. After a moment, one man stepped forward. "I swear fealty to the Queen Regent."

Another gave in, then another, until only Lord Neverly remained. Seanna met his eye, waiting. He widened his stance, his hand dropping to his sword.

"I recognize Udolf as king," Neverly said. His eyes hardened. "Not some Eadron bitch with a bastard in her belly."

The guards tightened their circle, expectant. Belrose waited for Seanna's command.

Show no mercy, else they will force you from the throne.

"Arrest Lord Neverly," Seanna said.

The lord nearly drew his sword, but thought better of it. He surrendered, his harsh gaze sending shivers down Seanna's spine. The courtiers muttered, but did not object. They trickled out of the throne room, some throwing loathing looks at her. Seanna did not back down, and waited until the room was clear before she let her shoulders slump.

"Would they behave that way if Henrik were still alive?" she asked Belrose as he walked her back to her rooms.

"I cannot say, Madam. But they're afraid, and rightfully so. Who knows what harm a siege will bring to all in the city?"

"Mm. I do see your point," Seanna said. "Did I make the right decision?"

"The lords have never had to bow to a woman on the king's throne. Neverly is one of many who resent you. I will ask the captain of the guard to set a stronger watch around you. We don't want Udolf and his allies to have any opportunities against you."

Seanna sighed. *That boy will be the death of me.* She sank gratefully onto a chaise lounge, rubbing her belly. "How many ships are in Dockside?" *Perhaps some of the people can escape by water.*

"The Lofalin ships have been spotted both north and south. I fear that their blockade would intercept our ships."

"Is there no way out of the city apart from the gates?"

"None that I know of," Belrose said, taking a seat beside her. "However...never mind."

"Tell me your thoughts."

"There may be a way to build off the caverns in Darkroad. They are many, and uncharted. With enough engineers, diggers, and mages, we might be able to construct an underground road away from the city."

Seanna felt a twinge of hope. "How long would it take?"

"I cannot say. But, it would be a way to escape the siege."

"Start tomorrow. Take my signet and gather whatever and whoever you require. Work night and day, in shifts if necessary, to make this happen."

"What of your negotiations? Are you hoping for surrender?" Belrose asked.

Seanna bit her lip and stared at her lap. "I hope for many things. I would surrender the city and give up my crown if it would save the lives of my people." She was almost surprised to hear herself say it, but knew it to be true. *How much I have changed since Riverfen,* she reflected. She continued, "It may still come to war. If it does, your plan may be the only thing that can save us."

"I will go to the caves tonight," he said, rising and bowing low.

"May the gods guide you," Seanna said. He left her, and she relaxed against the cushions. *Tomorrow,* she thought, *the real work begins.* She sank into a deep sleep, there on the couch, for she had never been so exhausted in her life.

CHAPTER THIRTY-ONE
Mavian

Renna screamed, her arms flailing in the sheets, hands hitting senselessly at Mavian. He tried to force her to be still, but she was strong in her sleep. She pulled away from him and cried out again.

"Renna!" Mavian shouted, grabbing at her wrists. "Wake up, it's only a dream!"

Her eyes flew open. She gasped, staring behind Mavian. "She's there, she's there!"

He whirled, but saw nothing in the darkness. Taking Renna in his arms, he tried to comfort her. "Hush now, it was only a dream. Shhh, my love, you're safe here. Nothing can harm you."

Renna stared up at him with wide eyes. "*I saw her!* She follows me wherever I go, I can't escape her!"

"Just a figment–" Mavian started, but Renna slapped him. He reeled from the strike.

Her expression – fury and fear together – made his heart break. "She's not just in my imagination, Mavian. She touches me, and my arm goes cold. She laughs, and I shiver. Even when I wake, I feel a chill, like she's behind me. She won't just go away with soothing words. You have to *do something*!"

"I don't know what to do!" Mavian shouted. He stood from the bed and ran his hands through his hair. "I can't stop a thing I can't see. What would you have me do?"

"Give me ardanim, that I might sleep better," Renna said. She pulled her dressing gown around her white shoulders and turned her back to him.

"Ardanim will only make your dreams deeper," Mavian said, coming around to her side of the bed. She shifted away from him, and he took her hands. They were so cold, he thought they should be blue. "I'll ask the curate what he thinks may help you sleep without dreaming. Would that be good?"

"Yes," she sniffed. "What about when you leave for Stonetree? I'll be all alone."

"I'll leave Merick with you," he said.

"That will only make it worse," she protested. "He makes my skin crawl, and he's as cold as I am! Take me with you, please!"

"I can't," Mavian said. "It's a siege, no place for a lady."

"I'll be far from battle. Please, Mavian. I can't stay here alone."

Mavian took her in his arms, his heart twisting. *If I leave her, she'll be alone and afraid. If I take her, and the siege goes awry...*At last, he kissed her forehead. "Alright, my love. I'll bring you with me."

She sank with relief and sobbed in his arms. He held her and stroked her hair, all the while fearing what the coming nights may bring. In the days since she'd woken, terrible dreams haunted her every night. Though he cared for her, his own lack of sleep was beginning to wear on him. He couldn't remember the last time he'd slept a full night through. *And now, my nights shall be filled with prowlers and the screams of the dying*. He shuddered, but didn't voice his worries aloud.

At dawn, Mavian began his work. Word had arrived from Stonetree of the army's arrival, and so that night, he, Rask, and the prowlers would finally go to war.

He went down, down into the caverns beneath the castle, to his red-lit workshop. There, he gathered his books and scrolls, his vials and experiments. Many he left behind, though he filled two satchels' worth of ingredients and supplies, along with a third satchel just for texts. With a drawn out siege, he wanted to bring as much as he could to prepare for any eventuality.

As he labored, the Merick wight stood behind him. It had

remained in the workshop at Renna's request. Mavian didn't quite understand why he did it, but he took care to visit the wight at least once a day, if only to tell it that he missed its company. Though it never spoke, and barely ever looked at him, he had grown used to its presence.

"You understand me," Mavian said, carefully stacking a set of vials in a satchel. "You've been to the other side, you know how it feels. I wish Renna could know the connection we've made."

A voice startled him. "Talking to the dead? A sign of a madman, I'd say."

Mavian glanced up at Chadron, who leaned against the hewn rock at the cavern's entrance. He shrugged. "Surely you've spoken to your weapons before. Thinking aloud, is all."

"Why spend any time down in the dark and gloomy when you have such a beautiful wife upstairs to entertain you?" Chadron's smirk made Mavian's skin crawl.

"She needs to rest," he answered.

"She'll grow tired of you," Chadron said. "I wonder who she'll seek when she realizes her husband cares only for things that crawl in the night?"

Mavian hunched his shoulders. "And you think she'll turn to *you*?"

"She and I share many common interests. You'd never understand our *connection*." Chadron drawled the last word, putting a weight on it that Mavian disliked immensely.

Without thinking, Mavian took hold of the white gem at his neck. He spoke the words of power, drawing runes in the air. In a moment, a dread portal snapped into existence, shaking the walls and rattling his teeth with its closeness. His shelves bounced, sending bottles and jars crashing to the floor.

At Mavian's will, black tentacles slithered from the void and wrapped themselves around Chadron. The knight swallowed, though his expression showed no fear.

"Don't speak of her like that," Mavian growled. The tentacles grew tighter, matched to his thoughts. In that moment, all he wanted was to see Chadron torn apart.

"Do it," Chadron goaded. "You wouldn't have the guts."

The tentacles writhed, and the knight let out a strangled sound. Mavian stared at him, everything inside him wanting to do it. Then Merick stepped in front of him, blocking his view. The wight laid a hand to Mavian's shoulder and shook its head. Somehow, in that small gesture, Mavian saw a glimmer of intelligence in the creature, perhaps even a hint of compassion. *It knows that Rask would have me killed for this*, he thought. *It doesn't want that.*

Mavian swept the runes aside, ending the spell. The tentacles vanished and Chadron fell to the floor. The portal flickered shut, the absence of noise making Mavian's ears hurt. The calls of the dead rattled in his skull before they vanished, leaving only his own thoughts.

"Coward," Chadron spat as he picked himself up.

"Leave me," Mavian said. "You're not coming to Stonetree; we have no cause to speak to each other."

Chadron's grin tried to be menacing, but it appeared more of a grimace. "Your wife and I–"

"She's coming with me," Mavian said curtly. "Now get out."

Perhaps the tentacles had actually scared the knight, for he turned on his heel and strode away, his shoulders rounded. If he had the strength to do so, Mavian would have savored the victory. Instead, he only felt hollow.

"Nothing is as it should be," he muttered to the wight. "Renna's dreams. Me. Even the prowlers are ill-humored today."

To his surprise, the wight spoke, "Live...today...fight...tomorrow."

"Something you used to say to Cara?" Mavian asked. The wight nodded. *A good thought, if an empty one. But he's right, in a way.* Mavian asked his creation, "Do you hate me? My magic killed you, then reanimated you. Maybe there's a bit of your soul still left somewhere in there. I'd hate whoever did that to me."

The wight regarded him with those cold, flat eyes. Something within those dark depths glimmered to life, and Mavian wondered if the real Merick was the one who said, "No...hate...only...pity."

Its words buried themselves in his chest, tightening his heart and making his breath catch. He staggered, staring up at the wight. "I'm sorry, Merick."

The wight nodded. "Protect...you...not...fight...Cara...again." That hint of a soul returned to its gaze, weighing it with hurt.

When he lived in Riverfen, Mavian had thought the wight to be no more than a tool. Now, he saw it for what it was: a monster of his own creation that didn't wish to be a monster. Truly, he had nothing against Cara. It had amused him during the Masque to send her undead master against her. As he took in the wight's words, he knew that he couldn't do so again. *I cannot become that wicked.* He said, "I promise, Merick. You won't have to fight her again."

As he said it, Mavian began to think of Merick as a "he" again, not an "it." The wight deserved that much respect.

"Let's go," Mavian said. "There's much still to do."

The wight inclined his head.

＊

The dread portal opened into an abandoned barn far from the army's encampment. First one prowler, then another emerged from the void and into their new home. They stared about with their red eyes, chittering to one another. Their skin shone white in the moonlight.

Mavian kept all his concentration on the void, silently counting the prowlers until all one-hundred-and-thirty-two had entered the barn. A smaller number than he'd had before, but enough to harry the defenders in their stone walls.

The prowlers milled about, sniffing at the high walls that surrounded them. They ignored Mavian. The gem pulsed at his neck, glowing softly as his will emanated over the creatures.

From within his coat, Mavian withdrew a vial of aromatic liquid that had hints of lavender and sage. He had instructed every man within the army to apply it at least once a day, for the prowlers would only discriminate using smell. From prowler to prowler Mavian went, letting them sniff the vial and telling them, in their tongue and with the gem's power, not to attack any who smelled like the liquid. *Let us hope Druam doesn't have his men bathe in lavender*, Mavian thought. He remembered his cousin's scent, always fresh and clean. Once, it had reminded him of home.

Mavian realized that he didn't want to see Druam's death. It came upon him suddenly, a cold wash of fear at that corpse laid out coldly on unyielding stone, the ancient life behind those grave eyes gone. He stumbled a little and dropped the vial. It shattered on the earth, sending up waves of the now-sickly scent. He gagged, the picture of Druam's body overpowering his fragile mind.

Shivering, he said without thinking, "*Harm not they who are your kin.*" His spell traveled over the prowlers, and they made their little chirps that told him they were compelled to obey. Though relief filled him that his cousin would not die by his prowlers, he knew that many an innocent woman and child hid within the keep. Would they be ravaged?

This is war, he reminded himself. *The men will do as badly or worse to them than the prowlers. At least prowlers don't rape as they invade.*

Slowly, Mavian regained his feet. The prowlers regarded him with fear and reverence – or as close to that as a monster could get – as he waded through them. The guards quickly shut the door behind him to keep the prowlers trapped.

Mavian walked slowly through the camp, his mind elsewhere. Attacking the Masque, which had been filled with sycophants and narcissists, was one thing. However this war, this theft of innocent rustic lives, made him ill. *I didn't start this journey into necromancy to harm those who need help; have my choices truly led to this? Is there no other path?*

It was *his* attack on Druam that had divided the earls and sent Rask on a warpath, *his* magic that had allowed for prowlers to reach Stonetree. How many deaths would be on his head?

The Lofalins would have come anyway, he reminded himself. *If Rask hadn't sided with them, they'd be sieging D'Clet too.* The thought brought him no comfort.

His feet carried him to the village house that Rask had granted him and Renna. All the officers of the army were given abandoned homes so that they wouldn't muddy their boots with the rest of the soldiers. Each time Mavian walked into the small house, he was reminded of those that had lived there before: the pots and pans, the carefully organized shelves, the clothes left folded in a chest at the foot of the bed. Who had lived here? Were they still alive? Had children laughed and played by the fire?

As Mavian walked into the bedroom, he cringed at the thought of seeing Renna. Fortunately, she was out, though he couldn't imagine where. He sighed in relief and sank onto the bed. He loved her, yes, and he was happy she was with him, but he couldn't speak to her about his concerns. She wouldn't understand or sympathize. Her nightmares had grown worse, and all she could speak about was herself.

He understood. He truly did. Yet he wanted her, for once, to listen to him.

Mavian fell into a deep slumber. He awoke in the hour before dawn to Renna's moans. She must have come in while he slept, but now her nightmares disturbed his rest. He cuddled up behind her, speaking fond nothings until she calmed and her breathing returned to normal. *Yet another night without true sleep.* Mavian tossed and turned until dawn, then rose to go to the war council.

Rask had commandeered the village's tavern for his council. The tables had been shoved together to create enough room for maps and diagrams, charts and reports. Rask pored over one of the maps. He nodded to himself, putting a finger on the parchment.

"Ah, Strilu," Rask said, glancing up at Mavian. "Are your prowlers prepared? Good. They'll attack tonight along with the first barrage from the trebuchets."

Mavian had seen the great war engines in the middle of the camp, huge machines with long arms and a heavy pendulum. He hadn't known what to call them before. "What do they do?"

"Same as a catapult, but with heavier loads and a longer

reach. None on the walls could ever hope to destroy one without leaving the safety of the fortress." Rask smirked. "Once the trebuchets have weakened the walls, your prowlers will enter the fortress and slaughter as many as they can until dawn."

"Then I bring them back?" Mavian asked. *Another long night ahead if I'm to corral the creatures from such a distance.*

"No."

"But the sunlight–"

"They can find places to hide if they're smart. Else they'll burn. The fate of such creatures is of no concern to me."

"So my prowlers are just an appetizer before the main siege? I thought–"

"You thought wrong." Rask's watery glare was chilling. "See it done, or I'll make sure your life is short and painful."

Mavian swallowed hard. *Another slaughter of my creatures in a single night. Gods help me.* "I understand, Your Distinction."

"Good."

Mavian tried to sleep more that day, but the *thud* of the trebuchets' loads and the screams of the defenders – even at such a distance – kept him awake. Renna had disappeared again, but he couldn't worry about her.

That night, once the sun had fully set, Mavian released the prowlers. They followed him, like a flock after their shepherd, until he stood at the bottom of Stonetree's hill. He looked up at the mighty walls and the field of debris from the trebuchet attack. Defenders crowded the crenellations, and he thought he could see Druam and Edsel standing together.

Scanning the walls, he spotted a possible place where the prowlers could enter. Speaking in the tongue of the undead, he ordered them to it. "*Go into the fortress and have your feast. When day comes, hide until nightfall, and do it again. Now go.*"

The prowlers howled and screamed, a blood-curdling sound as over a hundred filthy feet stampeded up the hill. The defenders shot at the creatures, but their arrows did not down them. Like ants, the prowlers swarmed the hole in the walls. Men's screams echoed in the night. The prowlers broke through to wreak havoc.

Mavian shut his eyes and turned away. He could bear to see no more.

The killing has started. How many nights until it ends?

For the first time, Mavian wished he stood atop those crenellations with Druam. Had he chosen the right side?

As Renna's dreams turned to shadow that night, so too did Mavian's thoughts and regrets haunt him. The light of day could not dispel the lingering darkness in his soul.

CHAPTER THIRTY-TWO
The Forest Witch

The days bled into seasons, red grass blooming and dying in turn, winter squalls that drove ice into grey-barked trunks while vicious winds screeched around any creature that dared to leave its den. The Forest Witch and Lintem settled into their shelter with its oven and cozy furs. They cuddled together limb over limb while the Woods outside bore the brunt of Frost's deep chill.

It was on a day like many that came before, cold winds and winter's reaching hands, that a knock came at the Forest Witch's home. Lintem snuffled in his sleep, and the Forest Witch climbed unsteadily to her feet. She lifted aside the heavy skin which blocked out the elements and peered outside.

Dona stood there dressed only in her simple smock, her skin unaffected by the chill. The Forest Witch raised a brow – none of the Witches had sought her out before – and nodded a greeting. Movement behind Dona caught her eye, and she startled at the two tiny humans huddling there. Their cheeks and noses were rosy with cold, their hands stuffed underneath their armpits.

"What is this?" the Forest Witch hissed. Lintem raised his head, a growl starting low in his throat.

"They are children," Dona said.

"Why are they here?"

"Our brother sent them to us for safekeeping," Dona replied. "Their mother is dead, and their father in no condition to raise them."

The Forest Witch didn't blink at Dona's mention of a brother. *Another forgotten Cythra.* She studied the children, their blonde hair curling over their blue eyes. A human impulse of protection leaked into her bones, and she tore her eyes away.

"Why have you brought them to me?" she asked.

"Have you no interest in learning more Songs of Humanity?" Dona's smile was knowing. "What better teachers than those who are pure?"

The Forest Witch drew back. "You want me to care for them? I am a caretaker of the Woods, not human children."

"We will care for the Woods," Dona said. "As we have since before you came, and as we will when you depart."

"I'm never leaving."

"Of course. Look at them; they're freezing. Will you not let them in?"

Though she glared at Dona, the Forest Witch stepped aside and the two children stumbled into her tiny home. Lintem scrambled to his paws and backed away from them, his large rear bumping into the bark wall. When the Forest Witch turned to Dona, the other Witch had vanished. With a heavy sigh, the Forest Witch let the fur fall back into place.

Her hut had a large oven built into the floor, its heat providing a cozy sleeping spot. Over the many years, she had accumulated furs and feathers to make a nest for herself and Lintem on top of it. She had widened the inside of the hut and laid leather over its dirt floor, and built shelves and alcoves into the knotted wood of the trees that formed her little shelter.

The two children, a boy and a girl, clutched at each other in the center of the room, their wide eyes darting from her to Lintem and back again. The boy had a determined tightness to his chubby cheeks.

"Are you a spirit?" the boy demanded. His voice was high and fluting, only a child's despite his brave words.

"No." The Forest Witch smiled in amusement. "Are you?"

"I'm a little man," he said. "So my mother says."

"She is wise indeed." The Forest Witch prodded at their

Songs. She had never known such pure magic before. A child's Song was not like that of an adult's, warped with time and cynicism, nor an animal's, filled only with instinct and experience. Their Songs flitted about like birds, fear and curiosity and imagination, dancing from one place to another. They had known grief, but couldn't put such emotion to words. They knew laughter and joy and pranks and spite, their world growing the more they interacted with it.

"How old are you?" the Forest Witch asked. She delighted in the innocence of the children's music, her hardened heart softening as she listened to it.

The girl answered this time. "Six."

"A very fine age."

Lintem still cowered by the far wall, his back arched, his stinger twitching. He had never met human children before. Though it had been many years, the Forest Witch remembered seeing children at play and giving sweets to calm them.

It's alright, Lintem, she hummed. *They can't hurt you. They are humans, only smaller.*

Slowly, the nightcat relaxed, though his ears still pressed against his head. He padded closer, leaning his head out for a sniff. The boy put himself in front of his sister, fear fluttering through his Song.

"Lintem is kind," the Forest Witch assured the children. "He only eats creatures of the Woods."

The girl reached around her brother and held out a hand to the nightcat. Lintem gave it a small lick, and she giggled. After a moment's hesitation, the boy put his fingers in Lintem's fur. He gasped.

"It's so soft!"

The wind blew harshly outside. The Forest Witch led the children to her nest and bid them to lay down. Lintem curled himself around them with a satisfied purr. *They are delightful, these human children.*

Indeed. The Forest Witch leaned against Lintem's comforting bulk while the children nestled further into the furs. She noted their good linen smocks and leather shoes, and the wool cloaks tied around their necks. *Not wealthy, but not poor either. They came from a loving home.* Though winter grasped at the trees, their shelter remained warm and safe, a solace from the blizzard outside.

"My name's Eaton," the boy said. "This is Elvy. What's your name?"

The Forest Witch frowned. She had a name once, far away on Earda, and she knew she had carried it with her to the Woods. Somewhere in those twisting branches and meandering paths, she had lost her name. She shook her head. "I don't have one anymore."

"So what do we call you?"

"Whatever you like, I suppose."

"You'll take care of us, right?" The boy waited for her nod before he said, "Then you'll be an Auntie."

Elvy clapped her tiny hands. "Auntie! Do you know any stories?"

"Oh yes," the Forest Witch said. She settled into a comfortable position. While she spoke, the Songs of Family and Comfort drifted serenely around them. The children's music filled with Wonder and Joy. The Forest Witch told them of the trees and creatures of the Woods, and of the strange man who had come for healing. She explained the Songs and the things she had learned.

Eventually, the children's eyes grew too heavy for them, and they drifted into sleep. The Forest Witch smoothed their hair and lay their cloaks over them, her heart beating with a new Song of Nurturing, buoyed by an ancient instinct deep within her. As she watched over the twins, she realized that this Song might be the most human of all.

She smiled as she recalled the boy putting himself in front of his sister, protective and strong. The thought awakened her grief from its frozen cage. Had she once had a brother?

No. The Forest Witch shoved the grief down. *I will not relive that anguish.*

She slept fitfully, her dreams full of vague memories that fled whenever she tried to catch them. When she woke, she quickly set about her chores, desperate to dislodge the grief from inside her. She warmed porridge with a Song, mixing dried fruit into it. Lintem slunk out to hunt his own meat, and the children dove into the simple meal with ravenous hunger. When they finished, they looked at her with shining eyes.

"Can we play in the snow?"

The Forest Witch peeked out at the glittering white glen. Icicles sparkled from the grey-branched trees, and the stream wove lazily between small floes. It was pristine and perfect.

Before she allowed them to wander, the Forest Witch hummed a Song of Warmth into their cloaks, encouraging the cloth to keep the children snug. She Sang out to the trees, forbidding them from allowing the children to leave the glen. It was not so large a space, and she was confident in her ability to guard the twins while she restocked her shelves.

The children bounded out into the snow, their shrieks of laughter loud in the quiet glen. The Forest Witch gathered her furs around her and stepped into the powder, her bare feet unbothered by its chill touch. She watched Eaton and Elvy from the corner of her eye as she walked through the copse of trees, Singing down fruit and collecting wild oats from the few surviving strands of grass. She coaxed fish from the stream and cleaned and gutted them in the frosty waters.

As she worked, memories of her own childhood, hazy and indistinct, fluttered through her head. She recalled throwing snow at the other children of the castle and screeching as the wet stuff slipped down the back of her shirt. The Song of Play was vast and freeing, its music as wild and imaginative as children themselves. The Forest Witch basked in her memories of playing, both in snow and summer, by herself or with friends.

A scream from across the glen interrupted her musing. The Forest Witch sprang to her feet and dashed through the snow, kicking it from her feet in flying puffs. The children cowered together by the trees, Elvy crying and Eaton waving a stick.

In front of them crouched a Woods wolf, its back arched with leather spikes, its jaws slathered with drool. Gleaming orange eyes gazed hungrily at the children. Its fur stood out in tufts from the leathery scales that coated its skin. The wolf was nearly as tall at its shoulder as the Forest Witch, its jaws large enough to close entirely around one of the children's heads.

The Forest Witch threw her hands out, Singing a wind that buffeted into the wolf's side. It snarled and snapped its head around. It howled, the cry as cold as winter's night. Songs hummed in her breast, their threads clear in her sight. The Forest Witch called for Lintem before she pulled on the Song of Fire. Flames grew bright in her hand, and she threw them at the wolf. It leapt back, the fire melting the snow.

Eaton and Elvy scrambled away toward the Forest Witch. As they ran, the wolf jumped at them, its jaws open wide.

The wolf never reached them. His muscles coiling beneath black fur, Lintem sprang at the wolf, sending it flying off course. They both sprawled in the snow, growling and snarling at each other. The Forest Witch gathered the children in her arms, terror in her throat as Lintem faced the Woods wolf.

The creatures circled each other, one large and brutish, the other lithe and quick. Lintem darted a paw at the wolf, drawing blood on its nose. The wolf bit back, its teeth scraping the nightcat's leg as Lintem leapt out of the way. The nightcat pounced on the wolf's back, his claws digging into the creature's hide. The wolf snapped and bucked, its teeth gouging at Lintem's forelegs. Still Lintem clung on.

The Forest Witch, her shock dissipating into instinct, grasped at the wolf's Song. It was bloodlust and hunger and violence, a wild evil found only in Woods predators. She had no time to follow its Song to its heart. So she reached for the first body part she found – a leg – and snapped it. The wolf howled in pain, and Lintem ducked his head down to the creature's throat. Blood drenched the once-clean snow as the wolf finally sagged in death.

The twins clutched at the Forest Witch, sobbing, and Lintem limped over to them. The Forest Witch touched his head, her gratitude carrying through the Songs.

"Come now, children," she said. "We must take care of our friend."

The party moved slowly through the glen until they reached their shelter. Lintem nursed a paw as he curled atop the oven, his green eyes glazed with pain. After settling the children in a corner, the Forest Witch set to work. She gathered herbs with healing Songs and ground them into a poultice. This she rubbed into Lintem's wounds, ignoring his whimpers of pain.

The Song of Healing was complicated, for tissue was far more easily broken than mended. She Sang the cuts and gouges closed, thankful that no organs had been pierced in the battle. One of his legs had been cut fairly deep, muscle showing pink in the firelight. The Forest Witch did what she could to weave it back together, but she knew that Lintem would always have a limp and scars.

When she finished, Lintem lay his head down to sleep, his body exhausted from the fight and the magic. As he snored, she turned to the children. She inspected them for wounds – luckily, they were more frightened than hurt – and fed them the warmest, most sugary porridge she could make. Much of her foraged food had been left out, and she would have to retrieve it after the children went to sleep.

The Forest Witch stroked Eaton's head and said, "You were very brave."

"I have to take care of my sister. Mumma said so." The boy's eyes drifted shut.

The frozen grief inside the Forest Witch exploded outward. *I have to take care of my sister.* The Forest Witch clutched at her stomach, her body roiling with the memories that assaulted her.

I had a brother named Wullum. He took care of me when our parents died. He stayed by me when I was ill.

Tears streaked through the grime on her cheeks. *He protected me, even until his death.*

His death.

The grief she had hidden for so long was agony over her brother's death. It had festered in her, growing unacknowledged, becoming more powerful the longer she ignored it. She had once tried to curse the Skals who had murdered her brother in front of her very eyes.

A curse didn't seem like enough now.

The Forest Witch keened softly, her pain a shadow over her heart. *Wullum, my brother. My protector.* He was gone, and she couldn't follow. The Song of Loss churned within her, leaving a bitter taste on her tongue and a weight over her chest.

A tiny hand took hers. Elvy crawled into her lap and leaned her head against the Forest Witch's shoulder.

"Don't cry, Auntie," said Elvy.

"I forgot an awful truth," the Forest Witch whispered. "I wish I never remembered it."

The girl nodded solemnly. "Papa Fred told us we might never see Mumma again. I don't like remembering that."

"I'm sorry, child." The Forest Witch stroked her hair. "I'm sure your Mumma's Song was beautiful."

"Can I tell you about her?"

The Forest Witch nodded, and the girl spoke slowly but lovingly about her mother. When she finished, she looked up expectantly. "Your turn. Why are you sad?"

"I lost my brother," the Forest Witch said. Grief tinged her words, but she pressed on.

To her surprise, her sorrow lightened with every word she spoke.

CHAPTER THIRTY-THREE
Cara

A crackle of lightning, the earth trembled beneath them, and Laris was there, his form silhouetted by the white-hot bolt. He stepped down and the sky quieted.

Cara's hand crept to her sword. She almost let down the beast's walls. "You're not welcome here, Stanthorpe."

He smirked. "Am I not? I told you I would return, and so I have."

As her eyes adjusted from the lightning, Cara saw that he had aged once more. Not so old as when she'd first met him, but his skin and hair had gained over a decade of wrinkles and grey. She quelled her beast, though she savored the sound of Laris's thudding heartbeat. *Soon,* she promised herself, *soon it shall be silenced forever.*

"I was hoping you'd return," she said. Her leg twinged with the memory of the healing he stole from it. "I didn't want to wait too long before I killed you."

The sorcerer scoffed. "You think you could? Go ahead. Try."

So be it. Cara lunged forward, drawing her sword. She went two steps before he uttered a spell that froze her in place, one foot hovering off the ground. Only her eyes could move, and she cursed her own impulsivity.

"Has the past taught you nothing?" Laris asked, circling her. He cast an eye over Darian and Jagger. "You've found new friends, but they can't stop me, either. You still owe me a great debt, and I mean to collect it." With another word, he released her. Her sword became scorching hot in her hand, and she dropped it with a curse.

"You can't steal any more healing from me," Cara said, trying to sound brave. Except her heart quivered and her beast shuddered. It, too, remembered the pain Laris had caused her. How could she fight back against someone with such power?

"Can't I?" Laris bent down and whacked her leg with a hand. "Last I saw you, this was broken and infected. It's remarkable how it's healed in the intervening quinns. Impossible, one might say."

He turned his cunning eyes to Darian. "Is this one a curate?"

Darian bowed low. "I am more acquainted with death than with life. It was not I."

"But someone did heal her." Laris's eyes drifted to Jagger. "This one looks more like a killer than anything else."

Cara raised her chin. "No curate has touched me, I can promise you that."

"Then how came you to be healed?"

That stopped her tongue. She gazed at Darian, pleading with him not to reveal her secret. His milky eyes stared at the sky, seemingly unconcerned with her plight. There was doubt and curiosity in Sandu's expression. He also wanted to know how she'd healed so quickly.

Cara didn't trust herself to lie well. So, she said nothing at all.

Laris stared at her a moment, waiting. When she remained silent, he sighed. "Nothing for it, I suppose. If the rest of you try to interfere, I'll call the skies down on you. Test me if you dare."

Raising one hand, Laris began an incantation. Cara stiffened as the magic poured over her. It slid through her bones and muscle to her leg. It flittered about, testing the sinew and marrow. The magic ebbed away, leaving her cold.

"Interesting," Laris muttered, crouching down. He gestured for her to sit, and she obeyed, if resentfully. Her sword lay just within reach, and she eyed it. Laris tutted at her, "Don't think about it, child."

Laris took her leg in his hands. He muttered to himself as

he felt the muscle. "Different working, I suppose. Yes, if I modify the spell..."

Though Cara wanted nothing more than to attack him, she stayed her hand. The beast cowered fearfully within her. *Remember the boar. You don't have the power to fight him yet.* Her eye caught Sandu's. *You're helping him now. If you try to hurt Laris, he could do worse to Sandu.*

Laris began his magic once more. Though the last time had shown a red aura and burned her healing out of her, this one was cold, freezing her to her core. Cara's teeth chattered, and she hugged herself.

The bone cracked, reopening the wound. It progressed from healthy blood to green-and-white pus, then a black infection, all in the course of mere seconds. Cara bit back a scream as her health flowed into Laris.

Laris cursed, drawing his hands back. Black-and-green mottled his veins, and though he'd grown younger once more, his skin had taken on an ill pallor.

"What have you done to yourself?" he growled, his hands trembling. "What did you do?"

"What I had to," Cara said with a strange smugness at his dilemma. Though her leg screamed with pain, she ignored it. He had taken some of the blood magic into himself, and she grinned at his dismay. *A darker consequence than you expected.*

"That's what a thief gets for his troubles," Cara said. She shuddered, the agony too much for her to bear. The beast surged within her, crying for blood despite its fear. The heartbeats all around her swelled in her skull, and her eyes clouded with the beast's instinct.

Her promise to herself was forgotten with her pain and hunger.

Laris backed away. The beast overwhelmed her, transforming her into a monster. She howled at the sky, then focused on Sandu. His neck throbbed with blood, and she saw only the inviting temptation.

She screeched and lunged, and he shouted in alarm. Even with the beast's help, her leg couldn't hold her. She collapsed to the ground, seething and thirsty, reaching for him still.

"Good gods," Laris uttered.

A soft touch descended on her head, and she knew no more.

✳

A cool, tender hand caresses her cheek. Cara opens her eyes, surprised to see torchlight flickering on marble walls around her. Instead of boiled leather and travel-worn cotton, she wears a blood-red brocade gown, tight around her waist and flowing into exorbitant sleeves and skirts. She lifts herself up to get her bearings.

Renna sits beside her. She, too, is clad in an elegant dress, though hers is white with gold embroidery, accenting the color of her hair. She places a lily-white hand on Cara's shoulder.

"How do you feel?" she asks.

Cara shakes her head, unsure. This must be a dream, for her leg doesn't hurt, and she's not filthy from the road. "I'm alright. But where am I?"

"In the world of dreams," Renna says, her smile gentle.

"It looks like the Cascade Palace."

"Dreams can oft feel like truth. If that's where you believe us to be, then it is." Renna stands and helps Cara to her feet. "Come, we're already late."

"For what?"

"The gathering of the dead."

Renna takes Cara's hand, leading her from the chamber and into the grand halls. Cara walks slowly, not quite feeling the swirl of skirts at her feet, her head in that trance-like state of a dreamer who knows that she dreams.

They come to a ballroom, one ten sizes that of the Masque. Inside, the dancers are dressed in black and grey. Hundreds of them, moving to music from an unseen orchestra, each with a veil covering their heads.

"Who are they?" Cara asked.

"They are the undead." Renna watches them with pity. "Those in black are the fampir *who have returned permanently to Autorus. Those in grey are the ones who remain."*

The fampir *clad in grey, as one, lift their hands to their veils and let them fall to the floor, revealing their faces. Cara sees Druam, tall and confident, guiding a black-clothed woman around the floor.*

"Where's Alex?" she asks.

"I don't know," Renna replies. As Cara follows, she descends to the dance floor. There, she takes Cara's arm and leads her into the fray, moving together effortlessly.

"Why am I here?" Cara asks.

"Must there be a purpose to dreams?"

Cara contemplates this and shakes her head. "I suppose not."

Renna's smile is serious. "This one does have a purpose. Each of these people here has walked Earda. Some are gone forever, but most are trapped within the Ossuary. Their souls can be freed, or doomed, by your hand."

"How?"

"Find me. I can take you to the Ossuary." As before, there is a gleam of something sinister in Renna's look. But, in her mistress's arms, Cara is content and safe.

"Where are you?" Cara asks.

"Go to D'Clet. I will wait for you there." Renna draws close, a hint of black within the blue of her irises. "Do not tarry, for I don't know what will become of me if Mavian has his way. You must come before he can stop me."

"Stop you from doing what?"

"Living as I must." Renna kisses Cara's cheek and turns her eyes to a group of fampir *in grey, their faces exposed to the light. "You see them? They are close to you, close enough to hunt. A coven of* fampir *waiting to be slaughtered. You can reach them tonight, before midnight."*

"How do you know this?" Cara stares at the fampir, *hungry. She wonders, for the first time, how a* fampir's *blood would taste. "Where are they?"*

"Due north of you, not even a league away. Search for a cave in the mountainside, its entrance marked by a dead oak." Renna whispers in Cara's ear, "Discover the delight of an undead's blood."

✳

Cara woke suddenly, disoriented by the darkening light. She stared wildly around the tent, moaning as she shifted her leg. Darian knelt beside her, finishing another splint over her calf with Jagger's help. Sandu crouched warily nearby.

"Where's Laris?" Cara groaned. She could still feel the warmth of Renna's kiss on her cheek, and shook her head to dislodge the dream. It remained resolutely present, goading her to find the coven.

"He's outside," Sandu said. "But I think he's sleeping."

"Then I'll kill him before he wakes." Cara started to sit up, but Darian pushed her down. For once, his gaze was stern, and she quailed under his displeasure. He turned to the other two men. "Leave us." Jagger and Sandu gave her one last look before they departed.

Darian thumped her broken leg. She swore, and he pressed down hard on the injury.

"What the veck–" Cara started, and he clamped a hand over her mouth.

"Do not think I came to watch you slaughter your way through the country," Darian hissed. "I know your dreams. The woman lies."

"I never asked you to come," Cara said, wrenching her head away from his hand. "I don't want your *help*."

"I came because you needed someone to guide you." Darian's blank eyes bore into her, heavy with the weight of his knowledge. He touched her cheek, and she heard them: the Songs of the dead and dying, a never-ending chorus of pain, grief, and relief. When he drew back, she inhaled sharply.

"*That's* what you live with?"

"Every candle of every day, every moment waking and sleeping. I hear them, and I help them as best I can. Your Song grows stronger with every drop of blood you consume, its melody tainted with darkness."

For the first time in his presence, Cara was afraid. His eyes held only death in their white depths. She wanted to know everything he knew, yet feared it. Did he know the day of her death? Could he foresee the success of her mission?

Darian's eyes filled her vision, and she could see nothing else as he spoke, "A time has come for your decision, Caralyn Gellder, Maid of Death. You have been given a second chance, though Laris does not know the gift he provided. Give up your bloodlust, seek your Song, and I will help you.

"If you pursue this coven of *fampir*, know that I will turn away from you. I will give you no more healing, no more words of wisdom. You shall become a phantom to me, though I will not abandon Sandu and Jagger. And when they ask what has happened between us, I will tell them the truth."

Cara closed her eyes, not wanting to fall further into his gaze. "How do you know about the coven?"

"Your dreams walk beside death, and so I hear them. Do not heed that siren's call; her words are poison to goodness."

"She's my friend. She wouldn't hurt me."

He snorted. "Has she not hurt you already? Have her actions not led to your injuries and Merick's fate? If you believe her, you may already be lost."

All I ever wanted was Renna beside me again. Cara clutched the memory of Renna's touch and promises, holding them as a drowning man clings to driftwood. *I tried, for Sandu's sake, to avoid it. But I can never be free unless I destroy Laris. And I can't destroy him without* fampir *blood.*

Darian sighed. "I have one last gift to grant you." He took a small knife from his belt and pricked his finger. He allowed one single drop of his own blood to grace the blade before he wrapped the cut. He placed the blade between them. "If you taste of my blood, you will have crossed the boundary and condemned your soul. It will heal you – utterly and completely – as no animal's life can. I am granting you this gift of temptation. Resist, and there may be hope yet."

With that, Darian took his cane and stood. Cara asked, "Blood gives me power. Can my Song do the same?"

He paused a moment. "I have seen what will become of you if you drink my blood. You will grow stronger than any *fampir* or mortal man. Your enemies shall fall before you in waves, and you shall have the vengeance which you so desire. Yet you will lose much in the taking."

"And what will happen if I don't drink it?" Cara eyed the blade, the beast within her urging her to taste his blood. *I will be healed and able to hunt once more. I will find a way to exact revenge on Laris and Druam and Mavian, yet what will I lose?*

Darian bent his head. "Your Song will bring balance to your soul."

"And I won't have the power to destroy my enemies."

"True. But–"

Before he could finish, Cara took the blade and raised it to her lips. She tilted the blood onto her tongue.

When she finished, Darian was gone. Her leg twitched and itched, burning with the warmth of his blood. She shuddered with strength. Every scratch and scar vanished, leaving her skin smooth. The beast roared through her, stronger than ever. It howled for *fampir* blood.

Cara slipped out the back of the tent, letting the beast guide her steps north.

First, the coven, she thought, the power of Darian's blood coursing through her. *Then Laris.*

She did not see the shadow of a man following her.

CHAPTER THIRTY-FOUR

Sandu

"Will she be alright?" Sandu asked as Darian emerged from the tent. He tried to peer inside, but the blind man blocked his view. As meek as a lamb, Sandu allowed himself to be taken to the remains of that evening's fire. Jagger waited there, his keen eyes piercing the darkness. There was no sign of Laris; Sandu supposed the sorcerer had left them once more.

Darian sat down on a stump, and Sandu rested at his knee, like he used to as a child listening to his grandmother's stories. "Will she be alright?" he asked again.

"Time will tell," Darian sighed. "She has made a decision which she cannot take back."

"What do you mean?" Sandu said, staring up at the blind man's milky eyes.

For a moment, Darian said nothing. He laid a hand on Sandu's head and said, "Bluston is not far."

"I know. Tomorrow, we'll find my children, and–"

"They aren't there."

Sandu's breath caught in his throat. "What do you mean?"

"You won't find your children in Bluston, or anywhere else on Earda."

Though the evening air was warm, a chill settled on Sandu's heart. He gripped Darian's knee. "You heard them die? Why didn't you say anything? I could have–"

Darian's milky eyes held no remorse. "They are not dead. But neither are they on Earda. Remember your dream?"

Sandu staggered to his feet. "It was just a dream!"

I have to see for myself. I have to find them.

Terror clouded Sandu's mind. He sprinted to the road, not caring whether Jagger or Darian followed. His breath steamed in the cold air, his limbs protesting as he ran and ran. His feet ached after half a mile, his lungs desperately tight in his chest. He denied his body's protests.

In the dark, he tripped over a branch. He went sprawling, dirt in his mouth. Strong hands helped him back up: Jagger. His friend signed, *Are you hurt?*

Sandu regained his breath, shook his head, and took off again. Jagger's feet pounded the path behind him. Sandu ran until he could run no more. His legs shook beneath him, his lungs heavy as iron. He fell to his knees and gasped for breath.

Jagger caught up and signed, *Not far now. Set an easy pace.*

It was hard to take such advice. Sandu's body cried out for him to stop while his heart urged him to *go go go* no matter the pace. He followed Jagger at a lope, covering ground without fully sprinting. His heart settled into a rhythm, his legs pumping steadily beneath him.

All thoughts of Cara had been dashed from his head. He only thought of his children, somewhere out there in the night.

The quiet town loomed over the road. A few lanterns shone from windows, but no one moved about. As Sandu jogged between the buildings, dogs barked. Somewhere through the huts and hovels he heard the clinking of a hammer on metal. *Frederick?*

Sandu followed the sound, moving in a daze. He hardly dared hope.

At last the smithy came into view. The forge glowed, and lanterns illuminated the workshop. A large man bent over his work, his bare arms sweating. Sandu held back and watched. He hadn't known the man well back in Kell, but Frederick had always held a good reputation. He worked hard and didn't drink, and many of the young women paraded around his shop hoping to catch his eye.

But he chose Tambrey. Sandu had never questioned

Frederick's decision. After all, Tambrey *was* the most beautiful woman in town, even after bearing children. Now, as the man labored, he wondered why Frederick had preferred her over the other lovely girls that had never been married.

"Best come out of the shadows," Frederick grunted. He lifted the metal piece from the iron and inspected it with a discerning eye. His glance darted to where Sandu and Jagger stood, half-hidden in darkness. "Sorry if my working late disturbed your sleep."

"It didn't," Sandu said. A wave of heat kissed his cheeks as he stepped carefully into the light, all too conscious of his bandaged stump. Jagger edged forward, his sturdy presence comforting.

Frederick doused the metal in a barrel and turned toward him. "How can I..." His voice trailed off. He tilted his head, sweeping his eyes over Sandu. "By the gods. Barty Barrow?"

"Nice to see you, Fred," Sandu said. He clutched self-consciously at his stump, shifting from foot to foot. Now that he was closer, he saw that the smith's eyes were red, the skin beneath them puffy.

"What's happened to you?" Frederick nodded to a chair and took out a bottle as Sandu sat. He took a swig, then passed it over. "And who's your friend?"

"Long story," Sandu said. He gave a weak smile. "I saw Tambrey."

Somehow, Sandu couldn't bring himself to ask about the children yet. He didn't know if his heart could bear the truth.

Frederick sat heavily by the forge. The burning embers flickered over his features. He was a handsome man, clean-shaven and strong-jawed. Tear tracks swept through the soot on his cheeks, and he wiped his nose with a kerchief.

"How is she?" Frederick asked.

Grief welled anew in Sandu's chest. He balled his fingers. "She passed."

"I see." Frederick took back his mead and drank heavily. When he finished, he poured a mouthful out on the floor. "She was a good woman."

"The best." Sandu's missing arm itched, but he couldn't scratch it. He settled for rubbing his leg instead. "I was there when she...when it happened."

"I wish I could have been."

"You took the children away. It's what she would have wanted." Sandu tried to catch Frederick's eye, but the smith took another long drink.

"It wasn't my idea, you know," Frederick said. "I liked her, sure enough, but never would have come between you. She said it was best for the children if you left and she remarried."

Sandu hung his head. "She was right." He sighed. *Always too late.* "Fred, where are my children?"

The large man made a strangled sound. He shook his head and stared into nothing.

"Fred, I want to see them," Sandu pressed. "Please. I won't take them away from you, but–"

"They're gone," Frederick whispered. "I got up one morning and went to wake them. And they weren't there. I always lock the windows and doors at night. None of them were open. They just vanished."

Icy dread filled Sandu's stomach. He rubbed his leg harder. "They must be somewhere. They're so small, they couldn't get far."

"I hired a Ranger," Frederick said in a tight voice. "Paid handsomely. He came, did his little spells, and said that the children hadn't left the room that night. Nothing in, nothing out. They just disappeared."

Jagger's hands flashed in Sandu's vision. *Rangers are rarely wrong. Their magic is specially used for finding lost people in the mountains.*

"I know," Sandu said softly. He shook his head, some part of him still in disbelief. To Frederick, he said, "Did they love you?"

"I hope so. I sure loved them with everything I had." Frederick hiccuped and took another long drink. "Can't sleep at night for worry."

"They're in a meadow," Sandu said suddenly. He tried to recall the dream, but it had slipped away. He thought aloud, "I saw them. When I nearly died. I went to this strange place, with stranger women. They said that the children were safe. But I don't know where they are."

Frederick turned away from him. "Don't give me hope, Barty. I can't live with the grief if I have to lose them twice."

Neither can I. Even if the children were alive, they were far away. Not on Earda, Darian had said. *I can never reach them.*

Sandu's stump ached, but it was nothing compared to the agony of his heart.

In the void of his soul, he knew what he should do. A quick thrust of a blade or a fatal drop. The way it would be done didn't matter.

I should have just stayed with Mumma and let myself die.

CHAPTER THIRTY-FIVE
The Forest Witch

While the children still slept, the Forest Witch crept from her hut to where the wolf had fallen. It lay still, its scaly coat dusted with fresh snow, tongue lapping at frost it would never taste again. Its glassy eyes stared through her.

The Forest Witch had encountered many Woods wolves before, and never had cause to kill one. They hunted lesser creatures among the trees, and she could not stand in the way of Nature's course. The wolves often scented her and Lintem and avoided them, knowing a losing fight when they saw one. This one must have been desperate in its hunger to risk broaching her glen.

She mourned his life briefly, then set to work. His leather-and-fur coat would make a good set of clothes, his teeth might line a stone knife, and his meat, though stringy, would last for many days. Her arms grew bloody with the gruesome tasks. After a time, Lintem padded out next to her, his injured leg still placed gingerly with each step.

Are the children awake? hummed the Forest Witch.

Not yet.

Watch over them. She shuddered with the knowledge of what could have happened had Lintem not reached them in time. The nightcat slipped back to the hut, and she continued her work.

When the wolf was properly stripped, its meat packaged and ready to dry, the Forest Witch found the spot where she'd left the previous day's supplies. She thanked the Woods that none had been stolen and quickly scooped it all up into her arms. As she straightened, her nose twitched. A foul smell carried on the wind, bringing a dark Song as it traveled over the glen.

The wind drifted past her, and the smell dissipated, leaving a sour taste in her mouth. The Forest Witch trudged back to the hut laden with the fruits of her labor, but her mind was not set to her tasks. She had heard that dark Song before, and still couldn't quite place it. The Song of Misery? No, its notes were too short for that. The Song of Despair? No, for this new melody had a finality to it.

By the time she returned, the children were awake. They played with each other and Lintem, tugging at his ears and rolling over his back. The nightcat gave them loving licks, contentment in his purr. Elvy slid off his shoulders and stubbed her toe, tears immediately springing to her eyes. Within moments, Eaton was there by her side, his comforting arms around her.

The Forest Witch turned away from them under the pretense of placing meat to dry on the shelves. Eaton's serious eyes reminded her too deeply of Wullum, and an ache built in her Song, drowning out all other music. Her pain was not sorrow alone. Rage burned in her, desperate to be unleashed against Olfrick Kron and the other Skallish traitors.

The Forest Witch did her best to set aside her wounds and care for the children. She made their meals and played with them, she told stories while they cuddled against Lintem, she helped them bathe in the cold stream. Like the rest of her life in the Woods, she didn't track the time, but she knew that many days must have passed as they all settled into a comfortable routine.

Yet, almost every day, while the children ran with Lintem or slept above the oven, the Forest Witch left the hut and sat alone by the slow-moving water, her thoughts with Wullum. She remembered now the vision the Witches had shown her of the Skals of ancient days and the wanton slaughter enacted on them by her ancestors. *I cannot kill all Skals,* she told the vengeance that lurked in her breast. *Just Kron. I kill him, and it'll all be over.*

Except she knew that it wouldn't. She had learned too many Songs of Humanity to content herself with blind ignorance. The other Skals would want revenge, and so take it out on the Demars. The Demars, subjugated and persecuted, would retaliate. And so on, and so on, forever, until they all killed each other off.

Despite the logic that she tried to use, the Forest Witch could not dislodge the vengeance that blackened her heart. She could not reason her emotions. The Songs she used to soothe others didn't work on her, for she knew their machinations and melodies too well. She couldn't fool herself into acceptance. So she sat alone each day, whenever she could slip away, and pondered whether vengeance was the final step toward humanity, or the last Song to completely break her away from it.

Some days, while she sat and thought, that foul wind returned. It never lasted long; it swept in, intrigued and frightened her, and carried away again before she could figure it out. She grew closer to the answer with each passing day, but its source still eluded her.

On a calm day, with blue skies over the white glen, the Forest Witch heard a Song from one of the trees. It called for her, begging for help. *The Witches said they would care for the forest.* As the day went on, though, the Song grew louder and more strained, and the Forest Witch couldn't ignore it any longer. She left the children in Lintem's care and sprang away through the trees, her heart lifting as she rushed through the grey branches.

This is where I belong. This is the true me.

The tree called to her, and she answered. When she came to it, her heart sank. This was the tree that she had once helped to root itself after it tried to move. It stood upright, but its branches drooped, and its face held only consternation.

The Forest Witch reached into its Song and recoiled. The same corruption that the wind had teased her with was in this tree, infecting it from the inside out. It shuddered as its sap turned rotten and its wood decayed.

What happened to you, Little Tree? the Forest Witch asked.

It came on the wind, it replied, sap tears leaking from its carved eyes. *I wanted to know what it was, but it hurt me. I see so many humans and elves. They're dying.*

With that, the Forest Witch realized her mistake. *That wretched foulness is the Song of Death.*

She stared, stunned, at the tree. The Song of Death was one she had heard many, many times, first when she had killed Lintem's mother to save him, and then with the deaths of creatures and plants in the Woods, deaths that held no malice, for they were simply the work of Nature. This corrupted Song did not bring natural deaths to man. It brought death through war.

The Forest Witch laid a hand to the tree. *I'm so sorry that you heard it.*

Can you take it out of me?

I'm afraid not. The Song of Death had wrapped itself too thoroughly to the tree's music. Extracting it would kill the tree as surely as Autorus. *But I can ease your passing.*

The tree sighed, and she hurried the Song of Death's music, slipping in Songs of Peace and Acceptance as she went. Soon, the tree had turned black and rotting, its soul forever departed from the Woods. The other trees shrank away from it, their branches shivering.

The Forest Witch touched the Song of Death, its foul melody grating against her skin. She drew back before it could infect her, and leapt away through the Woods. Her heart weighed her down, heavy with the knowledge of what men did to each other.

It is time, she realized. *The Witches wanted me to learn the Songs of Nature and Humanity. Death is all there is left.*

How could she learn of Death without dying herself? She had guided many into Autorus's domain, and had detected no way in for herself. She knew of the *fampir* and prowlers, creatures tied to the Underworld, but none were in the Woods.

When she returned to her glen, she found the Witches waiting for her. They stood passively as the children played.

When the Forest Witch descended to the snowy ground, they turned as one.

"I must go to Death," said the Forest Witch. "But I don't know how to safely return."

"You need a guide," said Tresa, the Witch who best knew the Songs of Death. "One who will show you the paths. If you travel through those Songs, Autorus will have no hold on you."

The Forest Witch nodded. "Where can I find this guide?"

"You already know him." Tresa held out her hand. In it was a single strand of hair. The Forest Witch took it carefully, her Song thrilling as she touched it.

"This is my husband's hair. Druam." She had not spoken his name aloud since she had come to the Woods. "I don't understand how he can help me."

"I think you do," Tresa said gently. "Search his Song."

The Forest Witch obeyed. The hair held little of its owner, only a whisper of a whisper, but its Song echoed with the same melodies as the ones brought by Alexandro Strilu before he was made mortal again. The Forest Witch swallowed. "He is *fampir*."

Of course. How could she have been so blind? Those nights in the poppin dens were not merely for sport, but to satiate his supernatural needs. That day on the tourney field when he'd collapsed, he had been too long in the sun, an exceptionally dangerous thing for one of his kind.

The Forest Witch steeled herself. *His lies don't matter now.* She clutched the strand of hair, holding onto the Song as a drowning man clutches to driftwood.

"Who will care for the children?"

"I will," said Dona, "until their father comes for them."

"Good." The Forest Witch's throat constricted, and she didn't quite know why. As she studied each of the Witches, she saw a raw, painful truth written there.

"I'm not coming back, am I?" she asked. "Once I leave the Woods to seek Druam, I won't return."

Una took her face in her hands, her expression kind and motherly. "You have learned all you can here. There are still many hundreds of Songs on Earda that you will discover."

"The Woods once dwelled on Earda," said Dona. "Perhaps you will bring them back again."

The Forest Witch nodded again, her tongue too laden for her to speak. *That is the only way for me to see this place again.* Through a raw throat, she said, "I want to bring Lintem with me."

"You control the Songs," Tresa said. "Take him if you wish it."

"I should say goodbye to the others." The Forest Witch turned to the children, but Una took her hand.

"You should remember your name first," Una said. She pressed a hand to the Forest Witch's cheek. "You will never lose that which you gained in the Woods. You will always have this wildness in your heart. Now, you begin your journey back to Earda. You should embrace what you left there."

The name echoed in her Song, murmured on Druam's lips and lovingly shaped by Wullum's tongue.

Gwen.

For a moment, the Forest Witch resisted the name, as if it were a cloak she could remove and throw to the ground. Then its familiarity washed over her, pure and true, completing her Song.

Gwen contemplated her hands, the smooth skin lost beneath layers of life in the Woods. *The Forest Witch is still in me.* She smiled. She was princess and earl's wife and sorceress, and she was Woods-wild, too.

One by one, the sisters stepped up to Gwen. Una kissed her right cheek and said, "For serenity, that you may find solace in the darkest of times."

Dona kissed her left cheek. "For bravery, that you may do what you must even when your heart rails against it."

Tresa kissed her forehead. "For mercy, that you may not become those who harm you."

Their kisses tingled on Gwen's skin.

"I will spend one more day here," Gwen said. "To part with my friends and the trees. Then, I will find Druam."

"As you wish," said Una. The Witches melted into the

Woods.

The children clutched at Gwen's hands, their eyes filled with tears. In their Songs, she heard the fear of abandonment. Their father had left them at a young age, and their mother had sent them away. She knelt to their level and held their hands.

"If I could stay with you, I would," she said. "But there are awful people doing awful things to each other, and I can help them. You have each other; never forget that."

She kissed their foreheads and held them close an extra moment. When she stepped back, Dona was there. The Witch took the children's hands and led them away.

Gwen and Lintem wandered into the frost-laden Woods. Birds with jeweled wings circled overhead crying calls of longing. Stones and trees murmured to her, assuring Gwen of their love. Animals darted out of the gloom, their fire-bright eyes telling her that they would miss her.

When she could take no more, Gwen held the strand of hair. She reached into its Song, and it carried her to Druam. One moment she stood, feet steady on the ground. The next, the world spun around her, a white-hot light forcing her to shut her eyes. She couldn't tell what was up or down.

The Songs of the Woods faded away, and she heard new Songs of Earda. Some were very similar, Songs of birds and grass and stone, but subtly altered, slightly different.

Gwen opened her eyes and found herself and Lintem in a cold stone room. A fire burned in the grate, and outside she heard screams and sounds of battle. In a mirror across the room, she caught sight of herself, and wondered at her reflection.

Beneath the grey-green-brown of the Woods, her skin was still youthful, as if she hadn't lived for lifetimes upon lifetimes. Her hair, loose and long, had wrapped itself in locks. Her violet eyes told of many years of survival and knowledge. Leather and fur covered her body, sewn together with a crude needle. She truly appeared a fae creature come to walk among mortals.

A grunt sounded from the bed. A man tossed and turned there, his blankets wrapped around him. Gwen approached him, enraptured by his Song. Yes, she could hear centuries in it, and life far beyond a mortal's. She heard Death and sorrow, ecstasy and hope.

She regarded her husband curiously. Once, she had desired his attention and affection. She wondered what it would feel like to be held again. Would it cause her heart to race, as it once had?

Gwen sat carefully on the bed and reached out to touch Druam. As her fingertip brushed his skin, he shouted and pushed her off. Fangs sprouted from his lips, his eyes glowing red in the darkness.

"Peace," Gwen said.

Druam's eyes glinted with fury. "Who are you? What are you doing here?"

Suspicion dripped in his voice. He looked her up and down, stunned into silence as he absorbed her strange appearance.

Gwen said, "How long has it been since your wife vanished?"

"I–" The abrupt question startled him. "Two months? Two and a half? I don't know, I've lost track of time."

"Two months," she murmured. "How little time here compared to the Woods." She shook her head. *The Songs truly are powerful.*

"This isn't the Cascade Palace." Gwen assessed their surroundings. No, this place was far too militaristic to be the lovely palace above the sea.

"No." Druam regarded her with doubt and curiosity. He sat up straight, the hint of *fampir* still in his features. "Who are you?"

"Don't you recognize me?"

"You're like an apparition from the wild forests," Druam said. "I've never seen anyone like you before. Perhaps I should be asking *what* you are."

"A Witch from the Woods," Gwen said. "I was a sorceress before that. I lived in a marble palace over a city glowing with lanterns. I was the earl's wife."

His lips parted as he scanned her again. "Your eyes." He leaned closer, hungry gaze locked onto hers. "Violet, just like hers. Gwen? Is it really you?"

He didn't wait for an answer. Druam drew her into an embrace, his arms strong around her, his Song bursting with exceeding joy. Gwen stiffened for a moment, unsure how to respond. *You are not just Woods; you are human too.* She loosened, drinking in the feel of him, the familiar slope of his shoulders, the crisp scent of his cologne.

"Where have you been?" he asked, his voice muffled as his head nested against her shoulder. "Why did you leave me?"

"I went to the Whispering Woods," she said, "I learned the Songs."

"Songs? I don't understand."

Songs. Lintem blinked slowly at Gwen. The Song of Death, foul and marked with clashing chords, sounded all around them. *Men are dying,* Gwen thought.

We cannot stay here long, Lintem purred.

I know. Gwen drew back from Druam, her thoughts already tuning into the intricacies of his Song.

"Gwen?"

"I'm sorry, my love," she whispered. "I still have many Songs to learn."

"Please, Gwen." His voice strained with urgency. "We're at war. Rask and the Lofalins are besieging us. If you have more power, we *need* you–"

"You have lived through many more battles than just this one," Gwen said. "*Fampir* tend to gravitate to war."

Druam looked as if she'd dealt him a physical blow. He gripped her hands. "I'm not a monster, Gwen. You must believe me."

"I do." She ran her hands over his face. "We are equals now."

"We were always equal." His hands were tight on hers.

"Were we?" She smiled. "I wish you had told me yourself. But it doesn't matter now. I must go to the Underworld to learn all the Songs of Death."

He froze, emotions flitting across his face in quick succession. He settled on stoicism. "You can't. Gwen, Autorus won't release you."

Gwen drew him into a kiss, stopping his protests. As their lips met, she found the melody in his Song she'd been searching for: his connection to the Underworld, a thread that would bring her to Autorus. She reached out for Lintem and allowed herself to flow into the Song.

For the second time, she abandoned Druam after a kiss.

Chapter Thirty-Six
Mavian

Fear clouded the air. It smelled of excrement and blood, tasted of bitter metal and sour vomit. A haze of dread wafted from Stonetree's walls.

The Lofalin army had run out of boulders to lob at the walls, and while some soldiers gathered more, others harried the defenders during the day. Day and night, those in Stonetree received no rest. Prowlers stalked their keep while the moon shone, and Mavian heard the screams from down in the village. He couldn't sleep at night knowing his creatures slaughtered so many. No rest came in the day, either, for while the trebuchets awaited their loads, troop after troop of elves and men attacked the breaches, coming away with blood on their spears. The dead littered the hill, too many to count. Broken pendants and banners fluttered in the chill wind, a marker of the dead lords and knights that lay beside their soldiers.

Yet still Druam and Edsel held out, their walls standing against the mortals that assailed them.

Mavian rose from an ill sleep, rubbing his eyes. Exhaustion weighed down his limbs, his eyelashes crusted with tears. Beside him, Renna mumbled in her sleep, finally resting after another bout of nightmares. He laid a hand on her head, praying for her release from the torment. Guilt lay heavy in his heart; was it the resurrection spell itself that had caused her suffering? *I freed her from death only to shackle her to dismay*, he thought, hanging his head.

Horns sounded from the hill, and shouts rang in the encampment. Though he felt too tired to move, Mavian sluggishly pulled on his boots and armor, then went outside to see the commotion.

Rank upon rank of elves and Rask's men assembled in the field below the hill, their banners held high and proud. Rask himself, clad in armor and wielding a sword, rode his horse behind the troops. A squire brought Mavian's mount. He spurred it to his commander, a thousand questions on his lips.

"What's happening?" Mavian asked.

"The trebuchets are ready once more," Rask said with a sadistic grin. "With a heavier load, the walls shall fall within candles. Once they do, our men will take the fortress."

And Druam will die, Mavian thought.

A horn blew from the fortress walls, ringing out over the valley. The troops peered around nervously, perhaps expecting some unknown reinforcements for the defenders. There was nothing; no hidden army, no magical force.

With a creak and a *thwup*, the trebuchet barrage began. Boulders, heavier than a horse and cart, flew at the walls. If the first barrage had been destructive, this one was cataclysmic. The boulders crashed into the walls and fortress, sending men flying into the air, showering the earth with man-sized debris of stone and plaster. The fortress groaned as its weight bore down on massive holes, though it still stood.

Another barrage, and the gates were torn asunder, the wood-and-iron doors crashing into the men that stood behind.

"Forward!" Rask shouted, his expression triumphant. "Claim Stonetree!"

The massed ranks of elves and men marched forward up the hill as the trebuchets continued their terrible work. The defenders shouted and screamed. Mavian tried to catch a glimpse of Druam and Edsel. The earls were nowhere to be seen.

At the rear, Mavian rode with Rask and the other officers. The vanguard broke into a run, shouting war cries and leveling their spears at the defenders in the breaches.

Another horn called from the fortress, and horses appeared

inside the fallen gates. A cavalry of a hundred strong assembled in front of the walls, led by Druam and Edsel. The charging army couldn't slow, but they were too far to stop the defenders.

With a yell, drowned out by the call of a hundred horns, Druam raised his arm. Mavian watched with dread fascination as the defenders' cavalry raced down the hill to meet their enemy. Druam's helm shined in the morning light, a beacon that drew all eyes to it.

The horses crashed into the spears, and chaos reigned.

Lofalins fell, their spears tumbling useless to the earth. Horses crashed as spearpoints found their mark, and still the cavalry came on. It plunged into the heart of the invader's army, pointed straight at Rask and Mavian.

"Fight!" Rask screamed. "Kill them!"

The victorious charge up the hill turned into a slaughter. The defenders' horses fell by the dozen, leaving their riders on the ground with their enemies. Half the attackers broke for the fortress, intent on breaching the walls, while the other half remained to fight Druam and his men. The earth churned beneath armor-clad feet, dust clouded the sky. Mavian coughed and peered through the melee.

In the center, Druam's horse had fallen. The earl's shining helm waded mercilessly through the morass of men. Druam bent for a moment, and Mavian thought he had fallen, but Druam rose once more, the unmoving body of Edsel Hawk draped across his shoulders.

"Come fight me!" Druam shouted as he drew ever nearer to Rask. His voice was hoarse and raspy, and he fought as *fampir*, his eyes red, fangs protruding from his lips.

The soldiers around Druam cowered, but the press of men forced them nearer. He wielded a spear in one hand, his other grasping with his claws. One soldier gurgled as Druam's hand closed around his neck, cutting off his air. Blood spurted from between Druam's fingers, and the *fampir* licked it.

Before Mavian's eyes, Druam grew faster, stronger, more fearsome. The *fampir* scythed through the army, biting and spearing and clawing in turn. Mavian's horse shied as soldiers fled the undead. Rask shouted for men to defend him.

Mavian had never seen a *fampir* in pure battle rage before. With gallons of blood pouring onto the field, Druam was unstoppable. Spears thrust into his sides, but he shrugged them off. Swords tried for his head, and he blocked them and gutted the wielder. He was a maelstrom of death, a crimson tide that brought Autorus's own hand onto Earda.

Mavian sat rooted to the saddle, unable to tear his eyes from the sight. Though the cavalry charge had failed, with horses racing riderless and defenders trying to stay alive while they fought on foot, he thought that Druam alone could turn the battle's trajectory.

New horns sounded from the walls: the Lofalins' horns. Victory had been won at the fortress.

Druam paused, his red eyes fixed on Rask. The invaders cheered and created a cordon of shields and spears around him. Blood stained his mouth, his armor's shine completely lost beneath the red.

Mavian thought he had never seen anyone so brave before in his life. Not for the first time, he wished he could have fought alongside Druam, reveling in his leader's courage. As Druam's eyes swept the officers and rested on Mavian's, Mavian blanched.

Druam leveled his spear at Mavian. His voice grated, "Witness my last stand, cousin, and see what Autorus's righteous power has wrought."

"You *lost*, fool," Rask said, riding closer to the circle around Druam. "Your power wrought nothing but failure."

Druam stood tall despite the weight of the dead Earl Stonetree on his shoulders. He glared at Rask. "Nothing is over until death, Rask. And even then, Autorus can change the course of history."

"Restrain him," Rask ordered, riding past him and up the hill to his new fortress. "Lock him in the dungeons until I decide what to do with him."

Mavian tried to catch Druam's eye as he went past, but the fallen earl's eyes burned into Rask. Shivering, Mavian tried to put the image out of his head. It obstinately remained.

With his officers and Mavian behind him, Rask rode over the collapsed gates and into Stonetree. Mavian stared at the carnage: corpses draped over cobblestones and walls, limbs rent asunder, blood painting the grey stone. Prowlers littered the streets, their bodies skewered with spears, their heads lopped off. *Did any survive?* Mavian wondered.

The conquerors rode through the double walls and into the fortress, dismounting before the keep. On its steps, Lady Stonetree stood resolute, her own gown stained with blood. *No doubt she served as a healer to the wounded.* She was past her prime, though still a handsome woman, with grey-streaked hair and large eyes. She looked nothing like her father Rask, yet Mavian saw the same resolute stubbornness in her stance. He braced himself for the coming argument.

Rask went up to the lady, his eyes hard. "Your husband is dead."

Lady Stonetree paled but did not weep. She replied, "He died bravely."

"Farrah," Rask said, a warning in his tone.

"You expect me to celebrate your triumphant entrance, Father?" Lady Stonetree blazed, her nostrils flaring. "You set prowlers and elves upon us, you endangered your own grandchildren and innocent people, and for what? A victory of stone?"

"Edsel chose his death when he chose Druam over me," Rask growled. "Stand down, daughter. I do not wish to see you dead."

"Then leave."

"I have taken this fortress by the right of battle!" Rask roared. He pointed a spindly finger at her. "Move aside!"

"Or what? You'll slaughter me? Slaughter your grandchildren? As long as I have breath, I shall not stand aside for an invader, no matter his blood tie to me. When you married me off to Edsel, you gave up my allegiance." Her eyes went past Rask as Druam was led into the courtyard, Edsel's body still draped over his shoulders. Her expression hardened as she turned back to her father, "Kill me or imprison me. But I will not yield."

Mavian watched Druam being led away. A pang of regret shot through him. *If only I had been as brave as Farrah Hawk,* he thought. He had never thought victory would bring such grief.

Rask's hands clenched at his side as he considered his proud daughter. She regarded him with a cool disdain. At last, he said, "Take her to the dungeons. Let her rot until she realizes the proper course."

Mavian's gut heaved. *How could he put his own daughter in prison?* he thought as four soldiers approached Lady Stonetree. She went without resistance, her head held ever high.

"Clear the halls of rustics," Rask commanded. "Tell them to get out by dusk or be killed. Tonight we feast in our hard-won keep."

The officers gave a resounding cheer, but Mavian didn't join in. His heart sank to his boots as he surveyed the ruins of Stonetree and all the poor souls who had died in terror. As the Lofalin soldiers began to clear away the mess, he couldn't bring himself to feel anything but regret.

Renna joined him that evening in the keep. She blathered on and on about such a righteous victory as she went through the wardrobe in their given chamber. She pulled out furs and woolen dresses, cooing at them between bouts of rapturous delight at the battle. Mavian sat morosely on the bed, barely listening to her.

"Mavian?" she asked. "Did you hear me?"

"What?"

"I asked if it was glorious to see Druam taken down. I wish I had seen him, his beastly self weak and–"

"Enough." Mavian stood, ignoring her aghast expression. "I don't want to hear any more."

"Surely you want to relive the glory? I–"

"You weren't there!" Mavian rounded on her. "You didn't see the way he fought, how he held his fallen man on his shoulders! Druam is a braver man than any I had the displeasure to ride with today!"

Renna's voice dripped with condescension. "Did I marry a traitor? How can you speak of our victory with such weak words?"

"I–" Mavian started, but she shuddered and gasped, dropping the furs to the floor. Renna shrieked, her hands clawing at her face as she sank to the floor in spasms. Mavian rushed to her, trying to hold her up.

"She's here!" Renna screamed. "She's inside me!"

"Help!" Mavian shouted. "Someone help us!" He cradled Renna's head as she wailed. "It's alright, we'll get her out, we'll "

His words died in his throat as Renna twitched and screamed. The black pupil of her eyes grew and grew, taking over the irises and then the white. Her cries increased, pitching through the ceiling, a sound that shattered Mavian's eardrums and tore through his heart.

She fell silent and went still, her eyes flickering shut. Mavian held her and prayed as an army curate dashed into the room. The curate ran his hands over her, noting her shallow breath and eyes twitching beneath their lids.

"What happened?" asked the curate. Mavian described as best he could, telling of her nightmares and the black of her eyes. He did not mention her resurrection. Leaning back on his heels, the curate shook his head. "This is dark magic. I know not how to aid her."

Renna inhaled sharply and opened her eyes. The black had receded, but a strange grey-red ring had grown around her pupil, tainting the blueness of her eyes.

"Renna?" Mavian crooned, stroking her cheek. "Renna, there's a curate here. You'll be alright."

Renna grabbed his hand and tore it away from her face. She glared at the curate. "Out. Get me Rask." A sinister tone tinged her voice, unfamiliar and terrifying.

"Renna," Mavian reached for her again, but she shoved him away with unexpected strength. He fell to the floor, staring at her as she climbed to her feet. She turned her hands over before checking her reflection in the mirror.

"My love–" Mavian started. Renna dealt him a swift kick to

the side that knocked the air out of him. She bent down, taking his chin in a hard grip.

"Renna is gone," she hissed. "And I live once more."

"The woman who haunted Renna," Mavian whispered.

Not-Renna laughed. "When you brought her back from the dead, you dragged me out of my tomb and into her body. She had a strong will, I grant her that, but no one can resist the first of the *fampir* for long." She licked her lips, darting her tongue over her teeth. Mavian's chest tightened, his mind reeling.

"Release him." Rask stood at the door, leaning on his wolfshead cane. For once, Mavian was grateful for the earl's arrival. He scrambled out from under the woman, panting.

"Rask, Renna's gone, she's been replaced with–"

"I know, boy," Rask said, his eyes fixed on Not-Renna. "I gave you the key to unlocking her, didn't I? And fool that you were, you raised her."

Rask bowed, lower than he ever had for the king. Mavian gaped, heart torn and head muddled, as Rask said, "I live to serve thee, Talnor Moertru, Queen of the *Fampir*. Welcome back to Earda."

CHAPTER THIRTY-SEVEN
Seanna

For the past two days, ships bearing Lofalin colors had ringed the harbor, each staffed with warriors and ballistae. The residents of Dockside had quickly fled into Darkroad, closing the doors behind them. As Seanna dressed that day, she smelled the smoke from the fires below as the Lofalins burned each one of the king's vessels.

No escape by sea.

That morning, Seanna had called for Seawind's outer gates to be closed, for the Lofalins would be upon them soon. Hundreds of people battered at the gates to no avail. Con Salur had shut its doors to its people, and the Lofalins would make their camps outside the walls before sunset. The Skals had already arrived with axemen and spearmen that shouted eerie cries, their screams floating over the walls to the cowering rustics.

No escape by land.

Before the gates had closed, a messenger had come through, his horse dying as he leapt off it. He brought a report of the North: Stonetree had fallen, Edsel Hawk killed and Druam Strilu captured, and Rask sitting as pretty as a hen on his new egg.

No help will come from the earls.

High Predicant Ropaz waited for Seanna at the great doors between Seawind and Darkroad, his cheeks thin. Walking alongside her litter, he said, "You must flee the city, Your Grace."

"And abandon the people? I think not."

"People who despised you a month ago, and who only look to you now because of Henrik's death. They cannot be saved, but you can."

One of the chairmen misstepped, his temporary lapse jarring Seanna. The baby stirred fitfully inside her. Cursing under her breath, she said, "I will not leave Udolf in sole charge of the city. Perhaps the Lofalins can be reasoned or bargained with. No matter our strategy, I will not flee. I don't think I could escape even if I wanted to."

"But, Seanna—"

"You will not sway me on this, Ropaz," Seanna said, tossing a coin to a begging child. "I stay. Besides, I thought you admired me for my conviction to remain with my people?"

"Think of the child. You could die before he's born. Our people need a king, and you think Udolf would do well on that throne? If you escape, and the heir is born safely, hope will live under elven rule."

"It is a risk I must take. Am I not Queen of Dotschar? And are these people not Dotsch? How many pregnant women are among them who may die before holding their child? If they have no way to escape the slaughter, it isn't right for me to flee."

With a sigh, Ropaz subsided into silence. Though the city was overcrowded with people, a hush had fallen within the walls. Dread and waiting. Always, the waiting. Waiting to see how long before the enemy attacked, waiting for the walls to crumble, waiting for sudden death or the long agonizing misery of a fatal wound.

After winding through the streets to the wall, the chairmen lowered the litter, and Seanna stepped from it, her rump sore from the ride. With Ropaz's help, she ascended the steps to the battlements where Udolf waited for her. Catching her breath, Seanna gazed out over the plains beyond Con Salur.

Her heart fluttered in her chest. The Lofalin and Skal army stretched from clifftop to horizon. They numbered in the thousands, with warhorses, ballistae, catapults, and the trebuchet. The news of that awful siege weapon had reached

Con Salur. Staring across the plains, Seanna marveled at the elves' swiftness and efficiency. Already, command tents had popped up at regular intervals, with the soldiers' tents raised in orderly rows all around. Smoke curled into the air from countless fires and smithies, drifting to the steel-grey clouds above.

"Look at them," Udolf said, sneering. "Like ants on a carcass. They scurry to and fro, but they shall be squashed. They cannot fell our great city. Many have tried, and many have failed."

"Have you seen the channel, Udolf?" Seanna said quietly. Her arms shivered with goosepimples, and she rubbed them nervously. "It's filled with ships. We are surrounded, and our allies are gone. My brother and Edsel are dead, and Strilu has been captured. Tell me, what hope do you see here? I see nothing but death beyond these walls."

"We have an impenetrable warren in Darkroad and a safe berth in Midtown. They cannot scale the cliffs, nor can they break into the caves."

"What shall we do if driven inside Darkroad? Mm? Starve slowly to death as our people are slaughtered in Seawind?"

Udolf stared down his nose at her. "That is why I shall be king. You are too weak for the crown. Neverly isn't my only supporter."

"Kings must also be wise," Seanna said. She hoped he bluffed about supporters. *Neverly is one of many; would they try to overthrow me before the siege begins?*

A blasting horn from below caught their attention. A small group of riders trotted up to the wall bearing a grey flag on a halberd.

"The ambassador has arrived," Ropaz said.

One of the riders called up, "Our esteemed ambassador, Hirren Fortir, has an audience with the Queen Regent of Dotschar. In a candle, he will enter the gates and ride to the Grand Novum. He asks safe passage in and out of the city while the grey flag flies."

Udolf opened his mouth, but Ropaz shouted, "We agree to

the terms of negotiations."

"You dare–" Udolf spluttered, and Seanna cut over him.

"Ropaz is right, Udolf. We are not in a position of power, and we cannot pretend to be. You can either sulk on the walls like a child or join us in the negotiations. Ropaz, aid me to my chair, please."

Seated once more in the uncomfortable litter, Seanna said quietly to Ropaz, "Don't let Udolf do anything rash. We may yet have hope of survival if he keeps his damn mouth closed."

The Grand Novum occupied the exact center of Seawind. It had nine sides, soaring spires, and a great dome that towered above its walls.

When Seanna had come to the Grand Novum in search of Predicant Manderly, the halls had been filled with supplicants praying for victory. Now, though, it was crammed wall-to-wall with bodies: the sick, the poor, the young, the old. Any who found more safety near the gods than near the soldiers.

With Ropaz at her back, Seanna proceeded through the temple, ignoring the prostrated folk around her. Here was the only place in all of Dotschar where the rustics and nobles would not have to scrape and bow to their queen, for even Seanna was a mere worshipper in these halls. Sweeping into the Exalt's office, Seanna searched for a comfortable place to sit. She finally settled on a cushioned chair while Ropaz sat beside the great desk. She noted him glancing at the Exalt's throne, but though she had made him High Predicant, he did not yet have the right to take the gold-covered seat.

"Udolf should be here soon," Seanna said. "And the Lofalin emissary. I wish to speak with you before either arrive. So I ask you, Ropaz. What would you have me do?"

Ropaz rubbed his temples, his cunning eyes squinted in thought. "If we surrender now, we may be granted leave to continue practicing our religion as we long as we pay tithe to the heathen god. If we fight, we will all be slaughtered or forced to convert. Those, er, trebuchets wreaked havoc on Stonetree. Even with heavenly interference, I do not foresee us winning this fight."

Hand on her chin, Seanna nodded. "I–"

The door swung open and Udolf swaggered in, sword gleaming at his hip. He stood in the center of the room, commanding attention. Before he could speak, Seanna leaned around him to talk to Ropaz, "It could take many negotiations, but we may be able to continue our religion under Lofalin rule."

"You're not suggesting surrender?" Udolf said in horror.

"I am."

"Weak woman!" Udolf exclaimed. He turned to Ropaz. "She knows nothing of war."

"And you do?" Seanna tried not to show her irritation. "We have been at peace for a hundred years, Udolf. *None* of our men know war aside from skirmishes. You have played at battle since you were a child, but you have not killed, you haven't seen the field strewn with the dead. You are a child, and if you insist on acting foolishly, I will not hesitate to confine you to the Silver Keep. Either stay silent or leave."

"I will be the king, you cannot treat me so!" Udolf shouted, his fingers twitching at his sword hilt. "You cannot command me, *aunt!*"

"Can't I? I am the Queen Regent. You are not king yet, child. Would you threaten a pregnant woman like a coward, or would you stand tall and accept defeat like a man? This is a battle we cannot win."

"I will not be trod beneath the heels of elves!" Udolf spun on his heels, exiting the room as suddenly as he'd entered.

"Fool," Ropaz muttered.

Seanna was inclined to agree, but she said nothing. Sitting up straight, she waited. The emissary would arrive soon.

Only a handful of minutes passed before a curate announced the ambassador. The elf flowed into the room wearing white-and-gold robes and exuding an air of confidence. Ropaz stood for him, and the emissary went straight to Seanna to kiss her hand.

"Master Fortir," Seanna said, inclining her head. "Please, be seated. Have you attendants or guards?"

"They wait for me just outside," the elf said. He had

startlingly bright eyes, with copper skin and dark hair held by a hundred tiny braids all pulled back into a silk ribbon. Taking an empty seat, he surveyed the room with a calculating gaze. "You know why I am here, then?"

"You bring terms of surrender, I assume," Seanna said.

"Indeed. And they are far more favorable than those offered to Stonetree, I can assure you that. We seek this city for its value in our religion, for our god's right hand was born within its walls. Upon hearing of your savagery, we also seek to bring our true religion of Amnah, the one god." The emissary paused, picking at his fingernails. "We are merciful. If any are unwilling to convert, they shall be allowed to practice their religion freely in their own homes. All novums shall be converted to worship Amnah, and all newborn babes shall be inducted into the true god's kingdom."

At that, Seanna rubbed her belly nervously. *My child, born to a religion different from his father's?* The thought made her ill, but she forced herself to listen to the elf.

"In addition, we shall allow your rulers to retain part of their lands and holdings, though our own lords shall take possession of two-thirds of all the estates in Dotschar. You, dear queen, will be allowed to keep your throne as a governor who swears fealty to our emperor. Your descendants will likewise be allowed to rule as vassals."

Swallowing nervously, Seanna asked, "And what if we refuse to surrender?"

"All your estates and titles will be forfeit. All of your clergy and nobles shall either be executed or enslaved, and your people forced to convert to Amnah. If they resist, they shall be executed. All novums shall be destroyed."

"How long will you give us to consider your terms?"

"I will return to the gates tomorrow for your decision."

"If we come back with terms of our own, will you hear them?"

"Of course. Negotiations are to be expected."

Licking her lips, Seanna looked to Ropaz. He gave a slight nod, and she said, "We will discuss your terms and draw up propositions of our own. At noon, you are invited back to the Grand Novum for negotiations."

"Excellent. A wise decision, Your Grace." Standing with feline grace, the elf bowed once more and swept from the room. Releasing a breath, Seanna leaned back in her chair.

"That went as well as could be supposed," she said. Ropaz seemed apprehensive, but didn't argue. "Let us take luncheon and reconvene to–"

Shouts and screams interrupted her. Steel on steel and cries of pain echoed through the corridors. Seanna rose quickly, but spasms forced her back to her chair. Ropaz rushed to her side as he called for a curate.

"See what's happening!" he ordered. He turned to Seanna worriedly. "Seanna?"

Seanna shook her head, gritting her teeth. The pain ran up and down her spine, the baby kicking and her insides contracting.

"Is it time?" Ropaz urged, holding her hand. After a moment, the pain passed, and Seanna breathed deeply, exhaling shakily.

"I don't think so," she said, waiting for another spasm that didn't come. "Not yet."

With the predicant at her side, Seanna adjusted to a more comfortable position. She wondered why she'd ever had cause to hate the man. *All those political battles are petty squabbles now.*

"What's happening?" Seanna asked.

"I don't know."

The screams and sounds of fighting had died down, leaving an eerie silence that consumed the Grand Novum. Minutes passed before the curate finally came back to the Exalt's office, drained of color.

"The prince," was all he said.

"What happened?" Seanna demanded, but her heart sank. She knew what her nephew done.

"He and his men...they ambushed the emissary...they killed all the elves." The curate stared into space. "They slaughtered them in the Novum itself."

"Gods help us," Ropaz uttered, making a sign across his forehead.

"I couldn't stop them. They're going to send the emissary's head back as an answer." Stumbling against a wall, the curate held his arm across his stomach. Gasping, Seanna saw that he'd been wounded.

"Bring a healer!" she shouted, but Ropaz was already at the curate's side. Easing the man to the floor, Ropaz yelled outside for supplies.

"We're doomed," Seanna whispered as Ropaz muttered healing spells, his hands reddened with blood. "Udolf has ruined us."

CHAPTER THIRTY-EIGHT
Cara

With each breath, the beast within her grew. It flooded from her chest, down her arms, into her pounding feet. The beast filled her head with the thought of blood, and she reveled in it. *This is what it means to be* sulpari, *to unite with my beast, to think as one.* She could still taste Darian's droplet on her tongue, tangy and oh so full of vigor.

Nothing could stop her now.

Cara raced through the moon-dappled forest of bare trees beside green-needled behemoths. Her goal was a beacon in her mind, the scent of the *fampir* so powerful that she needed no compass nor map to show her where to find them. She wondered how they stayed hidden with such a stench clouding the noses of those who passed by. *No, not all. Only those such as I, bred to hunt these monsters.*

Her breast filled with cold air, but she didn't shiver. The beast warmed her bones, making her complete. *How did I ever fear it? It is strength incarnate, my raw power.* For once, she didn't detect the beast's alternate moods or desires. They were so wholly her own that she couldn't tell where she ended and the beast began.

As she drew closer to the cave, Cara slowed. She unsheathed her sword, gripping the hilt with her taloned fingers. Before she went in, she paused, surveying a nearby tree. She hacked and sliced at the branches until she had a small pile of rudimentary stakes sharp enough to pierce flesh. These she tucked into her belt, ready in case she dropped her sword. *No mercy for Autorus's demons.*

With her heightened eyesight, Cara spotted the dead oak beside a rift in the rock. The rift was just tall and wide enough for a large man to squeeze into. She crept slowly to it, savoring the moments before the killing began.

The night hummed with tension. All the world held its breath, watching her. Once she started, the darkness would fill with screams of the undead, a delicious sound of righteous action.

Cara slipped into the cave, her footsteps silent against the soft earth. Her eyes adjusted to the dim light, her pupils large in her red-tinged eyes. She darted her tongue over her fangs and stopped herself from panting. *Not yet; I have to enjoy this moment.* Further into the cave, a band of twenty or so *fampir* clustered together, sharing wine and swapping stories. They looked like humans, but Cara could smell the taint of death on them. Confusingly, though, she also heard mortal heartbeats, loud as wind in the trees.

She stayed low, edging closer to the firelight.

"Where's Taline with lunch?" one of the *fampir* complained.

"She said she caught a whiff of deer in the north," said another.

"What, no travelers tonight?"

"The snows are almost here," the second replied exasperatedly. "We'll have to live on animals alone."

A small woman, huddled at the *fampir*'s feet, said, "You could drink from me or Yla if you have to."

The second *fampir* smiled. "I know, sweetling. Only if there is nothing to be found for quinns, though. We're not that hungry yet."

Cara counted the *fampir* and humans. Sixteen *fampir*, four humans. The humans weren't tied up or weeping, so they must have chosen to be there. She wrinkled her nose at the thought. *Lambs in the panther's den. If they don't flee, they'll die, too.*

Her mouth watered at the memory of Darian's blood. She could wait no longer. With an acrobat's grace, Cara vaulted the stones and struck at the nearest *fampir*, severing his head from his body. Unlike a mortal, where their blood spurts in gallons, only a little trickled out.

The rest of the *fampir* sat frozen in shock, staring at her. Then, as one, they scrambled away, crying for help. A couple of the braver ones edged forward, ready to attack her.

"Who are you?" a *fampir* shouted.

"Death," Cara said.

She whirled on one of the brave ones, slashing at his chest. Her sword cut two deep red lines through his shirt, and he stared in dismay at them. Too late, she wished she had coated the blade in garlic or onion. Her next swing decapitated him, her arm jolting with the force of it. His head bounced on the earthen floor, coming to rest at a human's feet. The girl screamed and hid behind a *fampir* woman.

The *fampir* huddled in the corner of the cavern. Cara waited at the entrance, ready for them to try and slip past her. She grinned, "Come on. Who's next?"

Three of the *fampir* – two men and a woman – shifted into their beastly forms, their red eyes shimmering in the darkness. They advanced on her, attempting to flank her. Cara watched them steadily. The beast within her shifted, and time slowed around her. She took a stake in her left hand, wielding her sword in her right. She had all the time in the world. While the *fampir* had slowed, she had grown quicker, a hummingbird moving through time.

The *fampir* woman hissed and reached for Cara's side. With precise ease, Cara turned into her, driving her stake into the woman's heart. She pulled it out and darted to one of the other *fampir*. His mouth gaped open in surprise, and he turned, but she was a blur as she struck him. As the first two fell, she reached the third, ramming her sword into his throat. She held him there, glorifying in the blood that ran down her blade toward her hand. Then, she pierced his heart with the stake. His eyes widened with pain before he slid from her weapons.

Time returned to normal for her as the third *fampir*'s body hit the ground. Heads and bodies surrounded her, blood splattered her clothing and armor; her hands were coated in red. Cara turned to the rest of the *fampir*. Her smile held no pity.

"Please!" one of the *fampir* begged. "What have we done?"

Cara spat on a carcass beside her. "Your debt to Autorus has yet to be paid. I'm here to collect."

"The mortals!" the *fampir* cried. "They haven't been turned. Let them go. Please."

Cara considered, her head tilted as she regarded the quaking humans, before she nodded. She stepped aside, leaving room past her to the exit. The four mortals huddled together, slipping on the blood, as they made a break for the door.

Just as they passed her, Cara turned. She slashed at the backs of two and cut into the chests of the others. They staggered, shouting in alarm, as she plunged her sword into one – a lad, only a couple of years younger than herself.

"I changed my mind," Cara said, stepping back in front of the three injured humans who remained. One of them drew a dagger and lunged at her. She blocked him easily, her eyes fixed on his throat: smooth, hairless, pumping with blood. She grabbed him, drawing him close, as she tore into the skin of his neck. Her dreams and nightmares had not prepared her for this.

Blood poured out of him, and he gurgled in her arms, staring at her in fear. His life spilled out onto her, coating her flesh, her clothes, her hair. It slid down her throat, ecstasy itself in liquid form.

The two humans who still stood backed away from her, nursing their wounds. They didn't get far before Cara's blade found them, and they toppled down together.

Stepping over their twitching bodies, Cara turned her attention to the *fampir*. "Weak, cowardly vermin," she said. She spat again. "Not one of you would stand up and fight me?"

She was powerful, the human's blood hot inside her. It buoyed her limbs, sharpened her eyes, made her move more quickly than before. A feral grin crept onto her face, and she raised her sword, licking the blood from the steel. She paused, realizing that *fampir* blood had mixed with mortal on the blade. It was cooler on her tongue, but no less sweet. Indeed, the *fampir* essence was intoxicating in its richness. She swallowed, and power welled in her belly.

Truly, this was the height of living. Why would anyone dissuade her from this course?

Cara lifted her weapons, preparing to take down the remaining *fampir*. She lunged, and–

"CARA!" Laris's shout echoed in the cavern, his spell sending her flying to the floor. Heavy air pressed on her, preventing her from moving, as the sorcerer skirted around the corpses toward her. To her delight, dismay filled his expression. He looked at the bodies on the floor, the blood on her sword and face, and her with open fear.

"What have you done, child?" he asked. He came to stand between her and the *fampir*. "These are no prowlers, mindless and feral!"

Cara growled, throaty and low. The beast and her raged against him, desperate to destroy him. From the depths of her being, something new welled up, a yet-unknown power unsealed by the lives she had claimed.

The birthright of the sulpari.

That power surged inside her, and she threw off Laris's magic. Heady exhilaration flowed through her as Laris gaped. *Your magic is impotent against me now*, she realized. She grinned at him.

"How did you–" Laris started, but Cara unleashed the power that burned at her hands and fingers.

Black flame exploded from her hands, racing out to Laris and the *fampir*. It singed her fingertips, a hotter fire than any she had ever known. Laris only had time to shout an alarm before it consumed him. The *fampir* scrambled to escape. The conflagration reached for them, not letting a single one escape.

Cara lowered her hands, awed and terrified by what she had done. The fire had been too hot for any to even scream. They died within an instant, their bodies burning to ashes in moments. The black flame burned out, leaving her untouched. She blinked, spots of the eerie fire still flickering on her lids. She collapsed to her knees, drained. Though she had consumed blood earlier, her stomach felt empty, as if the power had used it all.

She stared at the carnage around her, ashes and bodies and severed heads and blood. So much blood. The enticement had gone, though she didn't feel nauseated. If anything, a sick pride filled her. As the beast slithered down to its home in her belly, satiated at last, a small part of her was appalled at all she had done that night.

That part was soon silenced by rampant exultation. Laris was dead! No more would he haunt her with magic, no more would he harm her for his own greedy ends. She laughed, a madwoman alone among the corpses.

As she calmed, though, she thought of Sandu. He would be aghast if he had seen this. And Darian had promised never to help her again.

The beast, in its contented state, soothed her. *It's right*, she thought. *It doesn't matter now what they think of me. I have the power to make Autorus's minions pay for what they do to this world.* If Sandu couldn't see the beauty behind her actions, maybe Sandu didn't deserve to be by her side anymore.

PART THREE

CHAPTER THIRTY-NINE
Sandu

With tender, careful hands, Darian dabbed a cream over Sandu's stump. Sandu stared into the distance, the pain in his flesh nothing compared to the hurt of his heart. His shoulder twitched as a cooling sensation spread over it.

Across from them, Jagger poked a stick at their fire's ashes. He kept a wary eye on Sandu, perhaps waiting for him to go mad. Sandu didn't meet his gaze, nor did he consider the small signs his friend made. Nothing Jagger could say mattered. Nothing Darian could do mattered.

Darian leaned back. Sandu asked, "Where's Cara?"

"She left before you did."

"Where did she go?"

"You will have to ask her when she returns."

Sandu gritted his teeth, irked at Darian's half-answers. He stared into the woods blankly. His mind's eye showed him all the mistakes he'd made, everything he'd done that had led to these moments. Tears streamed down his cheeks, and he huddled over, gasping in between sobs. The grief built in his body, wrenching at his empty stomach. He retched and nothing came out. He felt Jagger's hands on his back, trying to be a comfort, but he shrugged them off.

When he regained enough breath to speak, he said, "You're a sick bastard, Darian."

"You would have gone no matter what I said," Darian replied. "You would have wanted to see with your own eyes."

Damn him, he's right. Sandu hugged himself, burying his head into his knees. He heard a rustling, and when he glanced up, he watched as Darian disappeared into the woods.

"Bring Cara back," he shouted, but he didn't know if the blind man had heard him.

What can Cara do? he asked himself. *Nothing. You should be glad she left.*

Another bout of sobs wracked his body as memories flooded into him. His childhood in the Valadi caravan, the prowlers...

In a haze, Sandu said, "I thought losing my mother and nan to the prowlers was the worst that could happen. I'd never seen such horror before. Blood and screams. My father brought me to Dunfrey, and he was too busy working for the lord's meadery to take care of me. I wandered the streets every day, I learned to gamble, I stole from people I envied.

"Then I met Tambrey. The whole world changed in a single day. There she was, perfect and beautiful, and she wanted me, too. *Me.* A no-good vagabond without a proper home to give her." He knew that Jagger understood that part. How Raven and Tambrey had married men like them were mysteries that would never be solved. Sandu rambled on, "I was never happier than when she fell pregnant. I resolved to turn things around, stop gambling, become an honest man. It lasted, for a time. But the children went hungry some nights, and I tried to make enough money at the card tables to buy food for them. Sometimes, I succeeded. I started going every day. I couldn't help myself. The debts grew and grew, and the lord's men came to collect on them. Father took my place, and Tambrey threw me out."

He coughed, choking on another sob. The image of that day burned clearly in his mind. Tambrey, her skin dirty from a day's work, and himself, drunk as could be. She slapped his bowl out of his hand, sending the stew flying, and told him never to come back. *You're dead to us!* she'd screamed at him. *I don't love you anymore!*

"I met you after that, and I betrayed you, too. Then I found Cara, and I dared to hope. Why did I do that? Everything that life's taught me has been that I'm not worth anything to anyone. What's the point of it all? Just death and pain."

Jagger pulled him upright, signing frantically. Tears clouded Sandu's vision, and he didn't try to interpret the gestures.

"I've been having nightmares," Sandu said. "Awful ones where I relive all my mistakes, all the things that have been done to me. I can feel..." He faltered, then plunged on, "...feel the queen's kiss. I didn't expect her to do that, and I know I should be honored, but all I feel is guilt. Like I've betrayed Tambrey somehow, and like I've been taken advantage of. I didn't want that kiss. Sometimes, I feel my lips burning as if she's still there. It turns into pain, and I remember the prowlers at the Masque, their claws in my skin, close to killing me but not quite deep enough. I wish they'd finished the job."

Jagger took his hand, squeezing it tightly. Sandu caught his signs, *You'd be a prowler then. A fate worse than death.*

"Maybe so," Sandu agreed. "All of it haunts me. Not just in my dreams, either. When I have those ill humors, those times when I can't breathe or speak, when my head is filled with memories, I can't stop them. They crowd inside me, beating at my insides. And now my arm's gone. I'm just a burden."

No, Jagger signed. *Let me help you.*

"You can't," Sandu said. "Not unless you can take away all of it. There's only one way to do that."

You let me walk to the mist-folk, Jagger signed, his eyes burning. *I won't let you do the same. You don't want to walk into death, Sandu. It's all your nightmares, but worse. And forever.*

Though he disagreed, Sandu nodded. If he wanted to kill himself, he'd have to wait until Jagger's back was turned. He didn't say more, and let himself be wrapped up in blankets and laid down in the tent. Sleep didn't come; how could it? Sandu tried to even his breathing, make it slow and steady. He listened until Jagger's breath had grown quieter in sleep.

Sandu crept from the tent, the blanket still draped over his shoulders. He headed back down the road to a point where a cliff's edge bordered the wagon-tracked path. The moon cast shadows through the trees, the wind carrying the calls of wild animals and prowlers. Sandu didn't care. Let them come.

His steps were purposeful, and he soon reached the cliff's edge. The earth fell away at his feet as he clung to a tree growing at the precipice. He stared down the dizzying height. How long would it take to reach the bottom? Would he die instantly, or agonizingly slow, a thousand injuries bleeding away his life essence? Should he throw himself head first, just to make sure?

Somewhere in the foothills below, a wolf howled. Sandu contemplated the vista and the plains beyond the hills. Lights, distant and small, showed throughout the night. He wondered if anyone had found Tambrey's ashes, or if there was enough left of her body to bury.

I'll just let go while I look, Sandu decided. *The last thing I'll see is beauty.*

He took a deep breath, leaning further out. Just as his fingers began to slip, and he resigned himself to the drop, hands wrapped around his waist and dragged him back from the edge. Sandu stumbled and collapsed into the waiting arms, shaking. Jagger held him tight. *Of course he'd follow me.*

Sandu shivered. He had been so ready to die, but now that the precipice had been taken out from beneath his feet, was he truly?

"Thank you," Sandu managed, his legs wobbly beneath him.

Jagger lifted him and carried him back toward the camp. Sandu clung to his friend, grateful for his friend's presence. As the sky lightened, he wished for Cara. She *had* to help him before he tried to kill himself again.

Exhausted by his grief and turmoil, Sandu fell asleep, comforted by his savior's steady pace, like a babe lulled as his mother walked him around the room.

CHAPTER FORTY
Mavian

"I don't understand," Mavian mumbled, cradling his head in his hands. He hid in the kitchens, the only place of warmth he could think of. The ovens blazed as the keep's servants bustled about, silent and tearful. More than one sniffled as they worked, and a few shot frightened looks at Mavian and Merick.

"It's all my fault," Mavian continued, staring at a cauldron in a fireplace. "My desperation, my *obsession*, my arrogance clouded my vision. I thought I'd done everything right. Perhaps I did, and it still didn't matter."

The wight laid a hand on his shoulder. Mavian sighed, grateful for his stoic presence. *I can see why Cara was so affected by seeing him like this. I stole him from her, just to prove my power. Arrogant fool.* His side ached from where Renna – no, not Renna, someone named Talnor – had kicked him.

I was an idiot, Mavian thought. *I believed I could overcome the curse of the ancient cultists by changing the name of the resurrected. All I did was bring her back with Renna.*

From the corner of his eye, he saw one of the kitchen maids approach. He lifted his head and shook his bedraggled hair out of his eyes. She gave a small curtsey and held out a bowl of broth. He accepted it and thanked her, but she backed away, eyes darting at Merick.

Mavian's stomach growled, and he downed the broth in a few large swallows, relishing the warmth as it flowed down his throat. It tasted of simple spices and vegetables that reminded him of home. The cook at Far-Eyes Castle had made such broths in winter, and Mavian would sit by the kitchen fire, sipping at his bowls and listening wide-eyed to stories of Autorus and the Dead's War.

Mavian placed the bowl on a nearby shelf. The nervous servants darted around him, not daring to meet his eye. *They don't want me here. I came with the army that slaughtered their friends and relatives, killed their lord, and imprisoned their lady.* He stood and departed, shoulders hunched.

As he walked, Mavian thought about the conspiracy he'd unwittingly deepened. *It's all because of Rask.* The more he contemplated, the more he realized how blind he'd been. *Rask must have had this gem for a long time and arranged for me to get ahold of it. When I wanted to raise Renna, he sent me after the sarcophagus. He* wanted *me to bring Talnor back. But why? Rask has never willingly served anyone in his life. Is he really so devoted to his family's cult that he'd do this? Or does he believe she'll aid him in getting what he wants?*

What does Rask want? Mavian paused, realizing that he'd never really analyzed the High Earl's motives. He had assumed, like most, that Rask wanted power and money the same as any other lord. But to bring back a centuries-dead *fampir*...what purpose did that serve?

Two courses presented themselves to him. The first was to try and reverse the takeover of Renna's body and bring back his love. The second, if that failed, would be to stay and determine Rask's goals. What he would do then, he didn't know. He doubted he had the bravery to defy Rask openly, but maybe, just maybe, he could find a way to do the right thing.

Mavian made his way through the keep to the room he was supposed to share with Renna. He hesitated outside, hearing voices within. With a gesture, he dismissed Merick. *I need to stand up for myself now.*

"...have I been gone?" came Talnor's voice with the beautiful tones of Renna's speech, but harsher, firmer. More demanding.

"Over seven centuries," said Rask. "I would imagine that the years became hard to differentiate in the sarcophagus."

"Hm. And you say you have reason to believe that the one who trapped me still lives?"

"He has haunted our world since your time. He could be the one."

"I will never forget his name and face. He's in the dungeons?"

"Yes." Footsteps and a cane's clacking approached the door, and Mavian backed away. Rask pulled the door open, stopping short as he saw Mavian. Talnor sneered over his shoulder.

"My *savior*," she drawled, her eyes glittering with malice. "Lingering at the threshold, are you?"

Mavian lifted his chin, determined not to let her get to him. *She speaks with Renna's voice, dwells in Renna's body, but she's not Renna. Never forget that.* "I came to gain answers."

"Leave disappointed. We have business to attend to," Talnor said, brushing past Rask. The old man coughed into a kerchief, then scrutinized Mavian.

"He can help us still," Rask said. "He knows the old tongue."

"Obviously. He couldn't have raised me otherwise." Talnor licked her lips. "But–"

Mavian grasped the gem around his neck and traced runes in the air. He had hoped to wait until she was sleeping or indisposed, but he had to try.

"What is he doing?" Rask asked.

"A vain attempt to bring his woman back, I should think," Talnor said with a bored expression.

Mavian's hand sweated, his fingers trembling, as he finished a rune and whispered the spell. The gem grew cold beneath his palm, and the air shimmered around Talnor. Without a flicker of fear, she reached out and brushed the runes away. They faded as she locked her claws around Mavian's throat.

"You have spirit, I'll give you that," she said. "But *that* belongs to me."

With her other hand, Talnor plucked the gem from Mavian's numb fingers, ripping it from around his neck. He staggered and gulped, his windpipe tight in her grip.

"Do you know what this was used for?" Talnor asked. He gurgled, and she smiled. "I don't know how, but Valder Riesk destroyed hundreds of my kin in one spell using this very gem. I mean to find out his methods."

"What will you do with him?" Rask stepped forward, his gaze unpitying.

"I need a pet," she said. "I'll keep him for now." She leaned down, the familiar blue of Renna's eyes tainted with the *fampir's* red. "If you disobey me, I will kill you."

Mavian nodded, and she released him. He gasped, massaging his neck. Talnor turned to Rask. "Will you join me in the dungeons?"

"I'm afraid not; there are matters with the Lofalins I must attend to." Rask went past her, his cane clicking on the stone floors. Talnor watched him go. She waved at Mavian.

"Come on, little pet." She walked quickly, moving so differently from Renna that Mavian had trouble remembering that his love had ever been in that body.

The scholar in Mavian wanted to ask this *fampir* questions, to learn about the Dead's War and the creation of her kind. The other part of him, the part that mourned the second loss of Renna, was determined not to gain any satisfaction from this ancient being.

"I must thank you for your gift," Talnor said, distracting him from his thoughts. She had slowed to walk beside him, hooking her hand through his arm like Renna used to. He pulled away, but her grip was iron. He gave up and didn't rise to her statement. She waited a moment longer, then said, "You brought me the blood of the *sulpari*. It is a greater gift than any I could have hoped for. The last *sulpari* died with my mate and a thousand others, and alas, I was never able to sway her to our cause. But this new one – Cara, was it? – she bends already to the darkness."

"How do you know about her?" Mavian asked, his curiosity overwhelming his resentment.

"Renna and Rask. You see, while I dwelled in Renna's dreams, I poked in her memories. Found out all I could. Dreams are a conduit between *fampir*, if one knows how to use them. And with the *sulpari's* blood..."

"You've been communicating with her?"

"In a way," Talnor replied smugly. "She doesn't know what Renna has become."

"She'll kill you," Mavian said. "She wants me dead for what I did to Renna. Imagine what she'd do to you."

"*If* she finds out," Talnor purred, stroking Mavian's cheek. Her long nail bit into the soft skin under his jaw. "But she won't find out, will she?"

Mavian gritted his teeth and nodded. *Whatever I need to do to find out the truth of all this.* He ventured, "King Landin made the *fampir*, correct?"

Her lip curled. "Landin did nothing. It was his sorcerers who made us. We slaughtered them once the war was done. Each and every one of them."

Talnor raised her hand, stopping Mavian's next question. They had arrived at the dungeons, and she stared at the far wall. Druam was strung up by chains, his hands anchored above his head. The cells to either side were full of captured officers and families. Mavian saw Lady Stonetree with her children, her head leaning against the wall as she slept.

"*It's him*," Talnor breathed, slipping into the ancient tongue. Mavian barely caught her words. He glanced between her and Druam.

"Who?"

Her grip on his arm tightened. "My mate, Galiyar, sired two Valadi soldiers before he was killed by Valder's spell. Those soldiers hunted me down and trapped me in a sarcophagus, condemning me to an eternity alone."

She strode down the dungeon straight for Druam. Mavian had to jog to keep up with her. When she stopped in front of Druam, the earl only glanced up at her, then at Mavian, before he stared back at the wall.

"What do you want, cousin?" Druam asked.

Talnor dropped Mavian's arm, her expression venomous. "*Cousin?*" she hissed.

"By name, not by blood," Mavian said, though he would rather have the stronger tie. "I suppose he gave his name to one of my ancestors whom he was especially fond of."

"Jeriku Lackname, who I made a Strilu," Druam said without emotion. "Your great-great-grandfather. A courageous man."

Talnor still didn't move. She glared at Mavian a second longer. She prowled up to Druam and asked, "Do you know who I am?"

"Mavian's bitch?" Druam offered. "Though I thought I'd killed you."

She took his chin. "He brought her back. And me with him. I remember you, Mordekai Strilu of Belleslye."

Druam blanched, what little color he had draining out of his face. His eyes flicked to Mavian and back to Talnor. "Even I had forgotten that name."

Talnor laughed, releasing him. "We have much to catch up on, old friend." She snapped her fingers at a guard. "Bring him down and relocate him to a more private chamber. I wish to speak with him without prying eyes and ears."

The guards obeyed as Druam stared at Talnor, no doubt a thousand thoughts and doubts running through his mind. They descended deeper into the dungeon, into a small, windowless room with a damp floor. Rats skittered through a hole in the wall as the door banged shut. Druam had been chained again to the wall.

"Who are you?" he asked Talnor as she paced in front of him. "How do you know that name?"

"Remember Galiyar?" Talnor asked.

Druam nodded. "My sire."

"My mate," she responded.

His eyes widened. "It was buried deep within the mountains, warded by runes and enchantments! You—"

"Rask's ancestors found it," Mavian said miserably. "They made the spell to raise her."

"And you—"

Druam was cut off as Talnor slapped him across the face,

her nails digging into his cheeks. He hung a moment before righting himself.

"You and your brother imprisoned me," Talnor said, enmity laid into every word. "When I'm done with you, I'll find him and destroy him, too."

"Too late," Druam said with a small smile. "Verdon's gone."

"I'll hunt him down."

Druam opened his mouth, but Mavian interrupted him, "He's right. Verdon vanished a long time ago, probably dead."

Without warning, Talnor backhanded Mavian. He stumbled against the wall, head ringing, as she turned back to Druam. From a small table, she picked up a flat-bladed knife.

"Then you'll have to take your brother's punishment. You condemned me to an eternity of suffering," she said in a lover's soft tone. "Your death will not be any swifter."

With careful precision, she placed the knife on the skin of Druam's arm. He shivered, remaining silent as she drew it up to his shoulder, flaying a sliver of flesh. It dropped to the floor, a pale snake coiled on the stone.

Druam's blue eyes met Mavian's. Hatred, grief, and anger lurked there. Mavian quailed. He turned and left. *I brought back the creature who hates him most,* he thought, his stomach churning. *Rask would have killed him and been done with it. She'll keep him alive for years as she exacts her 'justice'.* Without the gem, Mavian was powerless. He headed back through the dungeons, toward the light, when he heard a shriek of pain. It sounded again, utterly inhuman.

One of his prowlers! Mavian turned heel and ran toward the noise, not sure what he could do without the necromantic gem that had allowed him to control them for so long. He rounded a bend and came across four guards that had cornered one of the creatures. They goaded it with their spears, drawing its black blood. It hissed and squirmed, swatting at them but unable to get close.

"Stop it!" Mavian shouted.

One of the guards nudged the man next to him. "The prowler's keeper," he snickered.

Mavian reached unconsciously for the gem before he remembered. He had learned enough magic that didn't need the power of the Underworld; he cast a quick spell, blowing out the soldiers' torches. They shouted in alarm, and there was a scampering of feet and claws against stone. By the time they had relit their torches, the prowler had vanished.

The soldiers grumbled. Mavian held his head high, and they left, still muttering. He waited for them to disappear, then crouched down. He stared into the dark.

"At least there's still one of you left," he whispered before he stood and started back.

After a few minutes, he heard a pattering of feet behind him. He turned, confused. The prowler peeked from around a corner. It gurgled, its jaws slathered with saliva.

Mavian checked over his shoulder, but the hall was empty. Without the gem, he had no way to compel the creature. He took a deep breath and said in the tongue of the Underworld, "*I won't harm you if you won't harm me.*"

The prowler tilted its head, almost doglike in its confusion. It crept closer on all fours, one of its hands just lifted off the floor.

Then, it spoke in the same guttural tongue, "*Pack-mate?*"

Mavian startled, taking a step back. He had never, in all his years of studying the creatures, ever heard one speak outside of their own strange language of chirps and body signals.

"*A friend,*" Mavian said, surprised that his tongue worked. His heart beat rapidly, and he contemplated the creature before him. It looked like any other prowler: dark hair matted with blood and excrement, its human face distorted by feral features. Its long talons were coated in grime, and its clothes had long since shredded away. Ribs poked out from its thin chest. The man it had once been would have been around Druam's age when he died, Mavian supposed.

"*Meeaaaatttt?*" the prowler growled hopefully.

"*No. Pack friend,*" Mavian tried, hoping that the prowler would understand. His mind raced with the possibilities of true communication with prowlers. *Why are you so different from the rest?* he wondered. *What can I learn from you?*

"*Frrrriiiiiend?*" It tilted its head the other way, as if trying out a new word. It said, "*Ekkkkaaarrrrr.*"

"*Ekkar?*"

It gurgled happily. "*Ekkkkkaaaaarrrr.*"

"*Is that your name? Ekkar?*" That was another unique thing. Mavian didn't know prowlers even had names. It burbled and chirped, coming closer to him. The hungry gleam in its red eyes had vanished, replaced with an odd look that he'd never seen in a prowler before. He realized with a jolt that the creature gazed at him *trustingly*.

"My gods," Mavian murmured. "Where in the world have you been all this time?"

The prowler came within touching distance. It waited. Mavian hesitated, then pointed at himself, "*Mavian. Friend.*"

It slapped the floor, a gesture that prowlers did when they were happy. Mavian smiled and dared to touch the creature's claw. It froze.

"*Mavin. Pack-mate.*" To his astonishment, it took his hand like a child grasping its father's fingers.

Mavian should have shuddered at the prowler's hand in his. It was unnatural, unthinkable. They had only been tools before. As Ekkar gazed at him with those strange red eyes, amazement flood through him. *Such quick comprehension,* he thought. His grief had faded for a moment, leaving only the thrill of discovery. *This* was why he'd investigated the prowlers in the first place, *this* was why he wanted education and a new world, one which could help the prowlers rather than destroy them.

Ekkar trilled happily. Mavian straightened, wondering what Merick would think of his newest companion. *Surrounded by living, but my only friends are the undead.* He wanted to laugh, but heard a guttural moan from farther away in the dungeon.

Druam. Mavian stood there in the corridor, still holding onto Ekkar, and listened. He could not stop the shame that curled over his heart.

Chapter Forty-One
Seanna

Though clad in irons, Udolf leaned arrogantly on one hip, his head held high. Behind him, four more lords stood side-by-side, their hands chained to their feet. All of them were gagged. On either side of the throne room, nobles watched with guarded expressions. Their clothes hung loosely on them, an indication of their waning food supplies. Soon even they would have to join the bread lines all over the city.

Seanna sat on Henrik's throne, her neck sore with the weight of the crown. She understood now why Henrik had gone gray so young, why his temper had always been so short. *It is a heavy burden indeed.* High Predicant Ropaz stood to her right, with Dyle Belrose to her left, the two men she trusted most in the city. Strange, how she had hated one and ignored the other for so long, yet now she couldn't imagine the Silver Keep without them. To one side of the throne, the three rustic elders stood shoulder-to-shoulder, distinct in their simple linens.

With a wary eye, Seanna surveyed the crowd. She noticed the lack of certain prominent members of Con Salur society, and leaned over to Belrose. "Where are Lords Dunner and Preory? I don't see their wives, either."

Belrose gave the slightest shake of his head. "They left the city, Madam."

"When? How?"

"A small ship in the night. I believe they paid off the Lofalins for safe passage."

"Traitors." Seanna said with authority, "The Lords Dunner and Preory have betrayed their crown and their city. As of today, their titles and estates are revoked, granted instead to those who stand here today. If ever they are found, their lives are forfeit."

She waited for complaints or murmurs, but the courtiers remained quiet, staring at the floor or gazing at her with blank expressions. *What happened to the proud Dotsch of this city?* Of course, she knew the cause. Each of them was wondering if it would have been better to be branded a traitor, and possibly survive the war, than to be loyal and dead. *Too late now.* She glanced at Belrose from the corner of her eye. *He must succeed in finding us a way out of the city through Darkroad's warrens.* So far, the investigation into the tunnels had been fruitless, but Seanna remained positive. *We will find a way out.*

Now, to today's business. Seanna regarded Udolf with open disgust.

"You stand before me today as conspirators and traitors to the crown," Seanna said. She would have spat if it was queenly to do so. "You murdered an ambassador under the grey banner, forfeiting the city's right to negotiation and plunging us into heedless war. The death of every man, woman, and child will lay on your heads." She waved her hand, indicating the guards to remove Udolf's gag. "What have you to say for yourself?"

"Only that you sully my grandfather's throne with a woman's weakness," Udolf proclaimed, cocky as ever. "I did what needed to be done. We are proud Dotsch, we will never stand under elven tyranny!"

At his words, the chained lords behind him rattled their shackles, their eyes blazing. Seanna granted them a perfunctory glance before turning back to Udolf. "With what army would you have defeated the enemy? They outnumber us three to one and built machines we cannot counter."

"If we had met them on the open field–" Udolf started.

Seanna didn't let him finish. "You would be dead already!" She rubbed her temple, regretting the decision that lay before her.

"If I may, Madam?" Ropaz asked. Seanna nodded, ceding

the trial to him. He stepped forward, his predicant's robes swishing on the floor. "You murdered a man in the House of the Gods. Do you deny this?"

"I deny nothing," Udolf said haughtily.

"Do you deny that you saw, with your own eyes, the grey banner under which the ambassador entered the city?"

"No."

"Then why, pray tell, did you not await the Queen Regent's council in which you could voice your concerns and your strategies for battle?" Ropaz's clear, unthreatening tone sent shivers down Seanna's arms. *The man has listened to thousands of confessions in his lifetime,* she realized. *He knows how to break down a man's conscience.*

Udolf's smirk faltered. "That bitch would never have listened to me!"

"Would you say, Prince Udolf, that the gods look kindly on those who are unwise?"

"I'd say that surrender is unwise."

"For whom? For yourself? You are young. You seek glory above all else. Tell me, Your Highness, have you ever witnessed a Lofalin sacrifice?"

The prince paled. "Your Eminence, I wanted only to show the strength of the Dotsch."

"Let me tell you of the Lofalins," Ropaz continued, unheeding of the prince's words. "I visited their country some years ago on a mission to spread our peaceful religion. They laughed in my face. They allowed me to go free, once they had sacrificed my fellows. While the victim still breathes, the elves drug them, making them believe they are experiencing Lyael itself. Then, they tear out the sacrifice's still-beating heart.

"There are other methods, too, similarly vile. For some, they attach each limb to a camel, pulling the victim apart with excruciating slowness. Another is where they tie a man upside down to a wooden cross, leaving him for the vultures after they pull out his entrails to drag on the ground."

Seanna pressed a hand to her mouth, trying not to imagine the horrors Ropaz conjured. She watched Udolf, his arrogant facade slowly crumbling. Ropaz took Udolf's chin, staring into his eyes.

"This is what they will do to the people of this city. Your aunt's child will be torn from her womb and bashed against a wall. Each one of the people in this room will be sacrificed or summarily executed, if not raped beforehand. The Lofalins have conquered fourteen smaller countries in the last thirty years. They know war, a knowledge we have lost in a hundred years of peace. Tell me, other than glory for yourself, what did you hope to accomplish?"

Udolf looked away from the High Predicant. "I didn't want us to fall prey to those barbarians."

"Is that so? If you had listened to the ambassador's terms, you would have known how generous an offer they made us. You could have retained your throne."

At that, Udolf pushed the High Predicant away. He glared at Seanna. "I have no remorse for what I've done."

"Remorse would not change your fate," Seanna said. Ropaz came back beside her, and she thanked him. "Prince Udolf Bergfalk of the Royal House of Dotschar, you have confessed to crimes against the crown, the gods, and the people of this city. You and your accomplices conspired to murder the Lofalin ambassador within the Grand Novum, thereby subjecting a hundred thousand people to the ravages of war."

The ground trembled as she spoke, and the nobles cast terrified looks around. Seanna's heart quivered, but she pressed on.

"As Queen Regent of Dotschar, I hereby sentence you to death by beheading to be carried out at dawn. Make your peace with Autorus and the gods."

The quaking tremors continued as guards led Udolf and the chained lords from the throne room, the prince's face ashen and grave. *Mayhaps he learned his lesson, but too late.* Seanna sighed and turned to a soldier who stood nervously by the door.

"What news?" she asked.

"The Lofalins are bombarding the city, Your Grace," the soldier reported. "For now, they only use their catapults. We believe that the trebuchets will be finished soon."

"It won't be long," Belrose said as the soldier bowed and departed. "When the trebuchets begin their attack, no one in Seawind will be safe."

"I know," Seanna said. "Tell the generals to report the moment the elves load those machines. I want everyone in Darkroad or Midtown before the true terror begins."

"Of course, Madam." Delrose bobbed his head and left to carry out her word. Nobles filtered from the throne room, grumbling among themselves. The rustic elders bowed, their expressions grave. Only Ropaz remained with the queen, his eyes betraying some inner strife.

"What is it, Ropaz?" Seanna asked when they were alone. "Should I have spared Udolf?"

"No," he said, seemingly shaken from his thoughts. "His death is well-earned. I only wish we had stopped him before he killed the ambassador."

"If wishes were fishes," Seanna said, remembering her father's old saying. At that moment, she wished her father were there now to guide her. *He's with Henrik, and their troubles are over.*

"It's not the prince that troubles me," Ropaz said. He removed his red wool hat, rubbing the felt in his fingers. "Madam, I must ask a favor of you."

"Oh?"

"I have a sister, younger by a decade, who lives in Seawind near the walls. I ask that I may be allowed to bring her to the Silver Keep today; she won't be a nuisance, but–"

Seanna smiled at his fluster. *Of all the things I would have guessed, this one would never have crossed my mind.* She stopped his ramblings and said, "Of course she may stay. I'll take her on as a handmaid, and she will have a room beside mine."

"She's no noble, Madam, such an honor–"

"What has nobility ever given us? High graces and flowery shits? She'll be my handmaid, and that's the last of it," Seanna said, happy that she could provide some good news on this grim day. Ropaz opened his mouth to argue further, but wisely shut it and nodded.

"Thank you."

Seanna went to bed that night full of worry and dread, but at least she had done something kind for someone else. She didn't know the girl, but if she was anything like Ropaz, Seanna thought she'd enjoy the company of such a handmaid.

✳

The catapults pounded the walls throughout the night, but the mighty stone held firm. If the Lofalins had brought only those lesser machines, the people of Con Salur may have had cause to hope. As it was, Seanna was grateful for the respite when the bombardment ceased.

She donned her darkest gown, closing the buttons at her throat and draping her shoulders with a grey shawl. Though she had witnessed executions before, she had never been the one to give the command. Was this how Henrik or her father had felt? Guilty, morose, yet also relieved? *Neither of them had to execute their nephew for treason*, she reflected. *It's far easier to behead a wayward lord than an idiotic youth.*

With careful, deliberate steps, Seanna descended to the courtyard. A hasty wooden scaffold had been erected in the center, with a stone block and heavy axe in its center. The executioner with his black mask stood to one side, eyes hidden beneath his hood.

The five condemned men stood in a line before the scaffold, awaiting the queen's word. She took her place, holding the feeling of guilt deep in her heart. *Never let me be joyful for such a deed*, she thought before she said, "These men have committed the most heinous of crimes and must now face Autorus in the afterlife. May the gods have mercy on their everlasting souls."

Udolf came last. Though he had tried to keep a strained grin, his expression dimmed and dimmed as each of the lords lost his head. Seanna watched in a haze as crimson flowed and ball-sized heads stared up emptily from a large basket. The baby kicked, and she instinctively rubbed her belly, waiting for the executions to be over.

The four lords' headless bodies had been removed, and Udolf stood now at the block. He met Seanna's eye.

"Last words?" the executioner asked.

In the foggy morning light, Seanna thought she saw tears on the prince's cheeks.

Udolf knelt down, still staring at her. He said, "Here kneels the righteous king, murdered by his vicious aunt."

He stretched his neck over the block. He didn't blink, not even as the sharp blade sliced into his spine and through his throat, his eyes on Seanna until the very end.

Seanna waited until she made it back to her rooms before she vomited.

As she wiped her mouth, Belrose quietly entered her room. His face was grey. "Madam, the trebuchets have been finished."

His words hung in the air, a death knell for the city. Seanna bent her head and prayed to whatever gods might be listening. *Let us find a way out of this city. Not for myself, but for all the thousands of innocent lives that may yet be saved.* At the end of her prayer, she added a thought for Udolf. Whatever he had done, he had been a brash youth, barely out of childhood.

May all our ends be as swift as his.

CHAPTER FORTY-TWO
Cara

Dried blood cracked on her hands. Cara sniffed, the smell of death strong in her nose. She wrinkled her forehead as she sat up, her head aching. In the darkness, her human eyes couldn't see much. The beast rose enough to grant her its sight.

Corpses littered the floor, coated with ash, like snow but gray and lifeless. Cara had slept there among the dead, uncaring in the dark. Now, in the chill of dawn, the stench nauseated her.

Human bodies lay next to *fampir*, staring up with glassy orbs. All were young, in their late teens, with barely a wrinkle on their grimy faces. They lay draped over each other, a macabre display.

Cara stumbled to her feet and staggered out of the cavern. The wan light outside cast a somber feel to the mountains, the steel-grey clouds hiding the sun from the world. Even the sky seemed to know her crime.

With jilting steps, Cara made her way to a large stream. The water reflected the heavens, grey and distant. Each gurgle and trickle told her, *You are a murderer.* She threw off her blood-stained clothes and armor and waded into the water, shivering as it touched her tender flesh. With short, rough movements, she washed her hands and face, scrubbing the dried blood from her skin. It came off in brownish clumps and drifted downstream.

Though her raw flesh protested, Cara kept scrubbing. She rubbed herself pink, cleaning herself over and over. The water below her no longer carried a hint of brown, yet she kept going.

She dunked her head into the freezing stream, fingers working her scalp and short hair. When that was done, she went back to her arms, her chest, her head again. Her teeth chattered with the cold, goosepimples ran all over her limbs, but she scrubbed obsessively as if she could rub her very skin off.

The clouds had started to break apart, the meager sun shining through, before she left the water. Her breath hitched in her tight chest, and she turned to her clothing before she could think too much on the night's events. If she worked hard enough, perhaps she would forget it entirely.

The hard leather had absorbed some of the blood. The stain, she thought, could be mistaken for something else. Her clothes, though, were another matter. The creamy shirt, travel-worn and pit-soiled, had giant splotches on it. Without soap, she had no hope of getting those out. Her breeches, too, were a similar lost cause. She used stones to scour the linen until it nearly tore, the stains stubbornly clinging to the fabric, then hung it up to dry. Thankfully, her boots were as dark as her armor, and the stains could be safely ignored.

While her clothes dried, Cara sat by the stream and hugged her legs. She tried peering down into the water, but her reflection made her pause. She splashed it and stared up at the sky. It held no comfort. The trees, some bare, others green and dry, whispered in the wind, and she heard their cry of *Murderer, murderer.*

Cara shuddered. She leaned back over the stream, washing her hands, arms, and face again. Though her skin was clean, she thought she could still feel the dried blood pulling at the translucent hairs on her flesh. She would have sworn the stench of the *fampir* clung to her.

It was a chill day, and Cara's shivering grew worse. She didn't dare redress in wet clothes, nor did she have flint and tinder to start a fire. She huddled against a tree, the wind an enemy all around her.

At last, she couldn't stem the tide of her thoughts. *I killed them all*, she thought. *Humans and* fampir *and Laris. I drank their blood, and black fire poured from my hands.* The invigoration of such power was a distant memory, and Cara tried to hold onto it, to remember the ecstasy of that moment.

My enemies fell before me, and not even the great sorcerer could stop it. Cara grinned with dark satisfaction at Laris's final expression. *He'll haunt me no more. I've repaid my debt; he brought he into this world, so I took him out of it.*

Her thoughts turned to her parents, hazy memories of her mother flitting in and out of her mind. *I wonder if she ever loved my father, or just wanted to be the mother of such power. I wonder if she knows what's happened to me.* Sandu had gone to such lengths to free his father, yet Cara felt no inclination to find her own parents. *Even if my mother wants to find me, I don't want to see her,* Cara decided. *She knew the monster she would produce, and chose that path anyway. And my father never cared to find me. He could be dead for all I know.*

What would Sandu think of me? To see what I've become? She could imagine his fright, his disgust. He had forgiven one monster – Jagger – yet could he do the same for her? Somehow, Cara knew that Sandu wouldn't have the strength. *He's been through too much. I can't put this on him, too.*

Darian must know what had happened. He would have heard the Song as they died. *Let him judge me. I did what I must.*

Though filth coated her skin, Cara didn't regret what she had done. *It was a shame for human lives to be lost, but they allied themselves with Autorus's minions. They knew what their fates must be.* Cara couldn't shake the memory of those corpses beside her, so she embraced it instead. She thought savage things about each human, justifying why they needed to die.

The wind rattled the trees, stinging her flesh. Cara's teeth trembled in her skull. Her shoulders jumped and her ribs hurt from her violent shivers. Her extremities turned blue, and she watched them with fascination.

Am I going to die? she wondered.

The beast rose inside her, heating her from the inside out. Its roar consumed her, and she heard within it the desire to *live*. With the beast's vigor, Cara stood and pulled her mostly-dry clothes from the branches. The damp linen clung to her body.

She dragged on her armor and boots, then marched back to the *fampir* cavern, driven partly by the beast's force.

Inside the cavern, Cara gathered blankets and coats from the dead, piling them together to make a nest for herself. She climbed inside, bundling herself with layers of fabric. Her shivering faded and stopped altogether, and the beast descended back to its place in her belly. *It gave me the strength to live,* Cara thought. *It isn't all bad.*

She fell into a fitful sleep, and her dreams were plagued with ghosts.

Merick, his scars inky against pale cheeks, his eyes full of an unholy darkness. He contemplates her with those eerie eyes, a red glow behind his head. He says, slowly, haltingly, "You've become bad, Cari. Not like I raised you."

"I'm doing what's best for the kingdom," Cara says. She is dressed like his apprentice again, holding a wooden sword. "I want the evil in the world to be gone."

"How can it be, when it lives in you?" Merick presses a finger to her chest, and she falls backwards into blackness.

She lands on a down bed, naked. Turning, she finds Alex beside her, his nose crinkled as he sleeps. As she moves, he wakes, his eyes snapping open.

"Awake already?" he yawns, pulling her into his embrace. Cara wants to fall into it, to relive the peace of his arms, but she knows what he is.

"What's wrong?" he asks as she pushes him away.

"You are," she says.

Hurt fills his eyes. "You always knew there was something different about me. I know how the beast feels because I've lived with it for so long. Who else would make a better partner?"

"Anyone but you," Cara growls. She tries to escape the bed, but the sheets are molasses, the center a whirlpool drawing her back. Alex's arms close around her.

"Let. Me. Go." Cara mutters, squirming.

"Will you kill me, too?" Alex asks, his grip iron. "Will you slay me and pile my body with Druam's atop those humans who we call friends? Earl Stonetree and Lady Stonetree and Gwen and the king,

and all the world? When will it come to an end?"

"When Autorus's fiends are gone forever," Cara hisses back. She will not be cowed by this creature who had once claimed to love her.

Alex shakes his head sadly. "Then I should never have returned."

He and the bed vanish, and Cara finds herself in a cold, mildewy dungeon. She wanders it for a time, though its emptiness makes her afraid. After an eternity of exploring the maze of passageways and cells, she comes across a torchlit chamber. She enters to see Druam.

He hangs by his arms from the wall, his skin blotted with blood and trailing flesh. His eyes are gaunt, his hair in strings around his face. Some of his fingers and toes are splayed in an odd fashion, as if they've been broken without being reset.

As she enters, he looks up with genuine surprise and apprehensiveness.

"You travel fast," he says.

"This is just a dream," she replies. "When I wake up, I'll be gone."

"I wish I could say the same," he says. His blue eyes fix on her. "You're too late. Mavian is here in Stonetree."

Cara considers this. Perhaps she dreamt, and he did not. Perhaps it was all a lie. She picks up a torture device from a small table, running her finger over the crude edges.

"Your friend is here, too," Druam says, smiling. He's missing a tooth. "She did this to me."

"Renna would never–" Cara starts.

"Renna is dead," Druam says. At that, Cara whirls on him. She claws and punches. He hangs there, apathetic to the pain. When she tires, Cara steps back.

Druam stares at her for a long moment. At last, he says, "I hope I die before I see what you become."

The dream shifts once more, and Cara finds herself in a cavern of enormous proportions. The ceiling is high and dark, robed in shadows, and the far walls are difficult to make out. In the center of the room, two skeletons lay beside an altar. All around them, in every corner of the room, are statues of creatures. Fampir, Cara realizes.

Renna stands beside the skeletons. Cara goes to her, and notices that the altar is full of books and scrolls. Renna doesn't look up at her approach.

"What is this place?" Cara asks.

"The Ossuary. The grave of thousands of tortured souls, and the hiding place for all the secrets of Autorus." Renna turns to Cara with a gleam in her eye. "I can help you find it. Together, we can make the world better than ever it was."

She takes Cara's hand in hers, cupping her face with her other palm. Cara leans into it, savoring her friend's touch. Renna says, "I will be in D'Clet when you come. Together, we will right the wrongs of Autorus's creatures. We will bring about a new era."

"Druam said you were dead." Cara closes her eyes, breathing in Renna's fresh, clean scent. "I didn't believe him."

"Of course not," Renna coos. "I'm here, and I'll always be here for you. Come quickly, Cari. I need you with me."

The world faded into darkness, and Cara dreamt no more.

When she woke, she stiffened, immediately aware of another's presence in the cavern. A fire crackled nearby, smoke clouding the air. Cara shifted in her makeshift nest to see who it was.

"Just me," Darian said from somewhere nearby. "I came to give these people a proper burial."

Cara spotted Darian in the darkness. He labored with a shovel in the far side of the cavern, piling dirt beside a large hole. The bodies of the dead were stacked near him, ready to be interred.

"I thought you said you're done with me," Cara said.

Darian turned his milky eyes toward her. "I am. I came for them, not you." He struck the earth with his shovel, turning out another pile of dirt.

"Does Sandu know?" Cara asked. Her stomach roiled at the thought.

"No. He is mourning for his children." Darian straightened and felt for one of the bodies. "They are no longer on Earda."

"I'm sorry to hear of their deaths." Cara didn't know what else to say. Guilt washed through part of her that she'd gone killing while Sandu discovered the worst possible news. The rest of her knew that she'd done the right thing.

"I didn't say they were dead. Just not on Earda."

"That's impossible."

"Is it?" Darian dragged another corpse into the hole. "You brought black fire from the Underworld. Your father's soul broke to make you *sulpari*. Who can say what is or isn't possible?"

Cara pulled a blanket around her shoulders and turned away from him. *He'll never speak straight. It's not worth listening to him.*

"Sandu almost threw himself off a cliff yesterday," Darian said. Cara stopped short, listening intently. Darian continued, "Jagger saved him. Sandu's been asking for you ever since."

"He doesn't want me," she said. "I'm a monster to people like him."

"People like him?"

"People that see the world simply, who don't understand the evil within monsters like Druam."

Darian climbed out of the hole and continued his work. "And you do understand?"

"More than most."

"Yet not enough to have learned the truth."

Cara glared at his back. *He thinks he knows so damn much.* She said, "I'm going to Sandu. I'm not going to tell him what happened here, and if you breathe a word of it, you'll be sorry."

"It's not my truth to tell," Darian said. All the bodies had been carefully laid inside the hole, and he began to shovel earth over them. "There will come a time when he sees the real you. He will not like it."

"Then he'll have misunderstood." Cara turned and left the cavern. With each step, she contemplated Darian's words. The beast churned against him, and she agreed. *He's just a pompous, fortune-telling ass. He doesn't see the goodness in what I did.*

By the time she had returned to camp, Cara had justified to herself why not to tell Sandu – *He's grieving, far too fragile to comprehend it* – and why the murder of the coven had been good. After all, she knew no remorse for her actions.

Heroes must do the right thing even when the world calls it wrong. I'll be thanked for it someday.

CHAPTER FORTY-THREE
Mavian

Deep into the hours of the night, Mavian sat in the dungeons and listened to Talnor torturing Druam. The earl's moans turned to grunts of pain, but he never screamed. In the darkness, Mavian stared at the wall and imagined all the horrors Talnor must be inflicting. *Lashes and flaying and worse.*

If he were a brave man, he'd burst into the chamber and try to stop her. He dug his nails into his palms and brushed away tears. *I'm no brave man. I'm a foolish coward.*

Nearby, Ekkar chirped and whistled as he chased a rat. When he finally pounced on it, he dug his claws into its neck and sucked at the blood. After a moment, he held out the still-squirming rodent toward Mavian. Mavian closed his eyes and said, "*No. You have it all.*"

Ekkar burbled and turned back to his meal. Just as Mavian contemplated going upstairs, he heard the creaking of a door and the jangle of keys. Talnor had left Druam at last. He hid deeper in the shadows as the torchlight flickered in the connecting corridor. After a few minutes, the light vanished into the stairwell. Talnor had gone upstairs.

Mavian didn't quite know what he was going to do. He contemplated freeing Druam and escaping together, or perhaps attempting to murder Rask and Talnor in their sleep. His heart shuddered at each idea, warning him away. *It's suicidal.*

From Druam's cell, Mavian heard voices. He shushed Ekkar and listened. He hadn't noticed anyone coming back, but there was a female voice along with Druam's. The words were lost, and Mavian climbed to his feet on shaky legs – when had he last moved? – to come closer. With furtive steps, he moved to the corridor with Druam's cell and strained his ears.

The other voice was gone. He heard only a sigh from Druam. Before he second-guessed himself, Mavian opened the cell door and peered inside.

Druam was alone. A lantern burned in the corner, casting shadows over the moldy walls. Mavian stared for a long time at the fallen earl. Talnor had done much to him: his skin was shredded, some of his fingers and toes broken, a tooth missing. Mavian swallowed hard and hesitated.

Before he could retreat, Druam looked up. His blue eyes pierced the darkness, right into Mavian's soul. There was no love within them.

"Another late-night visitor?" Druam asked softly. If Mavian closed his eyes, he could picture Druam saying it from behind his desk in Riverfen.

Mavian felt like small child again, creeping in to see Druam after having night terrors. He wanted so badly to be able to go back to the trust they'd shared, the unconditional love. *I gave it all up for Rask's empty promises.*

"Come into the light," Druam said. Mavian obeyed without thinking, a chastised boy afraid of his cousin's cane. Behind him, Ekkar scurried about the stone, but the prowler didn't enter with him.

"Do you hate me?" Mavian blurted, glancing at Druam and down again at the floor.

Druam sighed, the same sound Mavian had heard so many times in his childhood. He said, "I pity you."

For a moment, Mavian simply stared at Druam. Then, clutching his head, he fell to his knees, his very core shattered. "I hated you," he said. "I hated you and your ilk, and I also wanted to be like you. To know all the secrets of man. Rask promised me that, he gave me coin and books and soldiers."

Why was he saying this? Druam wouldn't care. After all, Mavian had forsaken him.

Despite this, Mavian couldn't stop once he'd started. "Renna died, and I couldn't bear to be without her. I've learned so much about the Underworld and its magic, I had to try. I succeeded, for a time. I did it. She was alive again before Talnor took her. I was such a fool, I thought I'd outsmarted a centuries-old curse. I was wrong.

"And I watched Stonetree fall. I sent my prowlers to kill you, and the screams haunted me. On the last day of battle, when you rode out like a god from the skies, I thought, 'How incredible it would have been to stand by his side.' But I chose Rask. Such a fool. Such a proud, arrogant fool." Mavian hiccuped once, his hands wet with his tears. Any moment, Druam would wrap him in his arms, and he'd be safe, the small boy who looked to his cousin for help.

But Druam didn't comfort him. Druam was chained to the wall, and he was there because of Mavian's folly. *If I hadn't used the prowlers against him, if I hadn't helped Rask, if I hadn't brought Talnor back.*

The chains rattled. Druam leaned as far toward him as he could, his stare unpitying.

"Poor fool," Druam said. There was no sympathy in his voice. "You brought back a terrible evil, your creatures murdered my countrymen, and you expect me to comfort you? Many lives rest on your head: man, woman, and child. You must live with that, Mavian. After the blood flows in the streets of Riverfen and the lanterns burn, you must live with your mistakes."

"I just wanted Renna back," Mavian whispered. "Was that so grievous a wish?"

"Yes," Druam said. The word struck a blow through every one of Mavian's nerves, and he shuddered. Druam said, "You alone made the choice to raise her, and many will die because of it."

"I'm sorry," Mavian said, his voice tiny in the night.

"'Sorry' doesn't bring Edsel or his men back. It doesn't free Stonetree from Rask's clutches. It doesn't right the wrongs you've made."

"I know. But I don't know what to do." Mavian clasped his

hands. It was a strange sight: a young lord, kneeling on the floor, begging with a tortured man chained to the wall. Mavian pleaded, "I was wrong. I've known it for a long time, but I couldn't stop it. I've nothing left to lose. My prowlers are scattered, my love is dead, my gem is gone. I want to make things right, except I don't know how."

"So you look to me in your time of need," Druam scoffed. "You reek of desperation. You come to me only when you've lost all? I don't believe this act of contrition. It's another ploy by Talnor to torture my heart into thinking I have an ally remaining in this hellish place."

"She didn't send me!" Mavian shouted, rising now. "I came because I was wrong! Aren't you listening to me? If I could go back and die on that battlefield, I would!"

Druam opened his mouth to reply, then glanced behind Mavian. Confusion flitted over his expression. Mavian turned to see Ekkar crouched in the doorway, large red eyes glimmering in the candlelight.

"*Mavin?*" he chirped, crawling forward to take Mavian's hand.

"*It's alright, Ekkar,*" Mavian said. "*We should go. We aren't wanted here.*"

With Ekkar's hand in his, Mavian walked slowly back to the door. What had he expected? For Druam to welcome him with open arms? To have all guilt removed from his heart? No, those were the dreams of foolish children.

"Stop," Druam croaked. When Mavian turned, he saw an expression on Druam's face he would never have expected: complete and utter surprise. Druam's eyes rested on the prowler.

"Ekkar's not spelled," Mavian said. "He can speak, unlike any prowler I've ever met. I saved him."

Druam shook his head. "I don't care about that. *Look at him.*"

Mavian did, but all he saw was a prowler. One with trusting eyes and a rat's tail hanging from his mouth, but a prowler nonetheless. "I don't–"

"That's my brother," Druam said. His eyes lit with a strange fire, and he pulled at the chains, as if he could take them from the walls. "That's my brother!"

"Alex? No, it can't–"

"Idiot! *Look at him!*" Druam's face contorted into the *fampir's* feral mask, matching Ekkar's features. Mavian's confusion grew. Ekkar was just a prowler, he didn't notice anything strange.

It suddenly dawned on him. He studied Druam and Ekkar. Even in their grotesque forms, he saw a similarity between them: the same nose, eye shape, and fine dark hair.

"Cousin Verdon?" Mavian murmured, crouching down next to Ekkar. "It can't be. Can it?"

The middle brother of the Strilu family, Verdon had been missing for twenty years. His disappearance had fueled Alex's motivation to become a scholar, and Druam had sent many search parties over the years to no avail. Everyone had believed him dead.

"Wasn't Verdon a *fampir*?" Mavian asked. "You can't turn twice. *Fampir* can't become prowler."

"Let me down," Druam gritted out, still straining against the chains. "It may have been twenty years, but I'd know my brother's scent anywhere."

Though confused, Mavian did as he was asked. He retrieved a set of keys from the corridor and unshackled Druam. The earl fell to the floor, his legs unable to hold him after his ordeal. With his hands under Druam's arms, Mavian helped him up. Ekkar watched the pair warily.

"Verdon?" Druam asked. He reached out to Ekkar. The prowler let him take his hand at Mavian's nod. Ekkar sniffed at Druam's skin, wrinkling his nose.

"It's me," Druam said beseechingly. "It's your brother. You've come home at last."

The prowler licked at Druam's hand but otherwise gave no indication that he understood. He took back his clawed fingers and retreated to Mavian's side.

"Are you sure it's him?" Mavian asked gently. "Its been so long, maybe–"

"I know it," Druam said, rocking back on his heels. A deep, overwhelming sadness filled his gaze. "He doesn't know me."

"If it is him, how did Verdon turn from *fampir* to prowler? With everything I know about them, it should be impossible. Unless..." Mavian searched his recollection of his studies, trying to piece it together. "Unless some extremely powerful magic caused it."

"I don't–" Druam started, then stopped. He narrowed his eyes. "What magic could have done this?"

"Not mine," Mavian said hurriedly. "There could be someone, some great magician or other, who–"

"Laris," Druam said suddenly. "Laris Stanthorpe, the sorcerer. He and my brother met sometimes before Verdon's disappearance. I read their correspondences. All were written in code, I couldn't understand their messages, but I remember their signatures."

"The wizard from the Masque?" Mavian remembered the raw power the sorcerer had exhibited that fateful night. "Why would he do it?"

"There's something we're missing," Druam said. "But what?"

"Let's think about this logically," Mavian said. He paced the small chamber as he thought out loud. "Laris and Verdon wrote to each other about something secret. Verdon disappears, and Laris...what? What did he do after that?"

"Became the Guildmaster of the Peddler's Guild," Druam said thoughtfully. "An odd occupation for one of his power."

"Did Avallune ever worry about him?"

"No. Though he mentioned magic in his letters, he never showed any apparent power."

Mavian paced quicker, excited now. "Perhaps the same spell that turned Verdon into a prowler drained Laris of his magic! And prowlers didn't appear until about twenty years ago. What if Verdon was the first? Prowlers are just *fampir*, but missing that important soul link that gives you your humanity. Whatever spell it was, it severed Verdon's soul enough that he became like this."

"The first prowler?" Druam said with wonder. "I would never have thought it."

"Why did Laris come to the Masque?" Mavian had wondered it since that night, but Renna's resurrection had mostly driven it out of his mind.

"For Cara. He said she owed him, and that he'd find her. He helped her escape Riverfen."

That stopped Mavian short, his back to Druam. He trembled with his newfound realization. "Cara is about twenty years old."

"Laris isn't her father," Druam pointed out. "It has to be..." His voice petered out.

"Her father must have been a *fampir* in order to tie her soul to the Underworld. What if that same spell tore the father's soul to pieces? Made him into what we now know is a prowler?" Mavian stared at Ekkar. "What if Verdon was that *fampir*?"

"It can't be," Druam said. "Sura would have told me."

"Cara's mother?" Mavian guessed.

Druam nodded. "She told me I wouldn't know him."

"She lied. It's the only thing that makes sense. For Verdon to become a prowler, there would have been powerful magic involved. Laris is one of the few capable of that magic. Prowlers appeared around the time Cara was born, and if her conception tore her father's soul, then it all makes sense."

Mavian and Druam stared at each other, dizzy with their revelation. Druam shook his head with a small laugh. "Verdon and I always wanted children. He found a way to make it happen."

"And gave up his soul in the process."

"Not entirely. Verdon – or Ekkar, as he calls himself – speaks, if only the Underworld tongue. He is tamer than most prowlers. Perhaps there's enough of him left." Druam staggered to his feet despite his broken toes. "We have to try."

"We? I don't–"

"You have the magic, you understand the Underworld better than I do. You can bring him back!" Druam's smile was manic.

"Everything I have is in D'Clet," Mavian said. "I only brought a few scrolls."

"And I must go to Riverfen to prepare her for Rask's armies," Druam said. The excitement of their discovery drained out of the room, leaving only the dread knowledge of the days to come.

"You'd trust me with your brother?" Mavian asked.

"No. But I trust him, and he trusts you," Druam replied. "Go to D'Clet and do what you can for him. Isn't that what you wanted from the start? A way to help the prowlers?"

Mavian nodded. "But I can't leave yet. I need to discover Rask's plans with Talnor."

Druam hesitated, then nodded. "Once you do, send me a message. I'll do what I can with the knowledge."

Mavian wanted to reach out and embrace Druam, but there was still a gulf between them, filled with his betrayal. *I'll make it right*, he thought. He considered Druam's broken body and realized that the earl would never make it to Riverfen in this condition.

"Trust me with your brother, and I'll trust you with my blood," Mavian said. He held out his arm, baring it up to his elbow. "You have to move swiftly if you're to make it in time."

"Mavian..."

"Do it. I owe you that much, at least."

Druam carefully took Mavian's arm. Mavian shuddered as his cousin's teeth pierced his skin. His arm tingled, and his head clouded with fuzzy thoughts. It felt like the one time he'd partaken in poppin powder. When Druam released him, Mavian stared around the dungeon in a haze. There was a grinding sound and a few *pops*, and in front of Mavian's eyes, Druam's bones snapped back into place, his skin healing itself. A new tooth popped out from his gums.

Druam wiped his lips and clasped Mavian's hand. "Thank you, cousin. When I thought I could never forgive you for all you've done, you brought my brother back to me. I have hope yet."

"Good luck, Druam," Mavian said. "I'm sorry."

"I know."

Druam reached to Ekkar. "Keep him safe. No matter what

you do, don't trust Talnor."

"I understand."

With that, Druam slipped from the cell and out of sight, his *fampir* tread silent and quick. Mavian stood for awhile longer in the cell, his head thrumming with everything that had happened. Ekkar chirped, and Mavian squeezed his hand.

"I'll bring you back, cousin," he promised. "And I'll do it right this time."

Chapter Forty-Four
Gwen

The Song of Death carried Gwen from Stonetree, its melancholy sound all-consuming and inevitable. She held onto it, a twisting, purple-black rope that pulled her closer and closer to the Underworld. Her other hand clutched Lintem's fur, grounding her, keeping her from succumbing forever to Death's pull.

I am not dead yet, she told herself.

The world grew cold around her. Her breath steamed in the colorless void, where there was no up or down, no right or left. She had come to a world of nothingness. The Song's rope continued eternally in either direction, back to life or further into Death. Keeping a firm hand on it, Gwen took tentative steps toward the unknown.

A cool blue light shone ahead of her. She kept going, and the light grew larger and larger until it was all around her. In its glow, she saw a man. He was short and scholarly, with thin arms and simple robes of an ancient style. Grey dusted the hair over his temples, though his skin still had the smoothness of relative youth. The man regarded her.

"Are you Autorus?" Gwen asked. Her voice was faint in the void.

"No." The man spoke with a calm, measured voice. "Though many from my time would disagree with me. I am Valder Riesk. I lived in the Dead's War and created the undead wights to fight against the *fampir*."

A shiver passed over Gwen's shoulders. "That was a long

time ago. Why haven't you passed on to Lyael?"

Valder tilted his head. "Autorus asked me to stay. I understand the Songs of Death almost as well as he does, and so I can assist him in helping the dead."

"Will you be my guide?"

The scholar nodded. "You are at the borders of Death. The Underworld can be a cruel place, but it need not be for you. Take my hand."

Gwen hesitated. If she let go of Lintem, they could be parted. If she released the Song, would she ever find her way back to Earda?

"You came here with a still-beating heart," Valder said. "Your skin is warm. The dead may flock to you, but you are not part of them yet. Come; I have something I wish to show you."

His Song was muted by Death's. Gwen could not tell if he told the truth.

Can we trust him? she hummed to Lintem.

Do we have a choice? he whispered back.

Gwen let go of the Song-rope and placed her hand in Valder's. His skin was cold and hard, and he sighed when she touched him. He smiled. "It has been a long time since I have felt the living."

He led her through a darkness where time held no meaning. Gwen's feet did not ache from walking, but her heart yearned for daylight and Earda. Eventually, they emerged from the blue into an enormous cavern lit by magic sconces that emitted a pale orange light.

"What is this place?" Gwen asked.

"This is where I died," Valder responded.

In the center of the cavern stood two people, one an exact copy of Valder, and the other a woman, beautiful and strong. The woman's Song echoed with Death.

"She was *sulpari*," Valder said. "Like a woman you've met, I believe."

"Yes." Gwen's mouth was dry, and she clutched at Lintem's fur. "Is this a memory?"

"Indeed. Listen to the Songs."

Gwen tuned into the Songs, astounded at their power. They spun around the couple in a complicated dance, the music jarring and haunting. Another noise rose above the music, a pounding of many feet trampling the ground, with howls and the sound of claws scraping stone.

The memory-Valder reached for the *sulpari's* hand. "It's time, Alesse. Are you ready?"

The woman nodded, no fear in her gaze. "I'm ready."

Creatures flooded into the cavern, their foreheads wrinkled, fangs bloodied. Hundreds of the *fampir* surrounded the two people, their red eyes glinting hungrily.

A male *fampir* separated from the rest of the pack. "Our brethren wait above, Valder. Too many to count. We will not be stopped."

"You should not have come, Galiyar," said Alesse. "You could have been spared."

"*Sulpari*," the *fampir* hissed. "You would stand against your own kin?"

"I would stand against evil."

As they spoke, the memory-Valder began to Sing. His spell wove scores of Songs into the melody, a spell whose complexity she had never seen before. He held up a white gem set in a silver amulet. Gwen startled, knowing that gem. It was the same one Mavian had used for his dark magic.

The gem glowed. Songs poured from it, a conduit for their power. A bubble of energy formed around the couple. Though the *fampir* threw themselves against it, they could not break through. Their skin burned as they made contact.

A blinding flash of light burst from the gem. Energy rippled through the cavern. Gwen could feel the power of the Songs within it, and above all, the Song of Unmaking, its terrible force stronger than the rest put together.

In the aftermath, Gwen marveled at the sight. Each one of the *fampir* was frozen in place, their skin like white limestone. In the center of the room, memory-Valder lay unmoving. Alesse crawled weakly to him. The *sulpari* aged rapidly, years passing in seconds. Her skin wrinkled, her hair turning white.

"It's done, my love," Alesse whispered before she collapsed and turned to ash.

The vision faded, leaving Gwen, Lintem, and the current Valder in the dim blue light.

"You used the Song of Unmaking," she said.

He nodded. "There were too many of them. The Song took everything from me. I intended their souls to be ripped from the Underworld, for them to become mortal once more. But all I could do was freeze them in time."

Horror blossomed in her chest. "So their souls—"

"Were trapped in their bodies. Forever." His solemn eyes betrayed his anguish. "The Ossuary, with all my work, my library, and now a graveyard, was sealed away. I hoped it would be lost forever. My old foe has reawakened, and I fear the havoc she will wreak should she find the Ossuary."

"Is it possible to revive those *fampir*?"

"With a strong enough Song, yes. You've worked miracles with the Songs; you should know their power." He sighed. "There is more that could be done in the Ossuary. One could destroy the connection between Life and Death with the knowledge I foolishly left behind."

Lintem growled, and Gwen stroked his head absently. She said, "The severing of such a connection could have repercussions throughout Earda."

"And beyond." He gave her a level look. "We have tarried too long on my past, and we have a long journey to make before you meet Autorus."

He led her deeper into Death. Cold clung to her, a chill that could not be shaken off. The blue turned to an unsettling red mist that swirled around them. Shapes skittered by, silhouettes of figures trapped in the eerie fog. Gwen heard a cacophony of Songs, her ears hurting with dreadful music. The Song of Death had many melodies, and here she only detected Death after a terrible life.

"Purgatory," Valder said.

A woman passed by them, her arms heavy with gold. She twisted to hiss at Gwen and Valder when they accidentally drew too close. The woman muttered, "Must have more. Can't sail without more. Too little will sink just the same as too much."

Greed, Gwen thought. She touched the woman's Song, and recoiled from the Death she witnessed there. *The ship sank, and she would not leave her treasure behind.*

The woman melted back into the mist, but an elf trundled by, his hands red. He shook his head, staring unseeing ahead of him. His Song told of his desperation as he stabbed a street urchin to get the child's food. He had been slaughtered in turn by another starving elf.

"Does he really deserve this?" Gwen asked. "His hunger made him mad."

"You would have to ask Autorus," Valder said. He looked straight ahead, not sparing a glance toward the unfortunate souls that surrounded them.

As they walked, Gwen reached out to each person's Song. She didn't know why she did; she could not change their fates, nor would she find solace in their Songs. Jealousy and Vengeance, Cruelty and Malice, Murder and Torture, all were bedfellows in this red mist, their punishments meted out to the bearers in sadistically perfect ways.

Gwen stopped seeing their faces. She only listened to the Songs and watched the consequences, entranced by Autorus's method for dealing with the selfish or the truly evil. A Song called out to her, a Song of Spite and Uncaring. At first, she didn't realize why it spoke to her, then she detected other Songs within it that echoed her own Song in a way only family could.

She turned, and there, in the fog, she saw him.

Wullum.

CHAPTER FORTY-FIVE
Seanna

The Silver Keep shuddered, and debris tumbled down the cliffs. Faint screams carried down as the trebuchet bombardment continued its horrible work. Below in Dockside, flaming ballistae from the Lofalin ships burned down warehouses and homes. Smoke clouded the sky. Most of the trebuchets' munitions aimed for the walls of Seawind, but the occasional boulder carried too far, hitting homes or the cliffs above Midtown. Reports had come in of the damage to the Grand Novum, damage that would take years to repair. *The Novum is not as important as the walls.*

Eight days, yet the walls still stand. Ancient magic had been built into the stones of Con Salur, protecting it from damage. But the magic grew weaker with each passing day. Seanna sat on the throne as her general explained their situation.

"Three or four days, if we're lucky," the general said. "Then the walls will surely fall. Our mages work night and day to shore up the spells, but the Lofalins are trying to weaken them with their own casters."

"Double rations for each of them. Make sure they work in shifts to keep the walls up as long as possible," Seanna commanded. *If the walls fall, we are all doomed.* She sat awkwardly on the throne, her full belly sending shooting aches up her back. Faint contractions wracked her every few candles. Ropaz hovered nearby, ready for when the true labor began.

The general bowed. He would head back to Seawind to

continue the siege efforts. The moment the trebuchets had been completed, Seanna had ordered all remaining citizens to retreat to Darkroad and Midtown. All able-bodied men had been conscripted and given weapons to defend their city; only the sick, elderly, or young had been spared the decree. Immense guilt tore at Seanna for taking farmers and bakers and merchants from their wives and children, but Con Salur needed every soldier it could get. All except a bare minimum of the Keep's guards had also been sent up to fight back against the Lofalins.

Yet I fear it will be too little. Seanna grimaced at a contraction, but she had business to attend to. She wouldn't leave the throne room until Ropaz forced her out.

A steward bowed and came forward. "Your Grace, the staff have concerns about the rustics you've allowed into the Keep. There could be any number of dangerous people–"

"They're women and children, Edward," Seanna said. She had no patience today for his paranoia.

"But they could still steal–"

"Steal our silver? And do what with it, with no trade in the city and bread lines stretched to every corner? I'll risk some treasures if it means fewer people sleep on the streets tonight."

"But your safety–"

"I have guards around me at all times. Do as I say and bring as many refugees into the palace as it will hold." Seanna leaned back as the steward scuttled away. A headache had come on, and she hoped it would go away before her labor grew more intense.

She perked up as Belrose entered. Though he usually looked grim, today he had a small smile. He hurried up to her, bowed, and said, "We've found a tunnel. Very old – thousands of years, perhaps – that leads away from the city. My men are working now to expand it and build an exit far from the Lofalin lines."

Seanna took his hands, her chest bursting with hope. "Thank you, Belrose. This is the best news. The general believes we have only a few days before the walls fall – can you get it done in that time?"

"I will make sure of it," Belrose said.

"Good."

Seanna released his hands. He bowed once more and left as quickly as he'd come. Seanna thought of his bloodshot eyes, his trembling fingers. *He's worked so hard, yet he cannot rest. None of us can.*

"Seanna," Ropaz said, stepping forward. "Your time grows nearer. There is no one else today to speak with. I implore you to return to your chambers and prepare for the child."

Seanna was about to resist, but another contraction – worse than the ones before – beat against her insides, and she nodded. With Ropaz's arm around her, she waddled to her chambers. His sister, Portia, waited there with a clean shift and cool water. The handmaid aided Seanna to undress, wiped her down, and helped her onto a comfortable couch. Ropaz scuttled about preparing potions and compresses and all sorts of other things.

Seanna watched the siblings, wondering what it would be like to have her own brother and sister there. She knew her brother was dead, but she had no word from her sister's husband. *He was a vassal of Seastone's and would have been at Stonetree when it fell. Maybe Georgiana stayed home, safe and well.* Seanna dearly hoped that that was true.

More candles passed before the contractions became much worse. When they did, Seanna gritted her teeth and arched her back, trying to focus on her breathing.

"That's it," Ropaz told her, "In and out. There's a good girl." He spoke to her as he would any of the rest of his flock, and Seanna greatly appreciated him for it. She clung to Portia's hand during the worst of it, grateful for the girl's attention.

Between contractions, Seanna paced the room or stretched. She drank the potions Ropaz gave to her, but they didn't help when the pain came. Seanna sank to the floor, breathing heavily. Oh, gods, if she knew what the pain would be, she never would've agreed to be queen and bear the *stupid* child for the *stupid* dead king!

A candle passed, then another, each bringing with it more

pain and a stronger desire to just *get the damn baby out.* "Make it come faster!" Seanna shouted, gripping poor Portia's shoulder with steel fingers.

"I can't, Seanna. Now breathe and take some of this." The potion Ropaz poured down her throat didn't help the pain, not at first. Even after another candle, Seanna's cramping was worse than any moon cycle she'd ever experienced. Portia mopped her brow with a cool cloth, and Seanna resisted yelling at the poor girl.

Evening turned to night, the ballistae from the ships sending flaming javelins into the city. Some of the bombardments hit the cliffs below Midtown, causing the whole shelf to shudder as rocks fell to Dockside far below.

As the Lofalins pounded the city above and below, Seanna labored. She screamed and sobbed and was quiet as she went between bouts of intense agony and resting points. Still, Ropaz and Portia stayed by her side, brushing her hair from her face and murmuring soothing words.

The contractions were worst in the hour before dawn, and the Lofalin attack matched their intensity. The walls of the Silver Keep groaned and creaked, and people in Midtown screamed as boulders struck the clifftops above. Seanna screamed, too, pushing with all her might, squeezing until she felt she could squeeze no more.

"Damn...veck...vecking...veck...vecking damning–" Seanna moaned, her hand tight in Portia's. Ropaz crouched down at her nether, encouraging her.

"It's coming!" he said, his hand on her thigh. "Just a little longer, Seanna!"

Seanna pushed as she never had before. Her screams must have reached the bay and clifftops.

A new cry joined the tumult.

A new, high cry. Collapsing against her pillows, Seanna groaned as Ropaz swept away with her baby to clean it. Her innards still contracted, forcing her to purge what remained inside.

"I want my baby," Seanna muttered, but Portia ignored her

until everything was done. The bed was soaked with Seanna's blood, urine, and other unmentionable fluids.

With Portia's help, Seanna moved to a clean bed. She asked again and again for her child as the handmaid cleaned her and dressed her in a new shift. When she lay in the bed, still sore and hurting, she demanded again to see the result of her effort.

A minute passed before Ropaz returned with a baby wrapped in gold-threaded cloth. Holding out her arms, Seanna took the child. It cried out, and she shushed it.

"Is it...?" she asked.

"A new king," Ropaz replied, beaming down at her.

"A king," Seanna breathed, stroking her child's face. Not just her child. Her son.

Her son, the King of Dotschar. Tthe city crumbled around her as she stared into his little face, holding his tiny hand with her finger.

"What will you name him?" Ropaz asked. Portia stood next to him, beaming.

Seanna cooed at the infant and said, "He will be King Landin the Third."

It was the name of two strong kings who had led Dotschar through the Dead's War to victory. Seanna desperately hoped her son would continue the tradition.

"A good name," Ropaz said, bowing his head. "Long live King Landin."

"Long live my son," Seanna whispered, staring into her child's eyes.

CHAPTER FORTY-SIX
The Dead Men Walking

Alone again in the dark, damp dungeons, Druam stared up at the ceiling. He could imagine Talnor and Rask many floors above him, sleeping or drinking or whatever it was they did to celebrate. Escape should be simple, but he was tired. So very tired. Had the battle only been days before?

If he was to make his escape, he must do it before Talnor returned to sink her talons into him. She wouldn't tire as mortal torturers would, wouldn't hesitate to inflict greater and greater pain until he broke.

And he would break, that he was sure of. He was too old, too weathered. Too tired. Even with Mavian's blood coursing through his veins, he felt so exhausted.

With a sigh, Druam crept through the dungeons until he came across an elf soldier. The elf turned in surprise.

As quickly as his fatigued body could carry him, Druam sprang at the elf, pinning his arms to his sides. Before the elf could so much as gurgle, Druam sank his teeth into the poor soul's flesh, one hand over the guard's mouth. He drank, long and deep.

If this were one of the delirious poppin users in the tavern in Riverfen, Druam would have stopped before draining too much. He'd leave the sot alive and plant a false memory to hide his misdeeds. However, this guard couldn't be left alive, and Druam had a long way to go. He drank until the elf's skin turned translucent and thin, then dropped the corpse to the floor. Druam stripped the elf's clothes and armor, dressing himself in the stolen loot. After strapping the elf's axe to his hip, Druam left the cellars, striding confidently up the stairs.

Each *fampir* had their own abilities and strengths. Druam's had always been manipulation of the mind: false memories, persuasion, influencing emotions. As he strode the familiar halls of Stonetree, he exuded an aura that clouded the minds of Rask's soldiers so that they ignored him.

Still, he didn't linger. Talnor would sense his power and hunt him down if he remained for long.

Druam continued outside to the stables. Though he spied Rask's fine black charger, he knew it would be too great a risk. He glanced back up at the keep and pressed a finger to his forehead. *For Edsel. Goodbye, old friend. I wish we could have had many more years together.*

He took a plain brown gelding from the pen outside and saddled it quickly. With a kick to its flanks, it flew out of the keep and down the valley. His vision, adapted to the night, gave him clear sight along the road, and though the horse rolled its eyes back at his kicks, it obeyed him.

He rode hard for two candles, only letting the horse walk for small amounts of time. On a winding stretch of road, he didn't see a hole in the dirt until it was too late. The horse crashed hard to the ground, one of its legs snapping beneath it. As it tried to struggle to its feet, huffing and whining, Druam drew the axe from his belt and ended its misery in one quick blow. Hot blood spilled from its neck, and Druam stooped to drink. Though he had already had his fill from the elf, he knew that it could be days before his next satisfying meal. His stomach sloshed uncomfortably with the mix of human and animal, but he quelled the sensation and moved on.

The main roads would no doubt be crawling with soldiers in a few days. Keeping to the side roads and animal paths, Druam walked until dawn, where he found a small hollow to hide in for the day.

It's been a long time since I was confined to the night, he thought wryly. *I have grown too accustomed to sunlight and my high walls protecting me from its rays.* Especially at these altitudes, even if the air was cold, the sun could weaken him. He doubted he would suffer from sunfever, but he didn't want to tempt fate. After all, Shepherd Marin and his potions weren't there to help Druam heal, and neither was Gwen with her magic.

The thought of her pained him. She had suddenly returned, her skin filthy and hair matted, with a mythical creature at her side. He still wondered whether it had all been a dream, for nothing she told him made sense. She had kissed him – his lips burned with the treasured memory – and disappeared again, leaving him more wounded than if he'd never seen her.

She is not in the Underworld, Druam told himself. *It was a dream, and she is safe somewhere warm and welcoming.*

Sleep came at last, interrupted by snuffling creatures and disturbed by wayward sunshine, but restorative nonetheless. By this time, most of the blood in his stomach had been absorbed into his veins, fueling his fatigued body. If a *fampir* must choose between food and blood, he would always choose the latter. It pumped his undead heart, kept his brain active and his veins from freezing under his skin. Without food, one of his kind could last for quinns as long as they had blood; without blood...well, it wasn't a pleasant thought.

The moon shone over the forests and peaks, illuminating a sheen of frost on the ground. It spoke of chill and black hands. He wouldn't feel it, but his fingers and toes could turn blue and fall off before he noticed.

By the end of that night, Druam had traveled a fair distance south. His pace slowed in the candle before dawn, his movements sluggish. He needed blood.

A squirrel disturbed the brush in front of him, and without thinking, Druam dived on it. After snapping its neck in a quick, brutal action, Druam drained the tiny creature. His pulse quickened, but only slightly. He would need more before resting.

As dawn came, Druam crawled under an overhanging tree, the blood of two more squirrels and a bird making him nauseous. He wrapped their untanned skins around his feet and hands, protecting them from the frost.

Night after night passed in such a manner, though Druam lost count of how many. His features remained in his *fampir* state, for he hungered ever more for good, real, hot blood, coursing over his tongue, heating his veins, so delicious, so raw.

Druam licked his lips as he continued south, his red-tinged eyes flashing in the moonlight.

As dawn rose on a freezing morning, the River Valley spread out below him, its trees and grasses brown and dead with winter's chill. It was the most beautiful sight he'd ever seen.

Firelight glinted in a copse of trees. Even from that distance, Druam could see Valadi wagons in a circle, the brightly-painted wood the only splash of color in the dead forest.

Druam ran down the hill, heedless of tearing thorns and catching branches, yearning for a familiar sight at last. When Druam burst from the trees, the people in the caravan froze, one woman uttering a short scream. The men scrambled for their weapons, the children ushered to the wagons by their mothers.

"Prowler!" one man shouted. "Get the torches!"

"Wait!" Druam cried. He held his hands out, praying that they would heed him. "I'm no prowler."

"It talks," a man said, his axe at the ready.

Druam let himself relax, forcing his feral *fampir* side back inside himself. "Please," Druam said, keeping his hands out. "I'm hungry, and I've come a very long way. I wish to share stories by your fire."

"What are you?" the axe-man demanded. "I saw your face, I know something's wrong with you."

"I'm *fampir*," Druam said. It was still strange to say aloud. "Remember the tales of the Dead's War and the creatures it created? I am one of those, born of the Valadi tribe Dalscra eight hundred years ago. My blood still runs Valadi, my heart crying out for Belleslye."

"By the gods," another man said, coming forward. "That's Earl Seastone."

Letting out a sigh of relief, Druam said, "The very same. Please let me share stories by your fire and tell me the news of my valley. I have come a long way, and I don't know how close my enemies are."

The same man who recognized Druam stepped forward, a hand held out in greeting. "Welcome, Your Distinction. We have much food and good stories. My name is Lander of the Kirna tribe."

Shaking the man's hand, Druam smiled for the first time since his escape. "Around your fire, I am merely Druam."

Though many of the Valadi still gave suspicious looks to Druam, they fed him nonetheless with hearty stew and fresh bread. On most mornings, caravaners would swap stories or sing songs together, but they were quiet this breakfast. When Druam asked, Lander said darkly, "Too many listeners out there. We don't draw attention to ourselves anymore."

Lander's wife, a plump woman, bounced their fifth child on her knee and said, "Some folk blame us for the plague and the prowlers. They say they didn't have none of it afore our kind passed through. And with rumors of invasion, it's not wise to make ourselves targets any more than we already are."

Hearing such things broke Druam's fractured heart. How often had he lamented to Xandro of their people's plight, wishing the Valadi weren't treated so by their neighbors? No matter the laws he passed protecting them or the caravans he gave patronage to, the rustic folk still found reasons to distrust those descended from the people of Belleslye.

"Where are you headed?" Druam asked.

"To Skålland. Less disease and war," came Lander's answer.

Druam frowned into his stew. "I need to go to Riverfen. Rask and the Lofalin armies are coming." He met Lander's eye. "Our people must always give help when it's needed."

"And risk the lives of my children? That is no small favor." The other men nodded along with Lander, fear written plainly on their faces.

If he were a younger *fampir*, with less care for those under his protection, Druam would have used his power to persuade them otherwise. But he was old now, and so tenderly emotional. A dozen children were in this caravan, all too precious to send back into war. *How much I have changed over the many years. We weren't meant to live this long, to suffer so much.*

"Lend me a horse so that I may ride alone to my city," Druam said. He knew how much horses cost for those in poverty, but he *must* make it to Riverfen before Rask.

The Valadi shared a disgruntled look, and Lander shrugged. "If we had any to spare, I would. But–"

Druam stood suddenly, letting the *fampir* flash over his features. "Remember, Valadi, that I am your earl." If they wouldn't be persuaded, he would frighten them into compliance. "Never think that my reach is so small. You think you are frightened of war and plague? You have never encountered my vengeance. A horse is a tiny price to pay for your freedom."

The Valadi cowered away from him, the mothers holding their children to their chests as the men's hands twitched toward their weapons. Druam knew how he appeared, tall and dirty, his features distorted, but at that moment he didn't care. He felt no kinship for these people in his anger.

The sun had risen, casting light over the valley. It prickled at Druam's eyes, which had become accustomed to darkness. He turned to the mountains, knowing that Rask's army lay somewhere in their depths. *Too little time*, he thought. *Eight hundred years of leisure, and now I have too little time.*

Movement caught his eye, and Druam returned his gaze to the Valadi. A young lad brought him a saddled horse. None of the tribe dared to stop their earl as he mounted.

"If you have survived the snows and the journey north, my messengers will bring you gold as recompense," Druam said to them. Somehow, though, he knew that either the prowlers, the armies, or the weather would kill this caravan before it ever passed the Skallish border. He knew, too, that they would still try no matter what he told them. Such were the ways of man: doubt and stubbornness even in the face of death.

Digging his heels into the horse's flanks, Druam rode south, the sun to his left, finally in the daylight again. His belly full of food, his veins yearning for fresh blood, he didn't look back at the doomed Valadi. Deep down, he hoped some wayward bandit or highwayman might cross his path so that he could drink his fill with no remorse.

No such criminal interrupted his ride, but the miles vanished one by one beneath the horse's hooves, the sun making its slow way through the sky. With the animal's steady gait and the smoothness of the road – how grateful Druam was for spending so much of his people's taxes on such things – Druam lapsed into thought. Candles passed quickly for him, as short a length of time for him as a minute to a mortal.

Yet, with each candle, Druam remembered anew. First he thought of Gwen, his innocent wife, a girl of seventeen yet older for her suffering. His steward had balked at the girl's age until Druam had gently reminded him that all mortal women were equally as young in his mind; even a woman of eighty would seem a child to a man of eight hundred. Then Druam thought of the wife before Gwen, a witty Dotsch woman named Seren with hair that smelled of lilacs and smooth white skin. She'd never forgiven herself for failing to bear a child, and Druam had never told her that the fault lay purely with him.

Names and faces filled his memory, too many to recall. Wives, lovers, friends, family, enemies, allies. How many had he forgotten altogether? More than mortals met in a single lifetime, if he were honest with himself.

Yet none he loved as deeply as he loved Gwen. At least, it felt that way. Each wife he remembered, he compared to her: how Renina laughed louder than Gwen, how Ingrid spoke of embroidery with less passion than Gwen did magic, how Lianna sang with a lower voice than his Gwen. *And I never commissioned a portrait of my Gwen, as I had all the others. I have nothing to remember her by save my own mind, yet how can I trust it?*

How could it be that he loved Gwen so much when he knew her for such a short time? Many of his wives he had lived with for decades until their deaths, and loved before the end. Yet his heart had beat stronger, his nerves jolting like a youth's when he'd made the offer of marriage to his Gwen.

This is why men should not live this long, Druam thought,

realizing the truth. *The more memories I lose, the greater depths of emotions that come over me. The greater the hate, the greater the fear, the greater the love and the joy. It is like a youth infatuated for the first time, all humors going every which way. I have lived so long, I have forgotten the very experiences that should inform the wiseness of age.*

As the sun set, and Druam came to one of the many villages dotted throughout the River Valley, he forced himself to rejoin the present. *Too much to be done to squander my precious time thinking of the past.* There were soldiers here, and a hot bath and food for the Earl of Seastone.

Riding now with a fresh horse each day – courtesy of the stations along the road – and more and more soldiers to accompany him, Druam rode quickly through the River Valley, warning each village of the coming army. He ordered them to empty their cellars and scorch their fields, leaving nothing for the invading forces to scavenge. The people did as he commanded, traveling west to safer cities to escape the scourge.

And, at each station, Druam ordered his men to lay low. Those who didn't travel with him to defend Riverfen had an even greater duty to destroy the elves' siege machines before they could be used against his beloved city.

As Druam crested the dam overlooking Riverfen with his men behind him, he let himself marvel at the white-washed, blue-tiled beauty of the city. The sun sank into the horizon to the west, the fading glow shining on the mosaic-decorated roof of the Cascade Palace. Tiny spots of light filled the city, lanterns in all colors by the hundreds.

Druam was home.

✳

Jagger crouched by the fire, one hand on Sandu's shoulder. The lad slept in the dirt, his mop of hair tangled and matted. He shivered, and Jagger placed a blanket over him, soothing him with his touch.

Each of them had witnessed the other try to die. Yet now they were both here in this hellish world, scraping by without much care for tomorrow. *The gods have a cruel sense of humor,* Jagger reflected. *Puttin' us together and watchin' us suffer. Maybe I should'a let Sandu fall off that cliff. Maybe it would'a been less cruel than keepin' him alive.*

But Darian had told him, before they'd departed to find Sandu's children, that Sandu couldn't die. It wasn't his time yet, and there was more he needed to do before it all was over. Jagger didn't understand, exactly, but he obeyed.

Sandu mumbled in his sleep, and Jagger smoothed his hair out of his eyes. He wished he could sing something, or just whisper to ease the nightmares, but his resurrection had stolen that from him. Though Sandu couldn't see, Jagger signed, *We're all we've got. I'll stick with you 'til the end.*

Cara emerged from the woods. She was filthy, her clothes stained with blood. She crouched next to Sandu. "Is he alright?"

Jagger nodded. He signed, but she didn't understand all of the signals. He hovered protectively over Sandu, noting her stance, the look in her eyes. *She's killed tonight.* He knew that far-off gaze, the twitching in one's hands. *And she don't regret it.*

Cara sat heavily on the ground, breaking a twig in her fingers. "Darian should be here soon. He's, er, doing something first."

Burying the bodies, probably. Jagger wanted to speak with her, but without Sandu or Darian to translate, he wasn't quite sure how. It took him a moment to remember the parchment and charcoal in Darian's bag. He retrieved them, then wrote, *'Who did you kill?'*

He held it out to her, and she read it quickly before turning away. "No one."

'Liar,' he wrote.

"Is he asleep?" Cara asked, pointing to Sandu. Jagger nodded, and she said, "I killed *fampir*, alright? And a few humans that were with them. And Laris."

Jagger gave a low whistle. *Not bad for one night,* he thought. He wrote, *'What are you going to tell him?'*

"Nothing. And if you give him any indication that you know..." She left the threat hanging unsaid.

Jagger almost laughed. He scribbled, *'What makes you think you can defeat me? I can't die, and I've killed many a hotheaded young thing like you. You won't be telling me what to do.'*

Cara glared at him. "There are other things that can be done. Things you couldn't dream of."

Jagger poised his charcoal to reply, but Sandu muttered and turned over, his body shaking. Jagger dropped his writing utensils and bent to Sandu, making crooning noises and cradling him until he returned to a peaceful sleep.

"Why are you doing all this?" Cara asked. "I thought you hated him."

Jagger shrugged and wrote, *'I did. Death changed me. I have to make things right after all the bad I caused.'*

"What if you did bad things for a good reason?"

'Trust me, I didn't. I did it for coin or revenge, never for good. I'm starting to think there's no good reason to kill.'

"You're wrong."

Jagger shrugged again. *'Maybe, maybe not. Why don't you want him to know what you did?'*

Cara was silent a moment, her chin resting on her hands. She stared into the fire, and Jagger saw something in her look that made him shiver. *She's a killer, alright. Maybe a worse one than ever I was. She enjoyed it, and she isn't guilty for what she did. I may have been good at what I did, I may have liked the thrill of it, but I still needed Raven to comfort me in the long hours of the night.*

At last, Cara said, "He's lost his wife and children. He's about to lose his father. He doesn't need to worry about me right now."

Jagger contemplated this, deciding whether she was right. After some thought, he nodded. *'Alright. I'll accept that.'*

With a groan, Cara stretched her arms and torso and held her hands out to the fire. She said, "Darian told me that his children aren't actually dead. They're just not on Earda. But not in the Underworld, either."

Jagger nodded. *'He said the same to us. It still broke him.'*

Sandu whimpered again, and Jagger sat beside him, holding his head in his lap. Jagger stroked the lad's head as he thought. *If'n they really aren't dead, then there's a chance.*

He didn't know what he was meant to do after they rescued Sandu's father. Would he wander with Sandu forever, protecting the lad from himself and the world? Or did Darian have another duty in mind, one that would take him away from his only remaining friend? Jagger carefully wiped the sweat from Sandu's forehead. *I'm not leavin' unless I have to. That's a promise, Sandu. Everythin' else may have gone to shit, but I'll still be here.*

✳

The Woods closed behind him, their whispering branches giving him no advice for his journey. Alex realized that he had been brought to a different valley than the one he'd entered, for these peaks were smaller and greener. His now-mortal legs carried him to a path leading out of the valley, and when he turned to survey the Woods once more, he saw not the grey trees, but a large, crystalline blue lake.

As he stared confused at the peaceful waters, he realized where he was. This was South Farhen Lake, just beneath Farhen Peak, which overlooked the scholarly city of Mott.

The Witches had sent him to his second home, the home he loved far more than Riverfen.

The hike down from the lake would take a few candles at most, bringing him down and around the peak to Mott. Perhaps he would encounter his fellow scholars along the route, for many rare plants and animals made their homes near the lake. Shouldering his pack, Alex set off down the narrow, rocky trail, enjoying the sun on his cheeks.

Taking deep breaths, Alex reveled in the feel of air in his lungs, the bite of wind that made his eyes water, the ache that set into his legs and hips as he traversed the downhill slope. How glorious to be mortal once more! The thirst had vanished, leaving only a mortal hunger. The threads of the Underworld, so long attached to his soul, had been severed.

Full of joy, Alex had to laugh as he walked, scaring a nesting bird from its nearby perch. His steps light and bouncy, he sang an old Valadi traveling tune, his voice carrying over the bare trees and mossy boulders.

What a day to be well and truly alive!

Midday passed into afternoon as Alex rounded the peak, coming to a series of switchbacks above Mott. His happiness slid away as he rested at the top, for something was wrong.

Very, very wrong.

Black smoke curled up from Mott. It had an acrid smell to it, drifting over the wind to choke Alex's lungs and sting his eyes. Cries of terror rang in the air, loud even from a distance.

Without pausing to think, Alex raced down the trail, holding linen against his mouth and nose to ward against the smoke that eclipsed the hillside. He ran and ran, his body screaming at him to get away from the fire but his mind overriding all in his fear for the university. Tripping over stones and roots, he always regained his balance, his headlong dash as dangerous as the choking smoke.

Red and orange joined the black, flames that crept from buildings to the trees, sending animals running from their homes to escape the fire. Still Alex ran on. He dodged around burning trees and leapt over smoldering logs, coughing but not stopping.

As he reached the bottom of the trail, he stopped to take in the nightmare that greeted him.

Scholars ran every which way, some carrying priceless scrolls, others weeping as they faced their burning home. The towers of the University burned, cracking and tumbling under their own weight. Homes and business around the University were black and grey from ash and flame, the families that had lived there fleeing with whatever possessions they could save.

As the people ran, soldiers in dark armor, faces obscured by wetted rags, cut them down, blocking escape. There was a flash of silver in the chaos, and Alex peered through the smoke to see its source.

Sir Chadron Elliot whirled with a blade in his left hand and a silver prosthetic as his right, his tabard soaked with blood, his armor dark from ash. Two of the university's guards faced

Chadron, circling him warily. As one leapt forward, the other fell to Chadron's blade.

Stooping to a fallen soldier, Alex took the dead man's blade, a long double-headed axe. It felt strange and heavy in his hands, unwieldy at best and too slow at worst. But it was his only weapon, and he wouldn't back down.

The smoke cleared momentarily, carried away by a gust of wind. Alex dropped his pack, calling in a strong voice, "Chadron!"

The knight paused from his carnage, staring over the battlefield at Alex. Though his mouth was covered by cloth, Alex could swear the man grinned at him.

"No one touches that man save for me!" Chadron shouted at his men. The enemy soldiers paused in cutting down the defenseless scholars and turned to watch the duel. Many of the scholars and rustics fled while they had a chance.

Hefting the axe, Alex moved forward slowly, faking a limp. *Let him think the wound he gave me at the Masque is hurting me.* Chadron swept his sword up in a ready stance, his silver hand held just under the blade.

"You're too late, Strilu," Chadron taunted. "The University is gone, its secrets given to the flames. What will you gain from this?"

"The earl will not stand for this," Alex said. "He'll hunt you down and gut you for these crimes."

"Your dear brother won't have a head to give orders after the month is out. Even now he rots in a dungeon in Stonetree at my uncle's pleasure. Flee while you can, little Strilu, and perhaps I'll let you live."

Alex's heart dropped, his mouth going dry. Could it be true? Stonetree fallen? He couldn't think any more on it, for Chadron sprang forward with a raw cry, his sword arcing gracefully through the smoke.

Dodging, Alex instinctively tried to summon his *fampir* side to lend speed and strength to his movement. It didn't come.

Rolling under Chadron's swift blade, Alex swung the axe, but it moved choppily, a bear against a fox. Chadron stepped aside easily, smacking the axe with a playful swing.

"Come on, *fampir*. Show your true nature, else this will be too easy," Chadron laughed.

Too late, Alex realized that he stood no chance. All the swordplay and weaponry he'd learned, he'd learned as *fampir*, always able to coax out his wicked side to aid him. As a mortal, he was slower, weaker.

Alex stared death in the eyes for the first time in over a century, and his knees buckled.

His laughter fading, Chadron closed in again, each swing of his sword vicious and calculated. Alex barely deflected him, his arms growing fatigued, his back aching from the strain of lifting such a heavy blade. Still Chadron came, mechanical and merciless in his attacks.

Hefting the axe, Alex countered a particularly hard blow, but his hands throbbed with the strike. Sensing weakness, Chadron looped his sword around the axe shaft, pulling the weapon from Alex's hands and sending it flying away.

Weaponless, Alex backed away, his heart hammering. *No, I've only just begun to live again, I can't–*

Chadron's blade swept across the space between them, its finely honed edge tearing through Alex's skin. A shallow cut, but it stung nonetheless. Red seeped into Alex's shirt, and he couldn't stop to wonder at it.

"You were never a great warrior, were you? A scholar until the end." Chadron frowned. "But this was too easy. Where's the sport in it?"

Chadron threw Alex to the ground. He gestured at his soldiers. "Bind him. We'll take him back to D'Clet. I'm sure he'll enjoy seeing his love before he dies."

Alex's head snapped up. "Cara! Where is she? What have you done to her?"

Chadron stooped, taking Alex's chin. His smile was cruel. "It's not what's been done to her, little Strilu. It's what she's going to do to you."

Alex tore his head away and spat at Chadron's feet. The knight strode away laughing as his men bound Alex and tied him to a horse. The university burned and crumbled around them as the band of soldiers left the once peaceful town.

Alex struggled in his bonds, but he knew that Chadron was lying. *Cara will save me. She'll see what I've done for her, and she'll help me escape. Then Chadron will get what he deserves.*

CHAPTER FORTY-SEVEN
Gwen

"Wullum?" Gwen stood still, one hand still in Valder's, the other gripping Lintem's fur.

Her brother flinched and cried out as if invisible whips cut into his skin. He shook, his hands batting at attackers she couldn't see. *He shouldn't be here!* Gwen thought angrily. She whirled on Valder.

"Why is he in Purgatory! He was a good man, and the Skals slaughtered him!"

"Perhaps you should ask him yourself," Valder said mildly. "Remember, Forest Witch, our perceptions are not always the truth."

Gwen's anger simmered down. Too often had she met trees who claimed themselves to be victims when indeed they were the only source of their misery. She turned back to her brother and said, "Wullum. It's me."

For a moment, Wullum's eyes cleared. He blinked. "Little sister?"

"You're dead, Wullum. Do you remember?"

"Yes." He nodded fervently. "The spears. You were there with me. Did the Skals kill you, too?"

"No." Gwen summoned her fortitude. "Why are you in Purgatory, Wullum?"

"Because I was not a good ruler." Wullum whimpered, his back arching with another unseen strike. "I gave plenty to the Demars and left nothing for the Skals. I sent Skals to die in the mines and arrested those who protested against me."

Death, it seemed, had no room for lies. His Song corroborated his words. Gwen shook her head sadly. "You never told me, Wullum."

"You were still a child, sweet sister. And so compassionate. You would have objected to my treatment of them." His eyes glazed over once more, and he was lost within his punishment.

"Do you still think him a good man?" Valder asked.

"He was good to me," Gwen said. She turned away from Wullum, the vengeance in her heart faltering. *Perhaps he deserved his death.* The Forest Witch would not have questioned her resolve, but neither would she have been upset by Nature's cycles. *Violence begets violence, vengeance begets vengeance.* Gwen shuddered, knowing that Purgatory would await her should she give into the human urge that blackened her heart. *Knowing is not always enough to sway one's path.*

Valder moved on, and Gwen followed. The Song of Death changed, and they left the red mist behind them. Instead, they saw before them a series of campfires spread out evenly in rows. Some had Valadi wagons, others carriages and horses, and still others simple beasts of burden. People waited at each one, not noticing Gwen and her companions.

"What is this?"

"The place of Waiting," Valder said. "Some who die don't want to forget the loved ones they left behind. They don't want to experience the joys of Autorus's Halls or the unknown Lyael until everyone they love is with them."

As they passed through the rows, Gwen craned her head to see who she might recognize. As they came upon a fire with a grand carriage behind it, she startled.

"King Henrik," she said. The king sat on a log in his grand robes. Others surrounded him: Earl Stillmeadow and his wife, and a young man who looked like their son. They murmured to each other, their voices quiet as reeds, and paid little attention to her.

"King Henrik," Gwen said again. "You're dead?"

The king finally looked up at her. She hadn't spoken much

to him at the Cascade Palace, but she had seen him many times before. The wrinkles which had adorned his forehead had smoothed out, contentment in his eyes.

"Lady Seastone," the king replied. "I'm surprised to see you here."

"I'm not dead."

"No, I can feel your warmth." He gazed beyond her expectantly. "Did you bring them with you?"

"Who?"

"Seanna and the child," said Earl Stillmeadow. "We want to see if they survive the war."

His wife smiled vaguely. "She'll have given birth by now. Another grandchild for us."

"I thought you hated the queen," Gwen said to Henrik.

"I did. But we grew closer before I died. I want to see my child before I move on, and it's easier waiting with others." His attention turned away from her, and they all stared out into the night.

Valder tugged at Gwen's hand, and she moved on reluctantly. She asked, "Is it peaceful for them?"

"Oh yes," he said. "And if they tire of waiting, they can move on to Autorus's Halls. Which we must, if you wish to see him."

"What are his halls like?"

"Whatever you want them to be."

They left the campfires behind them and came upon a grand sight. Hills and forests stretched out before them. Homes and farms dotted the landscape, with large manors and wealthy towns spread haphazardly between them. A shining city glowed in the distance, its walls bright with gold.

"Autorus's refuge for those who don't wish to go to Lyael yet," Valder said. "A land of no want and no hardship. Some people like their death to be as simple as life, tilling the soil and reaping the rewards. Some want to learn more and study all the secrets of Earda. Others wish to have wealth they never gained in life."

"And everyone comes here?"

"In time. Purgatory is never forever; lost souls work their way out when their remorse is true, and they come here. Some people want to see Lyael, and they leave rather quickly. Do you see it?"

Gwen squinted, and there, beyond the city, she saw a road that stretched far beyond the distant mountains. "It leads to Lyael?"

"Yes. No one knows what's there. Perhaps a glorious heaven filled with the gods. Perhaps a worse torment than Purgatory. Perhaps nothing. Everyone is called to it at some point. I think it's human nature to want to see what's beyond."

"Does Autorus know?"

A new voice answered her, a voice that simultaneously held Death and comfort in its tones. "Not even I know."

Valder dropped her hand and drifted away, back to his duties with the dead. Gwen slowly pivoted until she saw him.

Autorus was not what she expected. Well, she hadn't quite known what to expect. Tales often spoke of the Cythra of the Dead as a tall, gaunt man with pale features and a long black robe. Others spoke of him as cold and terrible, winter in human form. Still others said that he took no shape and gathered one's soul with wind's gentle touch.

A man stood before her, his dark hair unkempt. He wore simple clothes and had a cane in one hand. His eyes were strange: one milky white, a blind man's eye, while the other was completely black, the void in its gaze. He was only a little taller than Gwen, his slight build making him appear entirely normal.

"I have never traveled the road to Lyael," Autorus said. Wistfulness filled his voice. "Though I have yearned for many, many years."

"Why not go?" Gwen asked.

He smiled indulgently. "And leave my domain unprotected? Who would care for the dead once I leave? Who would help those in Purgatory and grant desires in these halls?"

"I don't know."

"Precisely." Autorus came up beside Gwen and gazed out over the peaceful place. "I created this. All of it: Purgatory, the

Waiting Place, the Halls. But not Lyael, which was there long before the Songs found me. I was once mortal, you know. Then the Songs chose me, just as they chose you. They inundated me with all the melodies, harmonies, and adaptations of Death. They gave me the power to help the dead find peace. It is a startling thing, you see. Dying. Some people walk into my embrace with the knowledge of a life well lived. Most, however, are confused and angry. Some tragedy or disease or what-have-you took them before they had a chance to say goodbye." His eyes turned inward, sad and introspective. "Too many children. Too many in their prime. Life is precious, and I'm afraid that I only know that because I deal in Death."

Gwen took his hand, unafraid now that she saw his empathy and love for humanity. "I want to help you."

"Good. I tried to guide the *sulpari* to my path, but I fear that she is too far gone. She will try to sever me completely from Earda." His strange eyes turned to her, black and white and full of the trials of human history. "The Ossuary can stop her, and free me. You can free my sisters, too, and allow them to join me in Lyael."

"The Witches," Gwen said.

"Indeed. They, too, need a custodian to care for the Songs they have watched over."

"I will try to find someone worthy to replace you," Gwen said.

Autorus bowed his head. "Thank you."

As they stood together, hand-in-hand, Gwen opened herself up to the Songs that flowed through him. She heard the moans and whispers of the dead, and the cries of the dying. As the dead came into the Underworld, helpers like Valder determined where they should go. All humans made mistakes, had their cruelties and their flaws. Few, she saw, were banished to Purgatory. Most were forgiven, elf and human alike, from all stretches of Earda. She marveled at them all.

"It doesn't matter which gods they believed in," she said softly.

"Should it?" Autorus gave a wry smile.

She shook her head. "No."

The Songs of Death no longer frightened her. Some still had that foul whiff, but most were as gentle as they could be. Death was not malicious in itself. It simply *was*. As Gwen listened, she heard the melodies of the *fampir* and the prowlers, undead things that she thought should go against the Songs.

She asked Autorus, and he replied, "The Songs are not the arbiters of right and wrong. I have met *fampir* who use their immortality wisely, and *fampir* who use it to hurt others. They have that element of humanity. The prowlers are animals, they have no choice in what they do. I hope that Mavian finds a way to help them."

"Mavian?" Gwen nearly laughed. She hadn't heard his name in such a long time. "If there were a way, wouldn't you know it?"

Autorus chuckled. "I have been separated from humanity for far too long. You are an ingenious species; you will always find ways to use the Songs that I never thought possible. You created the *fampir* and the wights, and the *sulpari*, too. I have no doubt that a solution is in the Songs."

Gwen nodded. After a moment, she asked, "Is there anything left for me to learn here?"

Autorus shook his head. "You are armed with all the knowledge you need. You will find that, even with the Songs, life on Earda is complex and dangerous. Be cautious, but confident. Trust your instincts."

"Will I meet you again when I die?"

"Dear one, we will meet on Earda. I am not so far removed that I don't like to interfere now and then. Others know me as Darian." He gave her a wry smile. "Now, I can take you nearly anywhere you wish to go. Stonetree has fallen, and Druam fled home to Riverfen. Con Salur is under siege. The Skals run rampant across the plains."

Gwen pondered his question. Where should she go? Home to Riverfen, but would she do the most help there? Con Salur and Seanna, yet even she could not defeat an army on her own. To Demarren, where the Skals would execute her as soon as see her?

She asked, "What would you choose in my position?"

Autorus's mismatched eyes were unreadable. "I would resolve that which festers in my heart."

Gwen nodded. *I can't help the Cythra or the people I've come to love if I am still mired in doubt.* She said, "I will go to Lordstown, where Olfrick Kron has stolen the throne from my brother."

"Will you enact your vengeance?"

"I will do what needs to be done."

Autorus nodded, and Gwen took one last look at the Halls of Death. *Next time I'm here, I will have only one choice: to stay, or to move on.* The road to Lyael called to her, and she turned away from it.

I have much to do before I die.

CHAPTER FORTY-EIGHT
Mavian

In the dark hours of the night, Mavian paced his rooms. Thirty steps north-south, fifteen steps east-west. Ever since Druam's escape, Mavian had been unable to do anything else but worry. He'd packed his bags, unpacked them, then repacked, unsure if he should flee or stay. *I told Druam I'd try to discover Rask's plans, but that was a foolish idea. The old bastard needs to die regardless of whatever schemes he's cooked up. I should leave while I still have a chance.*

But he wasn't an experienced traveler. He'd always either taken carriages or dread portals, neither of which involved him tramping through the mountains with the threat of snow and starvation hanging over him. *If I leave, I'm likely to perish without ever reaching the River Valley, much less D'Clet.*

He had, at least, pieced together the semblance of a plan. He would return some of his stolen scrolls to Mott and gain their trust, then bring a few of their scholars with him to D'Clet to help him cure the prowlers. If Ekkar aided him along the way, he could gain a pack of prowlers and infiltrate the city through the very tunnels he'd once used for Rask's dirty deeds. *Chadron won't be able to stop us. I know those tunnels far better than he does.*

That was only *if* he could get to Mott before the snows blocked the passes, and *if* the prowlers would follow him without the gem's magic.

If he stayed, he could try and find out Rask's plans. What would Talnor do to him when she discovered Druam's escape?

Would she sniff out the truth?

Mavian glanced over at Merick standing stiffly by the fire. As always, the wight stared straight ahead, his arms at his sides. He could be a statue, save for his eyes, which followed Mavian around the room. Ekkar, meanwhile, had curled up on the bed, making a nest out of the blankets and pillows. He made snuffling sounds in his sleep.

The revelation still made Mavian's head spin. That simple creature that growled and twitched on the bed had once been a scholar, the brother of an earl. It had been a *fampir* that lived for centuries in secret until something drove him to try and make a child with a mortal woman. *What was it about Cara's mother that inspired him?* Mavian wondered. He thought of Renna. Had they been blessed with a child, he would have done anything for her and the treasure she carried. *Love can drive one to great or terrible things.* He shuddered and murmured, "We have both sold ourselves for the promise of a woman. I hope it was worth it for you; it wasn't for me."

The door burst open. Mavian jumped, his hand instinctively reaching for the gem that wasn't there. He stared at the intruder. Talnor. Her eyes blazed with fury, and she advanced on him.

"You released him," she hissed. She hadn't a *fampir*'s features, but her face still contorted with an ugly, terrifying rage. "Traitor!"

Mavian held his hands up, trying to look innocent. Difficult when one is guilty of all crimes. He said, "Slow down. What are you talking about?"

"Don't play coy with me! You were seen leaving the dungeons just before his escape was discovered!" Talnor closed the distance between them. She gripped his arm with one hand, the other closing about his throat. Mavian gurgled, his free hand faintly scrabbling at her.

"Luckily for you, a cell has just opened up in the dungeons," Talnor said, her fingers tightening. "You won't die. Yet."

Mavian stared at her, frightened. Her beauty had become a dagger thrusting deeper into him with each word. Renna had once been behind those eyes, combed that hair, draped that neck with jewels and gold. But she was gone, replaced by an ancient creature who cared not for him.

Talnor released him. Just as he regained his breath, she threw her fist into his stomach. He crumbled to the floor. She kicked him. He rolled away from her, and her awful hands pulled at him. She raised her hand for another blow, but the wight held her back.

Merick threw her away from Mavian, sending her crashing into the wall. Ekkar shrieked from the bed and scrambled to the floor, crouching protectively in front of Mavian. As Mavian coughed and struggled to breathe – his lungs felt as if they'd been crushed by bricks – Merick drew his sword and advanced on Talnor.

The *fampir* woman hissed and batted away the blade. A flash of her feral side came over her, but she didn't transform. She stared at her hands, a glimmer of confusion on her face. Mavian smiled despite his pain.

"Your soul may be *fampir*," he said, "but the body you stole isn't. I doubt you'll ever be able to truly turn."

Talnor stood back against the wall as Merick menaced her. He didn't swing again, but he held his sword out, blocking her from moving. At her neck, Mavian spied the white gem. He opened his mouth to tell Merick to get it, then Talnor spoke.

"I do wish I could stay and play," she said, "but Cara draws near to D'Clet. There will be no escape for you, traitor. Rask and his men know of your misdeeds; even if I don't kill you, they will." She clasped the gem and uttered the spell, her fingers drawing quick runes in the air. A dread portal opened behind her, and she fell back into it. When the last of her disappeared inside, the portal closed. Mavian's ears hurt with the noise, his bones rattling from the portal's savage presence.

Once she was gone, Merick sheathed his sword and bent to Mavian. Ekkar burbled and whimpered, clinging to Mavian's arm. With dedicated effort, Mavian climbed to his feet and retrieved his belongings: clothes, books, scrolls, and whatever else he had brought with him to the siege.

"We have to leave," Mavian said. He peered out the small window. Tents and soldiers crowded the valley as far as the eye could see. Druam had his *fampir* magic to slip through; Mavian had nothing. He ran his fingers through his hair, thinking.

As he did, Merick closed the door and blocked it with a heavy bar. Mavian nodded, grateful for the wight's presence.

"There may be a way." Mavian pulled out one of his books that contained spells of the Underworld. It also mentioned blood magic. He had never tried the latter, for it made him uneasy, but he was desperate now.

Riffling through the pages, he found what he was searching for. An old working had been scribbled on the page by an unsteady hand. *A passage through dreams*, Mavian read. *To transport the body from one place to another. It requires blood and a firm mind, one which will not wander lest it be caught and stay forever in the lands between life and death.*

Mavian traced his hand over the words, his mouth going dry. *Nothing for it but to try.*

Moving as quickly as he dared, Mavian drew runes on the floor with chalk from his bag. He said to Merick and Ekkar," I'll need your blood for this, too. I don't think I have the strength otherwise."

The undead creatures didn't respond, but neither did they retreat from him. When he had finished his preparations, Mavian took a knife and a vial. He made a small cut on his arm, near the marks left by Druam's teeth, and filled part of the vial with his blood. Then he did the same for Merick and Ekkar. After that, he went along the runes, sprinkling the vial's contents over the crucial junctures.

The runes sparked and fizzed, glowing with a faint light. Mavian stood in the center, his satchel over his shoulder, and held his hands out. Ekkar took one nervously, and Merick the other, staring impassively at the wall.

Mavian chanted the words to the working. As he did, his blood churned within him, energy draining out into the room. Ekkar whined, and even Merick grunted with the spell's effects.

Mavian closed his eyes and finished the spell. When he

opened them, they stood in a place unlike any he'd ever seen.

The land of dreams, Mavian thought. The world was completely white, with no shadows to show depth or distance. Flecks of grey swirled through the air like strange snow, though they didn't land anywhere; they just swirled and swirled, up and down and around, a never-ending blizzard.

Mavian took a step forward. Though nothing resembled the ground, his foot met resistance where the earth should be. Ekkar and Merick followed him apprehensively.

They saw no one. As they continued walking, the landscape remained unvaried. Mavian glanced over his shoulder, but there was no sign of their passage. He dared a shout, "Hello? Anyone?"

From the distance came a faint scream. He headed toward it, though he couldn't tell if he actually made any progress. He and his companions walked for what felt like candles and still saw nothing save white and grey.

Suddenly, a huge shape rose from the fog. His heart thudded as Talnor's sarcophagus loomed out of the mist, blacker than night in the colorless void of dreams. Its lid was glass, and he hesitated to look inside it, hoping that his suspicions were wrong. Mavian nearly dropped his companions' hands when he saw the woman locked inside the heavy tomb.

"Renna!" he shouted. She opened her dazzling blue eyes, tears streaking down her face. He stared at her, knowing that this was a land of dreams, yet still not believing his eyes. "What are you doing here?"

"I'm trapped," she said. "How did you find me?"

"I traveled here with magic," he said. "This isn't a dream for me."

"Neither for me." She blinked, and more tears cascaded into the stone. "She trapped me here. I can't wake up, but neither can I die."

"Talnor," Mavian whispered. Renna nodded. He asked, "How can I free you?"

"She must die. Then my soul will at last be allowed to go to Autorus." Her blue eyes held grief in them. "You didn't tell me that I'd died."

"I'm sorry," Mavian said. As he spoke, the sarcophagus and Renna grew fainter and fainter, the white and grey overtaking them. Dimly, as if from a great distance, he heard Renna's last words, "Don't linger, else you will never leave. Kill Talnor and free me. Please."

Nothing remained except the eerie grey. Mavian's heart faltered, and he said, "I will. I promise."

He drew strength from the Merick's stoicism and Ekkar's trust. He said aloud, "We're going to Mott."

Mavian took another step forward and fell through the white. He shut his eyes.

When he opened them, the world he knew had returned. He found himself with his companions on a road in the dark of night. Stars twinkled overhead, and he sighed with relief. *We survived.* He wanted to weep for Renna, but his grief couldn't help her now. He had to act if he wanted to rescue her from that horrid place.

Mavian walked forward. The wind shifted, bringing with it the smell of smoke and charred flesh. As he peered through the midnight forest, he realized that the scenery was familiar. Achingly familiar.

"Mott," Mavian whispered. He ran, heedless of the treacherous road in the night. "It worked!" he crowed, but he stopped short as the town came into view. His stomach dropped to the earth, and he half-believed he was still in the land of dreams.

No.

The dark night was lit by a multitude of torches and lanterns illuminating the wreckage of the town. Ashen-faced scholars and villagers walked about, collecting what could be salvaged and pulling bodies from the heaps that used to be buildings.

Mavian walked in a daze into the town. Ekkar and Merick hung back, staying out of the light.

"What happened here?" Mavian asked a scholar. "Who did this?"

"Sir Chadron Elliot," came the answer. "Him and his dogs."

He must have gotten bored waiting in D'Clet. Only two days' ride would have brought him here.

"How can I help?" Mavian found himself saying. Only a few months ago, his dread portal had led him to scholars of Mott, and *he* was the one who'd left destruction in his wake. All for the sake of obtaining scrolls and books to further his own selfish knowledge.

"Find what you can salvage. If you come across any corpses, we're putting them where the novum used to be."

Mechanically, his thoughts numb, Mavian set about his task. He cleared charred rafters from homes, pulling out the burnt bodies of innocent folk and carrying them to the ever-growing pile. Merick helped, too, though Ekkar remained hidden. Mavian knew Chadron was a bastard, but he had never imagined the man to be capable of this. *All these lives, all this knowledge, gone forever.*

Hundreds of thousands of scrolls and books lay in this great library, too many to be read in one lifetime. He asked a scholar who carried a painfully tiny body, "Was anything saved?"

"Not enough to fill a bookshelf."

Mavian shut his eyes against the storm inside. *Chadron never cared for knowledge or humankind's accomplishments.*

Gasps and cries went up behind him, and he turned to see Ekkar at the edge of the town, whimpering for him. The people drew back, some leveling weapons though no one moved closer to the prowler.

"*Ekkar*," Mavian called. "*Come to me.*"

The people fell back on themselves, one woman screamed, and the prowler crept forward to Mavian, his red eyes full of doubt and confusion.

The scholar next to Mavian had frozen. As he put a hand over Ekkar's head, Mavian asked the scholar, "What will you do now?"

"Rebuild," the scholar said. "Begin again."

As long as there is war, there will be those who destroy the knowledge of their enemies for destruction's sake. Scholarship is of no worth to them.

"You cannot build here," Mavian said, unconsciously stroking Ekkar's hair. "It's too dangerous."

"Where could we go?"

"D'Clet." It wasn't the plan Mavian had originally thought of, but it was still a good one. The city was walled, defensible, and a good fortress once Chadron was ousted from it. *And once the people learn what he's done, they'll stand against him.* Mavian continued, "I'll lead you to D'Clet once our work here is done. There, we will rebuild. Rask will not find his castle ready for him when he returns."

"And this monster?" The scholar's eyes flicked to Ekkar. The prowler stared down at a body, running its talons over the dead man's hands.

"He'll come too. We'll need him before it's done."

"For what?"

"For peace. And a cure." *If I can cure Verdon, I might be able to help the other prowlers.*

The scholar shrank back from him. "We don't need you, Far-Eyes. We've heard of your dark magics."

Far-Eyes. How long had it been since Mavian had heard his proper title? Ironic, how short-sighted he'd been lately.

"Come with me or don't. I'm going to D'Clet, and I'll rebuild the University's knowledge, scroll by scroll. If you come, the prowlers will protect you, and all my knowledge of the Underworld will be used to aid us. If you stay, the Lofalins or Rask will come to finish the job."

The scholar looked from Mavian to Merick to Ekkar and back again. "By the gods, you're a madman."

"Yes." Mavian fixed him with a determined stare. "Madness is what's needed when the dead walk the earth and war makes monsters of us all."

CHAPTER FORTY-NINE
Seanna

In the candle between dark and dawn, Seanna lay on the divan with her son in her arms, too exhausted to move but too awake to sleep. Portia stayed respectfully on the edges of the room, and Ropaz snored on a couch nearby. She smiled at him, immensely grateful for his loyalty.

Had something changed in her to inspire others to care for her? She felt another woman entirely than the one who'd departed Riverfen in a sulk, pouting and petty. Had she really been the one to denounce Gwen Strilu in front of the court, spewing lies of infidelity and barbarism? Had she spurned her lover in a fit of pique, disowning Maeria without a second thought?

Shame colored Seanna's cheeks as she held the new king. If this were a time of peace, he'd be blessed by the Exalt in a grand ceremony twenty days after his birth. But there was no Exalt, and the Grand Novum lay in ruins, a victim of the Lofalins' terrible onslaught.

With this new life in her arms, Seanna knew that she couldn't return to the petty, spiteful woman she had been. Even if by some miracle Con Salur won its freedom and she retained her crown, she couldn't descend back to the mockery and vicious squabbles of the past. All those times Henrik had scorned her and yelled at her, and she thought herself above his words. She shuddered. Henrik, with the weight of his crown and his people's lives on his back, had always been right.

It was a terrifying thought, knowing that she deserved all those rumors and hateful glares.

The baby yawned and wriggled in her arms, and Seanna cooed at him, her heart full for the first time in years. She had never truly loved Henrik, nor Larka or Maeria or any of the others, a string of women Seanna used and tossed as she pleased. That, too, made her ill now. If she had only allowed vulnerability in herself, she could have–

But no. That was all in the past, those women either dead or gone forever from her life, and she would have no other chances with them. *If the gods ever grant me another chance at love, I will not be so foolish*, Seanna thought. Yet in that moment, she thought that she'd need no one else save the babe in her arms. He was her soul, her body, her love, all wrapped up in gold-embroidered cloth with snot dripping from his tiny nose.

At long last, Seanna fell asleep.

She woke to shouts outside her door. Seanna immediately half-rose as people argued in her antechamber. Ropaz mumbled sleepily, waking only when Portia shook his arm.

"See what's the matter," Seanna said to Ropaz once he'd rolled to his feet. Ill humors coiled in the pit of her stomach, making her both sick and scared at once.

Ropaz opened the door, letting in a breathless soldier. The soldier bowed, but when he rose, he was clearly afraid. "Your Grace, High Predicant. The walls have fallen."

Seanna unconsciously drew her child closer to her, clutching at him as the world shattered around her. "So soon? But the general said we could hold for days."

The tunnels won't be ready yet. We're doomed.

The soldier swallowed. "We have barricades around the city between the walls and Darkroad. They won't get through yet."

"Return to Scawind. Tell them to give us as much time as possible."

As he departed, guilt weighed on Seanna's heart. *How many men have I just condemned in the hopes of saving the people inside Darkroad and Midtown?*

"Ropaz, send for Belrose," she said. "No, don't make him

come here. Send a messenger to him, tell him we're out of time. He has to finish the tunnel as soon as he can and start moving citizens to safety."

"Of course," Ropaz said. He left to do as she commanded. Seanna carefully gave her child to Portia while she dressed. When she was ready, she said, "Portia, pack belongings for each of us. Clothes for travel, supplies for the baby, food, water. Good linens and wools, not the courtly silks. We won't need such things on the road."

"Yes, Madam." Portia bobbed her head and began her work while Seanna fed the infant.

When Ropaz returned, his face was grim. "Seanna, you must leave as soon as the tunnels are ready."

"I know, Ropaz." Seanna held out a hand to him. "Let us pray that as many escape with us as possible."

"Belrose reports that there is a cavern near the tunnel's entrance. It will hold a few hundred; we can wait there until he's breached the other side."

"Fill it with others first. I will wait until the last moment."

Ropaz looked ready to argue, then nodded. "I will convey your orders."

A few hundred out of a hundred thousand. It's not enough. Seanna stared out over Midtown and the streets filled with her people. *Most here will die.*

One day passed, then the next. The people of Con Salur huddled together, listening to the fighting from above and the ballistae below. On the third day, Seawind went quiet. Seanna clasped her hands and prayed at the Silver Keep's novum for all the men who had died defending their city.

She returned to her rooms to find Ropaz and Portia. Ropaz said, "It's time."

Before they could move, the castle shuddered around them. The walls shook, the chandeliers on the ceiling tinkling as the glass collided. Ropaz and Portia ran to Seanna as she cowered on the couch. Together they weathered the attack until the floor came to a standstill.

Cries echoed around the city, screams of panic and pain. As

Seanna prepared her bag, her gaze constantly on the babe in Portia's arms, she listened to her people's suffering and wanted to weep. But she was queen, and she must be strong.

With the child held against her shoulder, Seanna rushed to the throne room. She arrived just as Belrose entered it, his face flushed. His robes were filthy, his light hair matted. He hadn't slept in days, with dark rings under his eyes and evidence of a recent bloody nose. By his despair, she knew that Con Salur had truly fallen.

"Tell me," Seanna said, determined to stand her ground.

"We've found a way out," Belrose began. "But it may be too late. They're coming down the cliffs."

More screams from the courtyard distracted Seanna, and she ran past Belrose, feet slapping the polished wood floors as she raced outside. She could see the ships far below and the great doors to Darkroad. The people around her craned their necks to stare fearfully up at the clifftops. Controlled as she was, even Seanna's hope shattered in her breast as she followed their gazes.

Hundreds of feet above, where the people looked like ants, the Lofalins had brought some horrible new machine. The cliffs thudded and groaned under the weight of them, and mighty chains began to descend the cliffs toward Midtown.

They won't try to breach Darkroad's doors. They're coming straight to Midtown.

The chains came slowly, slowly, for the Lofalins had to crank their machine, gaining each foot with a minute's labor. At Seanna's shoulder, Ropaz gaped, his throat bobbing as he swallowed.

"Con Salur has fallen," he said, and the servants and courtiers around them gasped and clung to each other, some sobbing, others bravely facing their deaths.

"We have to leave now!" Belrose said. "They'll be down those cliffs by day's end. We have to get you to the tunnels, Seanna."

Seanna didn't resist as she was pulled away from the Silver Keep. A cordon of soldiers formed around her small group, and the wisest of the nobles who had heard Belrose's words followed behind. Rustics, led by one of the elders, joined them. The ballistae had started up again, all of Midtown shaking as the munitions struck the cliffs below. Chaos filled the streets, the line between noble and rustic absent during war. Courtiers demanded aid, and the terrified people gave none.

"We must tell them," Seanna said as Belrose led her towards Darkroad.

"There's already panic," Belrose returned, his eyes darting about the stampeding people. "You and that child must be saved first. If others find their way into the tunnel, we'll protect them. But we can't risk you being trampled."

As he said it, a man shouted and ran at Seanna, screaming for help. One of the soldiers pushed the man aside, drawing his sword to deter anyone else.

Inside Darkroad, hundreds upon hundreds of people filled the walkways, cramped like insects in the small spaces. White faces peered from windows, and most of the homes and businesses had been barricaded, keeping the refugees out. The moans and cries of the masses echoed in the dim light, reverberating from the walls. Seanna didn't want to imagine how Darkroad would sound once the elves came to slaughter its denizens.

Belrose didn't stop as rustics begged him for help or cried out in pain. He led the way with dogged determination, never wavering. At last, he reached an alley leading into greater darkness, its corners untouched by the few lanterns or torches that lit the main thoroughfare. Casting a white, magical light, Belrose held it over his head as he went down the alley. Silent, eyes wide, heart racing at all the noise, Seanna followed, holding her baby close.

The alley turned into a rough tunnel, winding further and further into Earda, dark, mysterious, and small. As they went, the sounds of terror faded behind them, leaving only the tremors of the earth.

After awhile – Seanna couldn't tell how long – Belrose stopped, his breath coming fast. They were in a large cavern filled with people. As Seanna considered all the starkly lit faces, she saw that so few were inside. *This is all that remains of Con Salur?* Seanna thought, gazing at her people.

She realized that they all watched her, expecting her to say something. Swallowing her rising panic, Seanna turned to Belrose. "We can't stop for long. Where does the tunnel lead?"

"The hills west of the city. I've already checked; no enemy forces are camped there."

"Good. And what if the Lofalins find this tunnel?"

"They won't. I've rigged magical contraptions to collapse them once we've passed safely through."

Nodding, Seanna turned to the waiting group. "We may be all that's left of Con Salur come dawn tomorrow. Yet we are Dotsch, and we will not yield. We may flee now, but we will bring the fight to the Lofalins. No matter if it takes months or years, they will regret coming to our shores and taking our lands. If you stay with me, I cannot guarantee your safety, but I will promise vengeance for our lost families."

As she spoke, Seanna found that the words came easily and naturally. The people didn't cheer, though their eyes shone expectantly.

Turning the babe's large eyes to the crowd, Seanna said, "This new life represents our hope. He was born amid war, disease, and fear, but he will grow up in prosperity, in a Dotschar of our making. I have named him Landin after the great kings who led our people through the Dead's War, for he shall be a great king in his time."

Little Landin looked up at his mother with an uncomprehending gaze, and she kissed his forehead before saying to Belrose, "Take us to our freedom."

CHAPTER FIFTY
Gwen

Earda's bright sun shone down on her head, unimpeded by that strange magic which always diluted it in the Woods. Mountains rose in the distance, their crowns graced with snow. Forests lined the banks of a great river which stretched past the horizon to the distant ocean. Despite Demarren's natural beauties, Gwen's eyes were drawn to the city that stretched out below her feet. She stood on a hill overlooking her home, its familiar Songs washing over her with all the longing of childhood.

Lordstown, the seat of Demarren's rulers since her forefathers had made this land their dominion. It didn't have the splendor of Riverfen, its brick-and-mud walls long covered in filth, its poor living in squalor outside the city's walls. The keep rose in the center of the city, hard and unforgiving. Even from this distance, Gwen could see spikes adorning the walls, each carrying the head of a mage.

When at last she tore her eyes from Lordstown, she took stock of her surroundings. She was at the top of Boneyard Hill, a historic graveyard that held both Demar and Skals alike, united at last in the ground. Weathered stones whose names had long been washed away stood beside newer markers. A mausoleum dominated the western slope, its catacombs home to the royal dead. Gwen remembered the days she had walked inside it, first to bury her mother and then her father. She doubted the Skals would have had the decency to inter her brother with his family.

Autorus was nowhere to be seen. Gwen didn't particularly

mind that he had gone. She knew this land and this city; she needed no guide anymore. With Lintem keeping pace beside her, she descended down the hill on a packed dirt path, her legs used to the steady pace of a long walk. Her leather and fur clothes flapped around her, her braided locks bouncing with each step. Her bare feet made no noise.

The first people that saw her were a family of Demar who knelt beside a gravestone, their clothes threadbare, their shoes worn through. The children shrieked and dove into their parents' arms, and the parents trembled at the sight of Lintem. They backed away as Gwen approached. She stopped a distance away, reaching out to their Songs without thinking about it. She found hunger and suffering there, a family displaced from their home during the Trials.

"Where is Olfrick Kron?" she asked.

The father pointed a shaking finger at Lordstown. Gwen nodded. She hummed a Song of Sustenance, pulling forth tubers from the ground. She piled them at the family's feet as they watched with wide, terrified eyes. "These will last you a week if you cut and boil them in a stew."

"You're a mage," the mother whispered.

"A Witch," Gwen corrected. *I left Demarren a sorceress, and I return a Forest Witch.*

"They'll kill you," the mother said, concern overcoming the fear in her eyes. "With the Liegelord deposed, the Skals won't allow a mage to live. I know someone who can give you passage out of the country."

"Thank you," Gwen said, "but I did not come here to run away. Do not worry for me. It is the Skals who will flee the streets in fear."

The family stared at her as she continued past them, Lintem padding silently beside her. The cemetery path joined the main road, working its way through the slums toward the city walls. More and more people stopped to stare at them. A few shrieked when they saw the nightcat. The road cleared ahead of her, people huddling at the sides, regarding her fearfully. The Songs around her hummed of despair and fear. Always, the fear. It corroded every note, a wondering of whether their family will be imprisoned, or where they will find their next meal. Nearly all the poor people outside the walls were Demar. *When I left, the people here were Skals.*

The city walls loomed overhead, built of foreboding black stone. Gwen narrowed her eyes as she approached them. The last time she'd passed underneath those walls, she had been hidden in a merchant's cart, terrified that she would be found and brought before Olfrick Kron and his false Trials court.

Guards stood at the gates. They shifted nervously as she came closer, their hands resting on their weapons. All were Skals, their light hair flowing from beneath their helms. Gwen paused a few feet from them to analyze their Songs. Nearly all these men were recently out of boyhood, and only given their spears in the months since the Trials began. Mostly they dealt with drunkards or petty thieves.

"Who are you?" asked the bravest of the guards. His spear shook as he lowered it.

A crowd had gathered a safe distance away, the poor and the hungry, watching with deadened looks. They knew something miraculous could happen. This woman was clearly Demar beneath all that muck, and magic followed in her footsteps. A nightcat, a creature of myth, stood at her side. They wanted to see if such a being could defeat the Inquisitors.

Gwen tilted her head, regarding the guard. He was barely older than her, with a wisp of a beard on his chin.

"I am Gwendolyn Zaman, Princess of Demarren, sister to Liegelord Wullum Zaman, wife to Earl Seastone, and inheritor of the Songs of the Whispering Woods. I have come to take back what is mine." She waited for the guards' reaction.

A few gasps came from the Demar crowd. The guards shifted uneasily, clearly trying to decide what to do. One of the guards threw down his spear and stepped away. The others pressed closer together, their spears pointed at her.

"If what you say is true," said a guard with an audible gulp, "you are a sorceress."

The Songs were clear in Gwen's sight. She contemplated

which ones to use. *Force or persuasion?* She settled for a wind that spun around her, whipping her hair across her cheeks and rattling the guards' spears.

"I am a Witch, and you will not stand in my way," Gwen said. The wind grew faster and more determined, raising a cloud that assailed the guards with dust. They covered their eyes and coughed.

With a quick melody, Gwen urged the wind to die down. She regarded the cowering guards with contempt. Beside her, Lintem growled and raised his hackles, his stinger moving lazily back and forth.

One by one, the guards dropped their spears and moved aside, fear in their eyes and Songs. Gwen nodded at them and stepped through the gate. She could have taken a short route to the castle, but she wanted everyone to know that she had come. So she walked, steadily and sedately, up the main road that meandered through the city from the gates to the keep. The crowd of Demars grew behind her, some shouting her name, others striking up Demar songs of victory. Their feet pounded as drums that accompanied the singers.

Skals shuttered their windows and peeked from doorways. None of them tried to stop her or the Demar crowd. Some made holy gestures over themselves, their lips moving in a silent prayer. To Gwen's surprise, some of the Skals joined the crowd, standing side-by-side with their Demar neighbors. She chastised herself; was it not a Skal merchant who had spirited her from the city? Not all of them were like Olfrick Kron.

As the procession grew, Gwen held her head higher. Lintem raised his paws in a mock military style. Yet with each step closer to the place of Wullum's murder, vengeance festered in her heart. It called to her, urging her to destroy Kron and all the Skals. She had the power; she could raze the city if she so wished.

The road widened and grew straight, leading right up to the castle walls. A troop of thirty soldiers stood together in front of the portcullis, their pikes lowered and ready. The Songs of these men showed that they were no fresh boys. These were hardened fighters, the ones who pulled mages from their homes and drove out rioters with no regard to bloodshed. They would not be swayed by a simple wind.

The crowd grew quiet as the distance between them grew smaller and smaller. At last, Gwen stood before the troops, her chest mere feet from their weapon points. Lintem crouched low, his ears laid back, a growl deep in his throat. Gwen lay a hand to his head. *Not yet.*

Behind her, the crowd waited expectantly, their murmurs carrying over the still air.

A captain stepped forward, his helm boasting proud feathers. He said, "Magic is forbidden in this country. If you surrender quietly, you will be given a fair trial."

Gwen laughed. "A fair trial? I know what Kron and his ilk deem as fair. I will have none of it."

The captain assessed the crowd. His men had arms, but they were heavily outnumbered. He licked his lips.

"We will capture you dead or alive."

In the still air, the calm before chaos, Gwen could see a myriad of Songs laid out before her. Some melodies were quick and brutal, others fiery and harsh, still others subtle yet powerful. She could fight them, but would that leave her weaker as she faced Olfrick Kron?

A hum grew from her chest, up her throat, and into her mouth. She formed slow, steady notes, notes that evoked peace and deep sleep. She flung the notes out over the soldiers, the Song growing more powerful as she tugged its various strings. The soldiers resisted, blinking their eyes and shaking their heads, but the Song overwhelmed them. With a clangor of armor and weapons, they collapsed to the ground, all fast asleep. Only the captain remained standing, for she purposefully left him unaffected.

A wave of shock and confusion passed through the crowd, then a cry was taken up: "Hail the princess! Down with Kron!"

The captain sweated. He stared at his incapacitated men.

"What have you done?" he whispered.

Gwen drew close to him, wild-Woods grime next to his neat

uniform, and said, "They will wake by end of the day. You, however, I have yet to decide. Will you block my way, or will you order all soldiers in the keep to stand down?"

The command quickly swept through the castle. Guards on the walls and at the doors stood at attention, not daring to glance at her as Gwen made her graceful way through the gates, past the courtyard, and up the stone steps to the grand double doors. They opened for her, and she paused at the threshold to speak to the crowd.

"This is my battle, and mine alone," she said. "I will take back this land for all who wish to see the violence and corruption end."

A cheer rose from the gathered people, its joyous cry following her into the keep she knew so well. Gwen moved down the long corridor, her feet cushioned by a soft rug. The walls, which once held tapestries and portraits of her family, were now bare. She curled her lip. *Burned, no doubt.*

She had once run through this hall giggling and screaming as her brother chased her. She had walked it when escorting Wullum to each of his weddings, and she had carried his crown when he was coronated. She knew that at its end she would find the throne room, its peaceful memories shattered by her brother's murder. Had the Skals been able to clean up all the blood?

Fury bloomed deeper with each footstep. What right did Olfrick Kron have to uproot her life? His Trials had betrayed her brother and brought a schism to this city, deepening the lines between Demar and Skal. It would be just, a fair measure by any land's law, for her to take back her country and execute him. She could do it publicly, as he had done to her brother's wives and son.

Gwen pushed open the doors to the throne room. More guards swarmed her, and she didn't have time to think of a clever solution. She summoned a mighty wind, throwing them all back against the walls. They slumped to the floor in a daze. She didn't spare a glance at them.

Olfrick Kron sat on her brother's throne. He wore her

brother's crown. He was all she could see.

Gwen squared her shoulders and redirected her attention to the stone beneath her feet. She Sang, her words bringing flowers and plants all around the throne room. Vines curled around the pillars, flowers sprouted beneath the statues, ferns and trees grew up from the floor to brush the ceiling. The guards shouted and Kron stood, his words lost amid her spell.

Her words became a furious chant, a low, throbbing tune that evoked anger and loss. The tree roots grabbed at the stone underfoot, wrenching it aside like a giant tossing a boulder. Shards of stone went flying, and the floor shook as a chasm opened up in the middle of the room, widening and widening. Only Gwen and Lintem remained untouched, floating above the chaos. Guards cried out as they scrambled to safety. The entire keep shook around them.

Olfrick Kron tried to run as great ruptures opened at his feet. He shouted in alarm, retreating to the throne. It shook, but didn't fall apart.

Gwen walked over the chasm, her eyes fixed on Kron. She ceased her Song, allowing the ground to come to a stop. The chasm split the room in half, a deep, dark hole that dug into the very bedrock.

"Who are you?" Kron whispered.

"You murdered my brother," Gwen said. "You stole his throne."

The man shook, his furs no longer perfectly placed. "P-Princess Gwen?"

She nodded. "I stand accused of witchcraft according to the laws of this country. I come here today to confess my guilt." She leaned to look him straight in the eye. "Try and arrest me."

Kron stared out over the ruins of the throne room, his apple bobbing in his throat. "You vanished. The ambassador told me, you vanished during the Masque—"

"And now I've returned. Just as you once accused me, I accuse you. You murdered my brother."

"I did what I must." A stubborn glint came to his eye.

"You fueled the Trials, killing hundreds of innocents."

"It was necessary."

"So you admit to both?"

His eyes darted over his guards, all of them dazed by the walls. His hand drifted to the sword at his hip, and Lintem growled. Kron swallowed and said nothing.

Gwen allowed herself a righteous fury. The man who had caused her country's downfall and spurred her to flee her home stood in front of her now, quivering in his boots. With a word, she could stop his heart. With a thought, she could force the breath from his lungs until he suffocated.

The Song of Vengeance called to her, urging her to give in. Its unrestrained fury poured into her, demanding that Wullum's death be met with equal violence.

Gwen closed her eyes and reached past Vengeance to the other Songs that coursed around her. Songs of Earda, many familiar, some completely new. She had seen the bluntness of Nature and the whims of the elements, uncaring and thoughtless. Vengeance meant nothing in Nature's order. It was a human emotion, a human pettiness.

She had seen, too, the many wondrous Songs of Humanity. Selflessness and Hope, Nurturing and Imagination. Did she want to fuel one of the crueler Songs, or should she strive to help humans and elves achieve the incredible forgiveness that no other creatures could attain?

Finally, she thought of Death. It was final and inevitable. Kron would no doubt end up in Purgatory, but what of her? Did she want his death to mar her own soul? Lyael had called to her, and she could not go there if Vengeance still clouded her afterlife.

The Song of Vengeance whirled inside her, desperate to be unleashed. She lay a hand on Lintem's head, grounding herself in his calm Song.

After a long moment, Gwen let go of Vengeance. She dug it out from her heart and sent it away. Grief replaced the empty hole left inside her, and she knew she would have to resolve that someday. *But not today.*

Gwen regarded Kron without emotion. "You are spiteful

and cruel, and your ambitions have worsened the divide between our peoples. I could kill you, Olfrick Kron, if I so pleased."

Her enemy stared up at her, and she continued, "I choose to forgive. My brother mistreated the Skals, and if it wasn't you, one of them would have risen up against him. If I kill you, the Skals will demand blood from the Demars, and so the cycle will continue."

"What will be done with me?" he whispered.

Gwen said. "I am but one whom you have hurt. You will stand trial to face all the people whose lives you have destroyed."

Though fear still clung to him, he managed a sneer. "And what of you? Will you take Demarren for yourself, witch-woman?"

Gwen's fingers curled in Lintem's fur. She had thought long on this, but would need time to make her solution work. She said, "I will not. I am a Witch, not a queen. We are too divided a people for there to be one ruler, either Demar or Skal. We are not animals, to be ruled by the strongest, nor should we be slaves to tradition."

She looked out at the guards and past the doorway. She could barely see the crowd waiting for her at the end of the hall. "It will be a new era for Demarren."

CHAPTER FIFTY-ONE
Sandu & Cara

"Not far now. We'll be there in a few candles," Darian said, his tone encouraging. Despite this, Sandu didn't feel much excitement. He knew nothing but despair. His wife and children were gone, and for all he knew, they would arrive too late to save his father.

He both relied on and resented Jagger. While he was grateful for Jagger's support, he also wished that the damned man had just let him finish the job and throw himself off a cliff. *It would've been better that way. Simpler.*

He still dragged step after miserable step to D'Clet, his thoughts as brooding as the grey clouds overhead.

While they marched, Darian and Jagger came up with a plan to infiltrate Rask's dungeons and rescue his father. Sandu didn't oppose any of it, but neither did he think it would work. *Maybe the guards will do the job and kill me. Can't be any worse than living.*

Ever since Cara's return, she too had been stuck in her own head. She only barely spoke to Sandu, and when she did, her words were laced with guilt. If he had cared, he might have seen what was wrong with her. As it was, it meant he had one less person trying to make him feel better. He was almost grateful to Cara for this.

At their midmorning rest, Sandu went into the woods to relieve himself. He leaned against a tree, his thoughts elsewhere. A bird's cry caught his attention. He looked up as he laced his breeches, a task he still found difficult. A beautiful bluejay had alighted nearby. It watched him with a beady, human eye. Something told him that he'd seen this bird before, but he couldn't remember where.

The bird spoke, "Is Cara still with you?"

Sandu nodded, somewhat dumbstruck.

"Where are you?" it demanded.

"Near D'Clet?" Sandu said. Had he finally gone mad, now that a bird spoke to him?

The bird squawked once, spread its wings, and flew away. Its feathers disappeared into the woods, and Sandu immediately forgot about it. He looked down at his hand, wondering why he was taking so long.

He didn't notice Cara observing him from behind a nearby tree.

As the day passed, D'Clet rose, bleak and dreary, a weathered gravestone in the earth. The high walls around its outer farms were black and imposing, but no one stopped them as they walked through. A few men patrolled the ramparts, a bare-bones contingent meant only to guard from bandits. Their small group wound up through the valley between the mountains to the city proper.

Foot traffic traveled through the city and up to the ravine. Most of it filtered away by this point, but plenty of people still crossed the bridge to the fortress. They joined the crowd as it moved slowly over the chasm. Now that Sandu was so close to his father, a breath of renewed life filled him. *I'll do this, and then I can die.*

✳

Cara and her companions turned toward the barracks. As they passed the fortress's gate, she paused.

In the cold courtyard, a woman waited. A tall, golden-haired woman in a dress as blue as midnight, her hands folded contently in front of her, her blue eyes soft and welcoming.

Renna. But this woman was no longer the Renna whom

Cara had known in that quiet fief so far away. This woman's eyes were harsher, her smile not as warm. Yet the way she held herself, the scent of her, was achingly familiar. Cara stopped a few feet away, unsure yet quivering with anticipation.

As she looked at her old friend, Cara knew that Druam had been right. Renna was dead. Red tinged this woman's eyes.

The woman called out, "You won't find him there."

Everyone halted and stared up at her. Cara's hand strayed to her sword. She yelled back, "What do you want?"

The woman smiled. "I believe you came for Cadel Barrow, is that correct? He's inside. You'd best hurry before the stew grows cold."

Cara fingered her weapon, then went through the fortress's gate. She walked beneath the portcullis, half-expecting molten oil to be poured onto her head. Her companions followed, Sandu making concerned noises.

Cara stopped in front of the woman who'd stolen Renna's body. "You've become *fampir*."

"I have been one for many centures," the woman said. "I had hoped to have this conversation later. Well. I am not Renna. I have her body, yes, but her soul has departed."

"So who are you?"

"Talnor Moertru, one of the original *fampir*."

Cara contemplated this a moment. She hated the idea of allying herself with one of these monsters. She asked, "Do you work with Druam?"

Talnor's eyes narrowed. "He is my worst enemy."

Cara nodded. "We have that in common." She stared at this unknown *fampir*, wondering if she should continue with her plans. *The Ossuary is what matters. There I can make everything right.*

Cara made her decision. "Show us the way."

"Then come inside," the woman said, extending a hand to Cara.

Taking it, Cara followed the woman inside. The mighty oak doors closed behind Sandu and the others with an ominous thud.

As soon as they stepped inside the fortress, guards swarmed from all sides. They took hold of her companions' arms. Cara, however, they let go free. Sandu squirmed.

"What's happening?" he asked. "Cara?"

Cara looked at Talnor. "Don't harm them."

Talnor smiled. "I simply need to speak with you privately for a moment. Guards, put them with our other guests."

Though Sandu shouted, Cara went with the *fampir*.

✳

Sandu squirmed and fought against the guards, but it was no use. Their implacable hands held him tight. Darian walked quietly while a total of four guards surrounded Jagger, their spears ready should he move to attack.

The guards dragged them through the fortress. Not the carpet-lined corridors meant for nobles, but through long, low, dark passages. At last, they came to a small door with a heavy lock. The guards opened it and threw them in, then hurriedly locked it.

Sandu rubbed his sore wrist against his leg. They were in a small room without furniture, or much of anything else, really. The bare floor was slimy with grime. A high window let in a small stream of light, though not enough to illuminate the dark corners.

A bundle of rags moved in the corner. "Who's there?" A voice – tired, haggard, and strained – croaked out from the darkness.

"Come out," Darian said.

"Who are you?"

"Friends."

Sandu held back, his face hidden in the shadows, as a decrepit old man shuffled out from the corner, wearing nothing except a stained brown shift.

Though he'd always felt guilt at his father's imprisonment, never before had Sandu known such overwhelming regret and sorrow. *This is my fault. My father should have spent these last few years bouncing his grandchildren on his knee, not growing ill in his lord's dungeons.*

"Who's there?" Cadel Barrow asked. "My eyes aren't what they used to be. Come into the light."

Sandu's mouth was dry. He couldn't believe his father's appearance. In his memory, he always saw him as strong, ready for anything. This poor creature was a husk of his former self.

Darian and Jagger drew back, giving Sandu room. Sandu's tongue stuck in his mouth. What would he – could he – say to his father after so many years?

His father peered at him suspiciously. "Well?"

Sandu's courage failed him, and he stayed in the shadows, speechless.

"Come on, I'm old and going to die soon. Either tell me what you want or leave me be."

"I'm your family," Sandu finally managed to say.

"Impossible. My son's been dead these past years, and his wife remarried to a man who doesn't care for me. If this is a joke, I'm not amused. Put me back in my other cell and be done with it."

"Bartholomew isn't dead, though he hasn't gone by that name for many years." Sandu still shrank from his father's gaze.

"Stop playing coy and come into the light. If you know so much about my son, be a man and tell me face-to-face. Not that I'd believe you, of course."

Ashamed at his own cowardice, Sandu stepped forward at last, exposing himself to the light. He stared at the floor like a scolded child.

"Raise your head," Cadel said softly, inching closer. His papery hand touched Sandu's chin, lifting it. Cadel's eyes shone with tears. "By the gods. Barty, my little Barty, can it be? Is this a trick of illness, are my eyes deceiving me?"

"No, Da," Sandu said, his voice catching. "It's me."

They fell into each other's embrace. Sandu mumbled, "I've missed you so much. I'm sorry, I'm so sorry it's been so long, that I couldn't make enough coin to free you."

"My boy, my boy! The gods be praised!"

438

"I'm so sorry, this is all my fault, I–"

"I've missed you, my boy, I've dreamed of you every night–"

"–I wanted to free you, but–"

"–and now you're so handsome, but your arm–"

They talked over each other, Sandu holding his father up, their tears mingling on their cheeks as they pressed together, savoring the warmth of the other's touch. At last, Sandu pulled away, brushing his hand on his father's chin. "I'm so sorry, Da. I failed as a son, a husband, a father, a friend. I've failed everyone I've ever met."

"Oh, Barty," his father said, his eyes clearer now than they had been before, "don't speak of such things. You're here now, and that's what matters."

"So much has happened, Da," Sandu said, melting back into the scared little boy he'd once been, the boy who'd clung to his father after his mother's death. "I've done so many terrible things. I don't think I can ever forgive myself."

"Hush, son. I love you, and I've never stopped loving you. Whatever bad you've done, there is time to do good."

"But there's not," Sandu said. "Tambrey's dead, Da. So are the children. You're all I have left."

"No," Cadel mumbled, his hands slipping against Sandu. "Say it isn't true."

"I wish it wasn't." Sandu broke. He gripped his father tightly with his remaining arm, wondering if it had been right to come all this way just to break his old man's heart. *He'll never see his grandchildren again, even if he sees the light of day.*

Cadel's quiet sobs pierced Sandu's soul, and he desperately wished he hadn't come at all.

Darian coughed, and Jagger signed, *Someone's coming.*

*

Talnor and Cara walked side-by-side along a long, low corridor toward a fire-lit tower room.

"Where's Mavian?" Cara asked. Her hand was warm in Talnor's arm, but she still held hatred for the man who had turned Renna into this.

"Gone. He won't bother us anymore." Talnor's smile hid something, but Cara couldn't tell what. After her long journey, Cara had hoped to finish what she'd set out to do. *I'll find Mavian still. He can't hide forever.*

They entered the cozy room which held a fireplace, cushioned couches, rugs, and a table laden with food and wine. Cara's mouth watered, and she edged toward the table. Piling a platter high, she hunched over her food, eating quickly as she watched the *fampir* woman. Talnor stood beside the fire, gazing into it.

"Do you know what I want, Cara?" Talnor asked. When Cara shook her head, she continued, "I want peace. I have lived a very long time, and most of that imprisoned. Yet every minute of my immortal existence, I have sought peace. A lasting peace."

"There's no such thing." Even the peace of a hundred years had come to an end.

"Isn't there?" Talnor's eyes lit with some inner flame. "There are tools of the Cythra left in our world, tools from ancient times, crafted before the Dead's War. With these, you and I could force this land to its knees and rule as its immortal mistresses. No one could resist us; no one could bring us down."

"No." Cara discarded an apple core. "I don't want immortality. I want our kind scourged from this world. We're evil."

"Are we evil, Cara?" Talnor's hand darted over the flames, playing with their heat. "By whose standards? Yours? The rustics? The nobles who eat food and drink mead bought off the backs of their vassals? Undeath is no more evil than life. It simply *is*."

"I can't believe that."

"Look into the flames. Tell me what you see."

Apprehensive, Cara came to stand beside Talnor. "It's just a fire."

"Oh, but it's more than that. Tell me, would you call the fire in this grate evil?"

"No."

"Ah, yet its cousin, the wildfire, burns and scorches and ravages all before it, destroying with impunity. It is only the fire that leaps from its grate that becomes wicked. Fire contained and controlled is good. It gives us warmth, it heats our food, protects us from winter and the night's chill.

"Similar to fire is death and undeath. The former is necessary for life; if all beings were immortal, none could survive. And undeath is the leader that guides the mortals. Why, then, do we trust our kingdoms to those who see so little of life's bounties and griefs?"

"Druam has ruled thus," Cara said, but Talnor hissed between her teeth.

"Druam is too afraid to use his gifts. He's hidden his true nature from the world. Yet, for all his flaws, he has achieved that which all undead should strive for." Cupping Cara's cheek, Talnor said, "Do you want to be shackled all your life to those who would use you without understanding you? Merick, your childhood master; Druam, your would-be kin, whose secrets outnumber the stars; Laris, the feeble sorcerer who wanted only to use you to regain his youth? None of them found you to help *you*."

"And you would be my next master," Cara said, pulling away slightly, though finding herself enchanted by Talnor's words. The *fampir* was right. Never had Cara been free to do as she pleased, to live for herself and no other.

"No, not your master. Your equal. Your sister." Talnor said it, but it was Renna's voice Cara heard. "I can show you the secrets of your blood, the powers that slumber in your breast. Together, we can raze cities and depose kings, lead armies and discover ancient secrets. Together, as sisters."

Sisters. So long had Cara longed to hear that word from Renna, to be recognized as an equal, not a servant of the household. Except Renna had never said it, never seen Cara beyond their shallow relationship. *Even Sandu traveled with me for the bounty I would bring him. Yet does he truly care for me? He abandoned me, time and again, for his family. A family he loves more than he will ever love me.*

And Merick. I was like a daughter, but not his daughter. Not quite; after all, my mother sold me to him.

"Show me," Cara said to Talnor. The *fampir* smiled.

*

The key scraped in the lock once more. A guard stooped inside. Behind him came a brash young nobleman with a silver hand.

"Happy little reunion?" asked Chadron. He grinned scornfully at their bedraggled group. "You, with one arm. Talnor wants you."

"For what?" Sandu asked.

Cadel immediately grabbed Sandu's wrist. "You're not taking him."

Chadron looked bored. "Your friend is up there, remember? I'm sure they just want to talk with you. Now come along."

"What about my other friends?" Sandu asked. He backed away from the guard.

"They'll be set free. Your father, too. It's only you we want."

Sandu looked at his Da, his resolve shrinking. *If it gets Da out of here...*

"You promise they'll be let go?" Sandu asked.

"On my father's grave. Now come on."

Sandu squeezed Da's hand. "I'll be out soon." He turned to Darian and Jagger. "Take him to the place we agreed to meet. I'll see you there."

Jagger signed, *This isn't good.*

"I agree. But I'm not going to fight it."

As he emerged into the hall, Sandu gasped in surprise. Alex was there, his hands cuffed.

"Alex!" Despite his predicament, Sandu couldn't help but grin. "Gods, it's good to see you."

His old friend smiled weakly. "I've missed you too, Sandu. Is Cara here?"

"Yes."

With Chadron leading the way, the guards shoved them up the corridor. Sandu leaned over to Alex. "She's not what you remember. I don't think she'll be too happy to see you."

"She will," Alex said. He flashed that old, carefree grin. "I found a cure."

❋

Talnor drew out the white gem, which pulsed softly. "I took this from Mavian. He didn't know what he held. It is the key to the Ossuary and so much more."

Cara reached out, brushing the hard surface with a finger. "I remember this. It opened the dread portals."

"Indeed. And we will use it to travel north to Stonetree and rejoin Rask's forces. Together, we will take down Druam."

Her eyes fixed on the gem, Cara nodded. "And then, the Ossuary."

"Yes."

Cara raised her eyes to meet Talnor's. "When do we begin?"

"First, you must prove yourself to me," Talnor said.

Cara turned as Sir Chadron entered with Alex dragged behind him. Her once-lover was bound tightly, his eyes wide as he saw her. Sandu followed, his arm held by a guard.

"Cara!" shouted Alex. "You're here! I–"

Chadron slapped a hand over Alex's mouth, ending his sentence. All of them looked to Cara.

"Alex, your lover until he betrayed you," Talnor said. She glanced at Sandu. "And your companion in your quest to find Renna, your truest friend. But he always loved others more."

Cara stared at them. "I don't understand."

"One of them must die by your hand. Many more will fall before this war is at an end. You must prove your dedication to me. I recommend the *fampir*."

Cara stared into Alex's pleading eyes. She saw fear and hope within them.

You came far for a lost hope, she thought.

❋

Sandu watched in rapt horror as Cara drew her sword and leveled it at Alex. He screamed, "CARA! NO!"

Everyone turned to him. Cara's face fell for a moment before her expression hardened. Alex shook his head desperately, unable to speak past Chadron's hand. Sandu pleaded, "Please, Cara. Don't do this. He's our friend, the others are our enemies. Please."

"Go, Sandu," Cara said. A red light gleamed in her eyes. "This isn't your fight."

"You're my friend! I can't just let you–"

Cara shook her head. "I've done far worse than this. Alex *lied* to us. He's *fampir*, undead, just like the monsters who killed your caravan so long ago. He has to go back to Autorus."

Sandu stared at her. "This isn't you. Please. I know you've been struggling, so have I, but this isn't right. This isn't what we set out to do."

Cara hesitated. Talnor witnessed the whole exchange with a faint expression of amusement.

"Do it, Cara," the blonde woman said. "Choose one and finish it."

Sandu struggled and yelled, but he could do nothing. He knew that he was safe; Cara would always have chosen Alex. Still, he couldn't bear to see one friend slaughter another.

Cara indicated for Chadron to let go of Alex's mouth. She said, "I've granted you your final words, *fampir*. Say your piece before I kill you."

Alex stared up at her. "I'm mortal, Cara. I went to the Whispering Woods and broke my soul for you. Please, let us go. I just wanted you to–"

Sandu stared in fear and astonishment at his friend. *Surely Cara will listen to him!*

Cara shouted and swung her sword. Her blade sank deeply into Alex's flesh. He died without another word.

"NO!" Sandu shouted, squirming against the guard's implacable hands. "No! Cara, how could you?"

Cara's countenance reflected the beast inside. Talnor smiled. "Kill him, too. Just for fun."

As Cara pointed her sword at him, Sandu grew quiet. He met his friend's eyes, and in that moment, he knew that his death had finally come. *Not like this, not at her hands,* he prayed.

"You betrayed me, too," Cara said. "I saw you in the woods spilling our secrets. To whom?"

"I don't–"

She shook her head. "It doesn't matter anyway."

Sandu beseeched his friend with his eyes, hoping she would see the truth in them. *If I'm to die, don't let it be like this.* "Please, Cari," he said. "Please."

Slowly, Cara lowered her sword. She looked to Alex's head, then back at Sandu. "Let him live another day. He wants to die; he's no threat to us." She nodded to Chadron. "Throw him out the front gates. Make sure he doesn't come back."

Talnor frowned yet didn't protest. Sandu kicked and struggled, but was dragged away. His last sight of Cara was a monster staring without guilt at him.

CHAPTER FIFTY-TWO
As the Snow Falls

Too late for Stonetree, too late for Con Salur, thick white snowflakes drifted lazily to Earda, carried by heavy grey clouds. Some people lifted their faces, laughing with the cold snow, while others ducked their heads and muttered curses. All knew that with snow came peace and quiet, if only for a season. Campaigns must cease, battles stilled, until Earda's carpet of white turned back to brown and green.

At the head of his army, only a day's ride from Stonetree and still ensconced in the mountains, Rask shook his head and ordered their return to the fortress. Riverfen's reckoning would have to wait until the passes cleared.

Beside a river, on a hilltop leagues away from Con Salur, Seanna watched the snow fall. Its whiteness obscured the dark smoke that rose from her city. With Landin in her arms, she turned away from the sight. With no crown and no throne, she was no more than a beggar queen. A beggar queen who had no intentions of fading away into the night as snow melts in water. She would be the ice hidden beneath the snow, waiting for a stray foot to catch it.

Surrounded by scholars and wagons, Mavian felt the snow coming down, but he pressed forward anyway. They would find safety in the caves beneath D'Clet to plan their uprising. Ekkar remained at his side, flicking his tongue out to catch the falling flakes, while Merick rode silent as ever. The scholars gave Mavian questioning looks, and he only shrugged and kicked his horse. On the morrow, when he'd regained his strength, he would put cantrips on the horses' hooves that would burn the snow away, making their journey that much easier. Snow could not stop him, a creature of shadow, molded by darkness. After all, he knew the cold as well as the dead.

Stumbling through the snow, Sandu, Darian, Jagger, and Cadel paused to shake off the cold and warm their tired bones. Cara had betrayed them. Jagger and Darian supported Cadel, making sure his hands and feet were wrapped against the cold. In the back of the group, Sandu was silent. Morose, ruminating, he could no longer stomach this war and its undead things.

✳

As the snow fell, settling over the valley like a thick blanket, Druam worked. He couldn't watch the lanterns glow tonight for there was too much to be done. Rask's armies would besiege the city come spring, and Druam planned to send as many of his people to safety as he could before they perished in the whitewashed streets.

A knock came at his door, an unexpected visitor. She came without announcement or formal entreaties, simply appearing wraithlike at his door.

"Sura," Druam said without preamble. "Why are you here?"

The Corsair Queen strode confidently into the room, her dark eyes shining. "Con Salur has fallen."

Druam sighed. "Then we are alone against the enemy."

"I know."

"Are you here to tell me that my seas will be open for the Lofalins' use?"

She was silent a moment, and Druam waited. Finally, she said, "No. My ships will keep a blockade against the elves. They won't bombard this city as they did Con Salur."

"Good." Druam met her gaze, holding it unflinchingly. "You never told me about Verdon."

Sura froze, her expression guarded. "How did you know?"

"He's still alive." Druam wiped his forehead, remembering

all that had happened for that revelation to occur. "He's become a prowler; the *first* prowler."

"I thought..." Sura dropped into a chair, pain in her eyes. "He was so still when I left. The spell took everything from him. I thought he was dead."

"You still should have told me." Druam tapped his desk lightly, a storm of emotions flooding him. He wouldn't show this woman weakness. She was both friend and enemy, and not to be trusted.

"I have my reasons."

"Don't we all?" Druam murmured. He stood, wishing his bones would creak and ache as an old man's bones ought to. But he was as spry as the day he'd been turned. Going to the window, he said, "I would have liked to bury him if he had been dead. I could have also acted as uncle to Cara. You didn't have to be alone in this."

Sura shrugged. "I did what I thought was best. And now, we see if those were the right choices." She stood and stretched. "My ships are here, as I promised." Sura walked away, then paused and said, "For what it's worth, if I could go back, I would have told you." She swept away, leaving as suddenly as she'd entered. Dropping his facade of calm, Druam tried to weep, but couldn't. No *fampir* can cry.

Instead, he wrenched open the curtains, watching the snow fall on his beloved city, coating the lanterns to create pockets of color against the sparkling white. He prayed for Alexandro, for Mavian, for Verdon, and for Gwen, far away where he couldn't follow.

The snow blanketed Riverfen, bringing with it a tranquil silence and comfort.

✳

Cara looked down at Alex's body, bile rising in her throat. He had once held her and loved her, and she'd killed him.

Talnor stood beside her. "He lied, you know. Death is the only way out for a *fampir*."

"I know." Cara squared her shoulders and tore her gaze away. "It needed to be done."

Chadron entered. "He's been thrown out without being harmed, as you asked."

"Good."

The knight ran an eye over Cara. "You could always winter here rather than with the army. It would be much warmer than Stonetree."

Talnor smiled, but pushed past him. Cara gave a small shrug. "I follow her."

Chadron nodded, bowed, and left. With a graceful white hand, Talnor took the white gem. She spoke words of power, and a dread portal opened. Talnor walked through without hesitation. Cara dithered. *The last time I watched that woman walk through a portal like this, it changed my life for the worse.*

What choice did she have now? She had made her decision, and she couldn't go back. She stepped into the darkness.

✳

Sandu slipped away early in the morning. The snow blew about, angrier up here in the mountains than it was down below. His teeth chattered in the cold, but the snow was for the best. It would cover his tracks so that none may follow him.

He would leave Dotschar and never return. His father didn't need him now that he was freed, his wife and children were gone, and his friend had become a monster in spirit as well as form. There was nothing for him here in the snow-laden hills. Nothing but death.

As Sandu walked away, Jagger stepped out and stopped him. The tall man crossed his arms, waiting for Sandu to speak.

"I'm leaving," Sandu said. "This is no place for me."

Jagger only stared. The snow crunched behind Sandu, and he turned to see Darian and Cadel. The blind man gave him a sympathetic look.

"You're running without a purpose," Darian said.

"It's what cowards do," Sandu replied.

Cadel shook his head. "You're no coward, my boy. We've only just reunited. Don't leave me."

"I have to go, Da. I can't stay anymore." The memory of Cara murdering Alex seared his mind. "Why should I stay?"

To his surprise, Darian said, "You shouldn't stay. But you shouldn't meander out across the sea, either. Your children *are not dead*, Sandu. You just can't reach them yet. Not until you know your own Song."

"Enough of your riddles, Darian," Sandu said. He glared at the blind man, who didn't appear disconcerted.

A small smile touched Darian's lips. "The Songs will help you. Across the sea in Demarren is a sorceress who knows the Songs better than any mortal. She can help you find your children and regain yourself. She can help you resolve what Cara has become."

Despite Darian's words, Sandu didn't dare let himself hope. *I want to leave anyway. Perhaps I'll even find this woman.*

From deep in his memories, Sandu recalled a Demar woman in the Cascade Palace. He said slowly, "I've met her before."

"Yes." Darian laid a hand on Sandu's shoulder. "I'm afraid this is where we part. You must seek out this sorceress so that you may be whole once more. Jagger and I must help others to weather the winter's storms."

Cadel put a protective arm around Sandu. "And what about me?"

"You can't go over the sea, Da," Sandu said. "You're too weak."

"So fatten me up. I won't leave you."

Sandu opened his mouth to protest, then closed it. *It would be good to be with Da again.* He nodded, and Cadel leaned into his shoulder.

Darian nodded to Sandu. "Good luck. I hope you meet my sisters in the Woods."

"Your sisters?"

"The sorceress will introduce you." Darian gave a parting squeeze to Sandu's hand.

Sandu turned to Jagger. Grief and regret filled the tall man's eyes. *Funny, how hard it is to part after everything we've been through together. I'd almost forgotten that we tried to kill each other.*

"Well, then, it's goodbye. A proper one, this time." Sandu embraced Jagger. Jagger tensed before strong arms wrapped around Sandu, lifting him slightly out of the snow. "I'll miss you, you know. Take care of Darian. And, if you see Cara..." Sandu couldn't bring himself to say the words, but Jagger nodded. Jagger would take care of her as only a killer could.

"Goodbye, old friend."

Before he lost his nerve, Sandu strode off into the grey dawn, his hood raised against the blizzard, his hand wrapped in cloth to keep it warm. His father strode beside him, determined despite his shaking legs. Sandu glanced over his shoulder once at his friends, but soon the white made them vanish.

Days later, he and Cadel found themselves in a chilly harbor, its boats nearly frozen in the bay. One large ship, destined for Demarren, made ready to depart. He stopped on the deck to look back over his country, the only land he'd ever known. Never before had he left the shores of D'Ehsen.

Snow swirled down, coating the land in heaps and heaps of cold and death. Animals would freeze in their dens, starving children would perish at their mother's feet despite love and blankets and bone broth poured desperately down their throats. Hefting his sack, Sandu sighed and turned away. He had nothing but the shirt on his back and some few supplies in his sack.

Just like the good old days.

But he wasn't alone now. Da was with him, and if Darian was correct, then Sandu could still see his children again. He held onto that hope, a beacon that warmed his chilled soul.

"Come on, Da," Sandu said. "Let's get you out of the cold."

Coming Soon

The trilogy's thrilling conclusion:

The Enduring Flame

Sovereigns of the Dead: Book Three

Join the monthly newsletter list for sneak peeks, extra scenes, and much more at vistamcdowall.com.

GLOSSARY

Places:

Con Salur - a cliff city home to King Henrik

D'Clet - a mountain city overseen by Earl Hjalder

Dedaria - an elven kingdom of D'Ehsen, ruled by *Kair* Aremo

D'Ehsen - the large island and surrounding isles on which multiple kingdoms are found

Demarren - a kingdom of D'Ehsen, ruled by Liegelord Wullum

Dotschar - the largest kingdom of D'Ehsen, ruled by King Henrik

Eadrion Empire - a large empire to the west which rules a small portion of D'Ehsen

Mott - a town which is home to the only university in Dotschar

Novum - a temple of worship for Dotschar's main religion. Typically has nine sides for the nine gods.

Rengu - an elven kingdom of D'Ehsen, ruled by *Ameer* Voclain

Riverfen - a coastal city overseen by Earl Seastone

Skålland - a kingdom of D'Ehsen ruled by a chieftain

Units of Time:

Candle - roughly equivalent to an hour

Quinn - five days

Deshe - ten days

Creatures:

Fampir - an undead which used to be a human or elf, and can disguise itself as a mortal

Mist-folk - swamp-dwelling creatures which lure their prey into the marshes

Prowler - an undead which used to be a human or elf, but is now feral and predatory

Sulpari - a woman with a *fampir* father and mortal mother

Positions:

Ameer - the Rengu (elven) word for prince; their equivalent of a king

Clothman - a low-level cleric of the Dotsch religion; usually practices in small novums

Curate - a mid-level cleric of the Dotsch religion; trained in healing and employed in manors, palaces, or large novums

Exalt - the highest position in the Dotsch religion, either chosen by his predecessor or voted in by his fellow predicants

Kair - the Dedarian (elven) word for prince; their equivalent of a king

Liegelord - the sovereign ruler of Demarren

Predicant - the second-highest position in the Dotsch religion, there are three predicants for each of the four earls.

ACKNOWLEDGEMENTS

Mom, Dad, Michael, and Brandon, who would tell me they love it no matter what – thank you for always being there for me.

Allison, Kendra, Carmen, Paul, Don, Michele, Dave, Linda, Theresa, Janet, Matt, Ralph, Apryl, Bruce, and Wendy, who helped me polish up early chapters – thank you.

Rodney, for creating my beautiful map and bringing it to life – thank you.

Forest, who managed to read this during the catastrophe year that was 2020 – thank you.

All my readers: May you have enjoyed this journey as much as I have. I hope you'll join me for the next one. Thank you.

About the Author

Vista McDowall lives and works in the rural mountains of Colorado, where she imagines great quests over the snow-covered peaks. She also teaches young adults the love of literature and writing, and hopes that they, too, find solace in fantastical places and magical beings.

She can be found on Facebook, Twitter, and Instagram. Her website is vistamcdowall.com.

www.ingramcontent.com/pod-product-compliance
Lightning Source LLC
Chambersburg PA
CBHW021119260626
47169CB00005B/1360